The Servant

MAGGIE RICHELL-DAVIES

For Florence Richell, who dreamed of teaching but, as a Northumbrian miner's daughter, had to forego a scholarship and go into service in London.

CONTENTS

Chapter One

London, Spring 1765

'Let's have a proper look at you.'

I step within touching distance. The visitor has eaten something strong-smelling. Fragments are lodged between her teeth. And her breath, and what is happening, jolt me back to being ten years old.

Toasted cheese. The mouth-watering odour hit us as we were hustled into the room. Mary and I had been dragged from bed by one of the older girls and hurried, barefoot, to the overseer's quarters. There was a stranger with her, in a satin gown too bright and young for her face. From the plates and porter bottles on the table, they had just shared a meal.

'The dark haired one is the looker, with those striking green eyes,' said the visitor. 'Hannah Hubert, did you say?'

'Yes. A handful, though.'

The stranger yanked up my shift and, when I resisted, gave me a slap.

'Keep still.'

Fingers searched, hurting, and I bared my teeth.

The blow from the overseer knocked me to the hearthrug. Inches from my face was a brass toasting fork and I lunged for it.

'Don't!' A foot stamped on my wrist. 'Troublesome little bitch.'

I froze, the taste in my mouth bitter. Knowing I could be handled by strangers, like a donkey at a horse fair, and do nothing.

'I'll take the other one.' The stranger shoved a tattered shawl at the whimpering Mary, sounding bored. 'Can't be doing with trouble.'

'Want me to send for her boots?'

'We are not going far. Stones and filth under those bare feet will fix her mind on what running off would mean.'

'The parents are dead?' The voice is curt, dragging me back to Mistress Buttermere's elegant parlour. 'You are sure?'

In the chair opposite my mistress, the visitor is ramrod-straight. Hands twisting like snakes in the lap of her black gown. A figure fashioned from whalebone and iron. She means me harm, I know it. The eyes studying me are sharp as a skinning knife.

'I sent my housekeeper to look for Hannah's father after we took her in.' Mistress Buttermere shakes her head. 'There had been

1

fever in Spitalfields. She found no trace.'

The breath envelopes me again.

'What have you been taught?'

The poorhouse liked to say that it pleases God for a servant to be humble, so I compose my face to a meekness I don't feel. Not convinced the Almighty cares how I go about emptying piss pots.

'I know plain cooking. And the care of linen.'

'Then imagine I give you a gentleman's coat. Marked with spilled candle wax. What would you do with it?'

'Scrape off what I could with a blunt knife. Then use brown paper and a smoothing iron. Not too hot.'

She turns back to Mistress Buttermere.

'I presume the girl has not been interfered with?'

'Of course not.'

'No followers, then?'

'She is only fifteen, Mistress Chalke.'

'Being young didn't stop our last maid obliging anything in breeches.'

I concentrate on standing still, an unheard-of activity in my working day. Why must this happen after I had felt safe and happy these past two years? For the first time since Mother pushed out my stillborn sister and bled her life away.

Becoming this woman's drudge is the last thing I want. Being on the edge of her world. Making her life easy. While mine is menial work and always having to do what I am told.

'And you pay three guineas a year?' The woman's narrow lips compress. 'You are too generous.'

'I am sorry to let her go. But I plan to move to York at the end of the quarter.' Mistress Buttermere's voice softens. 'Maria is close to her lying-in.'

''Tis only proper to be with your daughter.' Our visitor frowns, an unnaturally black fringe visible under her cap. 'And the girl is available soon?'

'On Lady Day.'

'Show me those hands.'

I offer my palms, but instead she pokes long fingernails into my bodice and I shy away.

'She is only a scrap of a thing. I would need a proper day's labour.'

Mistress Buttermere's eyes stray to her French ormolu clock and I realise my future is just another chore for her before the move to York.

'My housekeeper says Hannah's strong for her age.'

'And eats like a carthorse, no doubt. I do not plan to fatten a waif at my expense.'

'She will not expect spoiling, Mistress Chalke. Remember where she came from.'

'Another parish bastard?'

'Her father was a respected silk-weaver, so she has gone down in the world.' Mistress Buttermere lowers her voice. 'There is insufficient work in his trade. Too many mouths to feed and a stepmother who despatched her to the poorhouse. At ten years of age.'

The visitor sniffs. 'It is no wonder the streets are awash with beggars. With all these foreigners flooding into our cities.'

The parlour fire crackles in the grate and I look at the women debating my future. They know I can hear every word, yet I might as well be the brass fire-irons for the interest they have in what I think. When Mother died, I became an object to be disposed of.

'Could you make yourself useful? In my house?'

I am sure it was Mary I had seen, a year after I came here, when Mrs Lamb took me to the draper's shop to teach me about fine-thread linen.

We had passed her, holding out a tin cup for spare change and dressed in rags. And though she had kept the bright red hair, her face was disfigured with running sores. She could be dead by now, yet lives in my mind as a reminder to keep my wits about me.

'Well?' The voice is brusque.

'Yes, ma'am.' I take a deep breath, to calm my uneasy imagination. Under that starched bombazine Mistress Chalke is just a woman, like myself. Not a devil.

'Then I shall give you a trial. But mind you give me a decent day's work. Or you will be sorry.'

It was a kind of magic, the weekly cleaning of the kitchen copper. I loved putting blackened pans in the stone sink, sprinkling them with salt and vinegar, then rubbing vigorously with a rag. Bowls and pans turned into rosy-hued mirrors that threw back an image of my pale face and dark hair. It reminded me of the *Genie with the Lamp* that my mother used to read to me at bed-time.

Everything had been unsettled since the housekeeper clattered down the stairs into the scullery, huffing to herself as she did when flustered.

'Quick! You're wanted in the parlour. And get yourself a clean apron.' Now all is changed; the copper is a chore and I hunch over it, sighing.

'Don't sulk, Hannah.' Mrs Lamb struggles to look severe. 'You had better start boiling that tongue. You need the practice.'

'I don't want practice.' I pull a face, remembering. 'Why must I work for that woman? She looked as if she planned to put me in the stocks, not in her kitchen.'

'Now, my dear. Show more respect.' The housekeeper leans forward to tuck a wayward curl beneath my cap. 'Be grateful the mistress has arranged another place for you. Many wouldn't bother. Not for a kitchen maid.'

'Couldn't I come with you? I would work for nothing.'

The household tabby winds around my legs, hinting for a bowl of cream.

'We will be in lodgings. By rights she should not be taking me.' Mrs Lamb studies her swollen knuckles and I wonder if she is uneasy about her own future. What if Mistress Buttermere moves in with her daughter and son-in-law, who will have a houseful of servants already?

I leave Puss in front of the fire and fill an iron pot with water. Boiling ox tongues is something I hate, always picturing the poor beast lowing in powerless protest as it is driven into the slaughterhouse yard.

I take myself into the scullery where the tongue is soaking in brine and carry it to the sink, turning my nose from its smell. Then I rinse it in clean water and take it through, dripping on Mrs Lamb's clean floor, to drop into the pot. There is an air of sympathy in the kitchen and nothing is said about the glistening trail as I throw in salt and bay leaves.

'It might not be so bad, Hannah. Mistress Chalke looks respectable enough. And that is what matters.' The housekeeper has her special face on, with brows raised and eyes intent. The one she saves for lecturing me. 'Our lady did not want you going to a household with young men. Footmen are good-for-nothings, often as not. And sons of the house little better.'

'I don't care for young men,' I say, airily, though I have scant experience of such creatures. 'But one might be useful for heavy work. Next door's manservant hauls water to the top of the house. The young ladies take hot baths. In their rooms.'

'Never mind the fancy ideas at Sir Christopher's. Magistrates are not like ordinary folk. If people must boil themselves like lobsters, there's nothing wrong with the public bath house.'

She sniffs; to her, cleanliness is the regular scrubbing of faces and hands with a soapy cloth and fresh linen once a week. My own views are different after two years in the poorhouse. Rat droppings and grit in our bread. Dishes caked with old food. Bodies unwashed. Clothing rank.

Mrs Lamb sighs as I place a saucer and spoon by the fire, ready for the scum that will form on the water. 'You are so young, with no mother to advise you. I should have prepared you better. The world is not always kind.'

'I know that, Mrs Lamb. I gave up fairy stories at ten years old.'

She nods her head. Knowing my history. Remembering my arrival at the Buttermere house half-starved and frightened, with lice in my hair.

'But with those looks, I fear you will be a temptation to some sweet-talking man. You need to be wary.'

I study a blister on my thumb. Being pleasing to look at is not as valuable to me as it would be to a young lady, needing to snare a fine gentleman for a husband. I have decided I need skills and experience so that one day I can have my own cosy housekeeper's room in some great house. Where I will have a full staff of servants under me and will organise grand dinners and splendid shooting parties for important people before retreating into my private sanctuary with a book.

I shall miss the Buttermere housekeeper, who has stood in place of a mother, taking me to be fitted for my first pair of half-stays and explaining how I must accept the discomfort of them. Telling me that being a woman meant bleeding each month and needing to hide it from the world as best I could. And that I must be guarded in my dealings with men.

'I bet Mistress Chalke beats her servants,' I mutter, prodding the seething tongue.

'Which you will deserve, if you fail to do a proper day's work.' Mrs Lamb eyes the water glimmering on the floor as if having second thoughts about a rebuke. 'You will be safer in a quiet household. In a year, when you are more experienced, you can seek out smiling faces.'

Then she opens a cupboard and pulls out a handsome carpet bag.

'The mistress thought you would find this useful, going to a new place.' She closes my calloused fingers around its pigskin handles. 'Our lady is done with it. See, the cloth is faded and there is a tear in the lining, though that is soon mended. Plenty of thread in the workbasket.'

It looks far from faded to me. The colours remind me of baskets of jewel-bright silks behind the loom that my mother used to tell me I was not allowed to touch in case my curious fingers dirtied them.

'She is sorry your place is going, when you are so young.'

The housekeeper pulls a handwritten recipe book, smeared with thumb prints, from her pocket. 'Take this, as well. Though Mistress Chalke knows you are not a proper cook. If she wants fancy tarts she can send you to the pastry-shop.'

She heaves a sigh. 'If anyone asked my opinion, which of course they never would, you are too young to be in charge of a household. But you are a bright girl. Perhaps you will please her. Perhaps she is kinder than she looks.'

She places my gift carefully on the table, away from the fire.

'It is said her husband is related to the great men at Court. But he disgraced himself and was disinherited. Maybe that is why his wife looks so sour.'

I turn back to the simmering pot. Life is not fair. Not for girls like me: alone in the world, and poor. Perhaps I will use that thread to embroider the words on the square of gingham I had cut from the hem of Mother's favourite gown, as a remembrance. Before my horrible stepmother sold it at the second-hand clothes stall. The only thing I had fought to keep at the poorhouse. I promised myself then that one day I would have a dress that was not a hand-me-down. That despite being a girl I would somehow have command of my own life.

'Will you think of me sometimes, in York?'

'I will remember you in my prayers, which is better.' Mrs Lamb pauses, clearly wanting to be encouraging. 'If you work hard and keep that cheeky tongue of yours in check, the worst that is likely to come your way is an unfair box on the ears.'

I only wish she sounded as if she believed it.

Chapter Two

Mrs Lamb frowns up from the written directions in her hand to the tall, narrow house at our journey's end.

'What was Mistress Buttermere thinking? Sending you here.'

Set behind spiked railings, little more than a yard from the public street, it is not somewhere you would expect a gentleman to live. The green-painted front door is chipped and flaking. The windows are grimy, with heavy curtains drawn tight across all those at ground level despite the sunny morning. Soapy water thrown over the steps has not been swept away, puddling dirty suds under our feet.

'Your new master may have fallen on hard times, but I did not expect this.' My arm is tucked in hers and she squeezes it. 'But it is only for a year, Hannah. By then we could be back in London. I cannot see Mistress Buttermere wanting to move under her son-in-law's roof. Being a widow all these years, she has lost the habit of doing any man's bidding.'

She gives me a quick hug before leading me down the steps to the servants' entrance and rapping at a tarnished knocker.

'Perhaps there is a magic carpet inside,' I murmur, 'and I will climb onto it and fly over the sea and far away.'

'The only carpets I suspect you will find in there will be ones in need of vigorous beating.'

My elbow is squeezed again as a rattle of bolts announces the opening of the door.

'Mistress Chalke…' Mrs Lamb starts in surprise at its being answered by the lady of the house.

The face is not welcoming.

'You have brought the girl.' Her hand grips my wrist and I catch a last glimpse of Mrs Lamb's startled eyes as I am jerked inside and the door is slammed behind me.

Then I am in the kitchen of my new home, flustered and with my nostrils twitching. The place stinks of old meals and rancid fat. Dirty dishes overflow the stone sink. The fire is a bare glimmer.

I am released and Mistress Chalke looms over me. Skirts lifted clear of the floor and her mouth turned down. Its preferred position,

I have decided.

'Don't just stand there. Make yourself useful. You can take your things to the garret later.'

'Yes, ma'am.'

I drop my carpet bag and start poking the embers. There is sea coal in a bucket and I select a few pieces and add them. Then grab the leather bellows and pump, hard. With only my wits and what Mrs Lamb has taught me, I must satisfy this hard-faced woman. Hot water will mean I can make a start. Though where is the other servant? Does the lazy slattern not know to sweep dirty water away from steps used by visitors?

Mistress Chalke turns towards the stairs, then pauses. 'And while you are at it, memorise my house rules.

'No dealings whatsoever with men or boys. On pain of dismissal.' Her lips twist with concentration. 'Jabber to anyone about our affairs and, again, you are on the street. Next door's maidservant has a nose the length of a poker. But the bitch will get it smashed if she sticks it in our business.'

She scowls as I blink at her language.

'No candle stubs. They are to be melted down for kitchen dips; not sold for your private profit. And we do our own laundry. I will not waste guineas hiring-in washerwomen. Old Peg can help you.'

With a final twitch of camphor and ill-temper from her skirts she mounts the stairs.

I grit my teeth. I am bound to this place for a year and will cling to Mrs Lamb's belief it will prove a step up for me. I must serve; it is my only respectable option. But I will merely pretend respect and plan for better things.

Grease from an iron pot sticks to my fingers as I fill it with water from a tub in the scullery and hang it over the fire. If this is to be my world, I will bring Buttermere standards to it.

A shadow looms in the gloom of the scullery doorway and my heart jumps, but it is only an old crone. A gaunt bundle of rags I can smell across the room. More like a beggar off the street than a servant in a decent household.

'I am Peg,' she says, revealing teeth like a broken fence.

The way she hunches back against the wall reminds me of a cur, hurt so often that only starvation will tempt it within kicking distance. I must be right about Mistress Chalke mistreating her servants. Perhaps the old woman fears me, too, now she is in my charge.

I will be kind to her but must first discover what kind of worker she is. Worse than useless, from the state of those steps outside and from what surrounds me.

Her bucket of slopping water is heavy and when she sets it down and leans for a moment against the kitchen chair, I see that she drags a crippled leg.

I find a rag to lift the pot of boiling water from the fire to refresh her pail.

'One other thing.'

My fingers are scalded and I squeal. The mistress is back.

I soothe my reddened skin against my apron. Mistress Buttermere never interfered in domestic arrangements, but this household threatens to be different.

Her eyes dart past me, to Peg.

'Away from that chair, you useless piece of shit! Before I kick you off it.'

Peg seizes a cloth from her pail and shrinks to her knees. A glimpse of leg beneath a torn petticoat reveals no stockings and men's boots stuffed with rags to stop them slipping off her feet. One of the soles is split from its uppers like a hungry mouth.

Mistress Chalke turns back to me as I struggle to keep my face impassive.

'Come.'

I follow her up the stair. Those drawn curtains, plus red flocked wallpaper, make the light so murky I need to watch where I put my feet.

'That door. At the top. Opposite the big mirror.' She points. 'It is the master's book room. He keeps it locked. You are not allowed in there.'

'Not even to clean, mistress? Or lay the fire?'

'Of course, you must clean.' Her eyes narrow. 'And naturally you must see to the fire. But you must never be in there unsupervised.'

'Yes, ma'am. I understand.'

I do not, of course, understand anything except that life with this foul-mouthed woman will be a nightmare.

'But when the master is out, perhaps…?'

My face stings from her slap and I have to grab the bannister to save myself from falling.

'What have I just said?' Her face mottles as she looms over me. 'Add insolence to stupidity and there is a leather strap I will introduce you to. You are only allowed in the book room when I am with you.'

I have visions of the master shouting with exasperation at there being no fire for him on a cold morning, but keep silent. In time, I will understand the ways of this house. I must, if I am not to end up without employment.

'Is that clear?'

'Yes, ma'am.' I dip a resentful curtsy, willing her to leave me in peace and let me return to her filthy kitchen.

At least they *have* a book room. Not a proper library of course, for I cannot imagine this shabby house will have anything like the Buttermere library with its walls of books. It even boasted a wooden lectern, like those in church, with a volume of Dr Samuel Johnson's *Dictionary of the English Language* on display.

Whenever I dusted I would pluck a new word to savour, happy as a lady selecting a sugared almond. And on my days off, if there were no visitors, I was allowed to go in there and read. Sometimes I would practise writing on scavenged scraps of parchment. I made it into my schoolroom.

'Well, then,' says Mistress Chalke. 'We understand one another. But do what you are told. Or I will flay the back off you.'

I have not been beaten since the poorhouse and I suppose life at Mistress Buttermere's has softened me. Mrs Lamb warned me servants sometimes get blows that are undeserved. It is how the world turns. Though the thought of being treated like a dog sickens me.

'Now get back to work.'

I soothe my scald again, relieved as the crackling of starched petticoats signals her departure. That locked room is a puzzle, but my flesh quivers at so much talk of whipping.

Downstairs, Peg shrinks into the shadows, water dripping from her cloth. Is it weakness that makes those knotted hands tremble? Or something else? Perhaps when we are alone she will explain the workings of this house, though it looks as if it would take thumbscrews to get a word out of her.

I want to be back in the familiar surroundings of the Buttermere house, but know that is not possible. Mrs Lamb said I was a bright girl. Perhaps if I prove I can run a household at fifteen this position will lead to better things.

Perhaps it won't be the calamity I am beginning to fear.

Chapter Three

The window is pulled down as far as it will go. All I can see of the outside world are the area railings and the legs of passing horses and people in the street. It is early and these are working folk, for the gentry are still abed. The air is busy with the rumble of wagons and handcarts hauling food into the city.

Already the kitchen is better and I proudly smooth the heavy wooden table with my hand. It is scraped and scoured almost white. The chamber pots are emptied. The water jugs filled.

A fire is set in the bedroom where the master and mistress are snoring so loudly behind their bed curtains that I am astonished they don't wake one another. I had worried the beef I roasted yesterday was tough when Master Chalke haggled at it with the carving knife, but nothing was said. The shortcomings of the girl before me have masked my inexperience and I am relieved.

He is a big man. Fleshy rather than fat, and must have been fine-looking in his youth. He wore an ivory waistcoat embroidered with flowers and butterflies, its tiny silver buttons cascading down the silk like rainwater on glass. It impressed me that he stuffed a linen napkin under his chin to protect it from the grease of his dinner.

He is a proper gentleman. I can tell from his voice and manners as well as his dress. More used, I can believe, to a great estate somewhere than to this gloomy house with only the crippled Peg and myself to wait on him. More used, surely, to fine ladies than to our mistress who looks like a poor relation brought in, for charity, as governess to someone's spoiled children. And uses language belonging in a stable yard.

I intend to discover what is so secret about his book room. The door was open last night and I glimpsed him at a great desk piled with papers, a quill in his hand. But as soon as he saw me looking, he levered himself out of the chair and whumped the door shut.

I hear Peg dragging her brush over the front steps, water slopping and the wooden bucket scraping, and smile that my pots are clean, if not bright. The mouse droppings are swept from the corners and the bread is baking, its yeasty smell chasing away the ghosts of sourness and neglect. My loaves will be nothing like Mrs Lamb's, but this household's standards are low.

There is a clatter outside. Hooves on cobbles. A deep voice.

'Wholesome milk! Fresh country milk!'

'Get to know the trades-people,' Mrs Lamb had urged. 'Sift the honest men from the rogues and be friendly. Encourage them to give you a fair measure. But don't let anyone think you a simpleton because you are young.'

I grab the coins I was given last night and hurry out, but although a bay horse and a four-wheeled wagon stand on the cobbles, the man selling milk must be busy with an order in a nearby house.

It is a beautiful blue-sky morning. Cold, but bright.

A dog's head pokes out from under the canvas cover, tongue lolling. He has such a broad, bony head that I move closer, to examine him.

'Good morning, dog,' I say, formally. He is brindle and white, with a patch of mottled colour over one intelligent eye. Handsome in a strange way.

'Get away from the dog!' The shout makes me jump and my fingers, about to stroke the animal, freeze in mid-air. A man is behind me, his boots surprisingly quiet on the cobblestones.

'I was not doing anything wrong, Mister.' I stiffen. He is a tall pillar in a coat the colour of burned toast. Black hair and a broad forehead. An expression between a frown and a scowl.

'He is not some lady's lap dog. He is there to guard the wagon.'

'I didn't touch your wagon.'

'Maybe not. But unless it is nailed down, anything of value around here disappears.'

'I am no thief!'

'Who is saying you are?' He clinks coins into the leather pouch at his belt and I wonder how he keeps customers if he is always like this. Maybe there should be a warning about him, not the dog.

'Hector can bite. You wouldn't want to lose your fingers.'

'Well, I need a quart of milk.' I remember my manners, even if he has none. '*Please.*' I hold out my money, which a large hand takes and tosses into the pouch.

'Hardly worth stopping for. Don't they like milk in your house?'

'I suppose not. It is only my second day.'

'You are the new kitchen maid?'

'Cook and housemaid.' I try to stand taller. 'And I am in a hurry.'

There is an almost imperceptible shrug of his shoulders as he transfers milk from his churn to my container with a tin pannikin. The wagon is smart, with yellow paint on its wheels and body. The man might look as if he has lost a guinea but picked up sixpence, but he is a good tradesman which is all that need concern me.

'But not so much of a hurry you can't poke your fingers into the jaws of a strange dog.'

Remembering Mrs Lamb's advice, I summon a smile.

'I thought Hector loved peace. Despite being a famous warrior.'

Black eyes stare down at me.

'Since when does a housemaid know about the Greeks?'

I stop myself asking how a man selling milk knows of them. But he is unusually well-dressed and well-spoken. This is the first proper conversation I have had since leaving Mistress Buttermere's and I expect I will see this man most mornings.

'I used to read stories about them, with my mother.'

'And you like dogs? As well as stories?'

'If they are friendly.' I look at the animal, who thrashes his tail. He doesn't look savage. 'His face is like the curve of a bowl.'

'He is a cross between a bulldog and a terrier. I bought him to chase the rats from my barn. The whole litter had those noses. Like faces on coins from the time of Julius Caesar.'

I take the jug from him, thinking I might ask Mistress Chalke if she would like a milk pudding. I can make those, if she will let me. All it takes is sugar and rice. These are cheap, which the bad-tempered witch will approve.

The dog leaps off the wagon and approaches us, legs splaying, as if bowing. He is quite a big dog. Muscular, but fast-moving. I could imagine him being an efficient ratter.

'What does it mean, when he does that?'

'He has seen us talking and knows you are not a threat. Now he wants a stick thrown for him.'

I am taken with the idea of this great, stern man unbending to play with his dog. People are not always what they seem.

''Ere!' A stocky maidservant from the next house stands by the area steps, hands on hips, apron flapping in the wind, two large pitchers by her feet. From the prominent nose, I presume she is the gossip Mistress Chalke warned me against. 'Come away, Farmer

Graham. Some of us don't have all day for tittle-tattle.'

The man scoops up the dog with one arm and pitches it onto the wagon.

'Walk on!' he tells the horse and they move off to their next customer without a backward glance.

I carry the milk down the steps, careful not to spill it. At least I have had a friendly word with somebody, even if it is only a farmer with a wagon.

Peg is back in the kitchen, avoiding my eye.

'What is that? In your hand?' I must not let her think, because I am young, she can take liberties.

She squirms against the wall, one arm behind her back and I wonder what she can have found to steal. There is little enough.

'Show me.'

She holds up the mouldy bread I threw out earlier for the sparrows. It is dirty from the yard and looks as if a rat has gnawed it. A rat with broken teeth and a leg that does not work properly.

'Are you hungry?' I frown at the thinness of her shoulders. The wrists like bird-bones. 'Hungry enough to eat that?'

She studies the floor.

'What I gets from the mistress only pays for where I sleeps.' She looks up, the crust disintegrating in restive fingers. 'But I wouldn't never complain about me wages. You won't say I did?'

If it only pays for her room, what does she do for food, for clothes, for heat? Peg gets a bowl of water gruel every morning and a heel of bread at mid-day. I hadn't thought – *why hadn't I thought?* – what else she might have to keep her from starvation.

I shake my head in reassurance and go to the pantry. On the floor are sacks of potatoes. Above my head, suspended from hooks, hang pieces of bacon and strings of onions. On a slab of marble for coolness, and covered with china bowls to save them from mice, sit blocks of butter and cheese. But they have been divided into squares with a knife by Mistress Chalke and her flinty eye will know if anything is taken. Yet under a cracked saucer is a bowl of dripping from yesterday's joint with rich jelly at the bottom and, next to it, a stale loaf that I am planning to use for a pudding.

I grab a knife. One slice will not go amiss. I carve off a chunk and thrust it deep into the dripping. It comes up rich with the smell of roast beef and makes even my mouth water.

'Here.' I turn a cautious ear towards the stairs, but all is silent. 'Take it into the yard.'

Peg's haggard face brightens and she seizes the food, devouring it already with her eyes.

'Thank you, Miss...'

'Don't thank me. Get it eaten, before we are caught.'

I stand the dripping by the fire to melt so that when the surface sets again nothing will show what has been taken. Then I go into the scullery to check the tubs of soaking laundry, guilty at my earlier lack of charity.

Our coarse-mouthed mistress may be able to command my body, but my mind is my own. I will somehow stretch the food to put some flesh on Peg and, while I am at it, find out if it is only beatings the old woman fears in this strange house. Or something more. Something in that locked room.

Chapter Four

'Be sure to put that into Goodman Twyford's own hand.' The master's fingers grip the package until I have acknowledged his instruction. 'Understand, girl?'

'Yes, sir. I must give it to Goodman Twyford. Nobody else.'

I have to stop my eyes searching the room. The best furniture is in here, some of it remarkably fine, but otherwise nothing to explain the room's mysteries.

A round table stands at the far end, surrounded by chairs and with an ornate silver candelabra standing at its centre. He had guests last night, though I failed to see them because he brought them into the house with him and, unusually, the mistress took up their wine. Perhaps they played cards around the table. They were noisy enough and I heard sums of money shouted out.

It must be what he does in here that is so secret. Is he composing something people will wonder at, like Dr Johnston's *Dictionary*? The desk is heaped with papers I would love to study. Or even help with. Then I hear the whisper of Mrs Lamb's favourite rebuke: 'Remember your place, Hannah.'

My father may have been a silk weaver and my grandfather a merchant, but that was all in the past. I am now just a girl wearing a coarse apron.

Master Chalke continues to stare, as if assessing my trustworthiness. He is a squint-eye, with one brown orb staring at me while the other wanders outwards as if utterly indifferent to my presence. As usual in the mornings he wears a striped green and pink banyan over his shirt and breeches. His matching silk nightcap is askew, though I wouldn't dare mention it. He is a clever man. An educated man. Perhaps a writer of important books.

'He will give you something in return. To bring back.'

'Yes, sir.'

He loosens his grip on the package. It does not feel weighty, but words don't need to be.

'Take proper care of both errands and there might be a farthing for you when you get back.'

I would like a farthing. My three guineas will not be in my hand until next Lady Day and Mistress Chalke has said, with a vicious pinch to my arm to drive home her point, that she never pays servants half-way through their term. All I have left from Mistress Buttermere's wages, after buying new boots for my growing feet, some dark blue cloth for a gown, and a fresh pair of stays, is one bright guinea and the shilling Mrs Lamb slipped into my hand as a parting gift.

Master Chalke slumps back in his chair. Soon he will shrug himself into a velvet coat and take himself off to Slaughters' Coffee Shop in St Martin's Lane. It has to be his work that must be kept secret. But why? Is he fearful someone might steal his ideas?

The neat parcel in my hand has been sealed with the master's gold ring to keep it private. Before I leave the house, I examine the impression in the wax. A strange beast, rearing up to display sharp teeth, with a ragged staff in its paw. The same creature inlaid on a shield into the backs of the hall chairs. They resemble some Mistress Buttermere had from her husband's old family house. An armorial, Mrs Lamb told me it was called. Reserved for lords and ladies.

I grab my shawl, not wishing to waste time. I have heard booksellers can have printing presses in their back rooms. Perhaps my new master is creating a masterpiece from the pages I carry.

Fifteen minutes later, as I turn into the square, I hear someone whistling merrily. The day is bright as a new penny and feels like a holiday, making me wish the booksellers further away, to prolong my outing. I have always loved to walk. It is a time to let my imagination soar. A pretence at being free. But remembering the chores awaiting me, I know I cannot dawdle.

The shop has small glass panes through which I get a tantalising glimpse of books and prints. The hanging sign shows the silhouette of a bewigged gentleman clutching a little girl's hand while studying a book.

A young man is perched at the top of a ladder, cleaning the upstairs windows. The merry whistler. He looks to be making a proper job of it as I smell the sharpness of vinegar in the water in his bucket and hear the squeak of his cloth against the glass. He has unusually fair and wavy hair, restrained at his nape with a navy ribbon. His rolled-up shirt sleeves show muscles flexing in strong forearms.

Startling blue eyes smile down at me as I step towards the doorway.

'Mind my water don't splash your clean cap, little miss.'

I pause in my stride. He is right; there are dirty beads of moisture falling from above. My only other cap is soaking in the scullery.

'Two minutes and I'll have this finished.' He eyes my parcel. 'Or I could take that from you.' He drapes the cloth over a rung and dries his hands on the backside of his breeches. 'It will be safe with me.'

He has full lips, almost like a girl.

'I must put this into Master Twyford's own hand. It is from Master Chalke.'

'One of his special deliveries?' There is a glint in the youth's eye as he retrieves his cloth, wrings it dry and wipes away the threat to my mob cap. Then he slides down his ladder, showing off I suspect, and bows me through into the shop.

'I am Jack,' he grins. 'Master Twyford's apprentice.'

We are surrounded by books, their spines gleaming with gold lettering. There is an intoxicating odour of leather.

I have never been in a bookseller's before, never so close to such a hoard of unread words. The master's books at home are locked in glass-fronted library cases and I am forbidden to linger near them when cleaning the otherwise ordinary-looking room. Always with Mistress Chalke's malignant eye watching. But one of these days I intend to at least study their titles.

The apprentice takes a step towards me and there is a faint whiff of male sweat.

'You have so many books,' I say.

'Hundreds. With more, upstairs.' He winks at me in a way I do not quite like. 'For our special customers.'

I cannot stop myself asking: 'Do you have the *Tales of the Arabian Nights*?'

'I believe so.' He grins. 'Though that doesn't sound like Master Chalke's preferred reading.'

'It is not for him.'

'For you?' His eyebrows rise and I think of my meagre store of coins. One day I intend to have a book of my own. Perhaps after I am paid.

'What is your cheapest book?' There is no harm asking.

'We have some poetry by Master Thomas Gray. At nine pence. About his cat, drowning when she tries to hook goldfish from a bowl. Not to everyone's taste, but you may like it.'

The youth's eyes are the colour of the sky. He is so polite that you would think I was a proper customer. Not just a maid on an errand.

'Would you like to see it? There is no obligation to buy.'

'I am here for my master.' I straighten my back. 'Not to buy books.'

The apprentice studies me with what feels like sympathy. Perhaps he has seen the hunger in my eyes.

'Why not? If you fancy one, there are less expensive books to be found on the market stalls in Cheapside. Or pawn shops have second-hand volumes they would be glad to sell. Reading can be found to suit the most slender of purses.'

I will not seek such luxuries for myself, not yet at least, but enjoy the novelty of being spoken to as someone who might appreciate a book of poetry. What is more, from the way he sticks out his chest and stands tall, I see I am expected to be impressed by his looks. As if I might matter.

But all I feel is envy. That he is a young man, not a powerless girl. That he is apprenticed to a good trade and will likely have a shop like this of his own one day. Even that he is happy enough in his work to whistle. But most of all that he is here, every day, surrounded by books with their wonderful smells and crisp uncut pages, full of stories.

Our talk is interrupted by a ponderous creaking as a barrel of a man lumbers down the stairs into the shop. This must be Master Twyford. A protrusion of shirt and belly threaten to erupt from his broadcloth coat like a punctured bolster. I wouldn't like the feeding of him.

'Trifling with maidservants, Jack?' His smile is indulgent. Then he notices the package in my hand and frowns. I am clearly not a customer about to part with guineas. 'What is it, girl?'

'I have brought this from Master Chalke, sir.'

'It is about time.' The fist that snatches the package is podgy from good living. 'What is he thinking of, keeping me waiting?'

'I am sorry, sir. I only know I was to bring it to you.' I study my feet to hide surprise at his lack of respect.

Master Twyford grunts, suggesting he thinks the delay, if there is one, must be my fault. Perhaps he is related to my mistress.

'Jack, fetch those proofs from my table upstairs.'

He stares at me while we wait, making me wonder if my cap is not straight.

Jack soon thunders down the stairs again, on legs younger and stronger than those of his master, and places another sealed packet in my hand. I suppose if I were a writer of books I, too, would treat the pages like something precious.

'Thank you,' I say, thinking what a pleasant way this is to earn a farthing.

Jack ushers me through the door into the street as Master Twyford labours back upstairs.

'We will meet again, little miss,' the apprentice says, pursing those fleshy lips and making a mock bow. Then he straightens to his full height and winks again, as if we are conspirators.

I almost skip back to the Chalke house, daring to imagine an alternative world, where I am not just a beast of burden. Invisible unless I do something wrong. Where people expect me to buy books of poetry. Where a young man with cornflower bright eyes treats me as an equal. Where there might be more in my future than ferrying stinking chamber pots to the necessary house.

Chapter Five

'Best watch yourself.' The voice behind me is coarse and low and I turn to see next door's inquisitive maidservant at my elbow.

The market around us is a hubbub, but it is as if we are alone in the throng.

'What do you mean?' I draw my basket tight against my body as if she might snatch it from me. Her eyes are more curious than threatening, but the mistress was right about that nose. I look away from it, in case she catches me staring and takes offence. She seems a rough character.

''Aint you scared of that place?' She sets down a wooden pail full of live eels. Cheap food for the servants' hall, I suppose. 'You should be.'

'I must not gossip.' My feet itch to run away from this woman with her eels. 'The mistress forbids it.'

'I bet she does.' Her breath is hot in my face. The gravelly voice indignant. 'I used to share a laugh with their last girl, when we had the chance. Until the silly bitch got taken by the constables.'

I study the silver bodies writhing in her pail, no more able to escape their fate than I am. I have thought of buying eels for Peg and myself, but hate the idea of slicing into living creatures.

'Everyone thinks them Chalkes are a queer pair.' The maid clears her throat and spits noisily into the gutter. 'There are gentlemen glad enough of Master Chalke's company. When it suits them. But nobody wants to know her. Even the son made off, as soon as he was old enough. Boy could not get far enough away, if you ask me.' She hawks and spits again. 'The raddled old bitch casts out servants like shit through a goose. Susan might have been a giddy trollop, but she didn't deserve to be hauled-off to Bridewell. Screeching she had done nothing wrong. But 'tweren't no use. She was took away, all the same.'

I stare at my feet. If the mistress knew about this I would be instantly dismissed. Yet the long-nosed maid's accusations fix me to the spot. Isn't this what I suspect? That the Chalke house is not as it should be?

'Susan weren't no thief,' the maid insists. 'But, after the stupid chit threatened to blab about the pair of them, they said she'd taken their spoons. A wicked lie!' Her voice squeaks with indignation, making a passing housewife pause, mid-stride, to stare. 'Branded with a 'T', for thief, she was. On the fleshy part of her thumb. Then shipped to the Americas as an indentured servant.'

She leans in, closer, and I smell dog on her. The family keep a brace of yapping King Charles spaniels who I suspect sleep in the kitchens.

'Because she knew too much.'

My fingers are so tight around the handle of the basket that I feel the pattern imprinted in my flesh. I should get away from this woman. She is clearly a troublemaker. Someone to be avoided. Yet she could explain things I do not understand so I cannot hold back the question:

'Knew too much? About what?'

She shakes her head and mutters, right in my ear. 'That I won't say. But I knows what I knows.'

I recoil as she wipes at a gob of snot with the back of her wrist. Then she hoicks the pail back over her brawny forearm and leans in, for a final warning. 'But if I was you, I would scarper. Smartish. While that pretty pink and white skin is still unmarked.'

Chapter Six

Mrs Lamb's round face is the deep pink of a squashed strawberry. A straggle of grey hair has escaped her frilled cap. Her apron of fine Holland linen, though white as a boil-wash can make it, looks limp.

Packing straw clings to my boots and the kitchen is stacked with corded boxes.

'I should not have come,' I say.

'Nay, Hannah.' She flops into a chair and eases off her shoes. 'I have been worried about you. How are you getting on?'

I breathe in the familiar scents of the Buttermere kitchen. Traces of the morning's bread, spiced with cinnamon from something baked for the upstairs table. Beeswax polish from the dresser. Rosewater from shifts airing by the hearth.

'Mistress Chalke is no lady. Her language reminds me of that groom Major Harper brought with him last summer. The one Mistress Buttermere made him send away.'

Mrs Lamb wrinkles her nose, no doubt remembering the man and his colourful oaths.

'When I was young, Hannah,' she says, 'I was sent as maid to an aristocratic house near Winchester. My employer was master of the local hunt and he and his wife rode out every day in the season.' She shakes her head, disapproving. 'Both of them swore like troopers.'

'This is different. The woman is vulgar and coarse. And I am convinced she dyes that hair. It is black as a lump of coal. At her age.'

'Even the finest gentleman can marry a woman he shouldn't,' Mrs Lamb shrugs. 'A governess. A shopkeeper's daughter. Even an actress. Perhaps that is why Master Chalke was disinherited. For making an unsuitable alliance.'

I grunt. Unconvinced she was any of those things.

'She never washes. Her armpits smell. And her house was a disgrace, though at least I have persuaded the skinflint to buy mouse traps.' I look around expectantly. 'Where is Puss?'

'Next door.' Mrs Lamb smiles. 'Little Sophy wanted her.'

25

I am pleased that Puss has found a good home. Sir Christopher is an old-fashioned man, said to be harsh as a wire brush to law breakers when he sits on the bench, but in thrall to five small daughters.

'They have oil paintings on the walls and fine silver on their table, yet every penny is turned over before it is spent.'

Mrs Lamb wriggles her toes and sighs. 'As I told you, your master is from a noble family, but his older brother got the inheritance. There will not be the money Chalke grew up with. But at least they are feeding you. You have filled-out since I saw you last.'

'I get enough. But there is an old cripple working there. So thin, you can almost see through her.'

'The scrub-woman?'

'Peg is not strong enough for rough work and gets beaten because of it. I am trying to put flesh on her, but it is impossible. The larder is checked every night in case I help myself. Even the eggs are counted.'

'A pity, because what your Peg needs is a fresh hen's egg beaten in milk. Every morning.'

'I will tell Mistress Chalke.' My lip curls. 'I expect she will volunteer some of the master's best Madeira to go with it.'

'Well, help yourself from our stores. We cannot take half of what is in that pantry.' Mrs Lamb leans forward. 'But tell me about the girl you are replacing? Was she really turned off for lewd behaviour?' Faded hazel eyes gleam at the prospect of spicy gossip.

'The maid next door says Susan was transported to the Americas. Not for lewd behaviour. For theft. She reckons that the Chalkes lied about her taking their silver.'

'Lied? Why would they do that? It is easy enough, more's the pity, to send a servant packing with no character if she does not suit.'

Mrs Lamb rests a plump hand on mine. 'It could be malicious gossip. Whatever the truth, they will appreciate someone like you all the more. But tell me about your master.'

'He is a proper gentleman. The mistress moans that he spends too much time at the coffee house, but what man wouldn't, shackled to such a wife?' I lean forward. 'I think he is writing a book.'

'If he is a lover of words,' Mrs Lamb smiles, 'you are in the right place.'

'But everything is locked away and I am not allowed near.'

I think back to how I was allowed into the Buttermere library. Dipping not only into books by Fielding and Swift, but old periodicals belonging to Mistress Buttermere's late husband. One wet Sunday, I devoured a *Gentleman's Magazine* of 1759 with an account of strange bodies, buried for centuries in ash, dug up somewhere in Italy. It said they were preserved where they fell when a great volcano erupted.

'At least he is not mean. Yesterday he paid six shillings for four bottles of port. And they are already empty.'

'Gentlemen can be over-partial to their wine.' Mrs Lamb's brow wrinkles. 'Let's hope he is not a drunkard.'

'Oh, no. It is for his friends. They shut themselves in his book room and it sounds as if he reads to them. I am sure I could help with his work, for I have a good secretary's hand.'

'Hannah, from what you say about the dirt, a maid is what that house needs.' She purses her lips. 'Remember what I told you: never draw unnecessary attention to yourself. Concentrate on pleasing your mistress.'

My basket is on the table and I grasp the handle with a sigh, thinking what an impossibility that is. 'Then, may I take food for Peg?'

'Aye. The mistress would not begrudge you.'

I step into the pantry and take a deep breath. Each smell is a memory. Of cutting lavender from the back courtyard and bunching it with string to hang from the ceiling beams to dry. Of boiling vinegar when we pickled the cucumbers. Of hot fruit and sugar seething on the hob after Mistress Buttermere's daughter brought plums from Yorkshire last summer.

There is a bustle behind me. It is Mrs Lamb, smelling faintly of the dried rose petals she sprinkles in the press holding Mistress Buttermere's clothes. It is no secret some find their way among her own under linen.

'Is your crippled woman truly starving?'

'She can barely drag herself about.'

We both know how it will end if she loses her work. The

poorhouse or the gutter. It could be us one day. Peg is at the bottom of society. I am one rung higher. Mrs Lamb two. And I know from experience how much easier it is to fall than to rise.

'Then take some eggs for the poor soul.' The housekeeper clucks disapproval. 'Does your mistress not care what the neighbours say? Letting one of her servants starve?'

'The old misery is hard as brimstone.' I pause, wanting to share my bubbling fears. 'Something bad happened between Peg and the Mistress. In the past. I am convinced of it.'

'Come, Hannah. Curb that imagination before it brings you trouble. Your mistress has given employment to an old cripple. How many ladies would have the charity to do that? She cannot be all bad. Can she?'

I nod my head, reluctant. What she says is true. Peg would otherwise be begging for scraps.

When I leave, I can barely heft the basket and over my shoulder is an old shawl, stuffed with cast-off stockings and a warm petticoat for Peg.

It grieved me to say goodbye to Mrs Lamb, with her soft double chin and kind heart. She is my only friend in London. In the whole wide world, for that matter. And soon she will be far away in York.

Walking down the street, I struggle to convince myself she is right about Peg and the mistress. If you are crippled there is only the poorhouse or the graveyard. Perhaps I am wrong and under that implacable whalebone Mistress Chalke does have something resembling a heart.

Yet my mind slips back to the night my friend Mary was taken away in the middle of the night, snivelling, to an unknown fate. That could have been me. Might still be me, if I am in the power of people who mean to take advantage of my being without friends or family. Why else was Mistress Chalke so anxious for my parents to be dead?

Chapter Seven

'Miss?'

Peg hunches in the scullery doorway. At least she is not afraid of me now, though there is still that odd expression in her eyes when I catch her watching me. Almost as if she is sorry for me, though that can hardly be.

'What is it?'

Hidden in a drawer is a clutch of eggs from the Buttermere pantry. Peg will get one while the mistress takes her afternoon rest.

'Can I put this in the embers of the fire?' She draws a bruised-looking potato from her pocket. 'They are hard to eat. Raw.'

I have not liked to stare at how she struggles with food or ask what happened to her mouth. A terrible accident presumably. The one that crippled her.

'Is it one of ours?'

'Lord, no, Miss! I wouldn't *never* steal from the mistress!' She sucks in breath, as if to calm herself. 'It was in the gutter when I walked through the market.'

'To take home? For your supper?'

She nods, still anxious. Quick to fear. Even over what will be her meagre supper when she returns to some miserable room after her work. Why is Mistress Chalke so cruel? To a pathetic creature like Peg?

'Of course, you may bake it in the embers. And take another from the pantry. I do not consider that stealing.' I suspect the skinflint would not agree, but don't care. That woman is as unbending as a poker and I despise her for it. 'Come, Peg. Mistress Chalke never checks the vegetables.'

The old woman hobbles away and I rake the embers aside to position her potatoes where they will cook, but not burn. Though she does not know it yet, today will be a feast day for the poor soul. A fresh egg in milk in the afternoon. Two baked potatoes for supper.

Half an hour later, I hold my tankard out to Farmer Graham, who has already filled my jug and pauses, one eyebrow raised.

'May I have a farthing's worth more, please.'

'Do the Chalkes not allow you milk?'

'It is not for me.' I dig into my pocket and glance at Peg, dragging the scrubbing brush across the front steps as if it weighs half a hundredweight. The wooden bucket contains only inches of water since she cannot lift a full one.

Farmer Graham fills the tankard. 'Keep your farthing.'

'I want to pay.' I thrust out my hand.

He accepts the coin and it shines in his palm for a moment before going into his pouch.

'The widow's mite. You have a tender heart.'

I know the Bible story as well as he does and bridle, disliking him knowing how much the small coin represents to me. Yet I see he means no harm and he *was* going to let me have that extra milk for nothing.

'If I am kind-hearted, it is my mother's teaching.'

'Then she will be proud of you.'

There is a pause, while I remember a long-gone life. A canary singing in a cage. The smell of my mother's hair. How can I admit she rots in a paupers' grave?

'What is it like, living on a farm?' I ask, instead. Life in the Chalke house is nothing but work and scolding, usually accompanied by a clip round the ear.

'How do you imagine it?'

'Not grey like the city and hemmed in by houses. Or noisy as a fairground with jostling carriages, horses and people.'

I half-close my eyes and try to picture it. There is an oil painting of the countryside in the book room, next to the locked library cases. It has a castle in the background and an arrogant-looking man posturing for the artist, a gun under one arm and a groom beside him restraining a black stallion. But such grand places hold scant interest for me.

'Meadows full of ripe corn. Cows grazing a field of buttercups. Trees as big as houses. Ducks on a pond, with ducklings bobbing behind.'

Something like a smile lights his face and despite the lines at the side of his mouth I see he's probably not as old as I thought. Perhaps twenty-five or thereabouts.

'The reality, after the winter rains, is mud with my cows still in their byre, knee-deep in tired straw. Hopefully, they will stay healthy until they are led out for the spring grass. But if we have a hot summer, the grazing could suffer and their milk dry up. There is always something to go wrong on a farm.'

I didn't think him capable of such a long speech. At least, not to me.

'It *can* be like your fairy tale,' he relents, seeing my disappointment. 'But more usually there is mud and a deal of hard work.'

I nod: familiar with hard work. He must get up even earlier than I do, to drive into the city each morning. It still surprises me he does not employ a man to do the round for him since his clothes and wagon are prosperous. He is educated. And he has a farm.

'You would like my cows,' he says. 'Some are mischievous while others are meek as spinsters in a church pew.' He holds up strong hands: tanned by the weather and calloused from the use of reins. 'They do not care for me to do the milking, but on occasion must make the best of it. Though they will try to knock over the milking pail or give me a sly kick.'

I rest the milk containers by the freshly swept steps and move to pat his horse's nose, loving the warmth of her breath on my stroking hand. Peg has finished her half-hearted scrubbing, swept the suds away and trailed back down to the kitchen.

'Peaseblossom trod on me last week. A cow weighs nearly half a ton. Have one stomp on your foot and you know about it, even if you are wearing a stout leather boot. I was hopping on one leg, in a temper. Like a bee, cross at being trapped in a bottle. Till I saw the humour in it.'

I cannot help smiling at the picture he paints. He is not solemn after all.

'She has an odd name.'

'My cow is named for a fairy. In a play by William Shakespeare.'

'Did you tell your fairy off? Give her a whack?' There is a riding crop on the wagon with a battered silver fox's head that looks as if it might have belonged to his father.

'She merely switched her tail and looked sideways at me. Like a young miss who has trodden on her dancing partner.' A proper smile lights his face. 'My animals all have stories attached to their names. Our Berkshire sow is Aphrodite. Because of her complicated love life and numerous children. She farrowed nine piglets only last week. My other horse is called Hercules.'

'Does he have a clean stable?' I ask, which provokes a brief bark of laughter.

I bite back a wish to say how I would love to see all this. But my place is in a kitchen not a farmyard. 'Do you have lambs?' I ask, instead. April is the time for such life-affirming creatures.

For a moment his face looks again as it did that first morning. Stern. Closed.

'No,' he says. 'I will not have lambs on my farm.'

He turns abruptly back to his horse.

'Walk on, Calypso. There is milk to deliver.'

The horse clops patiently towards the next house, harness jingling, her master at her side. Perhaps tomorrow I will ask him about that play, for although he can be moody, he is clearly a man who enjoys books and stories and I decide I like him. Even if, for some reason, he has an aversion to lambs.

Later, Peg settles into the ladderback chair and stretches thin ankles towards the fire. She grasps the tankard in both hands, raises it to her mouth and gulps.

I have done as Mrs Lamb suggested and beaten an egg into the milk, even sneaking a scrape of sugar from the loaf. Peg will get one a day until they are gone.

'Slowly,' I say, touching her arm. 'That will be rich for your stomach.'

She pauses, the rim of white around her mouth reminding me of Puss after she'd had her nose in a bowl of cream. There are what look like tears in her rheumy eyes and I wonder when someone last did her a kindness.

'You been good to me, Miss.'

'Take time to enjoy it. We will have ten minutes by the fire before getting the washing out of soak.'

She cradles the tankard in thin hands, like something precious. To her, of course, it is precious. Food is life.

'How did a nice girl like you end up here?'

'My mistress heard yours wanted a maid.' I shrug, as if I do not care. 'She was going to York and couldn't take me with her.'

'You needs to get away.' Peg licks her lips. It is unusual for her to speak unless spoken to and I stare, remembering the gossiping maid with the nose.

'What do you mean?'

'Find another place.'

'I will. At the end of my year.'

Peg studies the dregs in her tankard. 'The old bitch would skin me alive if she thought I was warning you. But you needs to be gone before then.'

'Why?'

'Because they are wicked, that's why. Young maids in their charge comes to no good.' She looks up and her eyes are bleak holes. 'But I won't say more. Just make sure you gets another place before the spring.'

I lean forward, busying myself poking at the fire and refusing to give way to fear. It would not help me. But nor will ignorance. What does Peg know, that she is afraid to talk about? And what am I to do? Ignore two warnings?

Chapter Eight

It scares me. Thundering at the front door when Mistress Chalke and I are alone in the house, close to midnight, with the master dining late with friends. Then, when I recognise his voice and open up, I nearly faint.

'Master!'

His hat and wig are gone. His coat is filthy. Blood oozes through the silver bristles on his head.

'I was set upon...'

He slumps against the wall as I slam the door and shoot home the bolts. It is pitch black outside and I worry that his assailant might be near.

'We must call the watch, sir. And a surgeon.'

I glance up the stairs, surprised Mistress Chalke has slept through the noise.

'Nay, girl. Let me get my breath.'

'But you are bleeding, sir.'

He shakes himself upright. 'Is the kitchen fire still lit?'

'It is. And I can stoke it to a blaze in a moment.'

'Then help me downstairs. We can manage without calling any interfering sawbones.'

He leans heavily on me as we stumble to the basement, the stink of his coat ripe in my nostrils. What has he been doing walking the streets at this hour?

'Was it a footpad, sir?'

He collapses into the kitchen chair. 'There were two of them. With cudgels.'

'Let me call the mistress.' I light one of the kitchen's tallow dips and put water to heat. 'She will want to know what has happened.'

'More likely she will abuse me. For not paying a link boy.'

The chair scrapes the stone flags as he stands again.

'Help me out of this.'

As I ease the coat from his shoulders, I see his waistcoat has lost its buttons. It is my favourite. The colour of egg yolk, its texture silky to the touch.

He sees my glance and frowns at the damage.

34

'You must mend this tomorrow. There are spare buttons on a dove-grey velvet upstairs in the bottom of Charles's old wardrobe.'

As I place warm water and a cloth before him, he empties his pockets onto the table, including his gilt snuff box.

'The scoundrels threw my possessions in the gutter, like rubbish.'

'Yet took nothing?'

'Quit chattering. Tend to my head.'

He winces as I clean the gash and I notice the glint of his signet ring. What footpads would ignore gold?

'They kicked me with their great boots after I fell.' His fist slams the table. 'Were I twenty years younger, wearing my sword, I would have skewered them.'

'You are sure I shouldn't call the watch?'

'To what purpose? The brutes will be the other side of London by now.' His voice turns petulant. 'Get me some burned wine. That should set me to rights.'

'Then I must rouse the mistress. For the wine cupboard key.'

He leans forward, making the chair creak, and hooks a brass key from the pile on the table. Slaps it into my hand.

'Go up to my Chinese cabinet in the book room and pull out the central drawer. In the space behind is a leather pouch full of keys. Bring the one tied with black ribbon. It is a duplicate of hers.'

The Chinese cabinet is the thing I admire most in that room because of the figures in strange costumes inlaid in the black lacquered wood. There is a river with two people on a hump-backed bridge, lovers perhaps, picked out in mother-of-pearl. A willow weeps from the sloping shore, with a building that might be a temple in the distance and a long-legged bird circling above. The lady holds a curious-looking umbrella and the couple look to be whispering beneath it. I would love to know their story.

I hurry to do as I am bid, glad to show how much better I am than the useless Susan. I cannot get the warnings I have had out of my head, but the house was a disgrace. I would have given notice to the girl myself if I had been in charge of her.

And that business about being falsely transported could have been invented by an ignorant woman keen to make mischief. As for Peg, there may be something wrong with her head, as well as with her teeth and leg.

When I reach the book room, open the door and locate the hidden pouch, I tip its contents onto the desk and extract the one with the black ribbon. As I replace the others, each tied with a loop of coloured silk, I wonder what they fit.

The best silver is under lock and key in the cellar, so what do the Chalkes keep hidden up here?

I snatch a glance at the bookcases, but the titles through the glass all seem to be in foreign languages and tell me nothing. The desk will be the place to look, but a quick tug at a drawer confirms it is locked.

The poker has been heating in the fire and when I get back to the kitchen, I break nibs of sugar from the loaf and drop them into a pewter tankard with cloves, adding grated nutmeg and cinnamon. Then I pour in the claret and some honey. When I plunge in the glowing iron, it spits like an alley cat and the aroma reminds me of Mistress Buttermere's Christmas punch bowl.

'Give it here.' Master Chalke snatches the tankard and gulps, smacking his lips and letting out a satisfied-sounding belch. 'By God, that's better. Now I will go up and try for sleep.'

He heaves himself to his feet, but pauses a moment, a large hand coming to rest clumsily on my head. 'You are an obliging girl, Hannah. I like obliging girls.' Then he belches again and wipes his mouth. 'You will have a coin for this night's work. Tomorrow.'

Mrs Lamb said there might be vails for me here, either from visitors or my employers. Small gifts of money for being extra helpful. And I need to squirrel away as much as I can, in case I am forced to leave before the end of my term.

That pat on my head was the first kind gesture I have had in this house. Yet I cannot help wondering where the master has been and why those ruffians would beat, but not rob him. Might it have been a grudge of some kind? But what dealings would a gentleman have with men who wear rough boots?

I need to uncover the secrets that are hidden in the book room along with Master Chalke's writing. The ones Susan gossiped about and Peg is so afraid of. But at least I now know where the keys are kept.

Chapter Nine

'You will think I have no manners.'

Glancing up from my brimming pitcher I must look puzzled, for Farmer Graham bends towards me. He is a good foot taller than I am.

'When you asked about the lambs.' he says. 'Yesterday.'

'I shouldn't stick my nose in other people's business.'

'On the contrary, it shows a girl who cares. I was churlish. Encouraging you to ask about my farm, then being rude when you did so.'

'It is not a kitchen maid's place to question people.'

'But you are a cook and housemaid.' His lips form a faint smile. 'Not just a kitchen maid.'

'Even so...' I should get on with my work, but I am intrigued by his farm, away from the city.

'Your mention of lambs brought everything back.' He gazes past me, over the rooftops towards the leaden sky. 'My twin sons wanted one to hand-rear. I had heard a farm across the valley had orphans, so I rode over one afternoon. My neighbour was growing clover and turnips for his animals and I was persuaded to spend the night so we could discuss farming matters.

'Then I took the lamb home next morning, tucked into the front of my old riding coat. It seemed content enough against my warmth and I was picturing the joy it would bring my boys.' He shakes his head. 'But when I reached Broad Oak everyone had the fever. Edmund. Henry. Even Elizabeth, my wife.'

The furrows beside his mouth have reappeared and I see that the look in those dark eyes is sorrow.

'It was over quickly. The lamb died, too. Poor creature. Nobody had time to tend it properly.'

Death is everywhere. Nobody is safe, from the greatest in the land to the least. Mrs Lamb told me that even our king's mother perished from ruptured innards. The preachers teach acceptance, but it is hard to see any plan to it. I remember my surprise at how much father's death affected me. More in some ways than losing my mother, though he was a disappointed man with an irascible

37

temper and I had adored her. Perhaps it was desolation at being alone in the world.

'My mother died when I was ten,' I say. 'And my father, soon after my stepmother sent me to the poorhouse.'

'Then we both know the pain of losing those we love.' His eyes are fixed on me with what I see is compassion. 'But you are a lesson to me. Despite being so young, it has not made you angry and bitter.'

I do not know what to say. The morning has turned serious and dark.

'I have made you sad,' he says, shaking his head. 'That was thoughtless of me. Let me set you a puzzle, instead. To distract that enquiring mind of yours.'

'What kind of puzzle?'

'My bull lost an eye as a young calf, in a dispute with a gatepost. It does not hinder him in his duties to my herd. In fact, the beast clearly thinks himself an exceedingly fine fellow.' Farmer Graham clucks at his mare to walk towards the next house. 'So, what I have named him? Think on it while you bake the morning bread. You can give me the answer tomorrow.'

I stare at his retreating back. A bull with only one eye?

'Wait,' I call after him. This is too easy. 'Cyclops! It must be.'

He turns his head to look at me, his ready smile telling me my guess is right.

Chapter Ten

Dust and the crumbled remains of camphor balls in the bottom of the wardrobe in Master Charles's room threaten to make me sneeze. It is stuffed with mildewed cloaks and black gowns that have rotted under the arms and should be given to the rag man. A heap of discarded waistcoats lie bundled at the bottom and I quickly discover the dove-grey velvet, pitted with moth holes, its ornate buttons black with tarnish.

Then, as I tuck it under my arm to take downstairs and snip off the costly buttons with the mistress's scissors, a flash of bright yellow flares at me from behind the dark garments. My curious hand quickly discovers the softness of silk and I draw out a magnificent gown, gathered into pin-tucks at the back of the neck to form a short train. Tiny satin-covered buttons adorn the sleeves. The fabric ripples under my fingers and has a strong, musky scent, like bruised flower petals. A creation fit for court, though the colour is bold and the neck looks shockingly low.

Intrigued, I feel around in the bottom of the wardrobe to see what else lies buried there and under some youth's breeches find three drawstring bags that my fingers tell me hold ladies' slippers. When I pull the contents into the light, the footwear is exquisite: fashioned from satin and softest kid leather, beaded and embroidered. Much too fine to jeopardise in the street, even with pattens. If their owner ventured out, it must have been in a chair, carried straight from one grand entrance hall into another like a precious object that must not be sullied by contact with the common ground. There are stockings, too. Gossamer fine, embroidered with clock patterns that shimmer in the dim light.

To whom can these showy things have belonged? They are not of the latest fashion and are, on examination, a little worn. But, not so long ago, they would have turned heads.

There are no daughters of the house who might once have worn them. Indeed, the Chalkes are unusual in having only one living child. Their son who, if the maid next door is to be believed, fled to the Americas to get as far away from his parents as he could. Why would a son do such a thing?

Then the bang of the front door makes me thrust everything but the waistcoat into the dim recesses of the wardrobe and hurry back to my domain in the kitchen and to scrubbing the master's muddied breeches from last night.

But my mind turns over yet another puzzle in the Chalke household. I am due to return to the bookseller's later and feel a skip of anticipation at the prospect of seeing Jack. He is always eager to talk – and if I am lucky might let slip something about what Master Chalke does.

Chapter Eleven

Jack looks almost the gentleman this morning. No longer cleaning windows in shirt-sleeves, but wearing a blue broadcloth coat to serve in the shop. His shoe buckles look like silver and the lawn of that shirt will be soft as a moth's wing.

'Does Master Chalke no longer care to frequent our shop?' he grins, as I walk through the door and hand him today's package. Jack is so clearly a trusted member of the bookseller's family that I do not feel the need to wait for Master Twyford.

'He is indisposed.' It is not my place to talk of his attack.

'Well, I shan't complain, when he sends such a pretty maid in his place.'

I ignore his nonsense. From the way his mouth turns up at the corners Jack enjoys making girls blush. Perhaps there is not enough work for him.

I watch him break the seal and open the package. Will it be the latest chapter of an adventure? Tales of pirates? Of long-dead kings? Doomed lovers?

There is a slender volume inside, wrapped in a sheaf of closely written pages.

'Is your master so busy with his pen that he returns our volumes?' Jack frowns at the book, his fingers obscuring its title.

'I expect he is particular about what he adds to his collection. He will not want to waste good guineas on poor writing.'

Jack turns enquiring eyes from the package to me. 'Does he show you what he reads? Or writes?'

'Of course not. Why would he?'

'He might. If he thought you would appreciate it.' There is a gleam in Jack's eye that I do not quite like. Mrs Lamb was right about young men being saucy around girls.

'The master expects me to dust his books, not read them.'

'Yet we discussed the poetry of Master Gray. Remember?'

'I do like to read.' There is no harm or shame in that, though I would not want him to think I am pretending to be above my station. 'But I am as likely to buy books as order a silk gown.'

'Clothe you in silk and those looks of yours would turn the head of any man who sees you.'

I feel myself flush. 'I am not here for foolish talk, Master Jack.'

'Call me Jack.' The full lips twitch, as if I amuse him, which I clearly do. 'And it is the simple truth.'

I stare at my feet and instruct myself not to fidget like a simpleton.

'It is hardly my fault you look the way you do,' he says, close to my ear, presumably concerned his uncle might overhear.

'I must not linger.' I edge away, remembering the chores back at the house. In addition to everything else, I have yet to finish rubbing the tarnish off those buttons before sewing them on the waistcoat. 'Is there anything to take back for Master Chalke?'

'There is, indeed.' Pulling a key from his breeches pocket he unlocks a drawer in one of the cabinets and removes a purse. There is a clink as he places it in my palm and closes my fingers around its weight. 'Tell your master this settles his account. Keep it safe. There is gold in there.'

I tuck the purse deep in my pocket, under my apron. This is surely proof

of Master Chalke being a published writer. Much about the man unnerves me, especially that squinting eye of his, but I recall Mrs Lamb talking of Dr Johnson visiting their house when old Master Buttermere was still alive. And of the odd gestures and tics that he had. Perhaps the result of long hours bent over a desk. I long to question Jack, but decide not to sink to the level of the gossipy maid next door.

'What is that noise?' I ask instead. A heavy rhythmic thumping is audible through the door at the back of the shop leading to the yard. It reminds me of my father's loom.

'The apprentice is running off penny pamphlets for my uncle.'

So, they do have a printing press. Presumably it will soon produce my master's book.

'But are you not the apprentice?'

'I am, but there is another.' Jack holds up hands that are soft and cared for. 'Since I prefer not to have ink-stained hands, or a back twisted from using a machine, we acquired a poorhouse lad for the dirty work of the business. For next to nothing.'

His words make me think of Davy, a wizened mite abandoned at the door of our poorhouse in a nest of lice-ridden rags. Always under-sized, he had been apprenticed to a chimney sweep at seven years of age. Also for next to nothing.

The old women in the laundry said later he got stuck in a chimney somewhere in Temple Bar. Another boy was sent up after him, to pull on his legs, but could not shift him. By the time a bricklayer was fetched to break a hole into the flue, with the sweep grumbling at the expense, Davy was dead from suffocation.

Jack kicks the door to the courtyard shut. Clearly the youth out there is nothing to him.

'My own apprenticeship is quite different, for Master Twyford is my mother's brother. He is easy-going and encourages me to read, believing a bookseller should be knowledgeable about what he sells.'

My envy returns. A life surrounded by books, where he is urged to spend his time reading. No wonder he whistles.

'We will see one another often, Hannah. Master Chalke is partial to our special editions and he and my uncle have other dealings. We can talk about books whenever you come to the shop.'

'I would like that, though I have read too few.'

The blue eyes study me. 'What do you do with your free afternoons?'

I stare down at my ugly boots. Mistress Buttermere was strict. I never went out alone and my ventures from that house were to the market, to her favourite milliner's, or to squirm on a hard pew hoping the Sunday sermon might end before Doomsday. And Mistress Chalke is even more severe.

'Would you not like to be shown something of the town?'

From my garret in the Chalke house I can see church spires and the roofs of houses, some grand-looking, stretching into the distance. I am consumed by curiosity about the city around me, yet conscious that Jack's interest might risk my position. The last thing I need is a young man paying me attention. Employers are wary of their maids having followers. It usually leads to trouble.

'Mistress Chalke would not approve.' I gaze into eyes that look innocently friendly. I can still feel another bruise on my arm where she pinched me yesterday for gazing out of the window at a youth singing for pennies in the street.

'Need your mistress know?' Jack's face remains open and smiling. 'I mean no harm, little maid. You would be perfectly safe with me.'

I do not know what to think. With nobody to concern themselves with my safety, I must shift for myself. Whatever Susan did, whether it was to steal or to dally with men, it cost her dear.

'Come,' Jack says. 'Do you like oysters?'

'I do.' I plan to buy some for Peg and myself. They are cheap.

'There are stalls selling them in Vauxhall Gardens. Would you not like to see fashionable London, parading its finery? There is free music.' He grins again. 'Dashing officers in scarlet regimentals.'

My life is so narrow that he sees I am tempted. 'Think, Hannah. We could meet on your afternoon off. As if by accident. Who could know it was otherwise?'

My mouth opens, to say I will have nothing to do with such a deception, yet on my first free Sunday afternoon I visited Mrs Lamb. When the next comes, I plan to explore the streets and squares near the house. I love walking and one day would like to go and look at the Thames. From my garret I can glimpse the masts of ships and when the wind is from the south smell the ripeness of the great river. Those vessels will have sailed back and forth from distant lands like giant white-winged shuttlecocks. While I rarely venture ten minutes from the area steps.

'Perhaps,' I say, lured by the prospect of being with a young man who spends his life surrounded by books. And telling myself I am not influenced by his looks. 'Let me think on it.'

Mistress Chalke has forbidden followers. Yet Jack is right. I could easily meet him by chance. He is a respectable young man with whom I have become acquainted while going about my master's business. It would be only polite to speak to him.

When I go to the door, Jack opens it for me and ushers me out. As we pause under the creaking sign, with its pretty child beside what looks like her doting grandfather, he takes my wrist, turns my hand over and drops the suggestion of a kiss onto my palm. Then he ducks back into the shop without a word, leaving me in the street. Astonished and disturbed.

Chapter Twelve

I am trying not to daydream of Jack and that disturbing kiss when the slam of the front door and a commotion on the stairs tell me there are visitors. More gentlemen. Several, from the clump of riding boots and the rumble of deep voices in the normally silent house. They must have come in with Master Chalke and have brought from the rain-washed street an air of damp wool, horse sweat and male bodies. Clods of mud and horse shit will need to be brushed off the carpet later after they have dried.

Almost immediately comes the impatient jingle of the bell, but I am ready. Visitors always need tending to and at least I am now allowed into the book room to serve them. Probably, I suspect, because of the lie I told the master last week.

There had been visitors that day, too, and after they departed, I remembered the need to clear away the wine glasses. The mistress was out, for once, so I tapped on the book room door and peeped around it. Master Chalke was hunched over a pile of crumpled papers. A hawk with a disembowelled pigeon.

'May I clear away, Master?'

Why did he look ill at ease? In his own house? About his own business?

'If you must. But be quick.'

As I removed the decanter and glasses he leaned back in his chair, eyes half-closed, squinting at the beams of the ceiling as if he had forgotten my presence. He has a noble-looking face and I wondered if Thomas might know about his writing. The farmer is well-read, after all. When I get a chance, I will ask him.

'Tell me, Hannah.' His gaze dropped to my face. 'Can you read?'

Startled by the question, I almost said: *I can read as well as you can.* But did not. Why? Because he wouldn't leave his papers around if he knew I could understand them.

'I recognise my name,' I faltered. 'And know how to write it down.'

He nodded, content. I do not expect Mistress Buttermere thought to mention the avid reading I was permitted in her library, or my early schooling from my mother. It was my industry with a scrubbing brush that mattered.

But now I am glad, because the lie means I am allowed in the book room.

Master Chalke stands outside the door, fingers drumming on the banisters.

'What can I fetch you, sir?'

'Bring the Madeira that came yesterday.' He holds out the key to the cupboard, its black ribbon gleaming. 'And do not keep my guests waiting.'

'I will not, sir.'

I fly down the stairs, unlock the wine cupboard and pour the wine into a suitably elegant decanter. Then I select fine-stemmed glasses and return as quickly as I can without risking the fragile cargo clinking on my tray.

It would make a welcome change to have lady visitors. But no gossipy females arrive to whisper the latest scandal. I think of the tea parties Mistress Buttermere loved: chattering society women, silk garments overflowing their chairs, often accompanied by tiny dogs on fancy ribbons. Talk of new fashions. Of whose daughter had caught a prospective husband with connections and wealth. Of the latest productions at the playhouses. Of whether the Queen might be increasing again.

I would love to create treats for tea parties, for there are instructions for macaroons in Mrs Lamb's recipe book. Something she had from Sir Christopher's fancy French cook. But Mistress Chalke has no friends, apart from one ugly old woman with a strange almost flat face who I can tell is no more a lady by birth than she is.

The kitchen door bursts open.

'Wait. Leave that.'

'Ma'am?'

'Take off your cap. I want to look at that hair of yours.'

Reluctant, puzzled, I put down my tray and do as I am bid.

She watches, twitching with impatience as I unbraid my locks and let them fall around my shoulders.

'Do you curl it, to make it so unruly? Put it in rags at night?'

'No, ma'am.' I am barely allowed time to wash it, never mind play the lady's maid with my appearance.

'Then you must keep it better hidden. I will not have you

flaunting curls in front of visitors. Not at this stage, anyway. Put this on, instead.'

The cap she thrusts at me is shapeless and inexpertly stitched from threadbare cotton. Smelling of someone else's greasy hair.

I hate the thing. And hate her for making me wear it.

'That is better. Now get yourself upstairs and keep those cat's eyes of yours decently lowered.'

There are four gentlemen in the room who mutter to one another, low-voiced, yet self-important, as I serve them. They sprawl in the chairs and stare at me as if I were a freak at a country fair. The youngest, a scrawny stick in a mulberry coat, his face pitted with smallpox scars, nudges his companion with a sharp elbow. The neighbour, with the bulbous nose and red-rimmed eyes of someone who guzzles more than a bottle of wine a day, laughs as if they are enjoying a secret joke. Their hands reach impatiently for the glasses, though it is obvious they have been drinking deep before coming here.

My mother would have called their manners rude, but gentlemen are habituated to doing as they please. It might be different if there were a lady in the room, though perhaps not much. Gentlemen are a rule unto themselves.

One of them fumbles a gold box from his pocket and takes a pinch of snuff from it with a tiny golden spoon, using it to sprinkle the powdery substance along the back of his hand. Then he sighs and lowers his head reverently, as if over a prayer book. He inhales deeply, up one nostril, then the other, closing his eyes in contentment before letting out an explosive sneeze. Tiny particles fly into the air, like ground pepper.

'Ah...!' He gasps with pleasure: 'Excellent!' Then he trumpets his nose into a lawn handkerchief and falls back into his chair.

I consider snuff-taking outlandish and pity the maidservant in his household who will have to get those black fragments from fabric too fragile to rub.

'Put the wine on the table, Hannah. Then leave us. Under no circumstances are we to be disturbed.'

I am getting used to being in a house with a man in it. Life is noisier than it was with Mistress Buttermere: an establishment full of soft-spoken, soft-footed women.

Despite fine shoes with elaborate buckles, Master Chalke stomps up and down the stairs like a bullock on a ramp. His smells are pungent: cedar wood from his clothes press, tobacco from his pipe and, in the evenings, a breath spiritous with brandy. He cannot close a door without slamming it and sometimes shouts and curses, not I think from ill-temper, but just because he can.

Mrs Lamb warned me that men are unpredictable. That even great lords can drink to excess, spend whole nights at the gaming tables, or chase after loose women. Some do all three. Even the best gentlemen have few occupations in London but paying social calls, gaming or attending coffee shops or playhouses. By contrast, Master Chalke's abrupt temper and noisiness seem trivial, for he is a man of learning.

In any case, whatever their failings, no man could frighten me the way his wife does. That speculative look she sometimes slides over me makes my palms sweat. She takes pleasure from tormenting Peg. Will it be my turn next? What dubious plan might she have for me, next spring?

I was behind her on the stair yesterday and had to fight down an urge to give her a vigorous push. As a lady, she wears skirts fuller and longer than mine. Fatal accidents happen all the time because of women's dresses. If not from stairs, from open fires or candle flames. If she broke her neck, Peg would get no more beatings and together we could look after the master in peace. Everyone would be happier, for how can he care for such a heartless creature?

Yet I am horrified at myself. It is a sin as bad as murder to wish another's death. My mother, up in Heaven, might be watching, revolted at how wicked I have become.

Chastened, I finish serving the wine, conscious again I have been studied as I slip from the room. As my feet turn towards the stairs a deep baritone voice says something that provokes a roar of laughter.

I pause, hand on the bannister. Are they laughing at me? But I can be nothing to these men, with their fine houses, horses and carriages. Country estates as well, probably, for from their wigs and finery these people are from the top of society. They have so many possibilities open to them, yet fritter their lives on pleasure. I would rather scrub floors. They remind me that I have never envied young ladies. For though tempted by their gowns and relative freedoms, I would not want to pass my days in frivolity until some velvet-coated fop deigned to give me a destiny as his brood-mare.

I leave the visitors to their talk, which becomes muted, with only one raised voice drifting after me down the stair.

'Don't tell me that fine chit spends all her time in your kitchen?'

My feet pause.

'Come, gentlemen. She is not what you seek. Let us return to the matter in hand. Who will make the first bid?'

To be the object of their scrutiny makes my ears burn as I hurry downstairs. But what was that talk of bids? What could that have to do with books and writing?

I think back to the curiously watchful look the Master had on his face last week. That swivelling eye is impossible to read, but at least he takes an interest in me and uses my name. I am not just a beast of burden to him, as I am to his miserable wife.

I wonder again about the hours he spends in his closet and those gentlemen who come to call. He is not a man of business or of the law, so perhaps they hold one of those literary salons Mistress Buttermere used to talk about. I suppose it is possible gentlemen might bid for book manuscripts as they do for fine horseflesh.

One day, after I have proved my worth in the kitchen and when he is in a good mood, might I admit to having an education? Tell him I am awed by anyone who can create so many words. Yet then he would know I had lied to him.

'Good,' he had said, with a nod. 'It is proper you concentrate on your duties.'

'Yes, Master,' I adopted my impassive face. It was the appropriate response and he seemed satisfied with it.

Then he held out his hand with a frown and I remembered the key and transferred it from my pocket to his broad palm before going back to the kitchen.

In some ways he seems a fair man, not someone with a house full of doubtful secrets. Yet why the contents of his book room must be hidden continues to baffle me.

As I return to darning the mistress's drab cotton stockings my mind returns to that tender salutation from Jack. I have not been kissed since I was a child on my mother's knee. It gives me a strange, warm, feeling that I might matter to someone after so many years alone. A young man like him, with prospects, would surely have scores of girls from whom to choose. Not, of course, that he would think of marrying a common maid. But any friends are welcome in my narrow and insecure world.

I think again about what was said upstairs. This is a gentleman's house and the visitors are aristocrats, I suspect, from their dress and manners. Does one of them perhaps think to offer me a position in his own household? As a lady's maid to a wife or daughter? That would mean not only escape from Mistress Chalke and her schemes, but a step up in the world. Servants are sometimes poached if a family lacks a good pair of hands. Yet I doubt the Chalkes would let me go. And why should the Master seem so relieved that I cannot read? Instead of concentrating on dust and cobwebs, I must find a way to unearth clues.

Peg has said no more about my leaving before the end of my year, but there is anxiety in her eyes when she looks at me. To her, Mistress Chalke represents danger and not just from the leather strap she is so fond of. If I could be alone in the book room, perhaps I might discover why.

Chapter Thirteen

'I have brought you something.' After filling my jug Thomas Graham produces a basket containing field mushrooms and two huge eggs. 'Fresh gathered and fresh laid this morning.'

'You have geese?' I touch the hard shells with a finger. Much larger than hen's eggs, Mrs Lamb used them when baking for a family visit.

'There is a flock in my yard, eager to peck any shin within reach.' A glint of humour lights his face. 'I have a farm. Remember?'

I scarcely know what to say. I imagine he has done this because I would not let him gift me that milk.

'I love mushrooms. And Peg falls on anything she can eat.'

I will shave butter from the crock and fry them to go with our bread and soup at mid-day. If I keep the windows open the smell should not drift upstairs. Fortunately, Mistress Chalke does not watch me as closely now. I tell myself she has realised I will not steal from her. Apart, of course, from that lick of butter, which is hardly stealing since servants expect to share the food in their houses.

'Keep the basket. I don't need it.'

'That is kind of you. I will think of your fierce friends while we enjoy our feast.'

'Geese are the best guardians. The Romans used them. They raise a noise to wake the dead if strangers enter my yard.' He glances at his dog. 'They have a running feud with Hector. He usually wins, but not always.'

I step across to give Calypso a stroke. The well-brushed feathers around her fetlocks are the colour of flax. As blond as Jack's hair, and nearly as well groomed. I look on the beast as a friend now, whispering endearments into her swivelling ears. She is lucky, with a kind master, a plump belly and probably a snug stable at the day's end. I try to picture where they live, a place without crammed-in buildings, rattling carts chased by urchins and speeding carriages with footmen hanging off the back.

'Who was Calypso?' I ask.

'A nymph in ancient Greece. In addition to beauty, she had a

51

voice that lured the passing Odysseus onto her island.'

'What for? To rob him?'

'To rob him of his free will.'

I frown, remembering stories read at my mother's knee.

'Those Greek gods were strange. Turning women into trees.'

'They did not need to work. Perhaps that is why.'

'I wonder if I would get into mischief? Without chores?'

'An unlikely circumstance with the Chalkes.'

I nod. 'It reminds me of the poorhouse. They lectured us on the goodness of work, but it was only to make us more biddable.'

'How long were you there?'

'Two years.' I study the cobblestones. 'I was with my parents until I was ten. But after my mother died everything changed.'

'A hard life for a child.' He glances at the house. 'I wish you had found a kinder mistress.'

I summon a smile. I was not looking to make the man pity me. 'I had a good lady in my previous position. And intend to find another, after Lady Day.'

He fills a leather bucket with water from a barrel on the wagon and puts it before the horse, who dips her muzzle and sucks deep, noisy draughts.

'Could you not find alternative employment?'

'I would like to, but it is difficult, without a character. And Mistress Chalke would withhold that if I left early, together with my wages. Every penny.'

'And you cannot, of course, afford to do that.' He grunts. 'Forgive me for thinking you free to choose.'

Her bucket empty, Calypso lifts her head and shakes beads of water over us, making us step back.

'I will be looking to employ another man soon,' he says. 'Work can be hard to find in the countryside, except at harvest time. Doing the deliveries myself denies bread to a labouring family.'

'I did think it strange...' I has become so easy to talk to him that I cannot stop my mouth running on.

'That I do it myself?'

'In your place, I would stay in my fields.'

'The man who used to do it had three of his fingers crushed by a wheel.' The farmer shrugs big shoulders. 'My house was as neat as a parson's parlour, without a hobbyhorse or wooden blocks to trip my feet. So it suited me to do the deliveries myself, and get away for a few hours.'

He turns to adjust the harness, I suspect unnecessarily, his voice almost inaudible. 'I still sometimes wake at night wishing to be troubled by a baby bawling over a tooth.

'They were young? Your sons?'

'Just over three years old. Our pastor tells me they are with God, but it is hard to fathom His plan in taking them. And my dear wife, besides.' He shrugs. 'I vowed never to wed again. To never risk making myself hostage to so much pain.'

Not knowing what to say, I concentrate on stroking the horse's warm neck.

'You lost your parents,' he says. 'I lost my family. I suppose we must be grateful to have had these bright people in our lives.'

For a moment there is only the sound of Calypso nosing at her empty bucket.

'What happened to the man whose fingers were crushed?'

'Jed? I have given him management of my cows. I could not risk him with a horse and wagon on the London streets. Not with only one good hand.'

He frowns. 'Our milk is of exceptional quality and Elizabeth always wanted to make more of our dairy.'

'You could still do that. Surely?'

'If I found the right woman to take charge of it.' He studies me. 'Do you like cheese?'

'Doesn't everybody?'

'I will bring you some.'

'The mistress would take it from me.' I cannot restrain a scowl. 'The Chalkes consider everything theirs. Like it is their right.'

He nods, clearly not surprised.

'So, hide it.'

'Then Peg and I would love some.' I smile at the thought of our conspiracy.

'It is best with fresh-made bread. And lots of butter.'

'Butter would be nice,' I say, aware of sounding wistful.

'Do they not feed you?'

'The mistress expects me to live on leftovers.' I shrug, embarrassed to admit I am not much better fed than Peg. The farmer thinks he knows about my life, but does not understand how my young appetite craves more than I am allowed. 'They begrudge every crumb.'

'I hear their son is away in the Americas. They no doubt miss him.' He grunts dismissively. 'We all tend to look only to our own wants. I expect they think they have a hard life.'

I imagine the son, across the ocean in a place so strange it must be like a fairy tale, and remember my mother's stories of distant lands. Of princes and princesses. Of happy endings.

'I have read it takes six whole weeks to cross the ocean.'

'When I was a boy, I dreamed of being a midshipman. I had an uncle who commanded a frigate at the Battle of Quiberon Bay, so I grew up with tales of battles and prize money. There was plenty to fire a boy's imagination.'

'Why didn't you? Become a sailor?'

'My older brother was lamed, hunting. The Church offered an easier life, so he went up to Oxford while I was left to sail the tides of my imagination in the family fields.' He shrugs. 'It was probably for the best, for I enjoy being a farmer. Or did, till I no longer had anyone to get up for in the mornings.'

'I will be sorry when you no longer come. But I would not spend my mornings in London when I could be in green fields.'

'I am glad you will be sorry.'

I should be getting back inside, but it is pleasing to talk to my farmer friend.

'Your horse is getting fat.'

'Feel her belly.'

I do as I am bid. She is a fur-covered barrel.

'There is a foal in there,' he smiles. 'I will soon harness my piebald and leave this lady in her paddock.'

I stroke the bulging flank, identify limbs, faint movement. You often see mares pulling carts with their young following behind. The drivers know the foal will stay close to its mother, but I have always hated to see such fragile creatures among the rough traffic of the public roads.

'Why the blisters?' he says, frowning at my fingers.

'Our washing tongs are broken. And the mistress refuses to buy new.'

'So your hands get raw?' He makes a noise of disapproval. 'My housekeeper swears by butter for sore skin.' He turns to the wagon and rummages in a canvas bag. 'Have this. From my own cows.'

I transfer the fold of paper into my pocket. Presumably it was part of his refreshment. It is a comfort to have such a generous friend, even though it will not be for much longer. 'You should call me Hannah.'

'And you must call me Thomas. I will feel less like a grandad, fit only to doze in a rocker by the fire.' He smiles again. 'Would you care to visit my farm, after the foal is born? When you have your full day off? I could come and collect you and Peg in my trap and take you to Broad Oak to sample some of my roast beef.'

'We would like that.'

It might not happen, but I will enjoy imagining it. Mother used to tease me about being away with the fairies whenever I helped with chores: hands doing one thing, mind elsewhere. But daydreaming is useful when you are eternally darning stockings or scraping egg yolk from encrusted fork tines.

So, Thomas Graham's countryside is not always a place of plenty. I should have realised, for there are ragged men on the London streets who have been cast off the land and are desperate for work. It is said they need to head north, where the new manufactures swallow men like a pig does swill.

Thomas will have many customers before he turns his pregnant mare for home. How cruel his own life has been. As hard as mine, though in a different way. But I hope it is not too soon that he employs his new man, for I will miss our talks.

Calypso clops a hoof on the cobbles and snorts, turning a soft eye on us. She clearly thinks it time to move on.

I turn towards the house. I may use that butter on my hands, but the temptation of sharing it with Peg on a filched fragment of this morning's bread is strong.

'I will bring your cheese tomorrow,' Thomas promises, taking up the reins. 'And do talk to Peg about visiting the farm after the foal is born.'

There is a lightness in my step as I go back inside. I have two friends now: Thomas and, of course, Jack. And two outings to look forward to. I should concentrate on them, rather than worry about things that are probably nothing to do with me and, in any event, that I will be powerless to change.

MAGGIE RICHELL-DAVIES

Chapter Fourteen

I am not used to arguments. Mistress Buttermere was a sweet-natured widow living alone with her few servants so there were no raised voices in her residence. The floors of the Chalke house are elm planks, its heavy doors of oak, so even loud conversations are usually muffled, but this afternoon is different.

I am rubbing beeswax into the hall panelling. It has not been given attention for years and though the hungry wood soaks up polish it is hard to buff to a proper shine. I am giving it much-needed elbow grease before returning to the kitchen when Mistress Chalke's voice slices through the air. At least, for once, her temper is not directed at either Peg or myself.

'This is our family house. I insist on having charge of it.'

I should not eavesdrop, yet cannot help myself. My days are so boring that this is the nearest I come to entertainment. How I wish for a book to read. But why do the Chalkes argue about how the house is run? The master never troubles himself with what goes on below stairs.

'Nobody disputes that, my dear,' he soothes, a rider nervous a fractious mare might unseat him. Every day I pity him in his choice of wife. Perhaps she was a beauty in her youth, before her face turned to porridge. Mrs Lamb said the ladies at court sometimes ruin their complexions with noxious face powders. Perhaps the mistress did the same, though I would not care about her looks if she had a pleasant disposition.

'The girl is our maidservant until Lady Day.' Mistress Chalke is not to be deterred. 'Until then, I do not want either you or your friends ogling her.'

My arm halts its rhythmic circling.

'You fret over nothing.'

'Do I? Must I dispose of another maid? You expect clean linen whenever you want it. Fires laid. Meals on the table. Would you have me do the work myself?'

'I merely remarked on her dumplings. What is wrong with that?'

'Don't take me for a fool.'

'If you wanted her ignored, you should have picked a less comely girl.'

'And what good would that be to us?'

'I am serious. If you don't like Hannah, there is a hiring fair at *The Black Bull* every other Saturday.'

'I am not interested in those who cannot find work. Or are without characters. Would you have us employ a blabbermouth? Poking her snout into our private business? Or another slut, like Susan?'

I am poised for flight if they sound like leaving the room, my polishing forgotten. Earlier, I was daydreaming of Jack's disturbing salutation on my palm. And those brilliant blue eyes.

Now I strain for every word. Why is the witch making lewd insinuations? The master has shown no sign of being a man who gropes beneath the skirts of serving girls. He simply appreciates my cooking. And how does having a pleasing-looking maid differ from wanting a handsome footman to answer your front door?

'Remember our agreement. Maids work their year, then go to Jarrett. They are not playthings. That nonsense with Susan cost us a good ten guineas.'

'Come, my dear...'

'Don't *my dear* me. It is bad enough being paupers, without you sniffing after girls under your own roof.' Her voice has an edge. 'You promised me a country estate, with a town house and carriages. Instead we live in cramped rooms with mildewed wallpaper and damp attics. Scrimping every penny.'

The silence that follows is broken only by the ticking of the hall clock. When it comes, the master's voice remains placating.

'Being the second born, of twins, my father's conscience was troubled about me. He swore that though I might not get his title, I would lack for nothing. So how could I suspect he would cut my allowance from his will? Simply because I refused to live like a monk?' He becomes truculent. 'Come, woman. Don't I labour long enough over that damned *List*. To make amends?'

Mistress Chalke's tone is no softer.

'Pushing a pen like a quill-sucking clerk will not restore our fortunes. Grow a backbone. Demand more. After settling with Twyford and Jarrett what remains barely pays our creditors, never mind Charles's allowance.'

I ease out my breath. The subject has changed. Talk of replacing me was spite from the mistress because I am not old and ugly, like her.

'And I want the auctions held elsewhere. At Twyford's.'

'It is more discreet to have them here.'

'The trade is hardly at risk. Where else could such habits be satisfied?'

'I still prefer to keep the business in our own hands. You know what Valentine is like. My brother will rip my guts out with his bare hands if I give him another scandal to cover up.' The master sounds weary, and no wonder. His wife is a bitch with a scrap of meat between her teeth. 'Come, I have proofs to check.'

'If you must. But remember our agreement. Do what you want outside, but respect our house.'

There is another silence. A truce, perhaps. I slip the pot of polish into my pocket and move to tiptoe downstairs. They must not catch me here.

'Let us not fight, Harriet.' The master's voice lowers. 'I wonder, do you still have those yellow satin garters...?'

'Don't try to cozen me with talk of garters. Finish your scribbling. I have better things to do.'

A chair scrapes and I scuttle downstairs, clutching my rag.

Back in the kitchen I sit at the table and force myself to be calm, for if I cannot be mistress of myself, how can I keep safe? But my mind is in turmoil. What trade were they talking of? What is being auctioned? What scandal might need to be covered up?

I may be young, but sense and Mrs Lamb's warnings tell me that if these goods satisfy men's weaknesses, and require secrecy, they must be something dark. Something from the underbelly of society.

Perhaps Master Chalke is not the good man I thought him. He may not have laid a hand on me, but perhaps he had dealings with Susan. Perhaps she really was sacked for lewd behaviour, with him? Perhaps she also talked about those secret auctions. And was silenced because of it.

And who is this Jarrett that the mistress talks of sending me to, after Lady Day? Can she pass me on to another employer, regardless of my own wishes? And why would Jarrett need a girl to be comely? I shudder. Do they have dealings with some house of ill-repute, where young women offer their bodies in exchange for money? Might that be my destiny after Lady Day? If it were, it would explain Peg's warning.

Master Chalke pens something called *The List*, which does not sound like any book I have heard of. Does it provide details of girls for sale? Sight of it might uncover the house's secrets. But when I think of what happened to Susan, I realise sight of it could put me in danger.

I glance down at my hands and my fingers are trembling. I expected this position to be a year of thankless work, but with prospects at its end of being able to say I am an experienced cook. That it would give me the opportunity to be employed in a better household where I might be valued. Where in some sense I could finally be mistress of myself. Instead I believe Peg and that maid were right. I am no longer safe.

Chapter Fifteen

My mind is feverish with the danger I might be in. Should I walk out next Saturday, find *The Black Bull* and hope some unknown housewife might give me work? With a live-in post I could survive forfeiting my wages, but how would I know who to trust at a hiring fair? When even Mistress Buttermere was deceived about the Chalkes?

I stab a needle into my sewing and wonder how many girls are forced to live in danger because they own nothing but shabby garments and a few coins. Who have no prospects and, most of them, little or no education.

For the time being I have decided to appear passive. To simmer, not boil. Lest someone slam a lid down on me. I will hide my fears until I can get away, for it appears I should be safe until Lady Day.

I am hunched over an old sheet that I have cut in two and am re-forming, sides-to-middle, so a tear will not end its useful life. Mrs Lamb would have let me use it to fashion rags for my monthly bleeding, but in this house nothing must go to waste and anything damaged is Peg's fault, or mine.

'Are you planning to spend all day on that?'

'It must be double-stitched, ma'am. For strength.'

I take care to look suitably chastened when criticised. Until I secure another place it should hide my suspicions.

'You've ruined that with harsh rubbing. I shall take its value from your wages.'

The woman knows no more of needlework than she does of kitchen matters. She must be schooled in some form of housewifery, though I have yet to discover what it might be, except penny-pinching.

Every day her ignorance confirms to me that she was neither born nor raised a lady. Mistress Buttermere rarely stepped into the kitchen, but questioned Mrs Lamb daily about what was purchased and what would be served at her table. She knew the price of a leg of mutton. The best shops for linen and where the finest candles could be purchased. She no longer had a husband to answer to, but considered it her duty to oversee everything that took place under her roof.

Mistress Chalke, on the other hand, knows less than a fifteen-year-old poorhouse girl. Mrs Lamb said there was some family connection with Ireland. Perhaps there, daughters of the gentry are differently raised. Or perhaps she really was an actress, before she lost her looks. How I wish Mrs Lamb might be right about the Buttermere household returning to London, but that would not happen for months. In the meantime, I intend to seek Thomas's advice about alternative work.

The Chalkes have been bad-tempered since receiving a rare letter from the son in the Americas. The master spluttered over his breakfast chocolate about its news.

'The boy would not expect so much if you had not spoiled him from the cradle. No word for months, then a begging letter. He is supposed to be mending our fortunes. Not whining after my hard-earned guineas.'

'He needs capital to buy more land. For the planting of tobacco. He is fortunate that his uncle gave him some useful introductions out there.'

Master Chalke sucked his teeth, as if they were troubling him again. I gave him oil of cloves yesterday and he thanked me with one of those smiles he slips me when the mistress is not looking. Is he really a lecher who needs to be watched? I bite my lip and wish I was older and understood men better.

'I cannot send what I do not have, Harriet.'

'Then tell Jarrett to find more merchandise.'

'How often must I say it? That would be risky.'

'Grow a backbone, you spineless loiter-sack. No wonder your father cast you off.'

I scurried back to the kitchen with their dirty dishes, pretending to be deaf as well as stupid. Jarrett provides the merchandise for those auctions and is also the man the mistress talks of sending me to, after Lady Day. But spring is a long way off. Time enough to get away from whatever the heartless woman has planned for me.

I take up my book of recipes, sniffing the scents of herbs and spices Mrs Lamb must have handled when using it and homesick for her friendship. A fragment of eggshell is stuck to a page and I pick at it with a fingernail, wishing I could use my education to earn my bread. If I were a lady, I might be a governess – not that enviable a life – but I am not, so I must strive to become as fine a cook as Mrs Lamb was. To hope to gradually better myself and become a valued housekeeper, like her.

Peg has been swabbing the scullery floor, but looking less bleak, probably at the prospect of spooning up the onion and potato broth simmering on the fire. It scarcely seems possible, but there is already a trace of colour in that gaunt face. I suspect it is also because she knows someone cares. But we both need to be elsewhere. When I escape, I must try to take her with me.

She puts aside her bucket and approaches the mistress, twisting her hands together, clearly anxious.

'Please, Mistress?' Her crippled leg drags. 'Me wages?'

Mistress Chalke stares at her with such contempt that I am more than ever convinced they have a history of some kind.

'The landlord is after me. For rent.'

Her look shrivels Peg back against the wall, but the expected blow does not come. Instead Mistress Chalke turns a sour look on me.

'Have you some coppers about you, Hannah? I have no change.'

'I do not, Mistress.' I make myself meet her eye. My modest store of coins is all I might have on which to exist if things go wrong here.

'Hear that, Peg? If you are short, go and collect some dog turds for the glove tanners.'

'There are pennies in the jar on the mantel,' I venture.

They are meant for tomorrow's milk, but I am sure Thomas will give us credit.

'If I want instruction from you, I will ask.' She divides a glare between us. 'Perhaps I should thrash the pair of you. Useless bitches.'

I go to the table, grab the rabbit I need to prepare for supper, and slide the kitchen knife into its belly. Seething that we are forced to work for such a monster. There are dogs who are better treated.

Peg's misery will not only be from hunger and unfair blows. It must be because of whatever happened between the two of them in the past. Despite what Mrs Lamb thought, mercy and charity will have had no part in it.

Chapter Sixteen

Being a wet day, the washing is festooned on rails in the kitchen and scullery making the air inside the house damp, but at least the Chalkes have left us in peace. It is a relief to see the back of them.

A discarded quill of Master Chalke's is clutched in Peg's scrawny hand and she is dipping it nervously into the ink pot on the table, her fingers already stained black. Later I intend to ask Thomas about finding work, but meanwhile am keeping busy, teaching Peg to write.

'What is your other name?'

'Don't have one.'

'But what were your parents called?'

'Dunno.' She scratches at a scab on her neck. 'Never did know.'

This is that terrible lesson I learned at the poorhouse. That children do not always know their parentage. Even by a name.

'You cannot remember them at all?'

'There was a woman was kind to me. When I was little. Before I was took to the city. I like to think she was my Ma.'

'So, you were not always in London?' It is hard uncovering Peg's past and questions make her mouth snap shut, like a bad mussel.

'Don't rightly know. I remember having my dinner once in a field. A juicy raw onion that made my eyes water, and some bread. Scaring crows I was. Flapping my arms to frighten them off a farmer's corn.' She screws up eyes with the effort of remembering. 'There was a cottage that smelled of piss and the pigs in the yard. But that was before I was took to the house.'

'What house? This one?'

'You ask too many questions.' Peg glances behind her, though we are the only people in the building. 'It will bring you trouble.'

She is probably right, but that is enough for now. For, while I am still here, I am determined to gather pieces of the puzzle of what happens in the Chalke house.

I smile encouragingly and guide her hand to form the capital letter, *P*. Followed, shakily, by the smaller letters, *e* and *g*.

'There. That is your name. *Peg*. Short for Margaret, I suppose.'

The browbeaten wretch was stolen away from her home and

family as a child. But why? Does she even know?

Chapter Seventeen

'Tell me how you became an apprentice,' I ask Jack at the booksellers next morning.

I missed my chance of speaking to Thomas earlier, since a whip-thin boy interrupted us then ran off, happy with scrounged milk in a battered tin mug. But I have until next March to escape and meantime need distraction if I am not to become as haunted-looking as Peg. And I still have hopes of learning about Master Chalke from my talkative friend.

It amuses me to see Jack puff out his chest and hold forth like a boy bragging to school fellows. But I encourage him. Peg remains withdrawn and the only other person I can talk with is Thomas Graham.

Mrs Lamb said apprentices were rough lads, best avoided, who love nothing better than carousing, breaking folk's heads and insulting honest womenfolk.

I am sure she is right, about some of them. Yet I cannot believe Jack is like that. I have never smelled even ale on his breath and he is the kind of young man any girl would be proud to be seen with. I suspect he is too careful of what he has to lose to misbehave. With such fine prospects, he would be a fool to put his future at risk. And Jack does not strike me as anybody's fool.

'I was bound to my uncle Twyford at fourteen,' he says. 'For seven years. I have completed five of them.'

So, he is nineteen. He looks older, but that will be because he dresses well and appears so worldly wise. Those are silver buckles on his shoes.

'Apprentices sign agreement to strict rules. And must be able to recite them, whenever asked.' Jack straightens his shoulders and stares up at the ceiling to aid his concentration or, more likely, set off his manly figure:

'I must do no damage to my Master, nor see damage done to him by others, without telling him of it. I must not waste his goods. Or lend them unlawfully to others.

'Nor must I play at cards or dice. Or frequent taverns.'

He pulls a face.

'Life is nothing but work, except on Sundays when I have my afternoons free.' He grins. 'To attend church and pray for help in leading a truly pure life.'

'But at the end of it, you will be your own master.'

'Aye. One day this shop and its commerce should be mine.'

'Is he a good master?' I hardly need ask, since Jack has an air of health and hands soft as any lady. Today he smells faintly of sandalwood, perhaps from where those fine clothes are kept.

'Good enough. My mother is a widow and was glad to have him act in place of a father to me.' He frowns. 'But I am not free. He expects me to walk out with my horse-faced cousin, who will not have opened a serious book in all her twenty-two years.'

He grins again. 'At least Uncle lets me attend the occasional cockfight. If it takes place in a tavern, so be it.'

'Jack...' His smile encourages me, though I do not like him being drawn to blood sports. Cockfighting is hateful, especially when they put steel spurs on the birds' feet. 'Do you know what it is that Master Chalke writes?'

Jack hesitates, the smile gone.

'He pens things for my uncle.' he glances upwards, where the family rooms will be. 'Bookselling is not as profitable as it used to be. The work is nothing to interest you.'

This is a disappointment, for I want to cling to my illusions about my master being a proper writer.

'We also deal in snuff and tobacco. From that shop next door.'

'I hoped Master Chalke might be writing a serious book.'

'His work is for gentlemen with special interests.'

'Is he a scientific man, then? Writing about rare foreign trees or plants? I have heard of such things.'

'Come,' Jack is brisk. '*The Maids' List* need not concern you. We still have not been for those oysters.'

I avoid his eye, so he won't see my gratification at discovering what the mysterious *List* is called.

'We could go this Sunday. Uncle's barometer suggests fair weather.'

He is persuasive. If I come across him in a public place, as if by accident, I can hardly be accused of loose behaviour. And since he has a prospective sweetheart, this will be a simple act of friendship.

I love to walk. It is an opportunity to pretend I can go wherever

I please. The nearest thing I have to freedom, for I usually only get out of the Chalke house to go to the market or on errands like this.

'I would like that,' I admit. 'As long as Mistress Chalke does not find out.'

'You are the prettiest girl I know, Hannah. But an odd little creature at times.'

Am I? Jack is so far from my experience that I sometimes think he talks in riddles.

'I am an ordinary servant, as you well know.' I smile. 'Though admittedly not tall.'

'Far from ordinary,' he says, stepping closer. 'A secret princess. Awaiting her prince. Like in a story book.'

With no sensible reply to make, I study the package in my hand. The third I have collected this week. No wonder Master Chalke spends so long at his desk. If only he could be a serious writer of books.

'And that hair…' his fingers tease at a curl that has escaped my cap. 'Like a blackbird's wing. A shame it must be hidden.'

I step back, refusing to look into those dazzling blue eyes. 'On the contrary. It is just as well, with young men like you about.'

'We will have our outing this Sunday afternoon, then.' His lips turn up in amusement. 'And you need have no fears, for am I not sworn to the best behaviour?'

He is right. How could I be in danger from him? And I am far too sensible to let those good looks make me do anything foolish. I have enough to worry about.

As I leave, a coach clatters up outside the snuff shop and an elderly gentleman clambers out on spindly shanks, leaning heavily on an ebony cane. He looks like a high churchman, or even a judge. As he hurries inside it surprises me that he conducts such an errand himself rather than sending his manservant. Perhaps he is particular about what he buys. Some men consider snuff like fine wine and are accordingly choosy.

Yet the place looks dark and shabby for fine wares, with the upstairs windows tightly shuttered. It is none of my business, of course. Just my habitual nosiness. Yet I have learned today that the master composes this *Maid's List* for Jack's uncle. If I can find and read a copy, my questions should be answered. It could be something totally innocent.

But what if that snuff shop is not what it seems? Could there be loose women in there, offering their bodies to men in exchange for guineas? Yet the brother of a lord would never be involved with such a disreputable trade. Would he?

Chapter Eighteen

Charred fragments, covered with looped writing, are folded in the scrap of rag in my pocket. I may not own lawn handkerchiefs, but was raised never to wipe my nose on a sleeve or the back of my hand.

Mistress Chalke left me on my knees at the book room grate while she fetched something from her bedchamber. I had already noticed the scraps of parchment under the coal scuttle and scooped them up before continuing with my work, my face suitably vacant. The more stupid she thinks me, the better.

There is fine furniture in here. As well as the Chinese cabinet, the master has a massive inlaid desk and glass-fronted library cases full of books. The ones beside the fireplace contain authors I recognise from the Buttermere library: Fielding and Smollett, Johnson and Sterne. The others appear to be in foreign languages: *Les Bijoux Indiscrets*, *L'Ecole des Filles*. *Margot la Ravaudeuse*. Mother spoke French, but apart from fragments of a lullaby about a candle and a moon that she used to sing to me, I remember not a word.

Though I have not read them, I am intrigued by books like *Gulliver's Travels* and *The Adventures of Peregrine Pickle*. But I cannot linger, with Mistress Chalke sure to return at any moment.

The desk has a tooled green leather top decorated with gold scrolling and my discreet fingers have already established that its drawers are locked. What else is there? That painting of the arrogant-looking man with the stallion, and the heavy silver candelabra on the table. But even though I know where the keys are kept, I could not snoop unless left here unsupervised.

Later, when I spread the parchment fragments out on the kitchen table, I am disappointed to find them unintelligible. Words. Phrases. A swirling loop that will have been the tail of an underlining. I recognise the master's bold handwriting, but are these extracts from a book? Edges crumble under my fingers like over-toasted bread while I marry pieces together like a lawyer squinting over the settlement of an heiress.

The mysteries of the house at least keep my mind occupied. The best part of a year remains before my service is done. Not that I mean to be here till Lady Day, for I am determined not to be passed to that Jarrett person. Like a parcel of used linen. There are households in this district I could apply to, though without a character from the Chalkes they would probably send me on my way. If I see that maid with the nose in the market again, I might just ask if she would put in a good word for me. Through her, or with help from Thomas, surely finding another place is possible?

Meantime, I intend to find out about *The Maid's List* and if these fragments will not solve the mystery, and Jack refuses to enlighten me, perhaps my other friend can.

Next morning, I hurry out to his wagon.

'Thomas...' Before long he will come no more. The realisation makes me sad, for I shall miss our talks.

'Yes?' His smile is reassuring.

'Have you heard of a book called *The Maid's List*?'

'I don't believe so.' He looks up from the pouch into which he has tossed the mistress's pennies. 'Who is the author?'

'Master Chalke, I think.'

'What is it about?' Raised eyebrows suggest he finds this hard to believe.

'I would like it to be about adventure or travel, but I have only heard the title. There is a mystery connected to it.'

'Perhaps the mystery is why it was written in the first place.' Thomas's lips twitch. 'A surprising number of men think themselves talented with a pen. Most are sorely mistaken.'

'But I believe it is to be published by Master Twyford, the bookseller. His apprentice, Jack, says so.' I look down at my friend's polished boots. 'It was being discussed by visitors the other day. They were drinking the master's best Madeira and incredibly loud with their opinions.'

'With your ear pressed against the door?' A smile suggests Thomas is not shocked at my prying and I am pleased I said nothing about the auctions. I must solve one mystery at a time.

'Why should it be secret? What man would not be proud of being an author?'

'Perhaps his book touches on political matters. Your master would not risk being accused of sedition.' Thomas shrugs. 'That might explain him wishing to publish anonymously. With a limited circulation.'

I think of the gentlemen who visit. They do not look like men who care about anything except their own pleasure.

'I saw scraps of paper in the grate. Partly burned. The writing was not about serious matters.'

No need to mention the hours they spent on the kitchen table while I struggled to join them together.

I frown at Thomas.

'Choice Selections. For Gentlemen of Discernment. That sounds almost like a tailor's handbill. But the master would hardly write about cravats and buckskin breeches. Would he?'

'Gentlemen can find themselves short of funds. Through losing money at cards or from extravagant living.' Thomas shrugs again. 'Which might force them to meet debts in ways they would never normally consider. And explain not wanting a family name on it. You say he thinks himself a fop. Perhaps he invents ways to tie a cravat?'

'He does care about his dress.' I kick my boot against the kerb. 'His tailor is forever presenting bills at the door.'

'He is probably dissatisfied at not being able to live to the standards he was born to.' Thomas does not sound sympathetic.

'But I wanted him to be a writer of books. It was the only good thing about the house.'

Thomas opens his mouth as if to speak, then closes it again. His brows knit and he looks suddenly weary. 'Best leave your master to his interests. Old men can have ill-advised fancies.'

I look back at the house. Perhaps this *Maid's List* has nothing to do with either his book or those auctions. After all, he works enough hours to produce writing of all kinds. Perhaps, too, he is a good man, with a wicked wife. Though he clearly knows all about that disturbing arrangement with Jarrett.

'I should not waste your time with foolish questions.'

I must get back to the pig's head simmering in our biggest pot on the fire. I am making brawn and if it boils dry it will have no flavour. When it is cool, I will pick off the meat, press it into a crock and pour calf's foot jelly over it before setting it under a weighted plate. My skills in the kitchen are improving at a gratifying rate. They are my best way out of here.

'They are never foolish, Hannah. Our talks are one of my few pleasures.' Thomas frowns over my shoulder at the windows of the house. 'I recall Jed saying the Chalkes never keep a maid more than a year. Less sometimes. It makes one wonder why.'

So, he, too, wonders about the house and its occupants.

Back inside, I chide myself for not asking about alternative work, for Thomas is surely my best hope. Much better than the woman in the next house. And a voice in my head questions whether I am holding back because of Jack.

Chapter Nineteen

'Best keep this between ourselves,' says Jack, when we meet at the corner of the square. I am wearing my new dark blue gown and pleased that I took so much trouble with its stitching.

'Who would I tell? Apart from the mistress, who would dismiss me on the instant?'

'Forget that miserable pinchpenny. The sun shines. The afternoon is ours.' He taps my elbow to hurry me along and away from the bookshop, since presumably Master Twyford must not know, either. I had dared wonder if this outing might be the start of a proper friendship. But how could that be, if it must be hidden? I accept that Jack is far beyond my reach, but the need for secrecy makes me feel something is not right.

I repeat to myself that I cannot come to harm, in broad daylight, in public places. With only Peg and Thomas Graham to talk to, I am hungry for distraction and companionship.

'Folk live for gossip,' Jack says. 'But what is it to them, if we go walking? We harm nobody.'

'You are right,' I say, still doubtful about what I am doing. 'And I have seen almost nothing of the city, though I have lived here my whole life.'

It is wonderful to be outside, away from the house. I love the light of these early summer days after living half-underground in the kitchen or in my garret, with its meanly proportioned window. But with so many streets and squares, I am soon lost.

'Where are we?'

We have reached a green space where cows graze in the care of a boy with dirty hair and a knobbly stick. The edifice across the grass is impressive, with curved perimeter walls and free-standing statues. Built of rosy red brick with white colonnades, there are garrets for servants high in the roofs with smoke drifting from tall chimneys. A fashionable couple stroll before the entrance with a giant wolf-hound on a leash, the lady's mantle rippling in the breeze.

'Is it a palace?'

'A palace for whores,' Jack laughs at my expression. 'Oh,

Hannah. How innocent you are. Forgive my plain speech, 'tis simply London talk.'

It is easy to forgive him. I have been protected for too long. It is time to learn to be a grown woman. Ignorance will not be my friend.

'That is the Foundling Hospital. Our city is full of strumpets and it was built to house their bastards.'

I study the cobbles under my boots. Such talk may be the London way, but I feel a blush warm my cheeks. 'And they leave their babies here? To be cared for?'

I remember the infants abandoned at our poorhouse, often on the doorstep in the dark of night. Most perished, some even before they were found at first light. Alive or dead, there was never any love for them and precious little care.

Jack shrugs. 'With a bastard, a woman cannot find respectable work. And she is shunned by decent folk.'

'Who built it? The King?'

'Farmer George has other concerns. I am told some old sea captain was horrified at seeing babies left in the gutter and raised the money. Fortunately for the whores, the city has deep pockets.'

I am pleased people believe in Christian charity, but shocked by the size of the building.

'Everything revolves around money, Hannah. Gaining it. Spending it. Losing it.'

'But what are those people doing there?' Finely dressed ladies and gentlemen saunter through the entrance, laughing and chattering. 'It is not a pleasure park. Won't those unfortunate women be shamed, to be gawped at?'

'They should not have been so free with their favours.'

'It is like a lord's mansion,' I say, wishing he would be more tender-hearted. The babies, at least, are innocent.

'People say so many mothers come that they must take part in a public ballot.'

'And the gentry watch? For entertainment?'

'It is the same at the mad house.' Jack at last looks shamefaced. 'The fashionable love visiting Bedlam. If they are diverted, their donations can be generous.'

'That is wrong.'

'It is how the world turns.'

A gaunt and bedraggled woman appears, creeping along the Hospital railings, and I clutch Jack's arm. She has a bundle at her breast and looks as if she has been crying.

'Will she be one of them?'

'Probably. Some penny-whore who got unlucky.' Jack places a hand on my elbow and steers me in the other direction. 'We should have come a different way.'

Moments later we are in the lee of the wall and his arm is around my waist as he draws me close. His mouth is on mine, wet and insistent, and I am suddenly aware of the blood coursing through my veins. Of a strange ache in my loins. My vision of the anguished woman fades until I recall what is proper and push him away.

'Come.' He grins, unabashed. 'I know how to divert you.'

I struggle to compose myself. Shocked by the kiss and by my body's reaction to it. 'Are we not going to Vauxhall Gardens?'

'The Gardens are best at night. This entertainment is nearer.'

We walk for several minutes, unspeaking, my mind full of his lips on mine and of the tragic-looking woman. She did not look wicked, but I am unfamiliar with whores. I expected a gown that failed to decently cover her. An unsteady step, from gin-drinking. A painted face and a coarse laugh. But the woman was nothing like that. She looked like someone who might have served me at a market stall or sold me a length of ribbon in a shop. Jack is right, I am unprepared for London ways.

With his grip firm on my elbow, he hurries me along as if afraid we might miss something. Perhaps the King is due to pass in a golden carriage. Or a military band is about to play, with the bright blare of trumpets and the rattle of drums.

'This is the place,' he says, as we turn a corner.

A crowd is gathering outside an inn – a great circle of forty or fifty people. They are mostly men, but a few women, too. Some hanging on the arm of their menfolk. Dogs bark excitedly. One of them has a bloodied rat dangling from its jaws. There is an air of expectation.

'What are they waiting for?'

Jack lifts me in strong arms and places me on top of a mounting block outside the inn. As if I were a child.

'You will be safer there, and get a better view.'

Now that I am raised above the crowd, I see a bull tethered by a short length of chain in the centre of the space. He looks alarmed by the crowd and strains to get his liberty. People are laughing at him, pushing to keep out of his way, yet staying perilously close, as if the danger thrills them.

It does not excite me, though I am relieved we have not come to see some public punishment. The crowd have a rough air – as if bent on mischief. I can smell slaughterhouses near-by and the bull is old. This will not end well for him.

There is a sudden roar from the mob and it makes me fearful. This must be how people behave at a public execution.

A shout goes up. 'A lane! A lane!' This must be a recognised signal, for they squeeze together to form a narrow avenue of bodies leading towards the frantic bull. Then a thick-set man brings a bulldog on a leash. The animal is powerfully-built, its flanks covered in old scars. The man sets the dog towards the bull, which lets out an enraged bellow.

'Pin him!' everyone cries, Jack included.

The dog lunges forward and latches onto the bull's nose with its jaws. Dark blood mixed with flecks of foam fly from the animal's muzzle as he tries desperately to shake off his assailant. It is horrible and my stomach heaves.

Frantic, his flesh torn and blood now streaming brightly, the bull somehow manages to dislodge his tormentor. The crowd pushes and shoves, disregarding danger in their need to see the outcome. Then the owner urges the bulldog back to his ugly task. There is to be no mercy. But as the dog runs at the animal again, the terrified beast somehow catches it on his horns and throws it high in the air.

There is a collective surge from the crowd, who close up together and catch the bull-dog as it falls, to save its neck being broken.

Agitated barking and snarling heralds a pack of mongrels who are now set on the poor bull, with active participation from the crowd, who throw stones and jeer. When, inevitably, the beast falls to the cobbles with a juddering thump, the dogs are pulled off its twitching body. A man in a leather apron leads forward a broken-down nag, its eyes rolling in terror at the stench of blood, and drags the carcass away with ropes.

Jack is flushed, his eyes bright. I know men enjoy this kind of spectacle, but what made him think I would want to see it?

'What jaws the dog had,' he says. 'I was sure he would hang on longer. Sometimes their teeth can wrench a bull's muzzle clean off. I won a shilling last summer on a hound with similar markings.'

I look up at the glorious blue sky, so perfect it almost hurts my eyes, then down to the trail of blood on the cobbles, and clench my teeth. I must not shame Jack by vomiting, but wonder if there is something darker behind his easy smiles to think this fit entertainment for me. So much beauty, and so much ugliness. How can it be a proper pastime for a Sunday afternoon?

'Come.' Jack has my elbow in his grip again. 'You look peaky. You need feeding. Vauxhall isn't the only place that sells oysters and the sport has made me hungry. Then I suppose I must escort you home.'

'You are right. Master Chalke will need his tea. I am going to make cinnamon buns.'

'You shouldn't put yourself to so much trouble.'

'Why not? He is my master, after all.' I still cannot believe him a lecher. His eye may be frequently on me, but he always keeps his distance. And my imaginings about those auctions could be wild of the truth. He is an aristocrat even if a disgraced one. How could the brother of a lord be involved with a bawdy house? The thought is laughable.

'Is he?' Jack turns those brilliant eyes on me and grimaces. 'The world is more complicated than you appreciate, Hannah. You must learn to take care of yourself. Nobody else will.'

He is abrupt, as if something has annoyed him. He can hardly be resentful of my attentions to Master Chalke, can he? But for Jack to have kissed me like that must mean something. It was not the salutation of a friend.

I need to be alone, to re-live that disturbing sensation. How soft yet urgent his lips were. I have never been overwhelmed by my body before, being dismissive of girls eager to catch some callow youth's eye. Now I have unexpectedly experienced the flame a kiss can ignite and it unsettles me. I remember Mrs Lamb's admonition that respectable girls must be virgins if they want a wedding band. And that if I really want to find different work, away from here, it means going away from Jack.

Chapter Twenty

The bruising hand over my mouth is no nightmare. It is flesh and blood. Soft-skinned. Redolent of the peppery scent of snuff. A gentleman's hand. And though he doesn't carry a candle, and there is just an outline against the moonlit window, there is only one man it can be.

I wrench my mouth free.

'Sir!'

Something unthinkable is happening. Master Chalke's weight is on top of me.

It seemed only moments ago that I locked up the house and crawled under my blanket expecting to dream of Jack and that kiss.

I choke out a strangled protest, my tongue dry in my mouth.

'Lie still, dammit.' It is a command. From someone I am used to obeying.

Fear and panic overwhelm me and I twist my head, gulping air.

This will be my fault. We are taught it is always sinful Eve who lures men to sin. Master Chalke has mistaken my manner. Has thought me a loose woman inviting an approach. Has thought me like Susan.

'I am a good girl, sir!'

'All the better.' He makes a noise that might be a smothered laugh. 'You can be good to me.'

I am frantic. To scream. To beg him to leave me alone. But the only noise I manage is a squeal.

I might as well plead for twenty guineas a year and jewels in my hair.

I sleep in my spare shift. It is all I have. His invading hand rips it from neck to hem and gropes at me. He is slobbering over my neck, his breath stinking of bad teeth and the brandy I carried to the book room hours ago.

I think of calling for the mistress, but she is no friend to me. Even if this is not my fault, that I would never flaunt myself before any man, especially an old one like him, it is just the two of us in the night.

I instinctively fight him, but he is too strong.

'Quit struggling. Or do you like to be hurt?' He labours above me. 'That's right. Cry. It excites me.'

I flail beneath him and instinctively try for his eyes with my nails. It is then that he punches me. Bunches his fist and strikes, like a pugilist in a ring. My nose gushes metallic-tasting blood and I am reduced to gasping wetly for breath as he thrusts with increasing violence.

Despite the noise we make, nobody comes. The house remains dark and silent. Only the clock on the downstairs landing measures my fate, as if nothing of significance has happened.

Now I weep, but quietly in obedience to his command, collapsed beneath him. He is the devil, come in the night to destroy me. Almost worse is knowing what an utter fool I have been.

How do women bear this? Must half the human race lie in subjection beneath the other half? Every mother in the street must have done it. My own included, though I cannot bear to think of that. Even our queen and king have children. How can God have decreed tender babes come from such an act?

At last, the master hoists himself off me with a grunt and bends to the floor for a knotted handkerchief he must have brought with him. From it he shakes pennies onto the bed, as if I were one of those desperate women who linger outside public houses. The shame stings as badly as the raw place between my thighs.

'One word to my wife,' he orders, 'and you are on the street. Without a character. Without a roof over your head or food in your belly. With no option but to open those pretty legs to anyone who offers.'

He opens the door cautiously, a thief in the night, before padding barefoot down to his own bed. Leaving me in a ruin of blood-streaked sheets.

I lie, shuddering with sobs. There is no bolt to my door, nothing to stop him returning.

The thought panics me. Clutching my torn shift, I scramble from the bed, grab my shawl, and flee down through the shuttered darkness, past the great ticking clock, my bare feet hurrying over wooden floorboards, then carpet, to the cold flags of the kitchen.

I stop at the door leading into the yard, palms flat against its rough wood. It is like pitch outside, for clouds have obscured the moon and it has begun to rain. I hear it tapping on the windows, like pointing fingers. I did not think to grab my boots and realise I cannot run through wet streets barefoot, in a torn shift. An affront to public decency. An invitation to any men lurking in the alleyways.

A church bell announces the hour. Two o'clock. Followed by disjointed ringing, near and far, from neighbourhood steeples and towers. So many places of worship, so many fine churches. When I observed them from my garret, I thought what an upright city this must be. With so many houses of God.

I cannot stay here, but where could I go?

Everyone knows the city's unlit thoroughfares are no place for honest men in the small hours. Honest women, never. Though I am no longer that. I am stained by what has been done to me. For my life long.

Yesterday began before dawn in the dank scullery and though I went to bed utterly weary I was innocent and clung to hopes for the future. Now there is only despair and shame, for I am spoiled goods. I cannot even weep, only shiver with cold and misery.

I think for a moment of trudging every long mile to find Mrs Lamb. She was the nearest thing I had to a mother since my own died. But Mrs Lamb is lost to me, and not just through distance. She would be repelled. It is as if I have been pissed on by something foul.

What would I do out in the night, a defenceless girl, with my shift in tatters and blood on my thighs? Yet how can I stay? Upstairs the master will be in bed with his wife and it strikes me that she has reason to be sour. I should have taken warning from what I have heard and seen. Instead of dithering, I should have begged Thomas for help and fled to the countryside.

For how can I stay safe from the master, who will likely come after me again?

All I can do is scramble to the hearth, grasp the cold, black iron of the kitchen poker and take it back with me to the door. I crouch against it, panting as if I have been running. My mind in turmoil. If he comes after me again, I will use it. I will kill him, even if I hang for it.

Chapter Twenty-One

There is a sour blade of light on the lime-washed wall. Dawn. The sparrows will be squabbling soon, as if this were a normal morning. But I am still crouched against the yard door, knees bent to my chest and arms tight around my legs. The poker still at my feet.

Everything is quiet, but my mind still rages at being turned to spoiled meat. The flagstones are chill but my tremors are more from fear and hate than from cold.

There have been long hours to beat my mind against the cage my position has become. Even if Mrs Lamb and Mistress Buttermere come back from York, they will assume I had forgotten their teachings. Decent housewives will slam their doors in my face. Even the poorhouse turns away fallen women. And after those two years under its merciless roof, I would rather perish.

I had been put in a narrow bed with Mary, younger even than my own ten years, who looked as if she still wet herself at night. The room was cavernous. Chill. Full of women and girls. Sleeping, snoring through snotty winter noses or coughing themselves awake from weak chests. Muttering with bad dreams that would likely come true.

'Tomorrow's our day for Chapel,' she confided, wet thumb briefly out of her mouth as she tried to cuddle into me for warmth. 'And we gets shin of beef, after.'

I had shaken free and wiped my eyes on the sleeve of my night shift. I had no handkerchief. They had stripped my own good clothes from me and given me others that did not fit, in scratchy fabric. Together with an apron. A cap. A pair of mended worsted stockings. All in a blur of rough hands, harsh voices, unwholesome smells.

'I want my mother,' I sniffled, but under my breath, in case the overseer heard. I had already discovered her sharp fingernails seemed to relish drawing blood from the earlobes of troublesome children.

'You have a mother?' Mary's voice was a whisper. She had bright red hair, though everything else about her was colourless.

'She is dead.' *If she were alive, I would never be in this bleak place.*

'But you had one?' There was a pause. ''Cos I never did.'

'Everybody has a mother.' I pictured the tall woman with dark, curly hair. Eyes like periwinkles. A laugh like sunshine. Arms always eager to hug me.

'Not in this place, they don't.' I turned to see the girl's eyes gleam in the near-dark. 'But I wish I could have had one. To remember.'

As I wrapped my arms around her, I vowed that one day I would get away from there. That nothing would ever make me go back.

I force my mind to settle. The Chalkes are creatures of habit. On wash-day, after breaking their fast, two chairmen arrive to carry them away until late afternoon. Until then, I must bite my lips and pretend respect while I decide what to do.

If I stay, that beast will surely come for me again. Turn me into his creature. But, were I to protest, the Chalkes would stand together and kick me into the gutter without a penny of my hard-earned wages. Without a character and destitute.

I have no idea where to find the local constable and if I went to him or even to the parish priest, have no confidence in being believed. What was done to me is an offence, but justice for the poor is rare. Even a fifteen-year-old knows that. I dare not risk being falsely accused of theft like the unfortunate Susan.

I unclench my fingernails from my palms. I should rouse myself before Peg comes. My shift clings to me and though I scrubbed myself with kitchen soap, almost relishing the harsh sting, I will never feel clean again.

Yet I remain immobile. Without money or anyone to whom to turn, the choice is between unsafe streets or a brute in a silken waistcoat.

It sickens me that I was raised to be obedient, to show respect, to be silent unless spoken to. This subservience, this seemly humility, is mightily convenient for monsters like my master. How can it be right for men to have such power because they are stronger and made in God's image?

What a fool I was to think Master Chalke worthy of respect. Even apart from those overheard conversations, the signs of what he was, what he would do, were plain in Peg's eyes. In the tales about Susan. The neighbouring maid's warning. The lascivious gaze of those visitors. I should have sought work scrubbing steps, like Peg. Yet I stayed, like a witless fool, and dreamed of working for a famous author.

I blot my swollen eyes with the hem of my shift and swear to survive the shame. To one day be revenged. To see the master dragged from his house with chains on his hands and feet. I know that could never happen, but to dream of it might just keep me from running mad.

Chapter Twenty-Two

A distant dog barks as the London bells begin to chime five. Hand carts jolt over the cobbles. The city is stirring. Peg will be dragging her way through the streets, eyes on the gutter for scraps for her hungry belly. What will she think to see me like this? I should drag myself to my garret for my gown and a clean cap.

But I fear going upstairs in case I grab a kitchen knife, run to the master's bedside and stick the blade into the lard of his belly.

A noise in the yard makes me flinch. The door latch rattles. Pressure is exerted against the bolt.

'Hannah?' The voice is low, fearful of waking the sleepers upstairs. It is Peg, of course, come early as it is wash-day.

'Why 'aint the door open?' The ironwork rattles again.

Shame keeps me motionless.

The scrape of ill-fitting boots on flagstones is followed by scrabbling at the window. She must be able to make out my white shift in the gloom, for she returns to the door.

'What's up? Let me in.'

I am usually the one giving instructions, but have to make myself leave the poker and work the bolt clear. I oiled it only yesterday, so it is easy. Yesterday, when I was still a pure maid. The knowledge makes me feel unclean, even before the lowly Peg.

But she has eyes to see as she limps inside. She drops her ragged bundle. Grasps me in bony arms.

'I warned you to get away.' She cradles my head against her shoulder. It is the first time we have touched and I do not care that she smells bad.

'You didn't warn me about *him*.'

She lets out a wheezing sigh.

'He is so scared of the mistress that I was sure you was safe. From that, at least.' She strokes my tangled hair. 'Flashed a knife at him, she did, over the Susan business. Made him swear on the Bible to never touch another girl under her roof. Or she would slit his throat.'

It sounds like something from a play, but I believe it.

'He went after Susan, too?'

'Does a dog cock its leg on every post? She ran complaining to the mistress. Who damned her for a liar, before throwing her out on the street.'

Peg steers me to the kitchen chair and makes me sit. Hands me a scrap of moistened rag.

I dab at my nose, thinking of Susan as the cloth turns from red to pink. The bleeding has stemmed. If I am careful the swelling might not be too bad.

'But the girl threatened to snitch. Not about being raped – she as good as asked for that – but about their other dirty business.'

'What dirty business?'

Peg dismisses my question with a grunt.

'They swore blind she had nicked their best spoons. A pack of lies, of course. But she was thrown in jail.'

Peg shakes her head.

'Then the mistress visited her in the public cell. Whispered the slags in there would finish her off in return for a silver shilling. Susan must have been pissing herself with fear, 'cos she took the punishment.'

Peg glances at the brightening light outside and sucks on her broken teeth.

'A chit scarce sixteen. Whipped. Branded with a hot iron on the thumb. Transported. For saying she would blab.'

She limps to the fire left ready-made last night, reaches for the tinder box and sets about striking sparks with the flint. 'It's freezing in here.'

I am still huddled under my shawl by the time she has brewed tea and brought me a bowl, wrapping my hands around its warmth.

'Get that down you. Or you will likely take a chill.'

'I don't care. I would like to die.'

That would be an escape. Yet the tea is welcome and as I gulp it, I find a burst of courage.

'I have read of men punished for rape. There was a major, once. A gentleman. He went to prison.'

Peg's brows furrow.

'Likely the girl he tumbled come from a respectable family. Nobody is going to care about a servant.' She sets a bowl of warm water in front of me. 'Clean yourself up. And watch that mouth if you don't want to end up in the river.'

'Must he get away with it?'

'What have I just said? Susan could have had a knife in her guts. Or even gone for the drop. For the value of spoons that she never took.'

I shudder. I have never seen a public hanging, but Mrs Lamb said women drew the biggest crowds.

'You needs to act normal.'

'How can I?'

'Surprising what a body can do, when she has to.' Peg thrusts a fresh rag into my hand. 'Clean your face while I fetch your clothes. They will be stirring soon.'

Sullenly, I apply the cloth to my face. It stings. His signet ring has cut my lip.

'He will come after me again. Won't he?'

'He might. If he thinks to get away with it.'

I want to go into the yard and puke. What is to stop him grabbing me whenever he wants? I will become his prey in the night, with the mistress asleep and him free to roam. If I cannot devise a way to protect myself, I am lost.

'Would the mistress stop him?'

'Maybe, if she found out. But you are the one who would pay. They would both swear you're an artful baggage. Or stole summat. Like with Susan.' Peg has resumed her defeated look. 'Don't risk it. Submit. Or run as far away as those legs will take you.'

I drop the cloth in the bowl. I must find a way to keep safe while I seek another post, perhaps through Thomas. I glance at my companion and a thought flutters through my mind. A desperate moth at a shuttered window. Mistress Lamb said I was a bright girl. I must use those wits to survive.

'The rich gets away with everything,' Peg mutters, at my shoulder. 'Always have. Always will.'

Destitution is fearful. Hollow-eyed misery you must pretend isn't there, lest it break your heart. The gentry no doubt, if they ponder the matter at all, convince themselves that is what the poorhouses are for. But I will never surrender myself to such a place again.

Peg surprises me with industry, fetching my clothes and setting the great cauldron to boil for the wash while I dress. As if nothing is wrong.

So much for my place in this house being my path to better things. Some servants do well if they stay with a family long enough. A few even stay their whole lives and are looked after with kindness in old age. If I had dreamed of anything, it was of becoming the valued housekeeper to some aristocratic family.

As Peg hurries upstairs for the chamber pots, I start viciously kneading the dough for the morning rolls. Outside the sparrows chitter their start to the day, eager for precedence. For the best perch, the best chance of crumbs. They have one another and a clean life. But everything is spoiled for me. I am spoiled. I doubt if I can even stay safe while trying to find another post.

Chapter Twenty-Three

Thomas Graham throws down his pannikin with a clatter and turns me towards him with a gentle hand. I had kept my head down, sidling close to the piebald's flank.

'Whatever happened to your poor face?'

Having seen my reflection in the parlour looking-glass, I hate to be studied. I resent feeling stained by what happened, when I was so foolishly innocent. My body still aches and I cannot even make water without it stinging like a nest of wasps. But the greatest hurt is to my pride. I no longer want this body to be mine.

When I raise my chin, I see anger in his face.

'Has Mistress Chalke done this?'

I shake my head. He must not suspect my shameful trouble. And he is, in any case, a man. I have learned about the evil thing they keep in their breeches and believe I hate every single one of them. Even Thomas Graham.

'I tripped. Struck my face against the banister.'

'The devil you did!' His eyes snap with anger. 'You tripped against someone's fist.'

'It was an accident.'

He does not believe me, but what could he do? Beaten servants are not unusual and, provided they are not killed, it is common knowledge there is no redress. Rape is another matter, of course, with harsh consequences. But Peg is right. No prudent maidservant will accuse her master.

Light rain starts to spatter the roof tiles and make the cobbles gleam which means I need to get inside and festoon the washing over the kitchen hanging rails to dry. I should ask Thomas about work, but am seized by an urge to creep into the furthest recesses of some dark cupboard and hide.

'You had best get back indoors,' Thomas shakes his head. 'Use cold cloths, to reduce the swelling. Then try to take things quietly for a few hours.'

I clutch the jug and turn towards the steps to the kitchen entrance.

'Does she often beat you?' The concern in his voice makes me turn around.

'Not often.' It sounds the lie it is. Though, for once, the mistress is not responsible for my hurts.

'I would be glad to think you will be all right,' he says. 'If I believed it.'

It is a comfort to see kindness in those dark eyes. It helps remind me not all men will be beasts.

'I am not surprised Mistress Chalke cannot keep servants. Her man should speak to her. Better still, you need another place. Why don't I make enquiries for you? In my village?'

That is what I planned to ask him about, but everything unknown is suddenly fearful to me and I am as knowledgeable about the countryside as I am about the Americas. Thomas Graham seems a good man, but what if he is another dissembler? I thought Master Chalke a Christian gentleman, didn't I?

'Our local gentry families are good people.' He is pressing me. 'Fair to their workers. Or there is an inn that might need help in its kitchen.'

I avoid his eye, wishing I had someone to give me advice. Wondering whether I could turn to Jack, who surely has tender feelings for me, but would be disgusted at what I have become.

I am no better than a beaten dog, desperate to crawl away and lick its wounds.

'The Chalkes would not appreciate interference and might take it out on you if they found out. But I would be discreet.' He rubs his chin, already darkening with stubble, though it is early. 'Calypso will have her foal any day. Why not make your visit to my farm on your next free Sunday? You can bring Peg, as your chaperone. By then I will have made it my business to talk to a few people about you.'

I lick my split lip, wordless. Chaperone? Does he think me a proper young lady? Little does he know.

He frowns at my silence. 'It could be your best option, Hannah.'

He turns towards the next house, where the maidservant has appeared at the area steps, her fresh cap and over-eager smile making me suspect she hopes to catch his eye. He is an unattached man who would give a wife a comfortable life. But he could do better than that raw-boned harridan, were he to change his mind about marrying again.

I drag myself back inside. I cannot afford to dwell on my pain and humiliation, though my mind is like a tongue worrying a rotten tooth. For I think of it, the whole time. The sounds he made. His sweaty stink. Being used like an animal.

But what can a penniless girl do? The world is divided between those with so many possessions they need stewards to keep records of them and those with little more than the clothes on their backs.

As Peg warned, the mistress, with her ruined face, would have no pity. I can picture her outrage. Accusations that I led her husband on. That he is a good man, though easily led astray like so many of his sex, while I am a lying slut. The dismissal for lewd behaviour. The impossibility of finding another position. Hunger and want.

To keep my place, to have a roof over my head and a crust in my mouth, I must bow my head. But there are too many months before my servitude will come to an end. Too many nights to avoid the master. I must pray Thomas can find me a position in his village. If I must put my trust in anyone, it should be in him.

Meanwhile I will only live to find a way to hurt Chalke. To pay him for my disgrace and pain. Uncovering his secrets before I leave might help me bring about some kind of justice, but for now I must face seeing the pair of them when they come downstairs.

Chapter Twenty-Four

Somehow, I help the Chalkes break their fast, positioning myself behind the mistress. As usual, she does not even glance up as I place hot rolls and the chocolate pot on the table. The master is across from me, but I avoid his eye and think him unlikely to remark on my bruised face.

By the time the chairmen to come take them away, my mind is scrabbling at my plan. With someone sharing my bed, the master would surely not come after me in the night. Could I use Mistress Chalke's hunger for money to keep myself safe? At least until Thomas finds out about work for me in his village?

'Do you think the mistress would allow you to share my room?' I ask Peg, as we finish off the breakfast chocolate that I had kept back in the heating pan. I no longer care about filching from the Chalkes. 'With you there, he could not come after me in the night.' I shudder at the thought of what will surely happen, come dark. I have wondered about trying to sleep in the wooden kitchen chair. 'Would you mind? Do you think she would allow it?'

Peg licks chocolate from her lips, then wipes her nose with her sleeve. She always seems to have a cold.

She blinks. 'There would need to be something in it for her pocket.'

'I could offer to work for less than my promised wage. It would be worth it, to stay safe till I find a new position.'

Perhaps Peg could go with me when I leave, but I must not promise salvation to her when I cannot yet see how to save myself.

'She would like that.'

'If she let us do it, you would save on your own rent.'

Peg scratches under her cap as she thinks it through. Pence matter to her. She has too few to feed herself.

'We would have to share the bed,' I say. 'Unless one of us slept on the floor.'

'I does that already. On straw.'

I look at her and wonder where this wretched place can be, where she sleeps on the floor, on straw, like some farmer's beast.

'It would be a comfort to me, to share,' I say.

'For me, too. And you are likely right, about it keeping him away.' She runs a finger around the inside of her bowl, though it is already spooned clean, then licks it. Perhaps there is a taste of sweetness left. 'And if I was allowed a bite of bread and cheese at night, I would be better off.' Peg sucks the finger, in case she has missed anything.

At the end of the afternoon, we face Mistress Chalke together. I need Peg behind me, shrinking in the parlour doorway, as I am still struggling to conceal my hurts, of body and spirit.

'I have a request, ma'am.' I force myself to sound like a dullard. That is my best defence in this house.

The unfeeling eyes slide over me. My nose has swollen and I suspect I am getting a black eye.

'Have you been in a brawl?' She fidgets with her lace mittens. It can be chilly in the parlour if you move away from the fire.

'I slipped on the stair, ma'am.'

'Did you break anything?' My hurts do not interest her.

'No, ma'am.'

'Then what are you asking? You are not getting paid before next Lady Day.'

'I wondered… If I took only two guineas for my year, instead of three. Might you let Peg sleep in my room? It would save her paying for her lodging.'

The glitter of greed in her eyes is immediate and gives me hope. 'Why would you give up a whole guinea? For that wretch?'

'I thought to do her a kindness.'

'A kindness! Then you are a simpleton.' She looks from me to Peg. 'The two of you? In the garret together?' There is an odd expression on her face that convinces me she has known about her husband all along.

She frowns down at the mittens, but not before I see she means to agree.

I bled for three days afterwards. I hoped, perhaps, that I might die from it, but I did not. So I exist, full of hate for Chalke and for a body that no longer feels my own. I have become his creature, even if Peg's presence in my garret has so far stopped him coming after me again.

I am convinced I still stink of him. That he has marked me, like a dog urinating on a post. And, as a final burden, what happened was a sin. The preachers insist on it. The flames of Hell surely beckon.

The old woman smells familiar now. Something to cling to in the night, for I feel in pieces, like broken china. But I cannot allow myself to be eaten up with bitterness and give the Chalkes another victory. I must cobble my fragments together and carry them away from here.

I listen for the master whenever he is in the house, but though he never tries to touch me in daylight and I curl up tight with Peg each night, his gaze follows me. He is careful whenever the mistress is near, but I sense his foul hunger. Shadows grow like bruises under my eyes and at the day's end I put off going up to bed. My nights are full of smothering dreams or of wakeful hours listening for the creak of his foot on the stair. Peg may not be enough to deter him, nor that chair wedged against our door. What if he were to order her from the room?

I loathe him from the top of my mob cap to the toes of my shabby boots and ache to empty the stinking contents of his chamber pot over his head. To scratch those invading eyes from his face with my nails. To find a way to poison him and see him clutch his belly in agony. But then I would hang as a public spectacle and go to Hell after. Which means that all I can do is piss into a jar in the scullery and trickle the contents into his tea. And wonder if Thomas might have found work for me.

Oddly, my weakness has given Peg strength. She does more about the house and keeps a rheumy eye open for the master.

'Watch yourself. He is wandering about, downstairs,' she will hiss, sliding into the scullery. It is a waiting game that I cannot win. I must do something. What if Thomas cannot find me a position?

The master calls for me. Peremptory. I am his servant and must obey, though my knees feel weak as I enter the hateful book room.

'Master?' My palms are sweating. If he puts his hand on me I know I will scream or swoon. Perhaps both.

'Do not think to avoid me.' He stands at his desk, thumbs thrust into the pockets of a green brocade waistcoat. Glowing with arrogance and expectation.

I wish I had the courage to fly at him, but am too slight to inflict harm. I am an insect to be swatted away. Or stepped on and crushed. And I have only one weapon: his fear of his wife.

He leans towards me. 'Come closer.'

On the floor above, the door of their bedchamber slams and he freezes as the mistress's footsteps stomp down the stairs and into the parlour next door. She is only through the wall from us. He scowls and slumps into his chair, lowering his voice.

'I have it in mind to dismiss the old woman.'

I take a quivering breath and lick parched lips. This is what I have feared. What I have prepared my mind for. Pretending boldness is my only hope. The mistress must think me stupid; the master a convincing threat.

'Then I will tell your wife.'

'You will do what!' The chair tips over with a crash as he leaps up.

Courage, or desperation, makes me jut my chin, though my tongue cleaves to the roof of my mouth.

'I will do it. I swear.'

In a stride he is around the desk and has slammed me against the wall. A meaty hand grasps my throat.

'You dare threaten me?'

'I ask only to be left alone,' I croak, a spurt of hot urine leaking shamefully down my leg.

His fingers tighten. I am starved of air. Blood pounds in my ears. My vision blurs. He is killing me.

Then the door bangs open.

'What the devil is going on?' The mistress is staring at us.

'Nothing, my love.' The hand relaxes its grip and I drag in a breath. If I was not against the wall I would collapse. The master's face is livid, but his recovery is quick. 'This imbecile forgot my tea. She needed a lesson.'

His wife stares at us, eyes narrowed.

'I will bring it immediately, master,' I croak, struggling to swallow. Terrified Mistress Chalke's sharp eyes will spot the damp patch on the carpet.

'Forget it. I am going out instead.' He glances at his wife. 'If that does not inconvenience you, my dear...'

'Do whatever you please.' She divides a scowl between us before turning to leave.

The master waves me from his presence with a muttered oath. But as I stagger downstairs, sodden stockings rubbing my thighs, I pray we have an understanding. For the present.

That night I gaze from my window at the new moon, high over the rooftops. It looks so pure, like a bowl of fresh cream, far removed from the cruel things that happen in its light.

I still dream he is in my room and wake in panic. But Peg is with me now and if she senses my nightmare her reassuring hand creeps to my shoulder to give me comfort.

At least Thomas should be making enquiries for me in his village. Someone surely will need a willing pair of hands. Living in the country would mean never seeing Jack again, but even if he could overlook my lowly status, he would never consider marrying soiled goods. Master Chalke has ruined my future in more ways than I can count. And, besides, marriage, even to Jack, would be utterly distasteful to me now.

Chapter Twenty-Five

I can hardly bear to return to the bookshop and face Jack. Even strange men in the street make me uneasy, and it is unthinkable to tell him what has happened. My face is less marked now, only swollen about the nose, but I feel everything about me shouts I have been despoiled.

'Best keep away,' I mumble, coming through the door. 'I have a cold.'

'I am glad you warned me.' He takes the package and retreats. 'I had trouble shifting my last chill. The only thing that eased it was a warmed treacle posset.' He shakes his head. 'My chest is delicate. Mother would put brown paper on it when I was younger. Spread with goose grease.'

Such talk might once have amused me, now I only want to hide myself away.

'Is there anything to take back?'

'Not today. The press is being cleaned. Ink clogs the letters. A dirty, tedious job.'

'Poor John.'

'The fellow is fed and housed. He has no cause for complaint.'

I move towards the door, not wanting to stay yet reluctant to return to the Chalke house. Jack is placing my unopened package in a drawer and I cannot help wondering about its contents.

He locks the drawer and shoves the key in his pocket. 'Isn't your next Sunday free? We could have another outing.' He grimaces. 'Assuming you are better.'

'I am going to look at the river. With Peg.'

'That drudge? Whatever for?'

'We want to watch the traffic on the water.' The lie comes easily. I do not want Jack to know about our visit to Thomas Graham's farm.

'Suit yourself.' He looks down his nose at me. 'I would have been a better companion than that old crone. Perhaps I will not ask you out again.'

I hesitate. He knows the world in ways I do not and will be familiar with Master Chalke's character. But he is also a man and they have become something to be wary of.

Yet with Peg still close-mouthed, is he not the best way of finding out about those auctions? To keep myself safe, I need to know.

'Jack...do you know someone called Jarret?'

His face changes. 'Where did you hear that name?'

'The mistress mentioned it.'

'To you?'

'I overheard talk...'

'Hannah.' He moves close and I flinch at his grip on my arm. 'Spying on the Chalkes is imprudent. Especially if they talk about that woman.'

Then he steps back, either remembering my chill or wondering if he has said something he shouldn't.

'It was just the once,' I lie, glad that at least it is not some strange man that they are thinking of passing me to. Yet women usually run brothels, don't they?

He watches me open the door, a frown creasing his brow. No salutation on my wrist this time, not that I could bear one.

Is he an honourable young man? He sensed my love of books at our first meeting and cared enough to show me something of London. I think he *is* good, but obliged to consort with others who are not. After all, he was apprenticed to his uncle at fourteen. With no more choice in the matter than I had.

Given time, if I can hide what has happened and prevent it happening again, perhaps we could remain friends who share an interest in books.

Yet I wonder now about the expression on his face when he looks at me. Mrs Lamb warned me that men can be unreliable. I would never want to understand them, if it were not necessary for my safety.

I even feel nervous about going to Thomas's farm on Sunday. Though Peg will be with me and it will take us away from the Chalkes for a whole day. Hopefully there might also be news of someone who needs a cook or even a scullery maid, safely away in the country.

Chapter Twenty-Six

Two more gentlemen have come, clumping their way up towards Master Chalke's book room. I stand aside on the landing to let them pass, with their odours of snuff, tobacco and horse sweat. The younger one, with a sallow, pock-marked face, pauses and leers. I remember him, from before.

'Ah,' he murmurs, 'the pretty maid.'

He grabs my chin in his hand and presses me against the wall so the buttons of his riding coat stab my bodice. There is wine and something sour on his breath.

I struggle, but am penned into a corner and feel the threat of that disgusting bulge in his breeches. A vein throbs in his temple. His hands are moist and urgent on my neck. What is there about me that makes men think me a slut? Don't I even possess my own body?

'Hannah!' The summons from the book room is loud and insistent. A reprieve. 'Where the devil is that wine? Get yourself up here!'

Master Pock-Face backs off, placing a foot in a polished riding boot on the stair leading upwards. 'Another day,' he says, sounding so determined that I shudder as I stumble to the cellar for the wine. I am convinced these men are no better than my master and suspect now that it is women who are auctioned off in that room, where gentlemen bid against one another like traders in the market. Yet these visitors, sprawled in the worn leather chairs with their wide-spread knees, are silk-stockinged men with gold-topped canes and lace frothing at their cuffs. Men of property and rank.

Peg believes she is protecting me by keeping silent, but ignorance will not help me.

I decide to fetch the wine, then creep back and listen at the door before going inside.

With a cloth on the tray to prevent the fine-stemmed glasses chinking and giving me away, I hurry back and approach the door on tiptoe. They have made it easy for me, since it stands ajar, tobacco smoke billowing out in pungent clouds. I must be careful it does not make me cough.

'You are a sly rogue, Chalke,' someone laughs. It sounds like the young one. 'Keeping the best for yourself.'

'Nay.' That is Master Chalke. 'I have said before, the chit is not what you and your father seek. Too old by far.' A chair scrapes. 'Where the devil is she?'

I rattle the glasses on the tray to signal I am coming through the door. The father has taken the pot from the cabinet and is pissing into it. He glances up from a feeble yellow stream and grins as if to say, *you will have the privilege of emptying this later*. Which, indeed, I will. Probably while it is still warm.

Two pairs of eyes assess me, a plump duck ready to be carved. Their talk has stopped, but resumes as soon as the door closes behind me. Though since I cannot make out anything comprehensible, even with the draught from the keyhole in my ear, I return to my kitchen.

These men do not trade in brandy, for who would consider such traffic evil when ministers of religion happily accept illicit barrels of the spirit at their back doors after dark? Loose women are probably involved, though why would they be auctioned like shipments of China silk? If Peg and Jack remain tight-lipped, my only way to uncover the truth is getting sight of *The Maid's List*.

But why the interest in me? I want to be mistress of my own destiny. Not passed on to that Jarrett woman, like a chattel. Or given into the hands of someone like Pock-Face.

After the men have gone, I remember that brimming pot of piss in the cupboard and trudge back upstairs, carrying a cloth to conceal its contents on its way to the necessary house. The sight must not offend any gentry who might be about, despite them being responsible for its creation. It is certainly not to protect my modesty, for I must tip away whatever it holds and scour any stains vigorously with sharp sand. What a nonsense that is. That if they are not seen, dirty things do not exist.

Tomorrow Peg and I go to see the foal at Thomas's farm. She thinks I should make eyes at the farmer and become his sweetheart, but I am more concerned with whether he has found me work. A place away from the Chalkes, and whatever happens in that room.

Chapter Twenty-Seven

'We are almost there.' Thomas glances up from the lane, lowering his voice to avoid disturbing Peg who is nodding in the back of the trap. 'Hercules has quickened his pace. Instinct always draws a horse back to its stable.'

In the traces is his sturdy piebald and I think of Calypso waiting, with her foal. Yet I feel awkward in my plain gown and darned stockings beside Thomas's broadcloth coat and buff breeches. This is who he really is, a prosperous yeoman farmer. Not the man delivering milk.

We have turned off the main road, hectic with mail coaches thundering in the opposite direction and gentlemen on mettlesome horses with smartly-dressed grooms trotting behind.

After passing brickworks and lime kilns, everything becomes green, the dappled light on the road like gold coins scattered in our path. There are trees in the city, of course, especially where the gentry live. In parks and public gardens. But they are hemmed in by buildings. Here the expanses stretch to the horizon broken only by random roadside cottages and farms. The hedgerows are studded with wild flowers and tree branches arch overhead like interlacing fingers.

To be away from the Chalke house is a relief, though I know I will never be free of what was done to me there.

'I feared I would never persuade you to come,' Thomas's eyes return to the lane ahead.

'Nobody has done such a kind thing for me before. Nor for Peg, either.'

I realise he does not frighten me. Instead he makes me long for an older brother, who might have taken care of me. Protected me.

'Well, they have been remiss.'

The air smells different. Cleaner. I close my eyes and feel something approaching peace.

'You should leave that place, Hannah. Those Chalkes are savages.'

'I want to. But they would refuse to give me a character.'

'That is nonsense. You are a hard worker. And skilled.' He

glances at me. 'There is a coaching inn, outside my village. Martha, the innkeeper's wife, needs a new cook. Her present girl has recently married and is in the family way.

'I am told their beds are clean and the food of exceptional quality.' He smiles. 'It should be, for their butter and milk are from my cows.'

I look at my chapped hands, clasped in my lap, and wonder if this could happen. A coaching inn would be a bustling exciting place to work, though the innkeeper's wife would reject me in disgust if she knew my history. Yet the place should be far enough away from the Chalkes to conceal my sordid secret.

I glance behind, at Peg. 'Might they have a position for someone to do rough work? Who would not need much in the way of wages?'

'I suspect not. But my own housekeeper would find her useful. She has a baby son. There are always clouts to wash.'

I stare at the horse's twitching tail and wonder again that Thomas comes so often into the city with a home in this clean countryside. A home that warrants a housekeeper.

Hercules has slowed to a walk. Across the quiet lane is an old stone church with a tower. We pass the churchyard wall and approach an open five-barred gate with a carved wooden sign: *Broad Oak Farm*.

'We are here.' Thomas guides the horse through. 'Betty will have refreshments ready. You must be thirsty after the dust of the road.'

I look around and my reaction is muted, for I had expected something different. A neat cottage, with half-a-dozen cows grazing in a field beside it. Perhaps chickens running in and out of a kitchen door.

The large yard we enter is a clutter of piled-up hurdles, with a broken wagon being used by chickens as a roost. Yet the farmhouse beyond is a handsome three-storey timbered building with ivy clambering towards tall chimneys, and outbuildings visible behind. It is too prosperous.

I sensed something like this when I saw Thomas waiting at the end of our street, dressed like a gentleman and holding the reins of this trap. I stare again at my stubby nails, ingrained with coal dust. How shabby I am, even in my one good gown. I am a servant. What am I doing here? Am I an object of charity?

'You have a thatch.' I do not know what else to say. 'I am not used to them.'

'After the great fire – you know of it? – when King Charles planned the rebuilding, he would not allow them in London. Flames spread too easily from one roof to another.'

'It looks like a painting.'

'A thatch is a mixed blessing. In wet weather, it gives off a fishy smell in the upstairs rooms. Though you barely notice when you live with it.'

He looks across at me as I struggle to make him out.

'Welcome to my home. I hope you will approve it.'

I hesitate. This man must be a respected figure in his community. Why bring a penniless kitchen maid to his house? Why care what she thinks of it? I remember Jack. The master. When men are interested in girls, I suspect now it is because they want their bodies. I must keep Peg near.

Loud honking approaches. From behind a rusty plough, geese waddle aggressively across the yard to investigate our arrival. They hiss at Hector, who jumps down, bristling, to bark at them.

'Come inside,' invites Thomas, helping us both down and placing himself between us and the stabbing beaks. 'But watch where you put your feet. The yard has its fair share of droppings.'

He offers me his arm. 'But before I take you back to town, remember we must agree about arranging a meeting with Martha.'

Chapter Twenty-Eight

Thomas is as welcoming to Peg as he is to me. She is silent, hunching her shoulders, her mouth agape at the house.

The stone-flagged entrance is a sensible three steps up from the mucky yard; the air inside fragrant from a jug of rosemary on a table by a tall-case clock.

Then we are led into a room with an inglenook fireplace. You would be able to see the sky if you craned your neck and peered up its massive chimney. A pair of battered pewter candlesticks flank a brass carriage clock on the over-mantel. Dark floorboards are underfoot, with lime-washed walls creating a pale, glimmering light. On one wall hangs an oil portrait of a stout man in an old-fashioned coat and bag wig, sitting in a carver chair with a dog of indeterminate breed at his knee. Thomas's father perhaps, or grandfather. A prosperous yeoman.

Everything is cool and clean. Wood shines. Brasses glitter. Windows are polished. His housekeeper must spend busy hours tending it. Yet I understand why Thomas seeks to spend time elsewhere, for the house echoes with empty rooms and ticking clocks.

'Come and meet Betty. She will have refreshments ready. Tea. Cider. Home-brewed beer.' He smiles. 'Even milk, if you prefer.'

We follow him back through the hall into a kitchen, where a plump woman bobs a curtsy. It is another fine room, with a stone-flagged floor and smoked hams suspended from the roof beams.

The goodwife has come from what must be the scullery, drying red hands on a clean apron. A baby sleeps in a wooden cradle in the corner of the kitchen and I assume it was her man feeding the pigs outside. The youth helping him is probably hers, too, for his sandy-coloured hair is identical to the strands escaping her frilled cap.

'I will be back in five minutes,' Thomas says. 'I need a word with Jed. Have your refreshment while I am gone.'

As he leaves, Peg limps over to the cradle, crouches down and peers at the infant, her wrinkled face softening. I had not suspected she liked babies. 'A boy?' she asks, voice low to avoid waking the child.

Betty nods proudly. 'My fourth,' she says. 'The others are old enough now to help on the farm in the mornings. In the afternoons Master Graham kindly pays a curate's widow to teach them their letters.' She sighs. 'I prayed for a girl this time. Perhaps the Good Lord will smile on me with my next.'

She urges us to sit at the scrubbed wood table, laid invitingly with a dish of saffron buns. Then, while the tea kettle boils, she pours lemon juice through a muslin cloth into a glass jug and carefully grates sugar over the top. I am impressed that she knows to use a long silver spoon to prevent the glass cracking when she adds hot water.

'Lemonade, Miss.' she explains, stirring the cloudy liquid. 'The master brought the lemons from town specially. I will leave it in the dairy to be cool for later, after you have seen round the farm. But will you take tea now?'

'We would love tea. But call me Hannah.'

'That would not be fitting. You are Master Graham's guest.'

'But I am only a servant. No different from you.'

'If you say so, Miss.' Her lips curve as she slides the saffron buns closer to Peg, who is eyeing them.

'What makes you smile, Betty?'

'Because I knew there had to be a reason Master Graham kept delivering the milk himself. When he didn't have to.'

I open my mouth to protest but Peg, her hand already on one of the buns, catches my eye and shakes her head. She is right. What could I say, anyway? Let Betty have her fancies. She will soon learn that is all they are.

'The single women of the village have been after him these last two years, as you would expect.' She shakes her head. 'But the young ones are silly, fluttery things, and the widows dull as ditchwater. Only interested in buying lace collars and inviting curates to tea. Though not one of them would bother to open the Bible, never mind the things the master likes to read. He needs someone to talk to about all those books he loves.'

This means Thomas must have spoken to her about me and our shared interest in stories.

'He is just like his father. Not a man to be impressed by ninnies with their heads full of nonsense.' She sighs. 'He spent the first year after his loss being bitter and angry at everything. Then he simply became sad. He has always been such a giving man. It is good to see him more like his old self.'

After we have had our tea and made a discreet visit to the necessary house, Peg stays in the kitchen while Thomas takes me outside. The old woman is in a chair by the fireside, her sound foot happily rocking the cradle and another saffron bun in her fist.

I cannot remember such a day in all my fifteen years. I am shown Aphrodite with her moist snout and curling tail, and scratched her rough back through the rails of the sty.

I have had the geese shoo'd away from my skirts by Thomas's silver-headed riding crop and taken care to avoid the slimy trail they leave behind them. And, on the way back from the open-sided shed where the cows are milked, have smelled the pungent muck heap.

'Liza always wanted me to shift our midden behind the barn,' Thomas nods towards it. 'Away from the house. I should have done it, instead of putting the chore off. Perhaps I will do it now. It would please her, if she is up there somewhere, watching.'

'Do you believe she is? Watching over you?'

'Perhaps. Religion is a puzzle to me, and I prefer sitting in an empty church to listening to sermons. Sunlight through stained glass moves me far more than words, along with knowing people have sat in those same pews, mouthing identical prayers for generations.'

'I sometimes wonder if my mother sees me.' I avoid his eye. 'I hope she does not.'

I used to kneel by my bed each night, hands clasped and eyes screwed tight.

Please God, help me be good. Help me to work hard. Help me to make something of my life.

But God cannot have been listening and now I have nothing to say to Him. I wish my life could be scraped clean. Scoured with brick dust, or sharp sand. Rubbed with coarse salt and a pumice stone. I want to be made-over into a pure girl again. One who can kneel and pray with a clear conscience.

'Why is that?' Thomas's brow wrinkles.

What can I say?

'I suppose because she hoped I might lead a more comfortable life. As her family did. In the old days, in France.'

'They were Huguenots?'

'They came from a place called Lyon. My grandfather was a silk merchant.' It sounds as if I am boasting, so I quickly add, 'Though that may be a tale. It was long ago.'

'But you remember your family? Your grandparents?'

'It is hard to picture my mother now, but I only need close my eyes to conjure a sense of her. The scent of her hair and how it curled down to her waist like a black curtain when she let it down at night.'

'Then you take after her. There is clearly a wealth of raven hair under that cap.'

'I am nothing like her, for she was spoken of as a beauty and a scholar. It was said my grandmother even had a governess, as a girl, in France. But that is all I remember.'

'They were wise to leave when they did. It was a cruel time. But it must have been hard for your family to lose everything.'

We walk past the pond, towards a field of grazing cows.

'I like the way you are training those two willows to arch over the water.'

'I planted them when our boys were born. It is strange to think they will grow to maturity, when my sons will not.' The lines in his face are back. 'Now they stand as memorials. There is a marker in the churchyard, but I have a preference for living things over dead stone.'

My smile dies. 'You have been so kind, inviting us here, and I repay you by reminding you of sad times.'

'Don't be sorry.' He studies the silver fox's head on the crop in his hand. 'It is good to talk about them at last. For too long I buried myself in grief. Life goes on. You cannot be a farmer unless you believe that.'

'Yet it is hard to lose those who make us happy.'

'My wife and I were certainly happy. When we wed, I was twenty and she twenty-two. We had known one another from county dances, which Liza adored.' He glances at me. 'Do you dance?'

'I do not know how.'

'You should learn. Those little feet would fly over a dance floor.'

I lift one of my boots. 'I would be a danger in these.'

'Then someone should give you some slippers.'

He hesitates and I suspect from his expression he had nearly offered to provide some. I want to be wrong, for I need Thomas as a friend. Not a man who views me as a woman who might dance.

'When will you take on the new man to drive your wagon?' I say, to change the subject. 'I would never leave this place to hawk milk around London.'

'Soon. Jed did it, before his accident. But it suited me to get away from my memories for an hour or two.' He studies the riding crop again. 'You are the first person I have been able to talk to about my sons. Thank you. It helps me.'

'So where is the foal?' I ask, after another pause. That is, after all, why I am here.

'In a paddock behind the house. With her proud dam.' He taps his pocket. 'I have something for Calypso. She cannot resist last season's lemon pippins.'

We pass through cows cropping grass under the shade of a huge tree, the ground under our feet rough and uneven from churning hooves.

'That oak is the tree the farm is named after. It was already grown when the roundheads were chasing the cavaliers.'

'Is it the one the king hid in? To escape the soldiers?'

'I believe that was somewhere in Shropshire. But ours is equally magnificent. And my cows appreciate the shade in summer. As do I. If I have a free hour, I bring a book to read beneath its branches.' He smiles. 'As I told you, I have never regretted being a farmer. I enjoy the turn of the seasons and seeing my crops and animals grow.'

Beyond, in another field, I finally see Calypso, with a beautiful long-legged foal at her side. The dappled charcoal creature darts behind the safety of her dam at our approach, to peep at us from under her mother's belly. When we reach the fence, the mare walks over while her foal leaps away towards the far hedge.

'Fillies are always more nervous than colts.' Thomas takes the apple and a knife from his pocket, slices the fruit into quarters and hands them to me. 'She will come over while her dam has the apple, if we are quiet.'

I am sure Calypso remembers me, for she readily comes to butt her nose into my hand to take the fruit. The foal edges closer. A perfect creature, bouncing on delicate legs.

I inhale the mare's warm smell and even manage a brief stroke of her foal.

'I did not realise farmers had such tender hearts. But Calypso is clearly used to being given treats.'

'I am not so soft. There is a squirrel who burrows into my thatch that I plan to slaughter. I cannot use my gun, in case of fire. But one day, he will be too slow jumping back into the old quince. And that will be the end of him.'

He wipes his knife on some grass and returns it to his pocket. 'What do you think of Aurora, as a name for the filly? She was the Roman goddess of the dawn.'

'Is she not too dark, to be named for the dawn?'

'Her father was a grey. And they are all that colour as foals. She will be creamy as milk when she is grown and ready to be ridden.' He glances at me. 'She will make a perfect lady's mount in perhaps four years.'

Turning back to the house we see a brindle cow standing in a stream at the boundary of the field, pulling grass from the bank.

'The famous Peaseblossom,' says Thomas. 'She often stands there to cool her hooves. She is the only one in the herd who does it.'

'Perhaps she suffers from corns. Mistress Buttermere liked to soak her feet in a basin of water because she always wore her slippers too tight.' I sigh, remembering. 'She liked me to embroider them for her. Delicate things, made from silk and brocade. Tied with satin bows.'

'You are a good needlewoman?'

'Fair. I have always enjoyed handling fine things.'

He glances at my rough boots. 'You never acquired cast-offs?'

'My feet were too small. And fancy shoes would hardly suit my work.'

'Finery has never tempted me. A farmer needs practical clothes, not the frippery those London popinjays favour. Though I have been thinking of treating myself to an embroidered waistcoat.'

I feel my face drop at the talk of fine waistcoats. I could never imagine Thomas as a fop, and am glad of it.

I peer into the milking shed, empty as it is not yet time for the cows to be brought in, and I am then plunged into the gloom of the dairy with its dark slate shelves and single mullion window, high up. Both have a strong odour: fatty, cheesy, slightly sour.

'Having the single window prevents sunlight turning our cream and butter, but we have to keep it closed.' He motions to the muslin covering the bowls on the shelves. 'Heat and flies. The foes of the dairy farmer.'

'If you fixed some of that muslin over the window, it would stop the flies while allowing you to keep it open.'

Thomas looks from me to the window and shakes his head. 'Not here half a day and you have solved a problem we have struggled with for years. I will send Jed's boy up a ladder to do it before you leave.'

We return to the yard, and there is contented snuffling from the pigsty as the great sow noses through scraps in her trough. Around her, piglets wriggle and squeal like over-excited children.

'What have you called them all? You must be running out of names.'

'I cannot bring myself to name beasts destined for the table.'

We pass an almost derelict structure and I peer in at tiered wooden racks, thick with spider's webs. It smells of dust and old saddlery.

'What was this?'

'A cheese shed. As a boy, I used to watch the women cutting the drained curd blocks, before salting and pressing them into muslin-lined moulds. They were stacked here to mature. Dripping on your head if you weren't careful.' He looks away. 'I always meant to return the dairy to how it was when my father was alive. But that was before…' He shrugs. 'Afterwards, I had not the heart.'

'Your cheese is better than anything I have seen in the London markets.'

His face clears. He nods.

'I know. I must have the place cleaned out. With landowners enclosing the land there is a great need for work.' He looks at me. 'When next you come, I will take you into the village to meet Martha and look over her inn. She is a woman with the strongest Christian values, so you would be in the safest of hands, working for her.' He smiles. 'And we would be almost neighbours.'

He looks happy to have found my salvation, though if I am to be employed by this lady, I must deceive her. Yet working in a country inn would not only get me away from the Chalkes, but give me a degree of freedom. Give me hope again.

So what choice have I, but to pretend to be what I no longer am – an innocent girl?

Chapter Twenty-Nine

'What was his wife like?' I ask Betty, after a feast of roast beef followed by baked apples. Thomas is outside again, consulting with Jed.

'The kindest lady. They grew up together, for her father's farm was only across the valley. It was a tragedy. He has never really recovered from it.'

I nod. After Mother's death I questioned how God could let such a thing happen. Now, after what Chalke did, my faith has wavered again.

'Can I not help you?' There are piles of dishes and pots waiting to be washed. 'You prepared a wonderful meal, but we have left you a mountain of work.'

'The master told me he has something to give you.' She smiles across at Peg, who has eaten so much that she is dozing, slack-mouthed, in a kitchen chair. 'I can wake your friend if I need.'

There is a rumble of iron wheels as her man trundles a barrow across the yard.

'That means they must have finished talking,' she says. 'The master will be back at any moment. You had best join him.' She touches my shoulder. 'It is good to see him interested in the farm again. It was beginning to look unloved.'

I step from the kitchen to find Thomas in the hall.

'Your clock doesn't work,' I say. It is a handsome thing, as tall as he is, with a peach-coloured face painted on the dial to represent a dreaming moon. There are too many signs of prosperity for me to think he could not afford to have it mended.

'It works,' he says. 'But I found myself lying awake, listening to its chimes and picturing the pendulum swaying away the night.' He shrugs. 'So I stopped winding it. A farmer needs his sleep.'

It saddens me to think of him lonely in his empty house.

'Come,' he says. 'I have something to show you.' He leads me back into the parlour. The ceilings are low, with beams thicker than a man's thigh, and Thomas has to duck as we pass through the doorway.

'Look,' he leads me to shelves on the far wall. There must be three dozen books there. 'Even a farmer has time to read, especially of a winter's night.'

I picture him, with a banked fire burning. Perhaps snow outside. Hector curled at his feet.

He picks out a slender book. 'I am going to ask Betty to put some ham and cider in a basket for you. While I am gone, look at this. It is to take away with you.' He places it in my hand. 'I hope you will enjoy reading it as much as my brother and I did, as boys.'

'How do you pronounce that first word?'

'It is the author's name. *Aesop's* Fables. He was a Greek slave. See the illustrations? The fox wants those grapes, but cannot reach them. And he is so embarrassed by his failure that he pretends he never wanted them in the first place.'

'I would be afraid to borrow such a fine thing.'

'It is a gift, Hannah. For you to keep.'

'I couldn't possibly take it.'

'Why not?'

'If the mistress saw it, she would say I must have stolen it.'

'I thought of that.' He flips open the cover and points to an inscription in a bold hand:

This book is the property of Hannah Hubert.
A gift from her respectful friend, Thomas Graham.

'Reading is a passion of mine,' Thomas says. 'Which is why I insist on Betty's boys learning their letters. Though I am fond of music, as well, and play the flute. Not especially well, but my neighbours tell me they sometimes recognise a tune.'

I glance at his large hands and he laughs. It is the first time I have seen him like this. Almost happy. Almost young-looking.

'You would not think it, would you? I will play for you when you come to meet Martha. Because you really must talk to her. You could be working for her before the summer.'

'It is four weeks before I have another whole Sunday free.' I stare at the book in my hands, wondering what might happen during that time. 'But I would be grateful if you could arrange for me to talk to her.'

Walking away from my position will mean giving up a year's wages. But work at the inn would provide bed and board, as well as safety, so I would not complain.

By the end of the afternoon my feet are reluctant as I walk towards the trap, and I stoop to rescue a bedraggled goose feather from the yard.

'May I have this? To make a quill?'

'There are better ones in the house.'

'A wash will have this good as new.'

Thomas picks another from the ground, brushes it off against his breeches' leg and hands it to me. 'I may be a farmer, but I dislike the harvesting of feathers. Most come from the Lincolnshire Fens, where they pluck five times a year. Even goslings of six weeks are not spared, to accustom them to what they must accept their whole lives. If the season is cold many of them die.'

Peg, ahead of us, has already somehow scrambled to her seat in the trap. The step is high and my legs not long.

'Let me help you.'

The brief pressure of Thomas's hands on my waist as I am lifted, the strength of him, unsettles me, then Peg grins at me from the back seat. Earlier she had not wanted to tear herself away from the baby. Has she had children of her own? She never speaks of them, so I imagine not. For would they not take care of her, if they existed? At least the old woman is happy today with a full belly and the basket of provisions on the floor under her skirts.

If she were able to come and help Betty, it would change her life for the better. But it is too soon to raise her hopes.

With one foot on the step, Thomas looks up at her, creasing his dark brows and pretending to be stern. 'Better not guzzle that cider, Peg. I make it strong. We don't want you doing a jig in the public street.'

'I won't, Master.' She is shy with him, but I sense her liking.

We sit patiently while he adjusts the harness and I begin to plan how to hide what we have been given: thick slices of delicious-looking home-cured ham; a crock of pale butter; eggs fresh laid this morning. The jug of cider.

'Don't lose your chance,' murmurs Peg. 'The man likes you. Smile at him. It could get you away. To safety.'

She thinks to make me his sweetheart, while I intend to let him find work for us both. In a little more than a month we could be leaving the city and starting new lives.

Thomas swings into the driver's seat, grasps the reins and

manoeuvres Hercules through the gate into the lane. Back toward London and bondage in the Chalke house. Where my fear is of being as much trapped in the power of heartless people as those Lincolnshire geese.

Chapter Thirty

After hiding our spoils on our return, Peg and I settle before the fire. Me with my darning and she on her knees polishing the master's shoes.

'That farmer fancies you something fierce,' she frowns over a scuffed toe. 'You should have made sure of him before we left his farm.'

'Thomas is sorry for me, that is all. A job is what I need from him. Not posies of flowers. And by my next day off, I hope to have one.'

She scowls at a silver buckle and dips a forefinger into the polish. 'Men lose all sense when they takes a fancy to someone. Look at Chalke's choice of wife.'

She applies the polish to the shoe, spitting on her rag, then making circular movements on the leather. 'You are a fine-looking girl. Educated proper and with a sweet nature. A man could do a deal worse.'

'I do not want a man.' I repress a shiver.

'The bed thing is not to my liking neither. But a husband would get you away from here. And some women seem not to mind it.'

'Well, I am not one of them. And Thomas said he will never marry again. He just has a kind heart.'

'That man is your salvation,' Peg says. 'Grab him. Before you regrets it.'

Next morning, Thomas brings me a fistful of right-handed goose quills.

'Do you have ink?' he asks. 'Something to write on?'

Remembering Peg's words, I avoid his eye. 'There are things in the house. The little I use is not missed.'

There is silence between us.

'Well? Did you enjoy your outing to the country?'

Remembering our visit, and his kindness, I cannot be stiff.

'Peg had a belly ache from overeating. But I suspect she enjoyed the unfamiliar sensation. I hope we didn't empty Betty's pantry.'

'She enjoyed your visit as much as I did. My house is too quiet for both of us.' He looks down at me. 'I have decided to expand my cheese production.'

'I am glad.'

'What is lacking is someone to oversee the extra girls I would need.'

His look is questioning, but he cannot be suggesting a fifteen-year-old undertakes such a thing. Unless he wants more from her than labour.

'Have you spoken to the innkeeper's wife yet?' I fiddle with the quills in my hand. 'About the position in her kitchen?'

'I was planning to ride over, last night. But when I started thinking about my own plans, I saw you would have a better home and fairer prospects working for me. On my farm.'

He is suggesting I move under his roof and I feel crushed, for Peg is right. His interest is more than Christian kindness.

'I would much prefer to work at the inn.'

'You would?' His smile fades. 'Well, I expect I can find someone else for my project. From the village.'

'And the position with Martha?' His kind eyes meet mine and I struggle to know what to make of him. 'Will you still ask her about work for me?'

I know I sound ungrateful, but who will look after my safety if I do not?

'So be it, Hannah.' He studies the cobbles and sighs. 'I promise to speak to Martha and arrange for you to meet next month.'

Chapter Thirty-One

In the afternoon a boy brings an urgent note from Master Twyford.

'I am to wait. For a reply.'

The lad is breathless from running, so I hurry upstairs and wait as the master breaks the seal. Mistress Chalke glowers across from her needlework. A tapestry of roses, the stitches ugly as a mastiff's teeth. My darning of stockings is finer.

'What?' her brows contract as she watches her husband and I wonder again what turned that complexion to lumps of curd.

'Twyford needs those proofs tonight.' He sighs. 'A knight of the realm wants something special. In a hurry.'

'So? An hour with your pen should do it.'

The master screws the missive into a ball and lobs it towards the grate. 'Don't I spend long enough at my desk, woman?'

I am as surprised at his combative tone as his wife is, for her mouth snaps open to scold. Then they remember me and the silence in the room is broken only by coals settling in the grate. I am so often in the background I suppose I am near invisible.

'Get back to your kitchen,' she snaps.

'The boy is waiting. For the reply, ma'am.'

'Damn Twyford!' Master Chalke heaves himself from his chair. 'I planned to go out. Now I must stay home and act the clerk.' He studies his wife's black brows before sighing and turning to me. 'Then you'd better say Master Twyford shall hear from me later.'

Mistress Chalke deflates. A bird of prey deciding against launching at a vole. She glares at me. 'Go on, then. Shift yourself.'

I scurry downstairs, send the lad on his way, then fetch the master's stockings from where they have been drying on stretchers in the yard. I am apprehensive. The streets will soon be dark and full of shadows, never mind scurrying rats.

At least Jack will be at the shop. Perhaps he will walk back with me.

I have never minded work, for there is satisfaction in ordering a clean house and having fresh linen snapping on a line. Yet something rots beneath the floorboards of this house and I worry about the three weeks I must get through before I can meet that innkeeper's wife.

Long after, when the sky is black, the bell summons me to the book room.

'Sir?'

I hesitate in the doorway, mouth dry, afraid of being within his reach. We made that agreement, but I do not trust him.

He stands at the desk in his mulberry-coloured silk banyan. He has draped his wig on its stand and candlelight makes his cropped hair gleam like bristles on a hog.

He softens a stick of wax with a candle and pools it onto a package like a glob of congealed blood. Then he presses his ring into it.

'Take this to Twyford. Quick as you can.'

Five minutes later, my shawl tight around my shoulders, I run into the dark street. It is ten minutes' walk, less if I hurry, and my speeding boots echo on the cobbles.

I need to rap several times at the bookshop door before a glimmer appears in the darkened windows and Jack opens up, clutching a candle. He is in shirtsleeves, wiping his mouth with his free hand. I smell beer and meat on his breath.

'Hannah? What are you doing here? It is late.'

'Didn't you expect me? Your uncle sent a message to Master Chalke.' I hold out the package. 'He needed this. Tonight.'

'I have been out all afternoon.' Jack looks in an ill-humour. 'I suppose you had better come inside.'

There is a smell of hot food in the shop and when he leads me into the back room I see the remains of a cook shop pie on a plate, with a tankard of ale alongside. A late supper. The fire burns merrily in the fireplace.

Jack wipes grease from his chin. 'Give it here, then.' The package is taken unceremoniously from my hand. 'Wait by the fireplace while I take this upstairs. Touch nothing.'

I had hoped for a friendlier greeting. If he is in this mood, how can I ask him to walk me home through the dark streets?

The uncarpeted stairs shake as he hurries up, two at a time, to rouse his uncle from bed and I stare at my anxious face reflected in a wall of glass-fronted bookcases. They will be locked, of course. There is a smell of melting beeswax from the candles on the mantel and a silver-gilt claret jug gleams on a dresser. I suppose this is their private sanctuary.

Minutes pass. Where is Jack? His supper will be getting cold. I wonder if I should put it before the fire to keep warm.

Then there is an abrupt noise through the wall. From the adjacent snuff shop, which is shuttered and dark. A tortured squeal. An animal of some kind? There might be rats in there. I shudder. London is running with them.

The coals shift in the grate and one of the candles gutters and dies. As I lick my fingers to pinch the smoking wick, the unsettling noise comes again. Loud. And it makes my heart lurch. For it is a girl's scream.

Where is Jack? I must call him back.

Even as I run to the stairs, he thumps back down. Yawning.

'Jack! Someone is being murdered. Next door.'

His shoulders stiffen. 'What did you hear?'

'A great cry. From a girl.'

Jack stares at the wall, then blinks. 'Do not upset yourself. The man who runs the snuff shop uses the upper floors for his daughter. The girl is touched in some way, so he has to restrain her. For her own good.' He pats my arm, as if I were a troubled dog. 'She is better off than most. Some would pack her off to Bedlam.'

'She sounded terrified.'

'Come, Hannah. Forget the noises through the wall. They have stopped. And they are not our business, anyway.'

I listen, then nod, my nerves raw from being on the streets at night. Those muffled noises were probably the result of the girl having a bad dream. They are something I have learned about these last weeks. And Jack is right that her father is doing his best by her. Plenty would have her committed to the horrors of Bedlam.

At least Jack has returned alone. There is an advantage in Twyford being so fat, for he is disinclined to labour up and down steep stairs. And I now consider him as bad as the Chalkes.

'At least your package put my uncle in a better mood,' Jack says, stifling another yawn. 'Now I had better kick John awake to set the type.' He stares at me. 'The old man will be asleep by now. We are alone.'

121

I do not trust the look in his eye. Must I fear Jack, too? Does my shame give off some kind of odour? Are all men like dogs in the street, scenting a bitch?

'I must get back.'

'You can spare ten minutes, surely?' He steps close, ale fumes on his breath and I think perhaps he is unsteady on his feet. This is a different Jack from the one I am used to.

'It is dark outside,' I say, still hoping he will be concerned about my return journey.

'But cosy in here.' His arm is suddenly around my waist. 'Will you not give me one kiss?'

'I will not.' I jerk away, revolted. Do I have *slut* engraved on my forehead? 'I will be looked for.'

He folds his arms around me and I panic at his male proximity.

'Why do you struggle? A kiss is not much to ask, surely? Did you not enjoy the one we shared that Sunday? Aren't you my sweetheart?' His manner seems different tonight and I hate his disrespect. As if he senses I am spoiled goods.

'Let me go.' I push at him, struggling to stay calm. 'Didn't you say your uncle wants you to court your cousin?'

'The girl is straight up and down, like a yard of pump water. And thick-minded as a barn door. I would rather spend my time with a pretty girl who has an interest in poetry.' He nuzzles my neck and my suspicions are confirmed, that he is the worse for drink. 'Think what pretty children the two of us would make together. If we could wait two years, why shouldn't I get away from Uncle Twyford and open a little shop somewhere? Must I always be at his beck and call?'

I catch my breath. Is he suggesting we might marry? But my interest in Jack was an ignorant girl's fancy. I break free and his face lengthens and becomes sullen. 'You have a cold heart, Hannah.'

I do indeed. It was turned to ice by Chalke. There is nothing in London for me now. Certainly not Jack, who must know what is sold at those auctions, even if he is not directly involved. My future lies in a country inn, well away from the Chalkes and their wicked activities. And although Thomas is a man, too, I believe he is one who can be trusted.

THE SERVANT

Chapter Thirty-Two

Thomas looks thoughtful as I approach with my empty jug. It is not long since our visit to the farm, but I am fidgeting with the need to secure my future far from here. The master keeps away from me, but for how much longer?

'Have you managed to speak to the innkeeper's wife?' I ask.

'I have and she is looking forward to meeting you.' He fills the jug. 'I will drive you over in my trap when you come to Broad Oak next month.'

'And she will take your word for my character?'

'She will. Though I wish you would think again about working for me. That idea about the muslin has already made a difference.' He leans towards me. 'I would take special care of you and of Peg. You have my word.'

'What's up with you?' Peg is mashing hard gums over an apple core left by the mistress.

'Oh, Peg.' I remove a hot loaf from the oven, drum the bottom with my fingers to check it is cooked, and sniff the crust. Almost to Mrs Lamb's standard. Once that would have made me happy for the rest of the morning. 'Thomas was talking again about wanting me to work for him, instead of at that inn.'

'Aint that good?'

'It would mean sleeping under his roof. And him with no wife or other woman in the house.'

'There is Betty.'

'She sleeps in her own cottage, doesn't she? With her man and children.'

'That she does.' Peg picks an apple pip from her lip and swallows it, never one to waste nourishment.

'So, you see why I am worried. He gave me such a look this morning. I don't know if I should trust him.'

I toss the loaf on top of the rolls already baked.

'But you will be at that inn, won't you? Not at his farm.' Peg rests the bucket of dirty water she was taking out to the yard on the floor. 'The important thing is to get away from here. Take your chance at the inn, but stay friends with your farmer. He strikes me as a good man.'

She hoiks up the bucket again and I could almost smile at the idea of Peg being a judge of men. If I were to trust anyone, it would be Thomas, but I still live in fear of every man breathing. And of what they want from a woman.

If he will get me that position with Martha, I will accept it with gratitude, and work from dawn to dusk to prove my worth.

Chapter Thirty-Three

'Tread careful.' Peg is anxious. 'The witch is spitting feathers. She lost something when she went off in the chair this morning.''

It is Monday. Where do they go, regular as clockwork toys? Peg refuses to say, but she knows. It has to be to do with their illicit trade.

'Was it money?' That will have put her in a filthy mood.

'That book she is always scribbling in.'

The little notebook in which she keeps her accounts. She is as careful with that as she is with coin. We had best avoid her till she finds something else to be vexed at. At least we cannot be held responsible.

I turn my attention back to gutting and skinning a rabbit for a pie while Peg drags her bucket outside to wipe soot smuts from our windows. But minutes later she is back, sidling up to me and pulling open the rags she has been using on the glass. Inside is a sodden calfskin-bound notebook.

'Look what I found,' she gloats.

'Where was it?'

'In the gutter. In a pile of horse shit.'

The cover is fouled and beginning to warp. Some pages are ripped, others stuck together. It will not be of much use now.

Peg smirks. 'Let's throw it on the fire.'

'No.' I wipe my bloodied hands, wrap the book in a scrap of rag and shove it deep in my pocket. Its contents would mean nothing to Peg, who cannot yet read more than her name and the simplest words.

The mistress would of course like it back, though Peg would never get thanks for finding it. But I am curious to see what the crow is forever writing in its pages. With a furrowed brow, and yellowed teeth chewing the end of her pencil stub, I would guess she struggles with accounting. I will study it later. Then burn it.

The master does not return to the house until after ten at night, his gait unsteady and his breath reeking of brandy.

'Sponge that,' he orders, fumbling off his coat and throwing it in my direction. 'Someone spilled Canary down the front, but I expect it like new by morning.' Then he clumps up to bed without a backward glance. Just as well, since each day it gets harder to hide my loathing of him.

I am relieved the stain is not the red wine that is nearly impossible to remove. After I am finally satisfied with my efforts, I shake the coat out and drape it over the kitchen chair before the embers of the fire. It should be dry by morning, when I will give it a final brush.

But as I position the shoulders around the curve of the chair back, the coat tails swing against the wood with a thud. My curious fingers feel a heavy metal shape in the pocket. The key to the book room door.

The temptation is momentary. I like to think myself brave, but not foolhardy. In two weeks, I hope to be safely away at Martha's inn. In the meantime, I cannot afford to make trouble.

I forget the notebook until I am undressing for bed and its rank smell in my pocket reminds me. Peg is already wheezing in sleep and I carry it to our rush-light to squint at the pages. Most are indecipherable, but some are only spoiled at their edges where the ink has run. There are entries dating back more than a year. Columns of tiny figures. Monies paid for coals. For comfrey, pennyroyal and liquorice from the apothecary. For a pair of silver shoe buckles set with brilliants. For copper sulphate, oak galls and gum, for the making of ink.

The witch's handwriting is crabbed and much of her arithmetic wrong. It pleases me to think the book's loss will inconvenience her. As well as the entries starting from the front, I notice others beginning from inside the back cover. More figures, but these are hefty sums rather than regular household expenses. I move closer to the sputtering light, but my eyes at first do not comprehend what they see:

Becky, from Seven Dials, Forty-five guineas.
Suzy Songbird, sixty guineas.
Irish Nell, forty guineas.

I turn the page. More women's names. More huge sums of money. They remind me, abruptly, of a bill I once saw belonging to Major Harper. Prices of bloodstock racing mares.

My head begins to spin and I sink onto the edge of the bed. These women are for sale. This must be the secret Peg has kept from me. The reason those gentlemen visit. The choice items put up for auction.

Are women sold like slaves from this house where *The Maid's List* is composed and deals are struck between arrogant gentlemen in that smoke-filled room? Are my suspicions right? Do the Chalkes run some kind of brothel for London's aristocrats?

I think of that key downstairs in Master Chalke's pocket. Nobody will stir until morning. This is my opportunity. I need to know for sure if the people I work for traffic in women.

I shudder. Was that what I was destined for, at the end of my year of service? Is that why the mistress didn't want her husband looking at me? To safeguard a saleable virgin?

In two weeks, I should be packing my carpet bag and leaving for ever. But I refuse to go knowing only half the truth.

I lace up my gown again and tiptoe back through the dark to the kitchen. Then I reach into the coat and grasp the key.

Chapter Thirty-Four

I stand at the book room door. Key in hand. Reminding myself to breathe.

My feet are bare, to make less noise, and I used my toes to feel for the edges of the stairs so they would not betray me with a creak. I have not dared bring a light.

The master will not rise for hours. Not after all that wine. The mistress never ventures from bed before ten o'clock in the morning. Peg always sleeps like the dead, which is just as well since she is still frustratingly secretive about what happens here. Yet I am still terrified of being caught.

Can the Chalkes really run a brothel? Is that where they go on Mondays? The thought makes me shudder. It would explain Mistress Chalke's lack of society connections and also her uncouth friend, Mistress Smith. I could imagine that woman running such an establishment.

I had wondered what the two of them were up to, heads conspiratorially close over tea and my saffron cakes. With Peg always anxious to keep out of their sight.

My palm feels sweaty as I ease the key into the lock. What if I am caught? I turn my mind from the thought of being dragged before the magistrates and accused of theft. Being branded. Transported across the oceans on some crowded, disease-ridden ship.

I have always done what others said I must do. Gone where they said I should go. Even worn the clothes I was told to wear. But when I think of the wrong that was done to me – which I cannot help, however much I try – I know those teachings have harmed rather than helped me.

I was to have been tied to this house until next March. Might still be, if Thomas has not secured that position for me in his village. What fate was planned for me? I intend to know before I leave.

The grain of the wooden floor is chill under my feet as I turn the key. The heavy door will be silent since I oiled its hinges with a feather only yesterday. At the master's request.

In the dark, I grope my way to the flint kept by the hearth and light one of the candles in the candelabra on the desk. Then I go to the Chinese cabinet, remove the hidden keys and spread them across the green leather top of the desk. One stands out: no longer than my thumb, tied with a scarlet ribbon.

I have not been alone in here since Master Chalke was attacked, except when I salvaged those scraps of parchment. I pause, gauging the size of the key against the room's furniture, before taking it to the central bookcase. In the candlelight the silk glistens like a flame as the key fits and turns.

Close packed on the shelves are books with handsome bindings and gilt lettering. *The History of Tom Jones, a Foundling,* I have heard of. But other titles are unfamiliar: *Satyricon*, which must be foreign. I hold the candle closer. *The Whore's Rhetorick,* and *Memoirs of a Woman of Pleasure,* will not be respectable books. I have heard men are drawn to such things. Women either pretend it is not so, or accept it. Might this be the kind of thing the master writes?

I lift one out, then recoil at black and white sketches. Disgusting portrayals of women with men. Their privy parts shown in detail that turns my stomach. I shove it back. If Chalke and Twyford publish such filth, Jack must at least know about it.

My instinct is to run back to bed, but I am no young lady, raised to swoon at the slightest shock. Nobody will bathe my temples with Hungary Water and urge me to spend the day in bed to recover from seeing something I shouldn't have. For my own safety, I am here to uncover secrets.

My trembling fingers explore smaller books with grey covers and white pages that look like copies of sermons. But they are not.

There is no sign of a *Maids' List,* but I find *Harris's List of Covent-Garden Ladies.* On the cover, a group of women flaunt themselves without a shift between them. Turning pages, I am reminded of the witch's account book, for here again are names, descriptions and prices, though for less outrageous sums. There is no doubt what these women are:

Sally R. The origin of this lady is obscure, but she sold sausages about the streets till above fifteen years old, when the celebrated Mrs Cole had sight of her maidenhead for thirty guineas; out of which she generously made Sally a present of five shillings, to cure her of the clap, which she got from her deflowerer...

Miss L. is nineteen years old. Her eyes, of a beautiful sloe black, beam a torrent of delight; her breasts are in the fullest proportion and will rebound with the more grateful ardour...

Even a kitchen maid knows there is a trade in whores, from the creatures lurking near disreputable inns, to finely-dressed women at court. Great men have the keeping of such creatures. There was salacious gossip about them from French lady's maid, Mlle Dubois, before the Buttermere staff began to be paid off. But my days in the servant's hall are gone. Mistress Buttermere has sent me to a den of depravity.

Perhaps the master visits such women on the nights he returns home in the early hours. But the signs tell me he is more than a customer. Is his involvement why Peg considers him the devil incarnate?

I leave the bookcase and examine the desk. Pigeonholes hold ink, quills, sealing wax, a shaker of sand and a knife for trimming pen nibs. What I would expect. Testing the keys, I open one drawer and find unpaid accounts from his tailor. Another contains play bills, a rolled-up map of London and loose silver coins. A third is stuffed with more demands for payment.

Then, on the landing, there is a noise.

I think I will faint. My heart thumps like a kettle drum. I cannot breathe.

Is it the mistress? The master, woken from drunken sleep? With the door ajar, the flicker of my candle must be visible in the hall.

I scramble into the kneehole under the desk and shrink into its tight space. Anyone entering will surely discover me. And why wouldn't they, with that unexplained candle burning?

Yet nothing happens. The thundering in my ears, in my head, slowly subsides. Licking my parched lips, I crawl to the door to peep into the darkness. All is silent. Was it a rat? A shutter caught by the wind?

I swallow bile and straighten up. Return to the desk to pick over the keys. If I do not find what I am looking for I will never dare do this again.

It is in the bottom drawer of the desk that I find the letters, their seals roughly broken, as if in haste:

If you will have the wench delivered to my London house tomorrow, Master Chalke, there will be fifty guineas for you.

Especially if the maid is of the quality of the last. A young miss, fresh from the country, and clean, merits a special price.

I take a deep breath. Mlle Dubois told us with relish that bawds meet coaches newly arrived to London, looking for unworldly girls from the countryside seeking work. Apparently, virgins in the capital are as sought after as bolts of China silk.

The impression in the seal is a heraldic device, revealing the writer to be a gentleman of quality. Someone the world will look up to.

The other letter, of only a few lines, is signed simply *Twyford*:

I look to receiving your proofs of The Maid's List as soon as can be managed. Remember, Chalke, we are now dividing the auction price for these chits between us equally, after Jarrett takes her expenses.

Although I loathe the man, I struggle to believe a high-born gentleman would procure virgins for society. Yet the proof is in my hand.

The letters were beneath a muddle of documents and are unlikely to be missed. I hold them in my hand a moment, then thrust them inside my bodice before returning everything else to its place. As I shut the drawer a faded scrap of paper falls out, with a smudged date that looks like December 1740. It is another bill, from a surgeon:

For attending to the injuries inflicted on the child, Margaret. Half a guinea.

On the back are closely written details of the number of visits made and the miracles performed in saving her leg, when she had not been able to put one foot on the ground for weeks afterwards. What had happened? Was this the child of some bawd? Or might it have been Peg? After hesitating, I stuff the note into my bodice with the other papers.

The City Fathers frown on the keeping of bawdy houses, but although their abbesses are regularly hauled before the magistrates they continue to exist and, reportedly, thrive.

So what likelihood is there, were a high-born gentleman implicated, of anything being done? Would it be worth the risk for his servant to betray him? If I cannot see a way to use this evidence against Chalke, it might be better in the fire. Yet I ache to stop the trade.

The stolen letters crackle against my breastbone as I lock the door, anxious to get downstairs and replace the key. But as I do so, a hand grips my shoulder and I let out a muffled scream.

Chapter Thirty-Five

A thin hand smothers my mouth and I realise, from the familiar odour, that it belongs to Peg. She must have woken and come to find me.

We huddle together, waiting to see if my cry rouses anyone. Then, when the house remains silent, I scurry down to the kitchen to replace the key while she returns to our garret.

Back in our room I undress and crawl in beside her. The sweat on the back of my neck has dried and chilled, making me shiver. The letters lie safe under a loose flagstone in the scullery. Taking them makes me a thief and I remember Susan and her branded thumb. But ignoring them was unthinkable.

Yet Master Chalke has powerful connections. What could a kitchen maid do against such men?

Even I know London has wickedness in its depths that polite society pretends does not exist. Churchmen rail against immorality and leading citizens call for reform, but as long as bad things are hidden nothing much happens. And servants are expected to avert their eyes from whatever their masters do, regardless of what it is.

Peg is hunched up in bed, fingers twitching at the blanket.

'You could have been caught.'

'I wasn't.'

She sets her back against the wall and drags the covers up to her chin. 'Peach on them two and you will end up like Susan. Or at the bottom
of the river.'

'They are selling women, Peg. Publishing their descriptions in some kind of list. Auctioning them to the highest bidder, like mares.' I tug at my laces. 'But you knew that, didn't you?'

'Women?' She evades my eye and licks her lips.

Knowing I will not sleep, I get up again, snatch my stays from the chair and begin to dress. Starting to pound the washing might work off my rage.

'The sooner we leave here, the better. Thomas said he would set you to work. For Betty. Would you not like that? Helping with the baby?'

She plucks at the blanket.

'I cannot leave.'

'Why ever not?'

'For one thing, I owes them money.'

I think of that surgeon's bill and wonder whether a debt like that could follow a little child through life. Probably it could.

'If that is the case, you might earn enough from Thomas to pay off the debt. You know you will never earn enough here to do it.'

'It is more than money.'

'What, then?'

'Chalke is from some grand family from Ireland. Filthy rich, from the labour of poor folk.' She hesitates. 'But they threw him off. For marrying a common whore. And they'd slit throats before letting people know what he does.'

'Marrying a whore?' My breath catches in my throat. I could believe Mistress Chalke abbess of some bawdy house, but never a woman of pleasure. She was surely ugly when she slid out of her mother.

'You would never think it,' Peg shakes her head, 'but she was a beauty once. That is how she got her talons into Chalke. Set the girl up in style, the fool did. Showed her off around the playhouses.'

I think of that yellow dress. The satin slippers.

'Which is why she hates anyone young and pretty, like you.' Peg struggles from bed herself and splashes water into our washing bowl from the jug. 'But after the family cast him off, their extravagance soon had them head over ears in debt. So, she visited her old abbess. To find ways to pay off their creditors. And, later, to have funds to send young Charles away from London. After the lad started asking awkward questions.'

I watch as she dabbles fingers in the water for a perfunctory wash.

'How could a whore make a gentleman marry her?'

'By knowing ways to pleasure a man. And giving him a fine son.'

I remember Mlle Dubois telling how the French king's mistresses were showered with jewels and palaces. How their power over him was so strong, they could even slight his queen.

'And now the pair of them run a bawdy house. And he composes a list of girls for sale?'

Peg nods, but still refuses to meet my eye. Can there be more? Printing and selling filthy books, I imagine.

'Whatever happens, Hannah, never let on you know their secrets. Susan had an inkling and it got her transported.'

I finish pulling on my clothes, queasy and muddled from lack of sleep. Pray God that position with Martha will get me away from here, and soon.

I remember Betty and her respect, affection even, for Thomas. Servants often understand the people they work for better than they do themselves. Would she have been so warm and talkative if she thought her master meant me harm? If Martha gives me a good report, I will remind Thomas about giving Peg work. I could not bear to abandon her in the depravity and cruelty of this house. Whatever she has done in the past, whatever her debts might be, I cannot believe they would pursue her into the countryside.

Later, when the milk wagon pulls up, I scurry out.

'Please, Thomas...' I must not sound desperate. 'That position at the inn? Might your friend let me start straight away? After we have talked?'

'I expect so. Though I still think you would be better off supervising my cheese-making.' He frowns at me. 'You would have more of a position in the world, with a higher wage. Martha can only offer you two guineas.'

'Two guineas would be plenty. I would take less.'

He sighs, clearly frustrated at my obstinacy. 'Then you had better bring your things with you when you come to Broad Oak. Martha's present cook is leaving soon, so it would probably suit everybody for you to start straight away. And you could leave a note behind for your present mistress, telling her you are leaving, without notice.'

Chapter Thirty-Six

'Take this to Master Twyford's,' commands the mistress.

I am up to my elbows in a washtub, sleeves pushed high, arms red and raw.

'Now, ma'am? I thought I was due to go this afternoon?'

She must be tired, for her slap has little force.

I abandon the tub, towel myself dry and tie a clean apron around my waist. I am still sickened by what I discovered in that room. It put me off my food and I ate no breakfast. I am now counting the days before I go back to the farm and can secure that job at the coaching inn. I cannot get away from here fast enough.

Peg still protests that she is unable to leave, but I think of that surgeon's bill. *For attending to the injuries inflicted on the child, Margaret.* Assuming that was her debt, how could a small child owe a surgeon for treating wounds not of her own creating?

The afternoon streets are quiet, though a town coach with glittering harness and matched bays waits outside the questionable snuff shop. Its liveried coachman honours me with a bored glance as I hurry past. The bookshop is empty when I arrive, though the outer door is not locked. After waiting a moment, I call upstairs for Jack, but softly. Master Twyford publishes lewd books and the fewer dealings I have with him the better.

But there is no response. The rooms feel hollow. There is not even the rhythmic thud of the printing press across the yard. Jack must be on some errand at this quiet time of day. But since I cannot leave my package unattended, I tentatively mount the creaking stair.

Then comes a small voice. 'Good day, Mistress.'

It is a tiny girl, of about six years, with a lilac ribbon threaded through her cap. She has appeared so suddenly, standing neatly on the top step like a porcelain-headed doll, that I am startled.

'I am seeking Master Jack,' I say. She is expensively dressed and from those vibrant blue eyes I wonder whether she might be his sister. 'Could you fetch him for me? I have an urgent letter.'

'Everyone is next door.' She beams at me, eyes wide and

sparkling. 'But I could take you to them, if you like. Next month I am to go and live in a rich household with my new uncle.' She jiggles up and down, humming with excitement. 'I have been promised a kitten. The finest silk stockings. And my very own spinet, so I can learn to play while I sing.' She pauses for want of breath.

'Then I must not interrupt,' I say. 'For that sounds important. But if Master Jack is upstairs, can you tell him Hannah is here with an urgent message? I will wait in the shop until it is convenient.'

'Oh, no,' she patters down the half-dozen steps to stand in front of me. She smells faintly of musky perfume. Has she been sitting on someone's lap, being petted? 'You can come with me.' She folds warm fingers into mine and tugs at me to follow her. She is so trusting and sweet that I cannot help thinking how wonderful it would be to have such a sister.

'Do you like my new gown?' she asks as we walk through the room where I waited for Jack that dark night. 'They say it is called *silk damask*.'

'It is beautiful.' Only a rich family would dress a growing child in anything so costly. She is lucky. But then I remember what she said about being adopted. Like me, she must be motherless. I tighten my hold on the little hand grasping mine.

'I am called Suzy,' my diminutive guide says, leading me up the stairs. 'Though my uncle may change my name. After I go to live with him.'

She leads me to a blue and gold tapestry at the end of a corridor and proudly twitches *Susannah and the Elders* aside. Behind is a heavy oak door and she nods her pointed chin towards it. 'Everybody is through there, but you had better knock, or they might be cross.' She giggles, revealing dimples and perfect teeth. 'I am not usually allowed out. But today they were too busy to notice.' Then her hand slips from mine and she skips away down the passage, humming to herself.

I hear the deep voices of men through the wood panels, together with that of one low-spoken woman. My mind is busy. Could that be some kind of housekeeper? Jack and Twyford must have someone to tend to their needs. Strange that I had not wondered about them being without a servant before.

At least it does not sound as if the troubled girl is with them.

Hopefully she is having one of her good days and is away with her father. I hope so, for I am afraid of meeting a mad person. Mrs Lamb told me they are unpredictable and violent. That the ones in Bedlam must be chained to the wall.

Footsteps approach the door and I frown over what I now know about the Chalkes. What really lies through there? A mad girl? A brothel? A dreadful place where a pretty child is locked away, awaiting collection by an uncle she seems never to have met. Could that be the man's coach outside?

As the voices get closer, I know I cannot stay a moment longer and fly back down to the shop, dropping my letter onto the counter. Relieved when nobody follows me. Then, in my rush to get away, my foot knocks over a leather satchel, spilling its contents onto the floor. A title stands out, crisply black against a buff cover: *The Maids' List*. In a panic, I shove the copies back, but not before thrusting one under my shawl. Then I run outside.

A glance upwards shows one of the shutters is ajar and I glimpse a familiar flattened face peering out, its shape now suggesting to me that the horrified midwife sensed evil at the birth and used her fist to try and thrust the child back into the womb. Is that Mistress Jarrett?

As I flee along the street, afraid to look at either coach or liveried coachman, a picture flashes into my horrified mind of that entry in Mistress Chalke's sodden account book. *Suzy Songbird...sixty guineas.*

My mind races back to the night Mary was taken. Though ignorant of what was happening, I had sensed it was something bad.

I could not help Mary. Must it be the same with little Suzy? That child is in terrible danger. I should go back. Drag her away. Find safety for her. But how could I put a respectable roof over her head and food in her mouth? Would these evil people not immediately accuse me to the constables of abduction? And even if I produced that notebook, who would believe my suspicions? Especially with a fat bribe thrust into their hand?

As I hurry back to the Chalke house, I could scream with frustration at being just a useless girl.

Chapter Thirty-Seven

When I stagger, breathless, into the kitchen Peg frowns up from the wooden paddle with which she is pounding the linen.

'I know everything,' I pull *The Maid's List* from under my shawl and wave it at her. 'There was a beautiful child at the bookshop. About to be sold to some foul old man.' I shudder at the recollection of that carriage. 'I refuse to let them have her. I must do something.'

She abandons the washing, her shoulders drooping.

'Like what?'

'If they knew, good people would surely be sick with horror.'

'Would they? Folk can be like blinkered horses, Hannah. There's things they cannot abide to see.'

'Then they should be made to.'

'By a fifteen-year-old serving girl? Even with that proof you say you have?'

A voice in my head sneers that she is right. That a nobleman's brother would never fear a nobody like me. Even if I manage to put my evidence into someone's hand, would it not be discreetly disposed of? Like slamming the lid on a noisome cesspit?

To get justice I must be resourceful. I had meant to wait until I was away from the house before using the evidence under that flagstone. But with Suzy at risk I do not have that leisure. I must find a way.

There is no sleep for us in bed that night.

'You should have told me that they sell children.'

Under our threadbare blanket Peg's hand clutches mine.

'I was too scared. For you and me, both.'

'But why did you stay?' I drop her hand and punch the rock-hard bolster serving as my pillow. 'Even the poorhouse would be preferable to working here.'

'I done something bad, Hannah. When I was little.'

'How bad?'

'I would have swung, if they told on me. Might still, even now.'

I shake my head. She must have stolen something valuable.

'They would never have hanged a little girl, Peg.'

Everyone knows a thief who takes goods to the value of twenty shillings risks the rope. But what jury would condemn a tiny child?

'There is no forgiveness. Not for murder.'

I recoil. *Murder*?

'It wasn't deliberate, Hannah.' She is shuddering. 'But they had forced me to swallow a poppy drink, so my mind was muddled. I only remember the knife in my hand afterwards. And the blood. Dark and sticky. Stinking like an old metal spoon. And the scrape and bump of them dragging away the body.'

Chapter Thirty-Eight

Peg sucks the edge of the blanket. A petrified child again.

'If I tells you, I might as well stick a knife in you. Like I did in that man.'

'I don't care, Peg. I need to know.'

'I never meant to kill him. That I swear.' She shivers. 'But though I wanted to hurt him, real bad, after what he done, I still can't believe I slit a man's belly. I must have lashed out. In fear.'

I make myself take her hands again. I had assumed she had stolen a watch or a ring.

'Tell me everything.' My words drag out, for I do not really want to know. 'From the beginning.'

'The whores said as how I was taken by the gypsies as a little 'un.' Peg seems to take strength from my grip. 'They would laugh and curtsy, saying I could have been a lord's daughter. Before making me scrub their filthy sheets.'

'What whores?'

'The ones at the bawdy house where I was took.' She sighs. 'But a lord would never have rested before I was found. Would he? So, I expect I was from some poor cottage.'

I struggle to picture Peg as a girl, toddling at her mother's knee. Old wives frighten children with tales of girls – snatched away to be raised by gypsies, it is whispered, until old enough to sell into slavery on the Barbary Coast. Or into London brothels. Mrs Lamb said the stories were lies, to make naughty children biddable. Now I know different.

'What happened at the bawdy house?' I cannot imagine Peg having been a harlot, even when young.

'One of the whores said I was being farmed. Like a suckling calf. That they snatch children up before they can speak proper, so they cannot say where they are from. Or who they belong to. But I understood none of it.'

Her fingers clench mine.

'Some months later, a man in a fancy coat took me into a room with a bed in it. Don't know how old I was. Don't know to this day when I was born, nor where. But I was small and had not bled yet.

Though I bled plenty that day.'

Her fingers pinch mine.

'He was rough and hurt me. I couldn't pass water afterwards. Only blood.'

She grunts. 'When he come back for more, not long after, I was so terrified that I kicked him in the crotch, hard as I could. It put him in such a fury that he hit me in the mouth with his cane. Then smashed me leg. They had to send for a surgeon.'

She wipes at her eyes with the edge of the blanket.

'They told me I took a knife after it happened and run into the passage after him. Flew at him like a demon. Not that I remember. Because of the poppy juice.

'The abbess was furious at having to cover everything up and pay the surgeon as well. She said I would owe them for saving me for my whole life.' She bites at her thumbnail. 'I remember it was the year our old king died.'

I count on my fingers. Can Peg be only sixteen years older than me?

'The girls said Ma Jarrett got rid of the body, in the river,' she says. 'And because the man was never missed, nothing come of it. But they only need tell the constables and I would swing.'

This is almost too much for me. A tiny girl? Killing a grown man with a knife?

'It must be a lie, Peg. And they were keeping you as someone to blame, if questions were asked. You should have run away.'

'How could I? With a crippled leg and insides that weren't right? I was no use to nobody. And Ma Jarrett said that unless I did what I was told, they would hand me over to the law.'

She gives a weary sigh.

'Soon after, Mistress Chalke turned up. Though her name was different then, of course. A fine-looking girl she was, with a pink and white complexion. Not a London face at all. No trace of the pox. Peaches they called her. And the gentlemen queued up for a touch of that skin.

'She got on with Ma Jarrett like a long-lost sister. Like iron nails, the pair of them.' She pauses. 'You have seen the abbess. The one with the squashed face.'

So, my guess was right.

'The ugly one, calling herself Smith?'

'No other. If a girl was difficult, she would burn them with a metal spoon on the soles of the feet. Heated over the open fire. She knew how to do it without leaving an ugly mark. They would scream at first, when they thought she had some kind of a heart. Then, when they knew better, they did as they was told.'

I think of the future planned for me and feel sick again.

'It was Ma Jarrett who found Master Chalke for Peaches,' Peg says. 'The pair of them had a fancy place in Covent Garden before she had that boy and sweet-talked Chalke into marriage.' she snorts. 'But the noble lord, his father, cast him off when he found out.'

I remember the signet ring. That painting. The signs of past wealth. Chalke's casual arrogance of manner.

Peg sighs. 'When they ran out of money, they turned to Ma Jarret for ways to pay their debts. And the trade in children pays well.'

I clutch her hand tight, willing her to spill everything, like a filthy flux. Someone needs to know what happens here, even if it is only me.

'I scrubbed floors in their brothel for years,' she says. 'Most of the time like a chained dog. Finally, they let me come and work here. I slept on the kitchen floor at first, before they kicked me out to sleep wherever I could. But I still had to come and scrub their floors. To be under their eye. Though they knew by then I was far too scared to ever talk about what they got up to.

'Later, the master had the idea of publishing a regular list, to keep the money coming.' Her voice falters. 'They had an agreement with Ma Jarrett about their maids, as well. Choose them young and pretty. Work them to death for a year. Then pass them to the abbess. They was supposed to be untouched. To fetch a better price.'

My mouth goes dry, remembering Master Pock-Mark.

'The mistress warned Chalke off the girls, of course. But once a bastard, always a bastard.'

She touches my shoulder. 'But you are going to escape, Hannah. To that job you was promised. By your farmer.'

The thought that Martha might refuse me makes me feel even more queasy. People worry about having their goods stolen. They fear being murdered in their beds and want to know servants taken into their households can be trusted. What if Thomas is wrong about his innkeeper friend giving me work without a character? What if I cannot get away? What if I am turned into a whore? And what will happen to little Suzy?

Chapter Thirty-Nine

I think of what is hidden under the kitchen flagstones. If only I could find the right man to whom to send those letters, and he saw how young the girls were, would he not bring these wicked people to justice?

But what kitchen maid knows people capable of acting against the aristocracy? Then I think of Mistress Buttermere's neighbour. The magistrate with five little daughters on whom he dotes.

If he believes my evidence, Sir Christopher will be outraged by what is going on and is a man with the power to challenge it.

I know he reads sermons to his family and servants every Sunday evening and is said to be that rare thing, an incorruptible magistrate. One who could take on Chalke and his clients, however high born.

I cannot know if a letter to him will achieve anything, but know I must try.

But I could never approach someone like that myself.

I gnaw my thumb and think that Sir Christopher is unlikely to take notice of a servant girl, even if I were somehow able to confront him. But if a letter in an educated hand was delivered to his house, written on good parchment and spelling out plainly what is being done, that should be a different matter. Especially one enclosing those damning letters and the account book detailing the money changing hands. Not to mention that copy of *The Maids' List* with the tender ages of the girls being sold.

There would be immediate repercussions, of course. But since Master Chalke does not know what I took from his desk he surely would not link me to his disgrace. He would likely assume a disappointed customer has made trouble for him.

Such a letter will not be easy to compose. I would have to dredge up the most scholarly words I can remember so that nobody would suspect it the work of a servant whom her master believes can barely scrawl her name.

I think of Mrs Lamb and wish I had her wise counsel, but suspect she would be horrified by my audacity. That she would counsel me to stay quiet and keep my head down.

I am taking a risk, but what choice have I? That girl is only six or seven years old and unprotected. It is time to stop being afraid.

I sit at the kitchen table after everyone is in bed and grasp one of Master Chalke's quills. This letter must convince the magistrate I am a gentleman of education and position, outraged at what he has uncovered, yet anxious to preserve his anonymity.

Dear Sir Christopher,

I write to you since you are a Gentleman Known and Respected for Speaking Publicly against the Immoralities of our Times. Someone furthermore who is considered a Protector of the Values of a Christian Nation and a Scourge of Dissipation and Vice.

If you will Peruse the Documents that I am Entrusting to your Care, you will Uncover an Outrage being Perpetrated against Innocents in our very Midst.

The Rules of Morality, Religion and Humanity Demand that the Virtue of Innocent Children is not Sacrificed to Debauched Men and those who Procure for them.

I beg you, Sir, to Consider the Miseries to which these Unfortunates are Subjected.

It is Against all Conscience for this to happen in a Civilised Country - and for Good Men to do Nothing.

As I wrote I found myself so angry that I could scarcely breathe and as I laid down the pen had to draw in a lungful of air. Then I sprinkled my missive with sand, folded it in parchment together with my evidence, and melted some of the master's wax to secure it. There was no signet ring to imprint in the wax, but I told myself that would be explained by the gentleman's wish to remain anonymous.

Perhaps justice will be done if I can get this letter into Sir Christopher's hands. If he believes it. If he takes action.

And if I am quick, and can work out how to have it convincingly delivered, there could be time to save Suzy. Perhaps then I will I be able to let this hatred of the Chalkes go, before it destroys me.

Chapter Forty

The letter is written, now I must get it safely delivered. Men of influence are the only ones with the power to challenge an aristocrat like Chalke, even a disgraced one. I have done my best with my letter. Now I must get it safely into the magistrate's hands.

The footman at Sir Christopher's will never take in a package unless it looks like a respectable missive. But my curling hand looks educated, elegant even, and the address is carefully correct. All I lack is a messenger, since I have no wish to approach the house myself and risk being recognised.

I think of the old clothes belonging to young Charles in that upstairs wardrobe. He must have been slight, for I think they would fit me. Well enough, at least. And I could borrow an old pair of the mistress's shoes. There is even a tatty wig that would look well enough under one of the master's tricorn hats.

In the afternoon, with the Chalkes both out and when Sir Christopher will be having tea with his family, I tuck the letter and its enclosures under my jacket and check my halfpenny is in my pocket, trying not to think of how much I might need that coin if things go wrong. Then I trudge to Sir Christopher's house, expecting at any moment to be challenged by a member of the public outraged at seeing a girl wearing breeches.

It feels strange wearing them. They chafe my thighs and it is a relief that the coat covers the shape of my legs.

I stood in front of Peg before leaving.

'What do you think?'

'That you will get yourself arrested. For offending public decency.'

'Don't worry. I won't risk going to the door myself. I will find a boy to do that. Just allow myself to be glimpsed by the footman, for when questions are asked later.'

It is strange not wearing stays and my breasts jiggle as I walk, but at least they are not pushed up make my clumsy disguise evident.

When I reach the magistrate's house I gaze at the velvet-draped windows and think of Puss somewhere inside. Spoiled and plump from kitchen scraps.

A figure in a frilled cap is looking out from one of the windows. Mrs Roberts, their housekeeper, I suspect, but she will simply see a nondescript youth standing down the street.

I beckon over a ragged boy who despite bare feet and threadbare clothes has a cheeky grin and looks resourceful.

'How would you like to earn a halfpenny?'

He squints at me, puzzled.

'What are you playing at? You are a girl.'

'Nothing you need worry about.' I do not want him frightened off, so I smile. 'I just need a letter delivered.'

'It looks big. For a letter.'

The package is bulky, from the enclosures. From that notebook.

He wavers, fingers flexing. Imagining closing around my halfpenny.

'Why not do it yourself?'

'My father disapproves of girls meddling in men's business. It is only a petition. Signed by concerned citizens. For a public pump. To provide water for washing.'

He shrugs, indifferent to such things.

'All you must do is hand it to the footman who answers that door over there and say you have been asked to deliver it. By a young gentleman. I will stay over here.'

He picks idly at his nose, clearly uncertain, before nodding. The halfpenny is too tempting.

'Give it me, then.' The boy grabs and bites the coin to check it is real, before swiftly disappearing it into his shapeless jacket.

'Tell him a fine-dressed gentleman has just given it to you.' I smile encouragingly. 'You can point to me, if you like. You might even get another coin from the footman for delivering it.'

I do not believe this, not for an unexpected package brought to the door by an unwashed urchin. But I cannot risk going to the door myself. The footman might remember me and I am already fearful enough that the package will cause me mischief. What if the Chalkes guess who has revealed their secrets? What if Jack tells them I have an education? That I might be a nobody, but I am not illiterate?

I watch the boy cross the street, jaunty with his errand and no doubt planning what he can buy with a halfpenny to fill a hollow stomach.

I have meant to do something like this ever since I took that evidence from the book room. Now I wait under a bare-branched tree as the lad rises on tiptoe to strike the gleaming knocker with a thump audible across the road. Then he speaks to the tall footman who answers the door. In the last months of my stay at the Buttermere house I remember that young man giving me tender looks and being scolded by Mrs Lamb for his presumption.

An argument seems to be taking place, with the footman gesturing at the scruffy boy to clear off, and my heart grows heavy. This was my great hope of doing some good. Of helping Suzy. Must my efforts and risks come to nothing?

But my courier is made of stern stuff. He stands his ground. Argues. Holds up my package, gesturing and waving it under the footman's nose. There is a pause as the young man takes it into his hand and scrutinises it. Can the footman read, I wonder? But even if he cannot, he will surely recognise the quality of the parchment. I hold my breath. The footman's gaze ranges over the street, uncertain, then hesitates at the sight of a fine dandy disappearing around the corner. He looks questioningly at the boy who, clever lad, nods vigorously. Even points after the man. Moments later, the footman carries my missive inside the house.

It is done. Now all I can do is wait and pray that some action comes from it in time to save Suzy. And that it does not have repercussions for me or for Peg.

Chapter Forty-One

I am not well. Perhaps it is the worry about Suzy and my letter. And not sleeping. Or maybe I have eaten bad meat since Peg and I are expected to finish scraps, even if they are turning green. I gnaw the hangnail on my thumb till it bleeds and try to turn my mind from what I fear.

But as time passes, I know it is nothing I have eaten. My breasts feel strange and tender. In the early morning I hurry to the slop bucket and vomit in spasms until I retch up nothing but the bitterest bile. I shudder at what it must mean.

Peg is awake as I rinse my sour mouth and splash my face. She must have heard me retching into the slop bowl.

'What is it?' she asks, swinging skinny shanks from our bed and squinting at me.

'A bellyache.'

'I seen them bellyaches before.' She scratches anxiously at her neck. 'That's not the first morning you have spewed your guts. You know what it likely means?'

I know enough, from the infants my mother had, alive and dead. Chalke has done even more harm than I thought. I will be unable to hide what I have become. Fingers will point at me for a whore. And that precious job at the inn will be an impossibility.

'Help me, Peg.' I turn to her, for who else do I have? 'I cannot have a child. I will be disgraced.'

My friend looks troubled, as well she might.

'It is said drinking a brew of crushed rue, morning and evening can help. Or pennyroyal sometimes brings a monthly bleed.'

I stare at her. Am I really thinking of killing a child, if one is lodged inside me?

'It takes money to buy,' she says.

I go to my carpet bag and fumble out coins. To add to my misery, this will eat into my scanty savings.

'You might still be all right,' Peg says. 'Women drop babies all the time. From heavy work.'

She is right. It is a hope to cling to.

'Or maybe those friends of yours will move back from York

soon. After the daughter's child is born.'

'And if they do? Would I be welcomed?' I place my hands on my belly. Flat, yet containing something shameful.

She gives me a sideways glance. 'A quick marriage would serve you best. That farmer likes you mortal bad.'

I flinch. 'How could I do that? And how hide what has happened?'

'There are plenty does it. Let some fellow have his way with you, swear they have got you in the family way, then rush them to the preacher. When the child comes early, pretend you had a fall.'

She sees my disapproval.

'Men cheat women all the time, Hannah. It is only fair for them to be at the receiving end sometimes.'

'No, Peg. You must buy those herbs.'

There is no time for despair. If I am with child, I will not be able to accept that position at the inn. As soon as my condition was suspected I would be shown the door, destitute, in the unfamiliar countryside. Perhaps forced to sleep under a hedge.

But if Peg can help me lose my unwanted burden, everything might still work out.

Chapter Forty-Two

Later in the week, I stand where the plain wood leading to the attics begins to be covered with patterned carpet and peer down the stairs. Above is my world of bare boards, broken furniture and mildewed walls patterned with damp. Further down, the treads become narrow again, and dark, though they are so familiar to my feet that I can climb them with no light at all.

Peg's herbs have done nothing. Nor does pummelling my belly with angry fists. My body has been stolen from me along with my hope of escaping this evil place.

My heart beats as if I had run upstairs with a heavy load. Indeed, I have tried carrying heavier and heavier burdens: double buckets of slopping water, sacks of root vegetables I have no business taking away from the kitchen, even lugging around a cumbersome trunk full of old riding boots. Nothing shifts what is lodged inside me. My body looks no different, though I suspect I am thinner than before, because of my morning sickness. But that intruder is still in my belly.

It is a long way down. I must not kill myself as I fall, since self-murder is the worst sin of all. Although an escape, it would condemn me to eternal hellfire. I would not even be allowed the shame of a pauper's grave. Suicides are shallow-buried at the crossroads, like dead dogs.

Afraid, yet determined, I stare past bannisters and newel posts whose wood gleams from my industry and smells faintly of lavender-studded wax. A boss smooth as an apple is beneath my palm. I am still young, with my whole life ahead. If I can lose my hateful burden and start working for Martha, I might be able to pick up my life again.

The fingers of my hand tremble. I must not let myself think about pain, in case my courage fails. Nor can I simply step off the top stair, for that would likely break my neck. Instead, I kneel, turning sideways in order to roll my way to the bottom, hopefully doing just enough damage, but not too much. I screw my eyes tight and launch myself downwards.

There is a blur of hurts as I bump down, banging head, shins, shoulders, ribs and knees as I tumble. There are buffets from all sides, as if the staircase is punishing me. Yet it is quick and I have the fleeting thought that I should have chosen the lower stairs, ending at the stone flags of the cellar floor. To make the outcome more certain.

Then, as if I have been thrown from a moving coach, I land with a thump that sucks the breath from me. I lie in a heap, taking shuddering gulps of air, thankful I am not dead.

No bones feel broken. The house is silent save for the ticking of the hall clock and muted sounds from the street.

I run a hand over my belly. Why no griping pains? Perhaps it is too soon. I cautiously hoist myself up and yelp as my foot takes my weight. A bad sprain. Then I limp into the kitchen and force down a few mouthfuls of small beer, to steady myself. There are Master Chalke's ruffled shirts to attack with the smoothing iron and I must busy myself with them, and hope, as my visit to the farm – and that meeting with Martha – is only days away.

Chapter Forty-Three

When Peg returns from scrubbing the floor of the necessary house she is cross.

'You could have ended up like me,' she chides. 'A cripple.'

I cannot argue, but I am desperate. If nothing happens after that fall I will need to lie to Thomas about the job.

Yet although I am covered with purple and yellow bruises and have a sprain that makes walking painful, I am still with child. Still on the brink of disgrace and destitution.

For a young woman dismissed for lewd living there is no respectable way of earning bread. I turn my mind from thinking of what most girls in my position are forced to do. Make their bodies available to men.

Death would be preferable. Carriages and heavy carts lurch and rumble past the door, frequently fast and reckless. What if I threw myself in front of one? Yet I shiver at the thought of being mangled by iron-shod wheels.

Another means of escape is not far: the evil-smelling presence of the river laps at my consciousness. I picture plummeting down, clothes billowing. Imagine the shock of the cold water. The struggle for air. Then oblivion. It is said drowning is painless. I do not believe it. For me, nothing in life has ever been painless. Why should death be different? But I cannot do the river. I am afraid of the dark water. And the fires of hell.

I am tempted to sob as I finish ironing Chalke's shirts. I do not want the life inhabiting my belly. I resent it and loathe thinking of how it came into being. But tears achieve nothing. I will have to tell Thomas tomorrow that I have changed my mind about that job and he will think me fickle or deranged.

Later, as Peg and I snatch a rest in the kitchen while the master is out and the mistress upstairs muttering over her accounts, I tell her what I mean to do.

'Tomorrow I will tell Thomas that I do not want that position. And that we cannot go to the farm on Sunday.'

Peg looks up from the stale crust she is gnawing and shakes her head. 'You know what I thinks you should do.'

There is silence in the kitchen apart from the noises Peg makes sucking at the bread.

'What will happen when my belly begins to show?'

'The old witch will throw you out.' A greasy rat's tail of hair escapes Peg's cap and she thrusts it from sight with a dirty finger. 'Like I say, make cow's eyes at your farmer while you still can.'

She retrieves a dropped fragment from the floor and swallows it, smacking her lips. Her reverence for the smallest fragment of sustenance is sobering.

'I have heard rumours of other ways of losing a child.' I stare into the heart of the fire. 'Don't crones, up dark alleyways, know things to do?'

'Nothing you would want to try. And if the constables found out, you would be in worse trouble.'

She places a scrawny hand on my arm. 'You have been my only friend, Hannah. If you will not go with your farmer, you should be able to manage a couple more months here, then go to the place I used to lodge. It is only a cellar, but you would have a key to your door. And it's cheap.' The rat's tail has escaped again, but she ignores it. 'Afterwards, when you are not pregnant no more, you might be able to find a yourself position somewhere.'

She is right, of course. No respectable house will hire a maidservant with a bastard in her belly. But if I hide my condition as long as I can, wait out my time in that cellar, then have the child and rid myself of it, I could pretend it never happened. Take up my life again.

'I refuse to expose it,' I say. Child of that hated man or not, leaving a living creature to die in the street is wicked. I do not want this wretched infant, but it deserves better than that. It is as innocent as I am.

'There is a place you can leave a baby,' Peg says. 'Near Lamb's Conduit Fields.'

I remember my outing with Jack. That distraught woman.

'The Foundling Hospital?'

'Aye.' Peg fishes a knuckle bone from the stock pot with her fingers and blows on it, to cool it. 'Though I still think you would make a good farmer's wife, if you played your cards right. Then you could keep it.'

'Why would I want to keep it? Or be anyone's wife?'

'One man is better than a score. Without a reputation it is hard for a girl to survive, except on her back.'

I let out a groan. This bastard child will come, whether I wish it or no, and then I will likely starve.

If I lace myself tight and hide my condition until I am six months gone, that would still leave three months' rent and food to find. I might earn a few coppers somehow, but not enough. I am careful with the money that I have, but have no confidence it will be enough.

'You are young and strong,' Peg sucks noisily at the bone. 'You will likely manage.'

What alternative is there? Work at the inn is impossible if I am pregnant. Should I do what Peg urges, and persuade Thomas to marry me? Even if I could bear the thought of a husband, what respectable man would accept a ruined girl? And what return would it be for that good man's unfailing kindness? To deceive him?

Peg recites what I need to do, like a catechism. 'Stash away scraps of rag and sew a quilt for the winter, since you won't be able to afford kindling. Mend your clothes while you still has needles and thread. And fatten yourself up as much as you can.'

I know her to be right. I might manage without heat, without clean linen or comfort, but not without shelter or food. Both of which will cost more than I have saved.

'This is the cellar where you used to sleep?'

'Aye.' She pulls a face. 'I would not put a dog there, but 'tis not for ever.'

'Have I silver for better?'

'The landlord is a piece of shit. But you will have a key to your door.'

I shrug my shoulders, struggling to hide hurt at falling so low. A roof over my head. A door I can lock. Something to sleep on. The occasional crust of bread. I can expect no more.

I thought myself poor before, now I am at risk of becoming a beggar. Every farthing will count.

But I refuse to resort to despair. The mistress remains impossibly mean. The meat, the cheese, the milk, are all carefully measured out, but the evil old witch cannot always be watching and I will become a mouse, nibbling corners from joints of meat. Trying to store fat against the lean times that will come. And I must think of ways to earn some money.

I return to my room and lay out my possessions on the pallet bed, for I have had an idea. My best petticoat was one of Mistress Buttermere's, barely worn and edged with lace. There is enough soft fabric to cut up and fashion into lavender bags using the dried plants hanging, forgotten, from the kitchen ceiling.

I will make as many as I can until the lawn is finished, then stash them away in my bag. People like to put such things with their linen to make them smell sweet and to deter moths. There is thread in the house and needles. Even some scraps of old embroidery silk. Perhaps I could even make a little business from them after I go into exile.

Chapter Forty-Four

'Have you chosen your new man yet?' I ask Thomas. Soon he will stop bringing the milk. He talks of it, but nothing happens and I am glad, for soon I will be in that cellar and friendless. Except for poor Peg.

He, of course, expects me to be seeing Martha at the end of the week and arranging to work in her inn kitchen. Instead I am taking care how I stand so he will not notice the bulge beginning to show under my apron.

'I have a lad in mind. Ruben is the eldest of seven. His father is crippled with arthritis, so a regular wage will answer their prayers.'

'I no longer pray.'

'Why ever not?'

'I do not believe Heaven exists for people like me.'

'You are charitable and good. How could you not go straight to Heaven? Though hopefully not for many years.'

Hector noses at my skirts, wanting his morning ear-scratch.

'More years in which to sin.'

'Come, now. What sins can a girl like you commit?' He looks amused. 'How old are you, anyway, Hannah?'

'I had my sixteenth birthday last week.'

'I thought you older. You make me feel like Methuselah.' He studies me as I ruffle the dog's fur. 'Do you never think of marriage? You are young yet, but when you meet the right man, would a loving husband not be better than the hard life you lead?'

'Exchange one servitude for another?' I hear revulsion in my voice. Husbands and wives share a bed until one of them dies, with the man having the right to do what he wants to the woman's body. With the Church's blessing. 'What woman would be a wife, who could be free?'

I am silent again, wondering from his stare if he senses the change in me. When I tell him that I cannot come to the farm and will not work for Martha, I would hate for him to suspect what is behind it.

The sky is dark, with prickles of rain in the air. At least it is not snow. In our garret under the roof the water in our jug freezes overnight.

'You think that badly of marriage?' he says. 'Of husbands?'

'It may suit some. Not me.'

'Do not dismiss the idea, Hannah. I would like to think of you finding happiness.' He clinks the coins in his pouch and frowns. 'I am, of course, much older than you and have paid too high a price to risk that path again. But in a year or two, you might meet a young man with prospects and a kind heart. You are wasted labouring in a kitchen that is not your own.'

He talks as if marriage were something to wish for. But loving is a sweaty invasion involving pain. No wonder it is done in the dark.

I know little of husbands and wives. Mistress Buttermere was a widow and gave the impression she was more than content to be so. Mrs Lamb was a maiden lady. My own mother must have found union with my father hard, with that temper like a red-hot poker. After her death he drank too much, then forgot her and married an unfeeling woman with three offspring of her own.

Yet I believe he loved her. Or, perhaps, loved having a beautiful woman in his bed.

Must love be coupled with such thrusting violence? Well, I want none of it. I cannot now help thinking of bitches in the street pursued by a pack of eager dogs, with a disgusted housewife hurrying to throw a pail of cold water over them.

'Wedlock is a game of chance.' Thomas's eyes have softened. 'But many couples take strength and companionship from one another. Some even find joy.'

'Joy!' I struggle with my face. It is different for men, of course. I have seen the satisfaction they get from mastering horses with whip and spur.

Thomas exhales. 'Well, some are not meant for it and I see you are one of them. We cannot all be the same.'

He makes another attempt.

'But country life should be good for you. Martha's establishment is full of laughter as well as work. She is really looking forward to meeting you on Sunday.'

'I cannot come. I have sprained my ankle. I am sorry.'

'Sprained your ankle?' He looks at me and I limp a few painful yards, to prove it is true.

'Has that woman been beating you again?'

'The house stairs are steep and dark. It is easy to miss your footing.'

'A sprain need not stop you coming.' His brows knit. 'I would collect you in the trap and drive you straight to the inn. You do not need two sound limbs to talk and reach agreement with Martha. She will know your hurts will soon heal.'

'I have been thinking,' I clutch my milk jug to my chest, wishing I were a more inventive liar. 'The countryside is too quiet, compared with London. Here, if I am lucky, I might get a good position in one of those grand houses in the square.'

Thomas looks at me and from his frown I see that he is struggling to understand.

'Please tell your friend I am truly sorry.' I lean against the wagon, to take the weight off my ankle. 'That I hope I have not let her down.'

'This is a puzzle, Hannah. You were adamant that job was what you wanted. Tell me you are not being pressured by someone. Or something.'

'Only by my wish to better myself.'

He expels a breath and I know he is about to question me, so I turn on my heel and limp quickly inside. To what comfort I can find from the kitchen fire and embroidering another lavender bag.

Chapter Forty-Five

'What is wrong, sweetheart?'

I flinch as Jack takes the latest batch of proofs from me. It is like handling hot coals. But why is everyone behaving as if nothing has happened? Why have the constables not shuttered up the bookshop and that terrible place next door? Why have they not even knocked on Chalke's door?

'I am just tired.'

'It is not that. You have lost your lovely bloom.'

'I spend my days gutting fish and scouring pots. In a basement. How should I look?'

'I know the work you do. But nobody would ever think you a kitchen drudge.' He looks disgruntled. 'I wish it were otherwise, but you are too often on my mind.'

He is like a beautiful boy eyeing a hobbyhorse he cannot have. I could almost feel sorry for him, for he is in his uncle's power as much as I am in that of the Chalkes. But my daydreams of him are dead. I only have to think of those ugly books and what happens behind those shutters next door.

'How could there have been a future for us, Jack?' The very thought is now distasteful to me.

'You are right. Uncle would forbid it. And the Chalkes will have plans for you at the end of your year.'

'Let them have plans. When my twelve months are up, I will run away.'

Far sooner, of course. But I must not mention that. Jack might say something to his uncle, who would likely tell my master.

'You can try.' He strokes my cheek with a soft finger and I back away, shuddering at being touched. 'Perhaps I should help you.'

His concern seems genuine and friends are what I desperately need, especially now I cannot escape to Martha's inn.

'I am in such trouble, Jack.' I tremble. The words are out.

'Trouble? Is it Mistress Chalke? I know the woman is a brute to her servants.'

I struggle to form words. Fail.

'Come,' he says. 'Tell me.'

'I cannot. It is too…shameful.'

'Shameful? How so?'

I feel my face grow hot under his scrutiny.

'Has something happened? Is it Chalke?' His eyes narrow. 'Has the old goat laid hands on you?'

I drop my eyes and know that speaking was a mistake, for Jack smacks his fist against his thigh. 'God damn him! Chalke has had you. Hasn't he?'

I wish the floorboards would crack open and swallow me.

'I should have known the rogue would not wait.'

Why did I think Jack might help me? He will know about *The Maids' List*. Will be part of everything.

He studies me. 'Take care, Hannah. The Chalkes tend to hurt girls who cross them. And that woman is a jealous old bitch.'

After that earlier flush of heat I am suddenly cold and shivery.

'The trouble was not of my making.'

'Sweetheart, you are a child no longer. If you do not want to be broken, you must learn to bend.' He touches my arm. 'I could help you slip away somewhere before your year is up. There could be profit. For us both.'

I edge away. 'Must everything be about profit?'

Jack's nostril's flare. 'I am telling you how it is. Look at yourself. To be poor is to be downtrodden and taken advantage of. My Uncle does not wear silk stockings from selling sermons.'

'I know what he does. He deals in female flesh.' I make a sickened noise, for though Jack clearly knows everything, there is no sign of guilt on that handsome face. 'I had a higher opinion of you than that.'

'He owns me, Hannah. I am not a free man. The bread that goes into my mouth, and that of my old mother, comes from him.' He plays with a loose button on his coat. 'And selling women is a trade, like any other. We buy things. We sell them. Whether they be leather-bound books or strumpets in satin petticoats.'

'Are tiny children strumpets? I met little Suzie. I know what happens over the snuff shop. It is *evil*.'

'I told you.' He spreads his hands, as if displaying a bolt of cloth. 'We are no more than dealers. We never touch them.'

'But you provide them for others. And they are so young.'

'Do not think to stop something that's happened since Roman

163

times, and probably before. Those girls would likely starve to death without Chalke and my uncle. This way, at least they get to eat. Some of them eventually make a fine living for themselves.'

He eyes me speculatively. 'With your looks, by next Lady Day the Chalkes will have lined you up with some fine gentleman with a taste in virgins. Though old Chalke has spoiled that, hasn't he?' Jack ignores the revulsion in my eyes. 'Second-hand goods fetch a second-hand price. Though you are pretty enough to still tempt buyers.'

'I am not an animal. To be sold.'

'You are wrong about that, Hannah. We are all animals underneath. And what other options have you? A life of patched clothes and wretched labour?'

Through the window I see people strolling by. The world about its business, while Jack speaks of me being traded like a newly broken mare.

'The trade is wicked. It should be stopped.'

'There is too much money involved. Too many powerful men with powerful appetites.' He places a fingertip speculatively on my bodice and I back away, shuddering. 'And Chalke cannot afford to stop. He sends half his income to that useless boy in Virginia and without what he gets from my uncle his creditors would lose patience. A debtor's prison would not suit him one bit.'

He studies me. 'Anyway, Chalke's family would never permit a public disgrace, so we are safe enough. You had better learn to give a little.'

His finger hooks into the laces of my bodice. 'I think I deserve more than a kiss, now you are no longer an innocent. Why not come into the back room with me?'

'For shame, Jack!' It sickens me to have suddenly become a girl who is considered easy. A girl who would welcome a man pressing his body into hers.

'Did you not enjoy your tumble?' He laughs. 'I cannot imagine Chalke being much of a lover. You would like me better.'

My tears are of indignation and revulsion. I decide I hate him.

'I thought you cared for me.'

'I do.' He sighs. 'But I am no rich guildsman with money for your keeping. Though I have daydreamed of it.'

'You wanted me for your mistress?'

'Did you hope to wed me?' He purses those fleshy lips together and I wonder that I ever thought him handsome. 'Do you not think I could do better than a poorhouse brat?'

He laughs, then slides his arm around my waist.

'Come, admit that you like me.'

'Leave me be! I am no whore.' I struggle, afraid he will force me, but his blows come as words.

'Yet that is what you have become. Though through no fault of your own.'

If we were beside the river, I would jump straight into the water. Never mind the preachers. Never mind the flames of hell.

Jack releases me with a shake of his head. 'It grieves me that you will end in some gouty old roué's bed. For another man's gain.'

I recoil against the wall. How can I have thought he had a heart?

'Use that clever brain of yours, Hannah. You are just a chit of a girl. Comely, but devalued by your master. Know your place. Put some rouge on your cheeks. Profit from those looks while you can.'

He is between me and the door or I would run into the street.

'Let me go, Jack.'

'For another tumble with Chalke?' There is a sneer in his voice, but he steps aside.

As I run from the shop, I decide that I loathe Jack as much as I do the Chalkes and wish I knew how to curse. To wish ill-fortune on every one of these people.

I am only sixteen, but even were I grown I could do nothing, for it is men who rule. Yet having those papers gave me a choice and I am glad I took it. My action could bring danger, but for once even a servant, and a woman, might make a difference.

Chapter Forty-Six

Someone is trying to break the door down and I think immediately of constables, come at last with a warrant. Yet when I pull the bolts a tall gentleman thrusts a fur-lined cloak at me and sweeps past with long-legged strides.

'Is my brother home?'

Everything about him speaks of entitlement and importance. A fine coach with liveried outriders is standing at the kerb and a retainer has followed him inside, a brass-bound wooden case under one arm.

I realise who this man must be, but not what to do, for he is already half-way along the hall.

I raise my voice.

'Sir? May I say who is calling?'

But I am invisible as he mounts the stairs, two at a time, his man close behind.

'You fuckwit, William! Show yourself.'

The book room door opens.

'Valentine? What are you doing here?'

I have crept after our visitor under the pretence of awaiting orders, but really to hear what happens. This must be because of my letter.

'Come into my book room,' the master says, and I see the sheen of sweat on his face. 'The stair is no place for private business.'

Then the parlour door opens and Mistress Chalke appears. For once she is speechless, but she edges forward as if meaning to join them.

'Bridger?'

'M'lord?'

'Get that drab out of my sight. If she objects, throw her through the nearest window. Into the street.'

The mistress shrinks against the wall, but Bridger grabs her and bundles her back into the parlour before slamming the door and returning to stand guard beside the book room doorway.

I am still frozen on the stair, my eyes glued to the pantomime reflected in the great mirror opposite the open door.

'This is ungentlemanly of you, Valentine. My wife and I deserve respect. You only hold your title, remember, because you beat me into the world by a paltry half hour.'

'Respect?' There is a sneer in the man's voice. 'Our father had hopes for you, before you met that slut. I should have had the bitch thrown in a ditch years ago. I still might, since it will be her fault if my name appears in the London scandal sheets.'

'Come, brother. We have been worried by troublemakers in the past. But they have always been silenced. It may have cost you, but you are hardly short of a few guineas.'

'A respected magistrate is not a nobody. Have you not heard? Evidence was laid before the authorities. How could I have my brother standing up in a public court? When I have the ear of our king? Our current sovereign takes a narrow view of immorality. I doubt he even knows a trade as foul as yours exists.'

'Then give me the income from one of your Irish estates, and a decent house to go with it, and my wife and I will cease to trouble you.'

'It is too late for that, William. Too many people know too much.'

He gestures to his man, who places the polished case on the desk and flips it open.

'Duelling pistols! You want me to fight you?' Chalke lets out a high-pitched laugh. 'If you fear a scandal, don't you think a duel between a marquis and his younger brother would set the city's tongues wagging?'

'I have no intention of fighting you, brother. Since this business is your own doing, I require you to salvage the family honour by putting one of these pistols to your head.'

'What!'

'You heard me. You must remove yourself. Permanently. It is the only way to get this disgusting business discreetly buried.'

Chapter Forty-Seven

'Does your household celebrate Christmas? Might you have a feast and a gift?

Thomas wears knitted mittens on this December morning, with a scarf tucked into his coat. It is bitter standing by the milk cart and I hug my wool shawl around me, watching the horse's nostrils puff smoke into the air. Winter is hard upon us and the bulge under my apron is growing.

The Chalke household remains tense after that visit from the marquis brother. The case of duelling pistols is still in the study, thrust under the Chinese cabinet. Unused.

Time passes and I daily expect something more to happen. But nothing does.

'They will have hashed mutton and a roasted goose,' I say, despondently. 'Followed by seed cake.'

'To share with you and Peg?'

I cannot prevent a grimace. 'We will get the remains of the carcass to pick over.'

'No lengths of dress fabric?'

I think back to the excitement of the female Buttermere servants on Christmas morning. Waiting to be given lengths of material with which to make themselves new gowns.

'A cuff round the ear is more likely.'

'Well, Betty will make one of her ham and rabbit pies for me to bring you. People need full bellies in this weather. I think there will be snow. If the milk freezes, I will not be delivering.'

'Why are you always so kind to us?'

'Why should I not be? Are we not friends?'

I have never had a proper friend, which seems a sad thing. But girls are not meant to have friends who are men. Not virtuous girls, anyway.

With no answer to make, I stamp my feet to get feeling in them. At least my ankle is mended. My boots are wearing thin, but it would be extravagant to have them repaired. My saved coins are too precious.

I am still careful not to stand sideways where my increased bulk might show. The swelling caused by Chalke's bastard horrifies me with its determination, its growing prominence.

'Why will you not come back to the farm?' The farmer's brow puckers. 'Surely you and Peg would enjoy a good helping of hot roast beef, in front of a roaring fire?'

I shake my head. 'Perhaps in the spring.'

'Now is when you need to come. There are shadows under those eyes. What you need is clean country air and a hearty meal.'

I pat Hector, avoiding a reply. There will be disgust in Thomas's eyes when he finds out about me. I used to welcome our morning talks, but now I am afraid to linger in case he notices my changing shape.

'I thought you enjoyed your visit in the summer.'

I don't help him. How can I?

'At least tell me why you changed your mind about going to work for Martha. I do not understand. You seemed so excited at the prospect. Yet you are still here working for those hard-hearted people.'

I hang my head. Silent. Within weeks my disgrace will be plain for all to see. If I had gone to work at that inn, I would have been dismissed as a loose woman by now. Staying here was the wisest thing. Time has passed, my store of embroidered lavender bags has grown, and each passing day is one less on which I will have to find rent money.

'I thought you liked the countryside? Did you really decide it would have been too quiet, after London?'

'I did,' I lie.

'But have you asked the nearby maids if they know of another position?' He glances at the other houses in the street, far more prosperous-looking than ours. 'Their mistresses might understand you not being given a character.'

'I will. Soon.'

I picture the thickset woman next door who warned me. It might have been worth trying if I did not have this bastard in my belly.

'You really should come back to Broad Oak. Betty often asks after you. Her boy is starting to crawl.'

'Not this side of Christmas.'

And by the New Year I am likely to have been discovered and

turned out. With the weather so cold, I huddle my shape under my shawl, indoors and out, but my luck will not hold much longer. Not only has this thing Chalke implanted in me swollen my belly, my gait has become graceless. Not for one moment will it let me forget its presence.

'If you could work up a liking for the country,' Thomas says, stamping his own feet against the cold, 'there is another vacancy you could fill.'

The look in his eye makes me quiver. Is he going to ask me to sleep under his roof again? I would have loved to make his cheese – if I had not had that fear of him wanting more from me than help with expanding his dairy. Though the child inside me makes everything impossible, I wish he could simply stay my friend. Then I might feel able to turn to him if things become too hard.

Thomas removes his tricorn hat and takes a step closer, smelling faintly of his farm and the sprig of dried rosemary in his buttonhole.

'There is something I must say, Hannah. I hoped you would come to Broad Oak, where we might have privacy, but no matter.'

He is desperately serious and I cannot think how to stop him, short of walking away.

'I could have spoken earlier. But I was really conflicted. You are so young. And you seem to have an aversion to marriage. What was I to do?'

My mouth has gone dry. This is unexpected.

'You said you would never wed again.'

'That was what I believed. But duties towards others give life meaning. I find I still have love to give.'

I stare at my boots and see the stitching around the welt is unravelling. Like my life.

'So be it. I must ask my question here.' Thomas twists the hat in his hands and glances to left and right. There is no-one near. 'I am older than you by ten years, but I think you like me. That you consider me a friend. But I more than like you. I have deep feelings for you, Hannah. And I worry that your life is so hard.'

I continue to stare at my feet. These are words that cannot be unspoken. Words to which he will expect a response and my heart lurches with regret that the time when I might have welcomed them – before that dreadful night – is long past.

He twists the hat again.

'I could give you a comfortable life. Though no farmer's wife is a stranger to hard work.'

He has said what he wanted. It is no plan of seduction, but something I thought never to receive. An honourable proposal of marriage from a man of property who is neither old nor ugly. Now he is waiting, hoping, and I feel the power of his expectation. This good and generous man thinks me something I am not. A pure maid. And I could weep for it,

Here is what I desperately lack. A husband. All I need do is deceive him. He would discover the truth soon enough, but with a wedding ring on my finger and vows exchanged before a priest, he could do nothing. Beat me, of course, which I would deserve, but I would be safe on his farm and I doubt he is the kind of man to turn me onto the street.

It is tempting. Every morning I could look into those brown eyes and know he would look after me and care for me. Only he would not, would he? Even if he did not turn me from his door, I would disgust him.

I look up at this man, who I realise matters to me, and know I cannot deceive him. He is the only person apart from Peg to have shown me real kindness since I left the Buttermere house. If I lied to him, he would rightly despise me for it, and I could not bear that.

'I have a farmhouse full of nothing but memories.' He pauses, the hat still for a moment. 'I have been thinking about this for months. You need a home, and a future, while I am without a wife. So why not be my helpmeet. My love?'

I shudder at that word. Thomas is a kind man and I more than like him. But I could not bear to be in his bed and have his hands on me.

'You are a bright and compassionate girl, Hannah. Life with me would provide opportunities for your talents. You could help me develop my dairy. Teach the children in my village to read and write. And in return, I promise to cherish you.'

'It is not possible, Thomas.'

'Please don't answer now. Take as much time as you need to think about it. You could bring Peg with you.' A ghost of a smile touches his lips. 'Make a lady's maid out of her, in lace mittens with ribbons in her cap.'

In the next street, a knife grinder is shouting and ringing his bell.
'I do not need time.'

He lets out a gusting sigh. 'I have lost the ones I loved before,
but without you I fear staying a sad man forever. How can I learn
to smile again, if the best thing in my life will not have me?'

'You must not say such things.' Despite what Peg says, this is
the last thing I want. 'I would only bring you trouble.'

'I am in trouble already. Whenever you are near, my stomach
swoops as if I were on the high seas.'

There is need in his eyes and I know I must stop him. He will
hate himself later when he remembers such foolish words.

'Gentlemen tend to bolt their food,' I say. 'But fennel seeds are
good for the stomach. Betty could pound some to put in your tea.
Or a strong dose of rhubarb might help.'

'Perhaps that is what it is.'

He is disappointed. Hurt even. It is in his eyes.

'I am sorry. But I could never be your wife.'

'I am sure you like me. And I would not rush you. You could
take as much time as you needed to find tender feelings for me. A
year. More even.'

'No, Thomas.'

'But what am I to do with myself, if you will not have me? I have
been lonely for a woman's voice. Not just any woman's voice,
Hannah. Yours.'

'You must persevere.'

'Do you not think I have tried?'

I start to shiver. Under my folded arms the thing lodged inside
moves, like a fish trapped in a bowl of water. Reminding me of its
hated presence. I need to get indoors and think of more ways to
earn money, but first I must destroy this hope infecting Thomas.
Release him to live his life and forget me. It is the only kindness I
can give him.

'There is someone I have met,' I say, hesitantly. 'Jack is an
apprentice in the Twyford bookshop.'

Thomas steps back as if I have trodden on his foot. He replaces
his hat, glances up at the bruised sky.

'Well, forget what I have just said. It was utter foolishness.' He
holds up his hands as if before a highwayman. 'I should not keep
you out in this cold. We will not speak of this again, for it must not

spoil our friendship.' He manages a stilted smile. 'I still think you need a husband. To give you a better and more fulfilling life. If it cannot be me, then I hope the young man at the bookshop might suit. It sounds as if he would.'

He settles his hat more firmly on his head and clucks at Hercules to move on, while I take myself inside, feeling as if I have strangled something precious.

Chapter Forty-Eight

How many minutes she has been watching I cannot guess, but her blow slams me against the wall.

The mistress has slid noiselessly into the kitchen as I am struggling to ease stays tightened until I can scarcely breathe. She has finally noticed the bulge under my apron.

'Look at that belly!' Her nostrils flare as if I stink. 'You have been whoring. With Jack Twyford.'

Her face is like a fist.

Shock makes me forget myself.

'That is untrue! This was your husband's doing.'

'Liar!' She strikes again. For a scrawny woman she has the punch of a coal heaver. 'Repeat that and I will have you in Newgate. For slander.'

'He attacked me. When I thought myself safe under your roof.'

'Shut your foul mouth!'

Her eyes are dark with fury and I almost believe she thinks him innocent. We stare at one another, spitting cats in an alley. The wind is moaning in the chimney and the kitchen fire dying, its heart turning to ash. It is finished, done with. Like me.

I grind my teeth, desperate with accusations, but afraid of what this wicked woman might do to me.

'I will not have you shaming my house. Get yourself gone. Before I fetch my husband's whip and flog that bastard out of you.' She kicks over a stool. 'Go on! And take nothing does not belong to you.'

I am incensed at her hypocrisy. In her youth, she sold herself to all comers. Afterwards, she was a kept woman and has now sunk to the filthiest of trades.

'If people knew...'

From under her skirts a slender knife flashes out and I freeze.

'Knew what?' The blade is a hair's breadth from my eye.

With no spit in my mouth I force my lips to form words. The tension in the house these last days has made me jittery. What would they do if they suspected I was responsible for that letter?

'That he...likes women.'

The blade is withdrawn, though not before stinging my cheek like a furious wasp. 'Spread such lies about your master and you will find that worthless throat of yours cut. Ear to ear.'

Then she backs off and storms upstairs, perhaps to find the whip. But, seconds later, I hear shouting and realise it is the master's turn. I hope she kills him.

Peg warned me.

'The minute she finds out, get away quick. Before the old bitch throws every last thread that you own into the fire. For spite.'

I must not risk that, so my preparations are long made, with my possessions always ready in my bag. The filched documents stitched into the lining. My lavender bags folded inside my spare shift.

As I scramble to the garret, I pass the master, stomping around in his book room.

'God damn you to Hell!' he roars at me.

I ignore him and hurry to the top of the house. The place has gone quiet, but the mistress will be lurking somewhere like a repulsive spider. My heart thumps as I seize my bag and remember I must collect my spare stockings from the line in the scullery. I will need everything I own to help me survive.

Peg is out, fetching the tobacco Master Chalke favours for his clay pipe of an evening and pastries for the couple to eat before bedtime. I will wait at the corner, for I need her to guide me to my hiding place.

On my return from the scullery with the damp stockings, I grab the cheese Thomas brought yesterday and the remains of this morning's loaf. It is unlikely to be missed and I cannot know when I will get more.

Outside, the sky is heavy with the threat of snow and as I slam the great door behind me hail spits on my head as if the weather, too, is incensed with me.

I have left through the front door, refusing to creep away out of the servants' entrance. I do not expect ever to return to this evil place and that, at least, pleases me.

I huddle under the bare branches of a tree, to wait for Peg. I would have gone on the errands myself, but the mistress seems to enjoy seeing the old woman limping along the road with her bad leg.

When Peg sees me with my carpet bag she limps over.

'They know?'

'Yes.'

'She cut you,' her hand moves to my face.

'A scratch. I would not care if she had paid my wages.'

The package Peg carries smells of hot cooked apple. There was a time I would willingly have baked such things for the Chalkes, but for many weeks I have only done what I must. Peg opens the paper wrapping and hawks disgustingly over its contents. After the briefest hesitation, I do the same. Then she folds the paper back over the food and grunts.

'I must take this inside. Then I will come back and show you where you needs to go.'

She will stay in the house, so at least one of us will be fed and she can let me know if anything happens about my letter.

In the icy wind it seems an age before she returns, placing her hand on my elbow as we walk, to guide me.

'It is a wretched place, Hannah. But you are strong. You will manage. And at least they had my old room available. I went to check, just yesterday.'

I am not strong. Inside, I am a whimpering infant, desperate to hide from bogeymen under her mother's petticoats.

'Of course I will manage,' I say.'

Peg takes my hand as if I am her child and we leave that hateful house behind us. We do not speak again, and I refuse to look back.

Chapter Forty-Nine

The sky is pewter rubbed with harsh sand as we trudge from wide streets, with gleaming front doors and clean windows, to where destitute families huddle in doorways.

Wheels and hooves spatter evil-smelling slush. Barefoot children and threadbare crones stretch out hands for coin or bread. Women clutching sickly infants slump on the steps of illicit Geneva shops, uncaring about freezing to death. Half-starved men slouch against walls, desperate for money to buy oblivion, and we cross the street to avoid a need so great they might try to rob women as poor as we are.

This London is beyond my imagining. Dilapidated houses lean across squalid streets, ready to collapse into one another. It is snowing properly now, dredging down like sifted flour, turning rooftops white and softening the edges of ruined buildings. Masking the piles of waste.

We reach a stinking network of courtyards, washing frozen into ragged shapes on sagging ropes, and stop before a derelict house. Wooden planks are nailed over most of the windows.

'Is this it?' My voice is barely audible.

'I said as how it was a dump.' Peg pushes at a warped door that refuses to open fully. Inside, the stench is like a buffet in the face and I bite the edge of my shawl to stop my stomach heaving.

Mortified at needing refuge in a place like this, I try to shrink into myself. Perhaps one of London's forgotten old rivers runs beneath the building, for damp mottles the walls as if they have a scabrous disease.

Yet people live here. Too many for decency. If I have been sliding down, this is the pit at the bottom. We step up to a battered door in the hall and Peg taps nervously on it.

The man who finally answers has a woman clinging to him whose bodice gapes indecently. Both stink of ale and Peg's diffident query is answered with a grunt and an exchange of coins for a key on a greasy string. Then the door slams shut again.

We gather up our skirts and Peg leads me down broken steps. People have used this hallway as a place to piss and I draw my shawl over my nose. At the end of an underground passage my feet sink into something moist and foul. The cesspit of the house next door must be leaching through the foundations of the wall.

'The good thing about this place, apart from it being cheap, is this.' Peg brandishes the key.

She unlocks the door and I see my future home is one of several partitions under what was once a grand staircase. It is the size of the scullery at the Chalke house, but makes that humble room seem a palace.

'The woman in the next room has a fire,' Peg says. 'Sleep close to that wall and there is warmth through the bricks. For free.'

A tiny window, high up, provides murky light and there is a heap of straw on the floor for a bed. There is nothing else but three pegs hammered into the wall and a stinking wooden bucket, brimming with the previous tenant's waste. The only thing to save me creeping out into the yard at night to do my business. Not a stick of furniture, not a stone to form a fireplace, not a rag for a curtain. All I have for comfort is the home-made quilt folded into Thomas's old rush basket and what I carry in my carpet bag.

The chill is like a tomb. I do not want Peg to abandon me here and clutch her arm.

'I must get back,' she says, smoothing my hand with hers. 'But I will come back tomorrow. Meantime, don't go wandering about after dark. It's a bad neighbourhood.' She prizes my fingers from her arm. 'But you are a strong girl, Hannah. You will manage.'

I feel anything but strong. I would sink down and weep, if the floor were not so filthy. I thought I knew about want. Now my ignorance chastens me.

'Best sleep in your boots,' adds Peg, as she turns to leave. I look a question. 'You don't want your toes bitten.'

I swallow down horror. Rats. How can I stay in such a place? But she is right. I will manage. Like prisoners in dungeons in olden times, I will make marks on the wall to count out the days of my captivity. I have been with child for six months and one week. That means eleven weeks remain before I am free of my burden. Though days and nights in a place like this will feel like years.

'Peg...' I bite down a sob.

'At least it is not the street. And you should be safe here,' she says touching my arm.

I take a breath and try to sound as if I could become accustomed to this squalor. 'You are right.' And at least I am away from the Chalkes.

After she leaves and I am alone, I can at last weep. I sink down on the straw as if on an island in a hostile sea.

How can I sleep one night here? Never mind more than eleven weeks?

Images from the past flood back. The warm and clean Buttermere kitchen, so vivid in my mind that it makes my heart want to bleed. Listening to mother's tales of my grandparents coming across the sea from France, having abandoned everything they had worked for. Her admonition that even if you cannot live as a lady, you should never stop behaving like one.

Then I jump, for I have been bitten. The straw is alive with vermin.

Chapter Fifty

There is no need to knock on the landlord's door, since it is open and inside he is crouched down, rattling the bars of his fire with a poker. At least that slut has disappeared.

The man is thickset, red-faced, and wearing a filthy waistcoat over a tattered shirt. Even from two yards away, he reeks of onions and stale beer.

'Is there a broom I could borrow?' I say. 'My room is heaving with fleas.'

His eyebrows arch as if I had said I wanted a coach and four to convey me to the court at St. James's.

'Brooms cost good money. If I lends them to everybody as wants them, they would be worn to a stump in no time.'

I am tempted to ask which of his miserable tenants has ever swept a floor in this pigsty, but must not offend him. 'I only want it for half an hour.'

'As I said. Things cost money.'

I finger the coppers in my pocket. 'How much for ten minutes?'

'A halfpenny.'

'I am not asking to buy it. And I need fresh straw. Should that not be included in my rent?'

He hesitates, perhaps calculating what I can afford, then grunts. 'You can have some for a penny. But the broom will still cost a halfpenny.'

'Even just to borrow?'

'As I said, you will wear it out, and I have a living to make.' He leers and fingers the buttons of his breeches. 'Unless you're offering *payment in kind*.'

I have to remind myself that not all men will be loathsome, though the majority seem that way. 'Keep your broom. I will just take the straw.'

I thrust out my penny and he shrugs. 'I was thinking to do you a favour, so no need to get on your high horse.' Dirty fingers grasp the coin. 'Fat Nellie, in the room next to yours, has a broom that she might lend you. It is not as if she ever uses it.'

He bends back to riddling his coals, addressing me over his

shoulder. 'The straw is in the abandoned stable across the yard. Take as much as you can carry in your arms, in two journeys. No more.'

I turn away. I would have slept on the bare brickwork, if necessary, with my rag quilt to give a suggestion of comfort. Anything rather than that flea-infested straw.

I return to my cellar and start ferrying soiled bedding to the common midden outside with my hands, shuddering at the insects that jump at being disturbed. Then my eye discovers a piece of wood, half-hidden in the slush near the door, and I find I can use it as a shovel to make my task easier. After I have finished clearing the straw, it can be a cover for the night soil bucket.

I refuse to waste money borrowing the wretched man's broom, for there are eleven hungry weeks to get through and necessities to buy. Perhaps it might be worth asking my neighbour about hers, after I am rid of the mucky straw. Eyes have been watching me since my arrival. I have felt them through the crack of the adjacent door.

As I get to the bottom of the steps on my final journey there is a thickset woman in the hallway, a stubby clay pipe between her teeth and a squalling child tucked under one arm. She is wearing a man's greatcoat, secured around the waist with string. She gives me the barest nod as she labours up the stairs to throw a bucket of swill into the street, somehow retaining a grip on the infant, but I am grateful at least she acknowledges me. She looks as if she might let me borrow that broom.

When she returns, I follow and stand in the doorway of her room. She must be a childminder, for there are infants everywhere, most bare-arsed so they can do their business on the floor and save the washing of clouts. In consequence, it squelches underfoot and a stench tells me what will be in the dark corners, where a small figure is currently squatting. Babies and toddlers sleep in baskets on the floor or huddled on the bed like puppies.

I have heard that many childminders scrape their existence by watching the infants of others. Her room is a disgrace, yet there is warmth from her fire and something simmering in the pot above it smells surprisingly enticing.

'Are you Nellie? The landlord said you might lend me a broom.'

'Did he, now?' I notice she wisely wears pattens indoors, to raise herself above what is underfoot. The hair escaping her cap is streaked with grey, but dark patches on the bosom of her gown suggest she is breast feeding.

'I have no money to pay for it,' I say, ready for a rebuff.

'Borrow it and welcome,' says Nellie. 'That room of yours is running with vermin. It would be a mercy to have fewer of them hopping along to bite me.' Behind her back I hear a baby whimper. How many can there be, squashed into her cramped space? 'But be sure to bring it back when you are done.'

There is the trace of a smile on her lips as she hands me a worn-out besom and the kind gesture fills me with hope. It gives me a spurt of energy to improve the awful place where I am condemned to live. The smell I cannot remove, but I sweep down to the brick floor, choking as I displace inches of dust and dirt. Now there is nowhere but my heap of straw for rats or mice to hide and the clouds of fleas the broom disturbed must surely be lessened.

I have forced open the tiny window to let in fresh air, but must soon close it again before it begins to freeze. With neither heating nor proper bedding, I will be sleeping cold. The fresh straw from the landlord will help, but there is not enough of it and I long for even a single blanket to add to my rag quilt. I lay the flat of my hand against the wall. Peg was right about there being warmth from the bricks of Nellie's fireplace.

At least I have a neighbour with a scrap of fellow-feeling, though I did not dare say much to her when I returned her besom. She must guess I carry a bastard under my petticoats and presumably decided to ignore it, though she might easily change her mind and refuse to have anything more to do with me.

I told her my name was Anne. The landlord had not asked and clearly does not care as long as I can pay him. Close up, Nellie's curdled smell made me want to gag, but it is a comfort to know who lives on the other side of the wall when I feel so desolate.

Life is not fair. But whoever said it would be? This is my lot and I must make the best of it. I realise now what a blessing my early childhood was, even if it did not last beyond my tenth year. To have so much love and the beginning of an education. It gave me something to build on.

I think of the Chalkes and their hypocrisy. Without my mother's urging me to always keep learning, and that *Dictionary* in the

Buttermere library, I would never even have known what that word meant. I have also been taught how to do accounts by Mrs Lamb, as well as kitchen skills. One day these things must help me, for I refuse to be like Peg, forever scrubbing and sweeping. Forever hungry and in rags.

I must somehow survive, hidden here, and hope to pick up some kind of life after the child is born. Hope, too, that Peg will bring me news of the Chalkes being brought to justice and possibly of some kind of reprieve for little Suzy. Of whether she escaped the clutches of that dreadful uncle.

Chapter Fifty-One

I gave up counting the flea bites this morning. My legs and body are aflame with bumps I cannot stop scratching, but I tell myself they are just one more thing to be endured. At least I wasn't troubled by rats, though I heard scrabbling in the night and lay rigid with fear in the dark. I have never been completely without the means to make light before and am grateful for the layer of snow that has fallen, since it reflects a pale gleam into my dungeon.

I barely slept, from the terrible cold, from the scurrying of creatures under the floorboards, and the all-pervading noise: children crying, men's angry voices, women shrill with drink, boots stomping up and down the stairs. I feared somebody might break in, despite the lock on my door. Not to rob me, for I have so little, but to put hands on me. The biting things that found their way into my clean straw, into my hair and my clothing, were almost a welcome distraction.

This cellar is even worse than I feared it would be, but Peg used to sleep here and survived. At least it is cleaner than it was. Then there is the landlord, Doggett, who is not someone you would buy a second-hand chair from, for fear it would collapse under you. I grip the key, on its string around my neck, and pray he does not have a duplicate.

I think about my letter and wonder whether Chalke's brother has managed to hush everything up. Whether things continue as before. My flesh prickles with fear at the thought that they might suspect me and try to track me down. And I think about little Suzy and wonder where she might be.

Meanwhile, I must do what I can to make this new existence tolerable. There are things to buy. After that, perhaps I can turn my lavender bags into money to help me through the bitter winter.

Chapter Fifty-Two

In the afternoon I trudge to the second-hand stalls to sell my hairbrush, my spare flannel petticoat and my carpet bag to pay for necessities. A bowl to wash in, a jug for water. A spoon. A knife. A dish and a tin mug. I also need an old blanket, for the cold in that cellar is frightening and my rag quilt offers insufficient warmth. With my swollen belly I am beginning to move like a farmyard goose, though pregnant women are commonplace and nobody gives me a second glance.

I lay out my possessions and the trader surveys each carefully. Turning them over, holding them close under his eye, frowning. His expression is dismissive. He is clearly a shrewd man, who will guess my plight and seek to take advantage of it. Why else would I be offering him these things? I know this, but have no alternative.

He offers under a shilling for the first two items, though the brush once belonged to Mistress Buttermere and the petticoat is in good condition, but lingers over the bag, unable to hide an avaricious gleam in his eye.

'It has been mended,' he says, squinting inside.

'*Invisibly* mended,' I stress, knowing the superiority of my needlework. 'The stitches barely show. Anyone can see it belonged to a lady of quality.'

'Nicked from some house where you was working, was it?' He does not sound judgemental, only interested in what he must give for it.

'Of course not! It was a gift.'

'So you say.' He grunts and runs a finger over the silk lining. 'I expect I could sell it, given time. It would be useful for someone wanting to travel. I am prepared to give you five shillings. No questions asked.'

'I want more than that. It will have been costly. And it was not stolen.'

'Seven and six.' His eye runs over me again. 'That is a generous offer, girl.'

'A guinea.'

He rolls eyes heavenwards, then he thrusts the bag back at me and returns to re-arranging the things on his stall.

I need money to keep a roof over my head until February, when the child will come and I will at last be free. Meanwhile, work will likely be impossible to find, but the rent will be due every week and the landlord will come banging on my door for it.

I grasp the bag by its pigskin handles. It is worth a great deal more than what is being offered. There are other stalls nearby, though the customers looking for bargains are poor folk, unlikely to buy fine bags.

'It is worth at least a guinea,' I say, making myself sound firm. I can always come back with it, tomorrow. He will still be here. 'I will just take what you are offering for the brush and petticoat. Others will be interested in a bag that clearly belonged to a member of the gentry.'

'Fifteen shillings.' He sounds disgruntled at being bested by a slip of a girl. 'Take it. You will not get more. Not around here.'

I hesitate, then nod. I need to get back to my cellar, for my bladder is bursting. 'I'll take it. But you rob me.'

He counts the money into my hand, glancing at the livid flea bites on my wrist. 'That gown of yours,' he says. 'I could give a fair price for it. It is hard-wearing fabric, and well-made. And you are going to burst out of it soon enough.'

For a moment I do not understand. Does he think I will sell the clothes off my back and walk away half-naked?

'It is the only one I have.' I give him a sour look. 'I do not intend parading around in my shift.'

'There are others here you could exchange it for.' He gestures behind him. 'On the trestle table yonder. You could do a trade and walk away with the difference. In coin.'

'Not today,' I shudder at the thought of dragging another woman's unwashed gown over my head. Of wearing her dirt and smells pressed against my skin. At least the sweat saturating my clothes is my own.

He nods, but I see he expects to see me again.

I will need to look respectable when I am ready to search for decent work again and wish I had not cut down my other gown for Peg after the bodice of her own was badly ripped for some transgression. Yet my priority for now is to keep that miserable roof over my head and put food in my belly. When my money runs out, which it probably will, I might be glad to raise a coin or two by trading my gown. It is well-sewn, by my own hand, and someone will be glad to buy it. I must take care to trade it before it loses its value by becoming ragged. And this man and his stall will still be here.

Soon I will take my lavender bags, door-to-door, to some of the better houses. Anything to increase my meagre store of coins. If people like them, perhaps I could buy fabric and make more. But to do that I would surely need a table and scissors, as well as more fabric and lavender. If only I had some spare money, I believe I could make life better for myself.

Returning to my cellar from the second-hand stall, I approach Nellie's open door again and peer inside. Dim light shows her eating her dinner on a rickety table, with a gin bottle and a spoon by her hand. A pot simmers on the fire, probably a permanent fixture into which she throws whatever scraps she can scrounge. All I have eaten today is that last heel of bread I snatched from the Chalke kitchen and some of Thomas's wonderful cheese. Thinking of him makes me wince. What would he think, to see me now? What will he think when he hears I have been dismissed, and why?

Nellie looks up and noticing my hungry gaze grasps the ladle and measures an inch into a none-too-clean bowl. She hands it to me and I do not care and scald my mouth spooning it down. It is potato and onion, with shreds of what might be rabbit, and tastes surprisingly good.

'You are a kind woman, Nellie.'

Every surface is jammed with babies and infants, most in soporific sleep. She leans over to the bed and spoons clear liquid into a fractious mouth that makes the infant splutter. It is clearly true childminders use gin and water to keep their charges from being a nuisance. Perhaps that explains the relative quiet in the room.

'Do you know of any work?' I put down the empty bowl. 'I am not proud. I will put my hand to anything honest.'

She studies me. Breasts like swollen udders leaking dark patches through her gown. 'What can you do?'

'Sew. Cook. Scrub.' Best not say I can read and write.

I am aware that needlework, like most home work for women,

pays only starvation wages and that my room is unfit for making more lavender bags, even if I could scrape together money for what I would need. But that might change if only I can earn something. Cooks work in households or inns, where a character is required. Casual cleaning jobs are easier to find, but women with growing bellies scrub less efficiently than those without them, so why employ them?

Nellie tamps down the bowl of her pipe and frowns thoughtfully.

'You could maybe plait straw for bonnets. It is hard on the fingers, and the pay is bad, but it would bring in something. Though the light is poor in that room.' She sucks on her pipe till the tobacco flares, a coil of smoke rising.

'I could sit on the floor under the window.'

'Aye. You could.'

She eyes my shape. 'Sweetheart let you down? Men can be bastards, can't they?' The baby starts grizzling again and she scoops it up and rocks it, roughly but not unkindly. 'I suppose you know you could call the law down on the rogue responsible? To make an honest woman of you?' She grunts. 'Though it probably takes an angry father behind you to make that happen.'

'And who would want to be tied for ever to such a rat?' I shake my head. 'The man, in my case, has a wife living.'

She eyes me. 'I bet it were a gentleman. They consider maidservants like sweetmeats. To be fingered and devoured.'

'The man I worked for came after me.' I make a noise of disgust. 'In the dead of night.'

Nellie gives a gusty sigh. 'Wish I had a guinea for every time I have heard that tale. A poor man can be whipped for stealing turnips for his starving family and a poor woman transported for lifting a silk kerchief. But toffs with money can tumble an innocent girl, ruin her by getting her in the family way, and saunter away laughing.'

The gin seems to have done its work and she settles the quietened baby back on the bed and moves a basket from a rickety chair onto the floor. Another baby is sleeping soundly inside it. 'Nothing much women can do about it, except stick together. Here, you can borrow this chair, to sit on. The floors in these cellars are mortal cold, Annie. You don't want the rheumatics.'

She dusts it off with the skirt of her gown. 'I will ask about straw plaiting for you. And find out if the skinflint on the top floor might pay something to have his shirts mended. They have more holes than a colander. He's only a clerk, but he has coin in his pockets.' She sniffs. 'Or he might bring something from the warehouse where he works. A packet of tea sweepings, maybe. You could trade that for bread in the market.'

'You are very kind.'

'Like I said, Annie. We must stick together. My man went off with a tavern wench half his age, leaving me with five little ones and another on the way.' Her chins wobble with a snort of laughter. 'But I find I am better off looking after other women's babies instead of sprouting my own every year. My daughters are in service in good households now, and remember their old mother when they gets paid. I have no complaints.'

She ladles more soup into my bowl. 'You are pretty, Annie, but better still, you are bright. No reason why you should not do all right for yourself.'

I pray she is right. I intend to try.

I sold my lavender bags with surprising ease the next day. They were admired, for I had embroidered tiny butterflies on them with scraps of silk from the bottom of the mending basket Mistress Chalke probably did not even know were there. They earned me over a guinea, which I added to the coins in the glass jar hidden under my bed straw. I could buy more food with it, but my priority must be settling the rent, week in, week out. Going hungry, I can probably bear. Sleeping in the street, I could not.

Chapter Fifty-Three

If I cannot find a place soon, I will have to lift my skirt to squat and make water in the open street. Up some side alley, in the gutter, like the beggar women.

There is a tumbledown inn on the corner with a sour-faced woman sweeping the yard cobbles. A necessary house is at the side of some ramshackle stables.

'May I use your privy, Mistress? Please?'

Desperation is in my voice, my face, my rigidly held body. She gives me a quick sideways glance, pauses a second at my shape, then nods me towards the rough plank door. I only just make it. These last days I want to go all the time and trudging the streets only makes it worse. Men are spared this, as so much else, since even a great lord will piss freely against any wall –

at the side of a church even, if nature calls – and none will think twice about it.

When I come out again, breathing through my mouth rather than my nose, and holding my skirts tight against my body to avoid touching anything, I bob the woman a curtsy by way of thanks. The place was only a befouled wooden seat over a stinking pit, but it was not the public way.

'I went like the parish pump with my last one,' she says, with a shrug. 'They say 'tis how they lie in your innards.'

Through an open door I can see a shambles of crocks in what must be the inn's scullery.

'I am looking for work,' I say, hope glimmering. 'Cleaning, scrubbing. Or I can cook. I will do anything you need, and do it well. I am a hard worker, and honest. For just a few coppers.' I stop gabbling and we both hear my stomach growl and know I am in no position to bargain. I have not eaten since yesterday and that was only a heel of bread so rock-hard, I feared for my teeth. I lower my expectations. 'Or I will put your scullery to rights for a bowl of broth.'

She peers at me and frowns. My dress grows shabbier by the day, but is too good for a vagrant. Then her eyes reach my left hand and narrow with contempt. Perhaps Peg was right. I should have used a few of my precious coins to buy a pinchbeck ring.

'Honest?' Her nostrils flare. 'With that great belly, but no wedding band to excuse it?' She makes a motion in my direction with her besom as if to sweep me from the yard. 'Do some more whoring, if you are hungry. Our pots are too good for the likes of you.'

I turn to skulk away, my cheeks flushing at the unfairness. Not long ago, this woman would at least have treated me with respect. Now she regards me like dog mess on her shoe.

'I am going,' I say, striving for dignity. 'But your scorn should be for the church-going gentleman who forced himself on me. In the dead of night. When I believed myself safe under his roof.' I am tempted to spit my disgust at her feet, but remember mother's attempts to make a lady of me and merely look my defiance. 'Were he here now, you would bow and scrape to him. Though he is no better than a beast.'

I shrug my shawl around my shoulders because the wind is keen, and regret letting my mouth run off. It does no good and will likely bring more trouble on my head. As I turn to leave, I try to make amends. After all, the woman helped me when I had a need. 'But thank you, Mistress. For letting me use your privy.'

'Wait.' She stands, head tilted as she studies me. 'How old are you?'

'Sixteen.'

She scratches absently at her back with her free hand. She looks none too clean.

'And this is true? About your master?'

'As God is my witness.'

'Men.' She scowls in the direction of the inn, not a prosperous-looking place. 'Every man Jack of them ruled by the itch in their breeches.'

She grasps her besom between strong hands as if it were a troublesome fellow that she would enjoy throttling.

'They cannot abide being guided by their womenfolk, either. But marriage teaches you to manage them. Master Haggerty would not let me give work to the likes of you, but since he never goes near the kitchen, what need for him to know?'

She sweeps her pile of rubbish towards the corner of the yard and then turns her back on it, indifferent to the fact that the wind will swirl it back across the cobbles within minutes, and has another vigorous scratch. But the biter, whether flea or louse, is too deep behind her stays to reach, so she gives up. Instead, she jerks her chin towards the open doorway.

'Get inside and scour them dirty pans. If your work is to my liking, there might be some coppers for you. Meantime, help yourself from the pot on the kitchen fire. 'Tis only horsemeat and onions, stewed in the dregs of our beer, but none the worse for that.'

The stew scalds my mouth, I am so anxious to spoon it down. The meat is stringy, the gravy thin and there is a taint to the food suggesting the ingredients were less than fresh, but I do not care. I crave meat. Of late, I have felt as if my innards are pressing against my spine from emptiness. I understand Peg's reverence for a full belly.

I have made a start with the cleaning, not liking to fall on the food before I had done anything to earn it, and it is satisfying to have proper work. The straw-plaiting I have been doing will not earn enough to cover my rent, never mind food.

Although the place is shabby and the pantry stores stale, they are plentiful. I mix a lump of butter into flour, soften it with some of the gravy, and then stir it into the great simmering pot on the fire together with some extra salt.

The customers in this place are working men, looking for quantity rather than quality in their victuals, but everyone likes good food if they can find it.

Mistress Haggarty has been watching me and reaches across for the spoon for a taste.

'Much better,' she says, smacking her lips. 'You did not lie about being able to cook.'

'You have butter about to turn,' I venture. 'I could use it with flour to make sheets of pastry. Then, if you cut them into squares, you could sell them alongside the stew. Hungry men would love something like that.'

Mistress Haggarty's hand strays around to her back for another absent-minded scratch. If I were her, I would give those stays a long soak in some lye.

'At a farthing apiece…' she muses, and her eyes glaze over as if she is struggling with calculations. 'That might put my man in a decent humour, for a change.' She gathers up the armful of jugs I have just washed and turns to take them to the cellar to fill with the inn's watery ale. 'Do it. Make as much as you can manage. We have a cock fight tonight. That always stirs appetites as well as thirsts.'

I had noticed the brick-built pit earlier, with rough wooden benches piled to one side, ready for those watching and placing bets on the fighting birds they fancy.

I am glad to leave before the men begin gathering for the fight, since I hate seeing innocent creatures torn to pieces for sport and, anyway, am dropping with fatigue. But I have done a good day's work and the kitchen is piled with scoured pewter plates and a basket of pastry squares sits, close to the fire, under a clean cloth, to keep warm. In my pocket to take away with me is a battered penny and two pastry squares wrapped in a scrap of paper. Today has been a promising day and I feel the possibility of hope. Perhaps I can manage to get through these weeks. Perhaps make it through until the child is born, and afterwards find a way back into service in a respectable house.

I have to hope that fortune is smiling on me at last.

Chapter Fifty-Four

Work at the inn is hard and long, not helped by the burden under my apron. By the end of the day my back and legs ache and my ankles take the imprint of a finger, like fresh dough. In the hot kitchen, sweat collects under my cap until it is sodden. My hair is stiff with grease and I am glad it is hidden. I could weep for the state of it and of my under-linen, itchy and smelling unclean. Anything I have tried to wash remains damp in that cellar and threatens to disintegrate from rot.

Yet I revel in being in this kitchen, for it surely proves I might survive my trouble. I have improved the cleanliness, taking care not to let Mistress Haggerty see my disgust at the dirt. It is better than it was, but there are still corners calling for a stiff broom and walls that have not had a lime-wash in years. The foods I cook are from the cheapest ingredients, from spoiled flour and flesh that often smells tainted. Master Haggerty refuses to let his wife buy anything but the leavings of the market stalls.

How I wish to be at a clean-scrubbed kitchen table, flour on my hands and a loaf of hot, sweet bread in the oven, scenting the air. As my work here is rough, I wear a swathe of sackcloth to protect my solitary gown rather than an apron. Nothing is said, but Mistress Haggarty and I both know it is also to disguise my shape. My hands and arms are raw from washing pots and tankards, but hunger is a thing of the past and I am allowed to eat my fill from what I prepare for our customers. Business is looking up, because of my pastry squares and a suet duff I have introduced. Poor men crave full bellies and plates of cheap pudding are popular, especially if the man can afford a dribble of jam to spoon over it.

She was right that Master Haggerty never enters the kitchen, though I hear his rough voice serving customers or chastising young Sam, who tends the horses. I have seen the innkeeper out in the yard, through the window. He is older than his wife by a score of years. Barrel-chested, with big ears and a weather-beaten face.

If it were not for him, I would be tempted to ask to sleep in the hayloft over the stables, though their son Sam spends much of his time there. He is a great, lanky lad with freckles and a shock of rust-coloured hair who never speaks.

Anywhere would be better than that cellar, but I must keep out of Master Haggerty's sight. To lose this position would mean hunger again, for although there is money in my jar, I doubt it will stretch through until February. Most weeks see me selling something, the latest being my wool shawl. I have made a calendar of sorts on the wall, using the end of my spoon to scratch crosses marking the likely days until Peg and I think my child is due. But they stretch impossibly far and I do not like to dwell on their number.

Mistress Haggerty returns to the kitchen while I am roasting a great tin of pig's trotters. She is carrying a sweet pie from the corner pastry shop.

'For my Sam,' she says, nodding in the direction of the yard, where the boy is rubbing down a customer's nag. She shakes her head. 'The poor lad got kicked by a pony when he was barely walking. Never spoke after. Not a word. Not to this day.' She shrugs. 'Yet the boy dotes on horses. Even after what happened.'

'I could make fruit pies for him, if you like. They sell dried apple rings in the market.' I check the trotters. Nearly done. Then turn back to her. 'And when I do the suet pudding, I can make extra for him, with sugar and currants.'

'People are beginning to talk about our food,' she says. 'Better be careful. We don't want Haggerty getting curious.'

I nod. She is a bright woman, probably more so than her clod of a husband, and although she is unkempt and dirty, I welcome her friendship. It seems to me sometimes that it is often the poor who are the most generous with what they have.

Later, I cut two pastry squares, brush them with butter and then sprinkle sugar and a grating of nutmeg on top. I leave them on the windowsill for when Sam comes over to collect his dinner. He is a good lad. Helpful to me, kind to his mother.

At the end of the afternoon, men begin to gather around the gaming pit, leaning forward on the wooden benches, excited, placing bets while they wait for the arrival of the fighting cocks. Many have rolled out of the inn the worse for drink and a black bottle or two have changed hands. They are like overgrown schoolboys intent on mischief, but there is a dark undercurrent of cruelty. Blood will be shed and they cannot wait to see it.

Mistress Haggerty has set up a trestle table close by, with jugs of ale and some of my horsemeat patties to tempt their money before it is gambled away. She has also mixed a paste of powdered charcoal for the owner of a cockerel, Black Spur, to mask a weeping sore on the bird's leg.

I slip along the side of the inn wall with a platter of sliced blood pudding to add to the spread and she takes the dish from me and nods for me to get back out of sight. I am usually long gone by now, but have been promised some farthings to stay and help.

Hurrying to the kitchen, I glance back and freeze to see flax-blond hair gleaming in the lamplight of the inn yard like a bronze helmet in a painting.

Jack. This must be one of his haunts. I remember him offering to take me cock-fighting.

I make my ungainly way back to the kitchen, unsettled. He has not seen me. One more girl in rags with a protruding belly would be beneath his notice. Usually I try not to dwell on what I have lost. How much further I might sink. But seeing Jack brings everything jolting back. He is far from the kindly youth I thought him and I suspect he would sneer at how low I have sunk.

When Mistress Haggerty comes in to refill the great jugs with beer for her customers, she gives me a keen look.

'What's up, Annie? You have a pain?' She opens the bung on a keg of ale and tops up the first jug. 'Set yourself down a minute. Take a sip of this ale.'

'I am fine.' Under that sour exterior, she is a compassionate woman. I was lucky to find her. 'But I saw someone outside. From my old life.'

She closes the spigot and frowns over at me.

'Not the bastard who attacked you?'

I shake my head. 'Some else who thought to take advantage of me. A young man.'

She sets the full jugs on the table and peers through the open doorway. 'Where?'

'Bright golden hair, blue eyes,' I say. 'Imagine St George in a church window.'

Mistress Haggarty makes a rude noise. 'Good lookers are often the worst. They get away with more.' She balances her brimming jugs with practised care and purses her lips. 'Best keep out of his way.'

On yet another trip to the necessary house, as the contests are about to begin, I step aside for a man making his way back across the yard, still fumbling with his breeches. I rarely see the inn's customers and avoid them, not wanting anyone mentioning me to the innkeeper.

'Hello, sweetheart,' the man says, ale-sodden breath gusting into my face.

'I am a widow,' I say, not liking his expression or his proximity. 'And expecting a child. As you can see.'

'Some of us like a belly on a wench,' he hiccups, unsteady on his feet. He looks like a tradesman, slipped away from his counter for a drink. Maybe his customers don't mind the smell of beer on him. Or more likely he does not have any because he is a drunkard. Yet though not prosperous himself, a surfeit of ale does not stop him recognising someone too far below him to complain of coarse behaviour.

He leans in closer, swaying. 'Shows she knows what she was made for.'

I may be ungainly, but my feet are still fleet enough to sidestep a sot, so I shove past him and hurry back towards the kitchen, taking care not to look back.

I can only suppose the drunk distracted me, for I jump with fright to find myself face to face with Jack.

He must have come from the pens where the birds await their turn for the ring.

'What the devil!' There is shock in his eyes. 'Little Hannah?' Then his expression changes. He looks almost amused, though his smile is cold. 'Though not so little now.'

'Did nobody tell you of my misfortune?' I say, my cheeks hot with humiliation.

'Sara, the Chalkes' new girl, prattles of little else,' he says, with a snort. 'But she is too coarse for my taste. I doubt she can even read her name.'

He tugs at his neckerchief, then jingles coins in his pocket. 'You work here?'

I nod. It may be a poor place, but my labour is honest.

'Then what do you know about today's birds? Is there a

favourite?'

He has no more interest in me or my situation than he had for little Suzy. At least there appear to be no suspicions about me. Though why would there be, since nothing appears to have happened about my letter except that brief visit from Chalke's brother.

'Black Spur is thought the strongest,' I say, clutching my sackcloth shawl around me and wishing him ill.

'Then I will risk a wager. Uncle talks of us having to tighten our belts. Perhaps even move the shop elsewhere.' About to walk away, he turns back. 'There was a farmer asking after you at the bookshop the other week. Grantham, or some such name.'

'Oh.' My hands tighten on my hessian shawl.

'You are a dark horse, Hannah. With all these men after you.' His eyes run over me. 'Though for some reason he thought me the father of your brat. Had the brass cheek to threaten me for not making an honest woman of you.' He laughs. 'But it gave me considerable pleasure to tell him your belly was the result of a convenient arrangement with your master. That the two of you were at it as regularly as rats up a drainpipe. That shut him up.'

My mouth falls open, but with only the briefest nod, Jack turns on his heel and heads towards the ring and his wager.

I could cry with vexation. Why be so needlessly cruel? Mistress Haggerty is right. The handsome ones are the worst. Thomas was looking for me, must have thought he was helping me, but will now despise me as a loose woman and look no more. Not that I want him to find me and see how low I have sunk. But I realise the thought of him searching would have been a comfort.

I drag back towards the kitchen, hoping Jack wagers the whole contents of his purse on the sickly Black Spur. Praying the bookshop and its adjacent brothel might soon be closed.

Chapter Fifty-Five

Next morning the kitchen door crashes open.

'Where is she! Where is the slut?'

Freshly scoured pewter plates clatter from my hands to the floor. In a stride, Master Haggerty is looming over me, his wife at his heels. A row of livid bruises on her cheekbone mark where knuckles have recently landed.

'So, it is true,' he says. 'Not only lying to customers about the fighting birds, but flaunting a whore's belly in my kitchen. I have a mind to take my boot to you.'

I stoop to retrieve the plates, afraid of his meaty, bunching fists, and do not see the foot coming. Then I feel a thwack to my buttocks and am knocked face down on the flags. Through my threadbare clothes a boot is slamming into me and I curl up to try and protect myself.

To be kicked. Like an animal. Like a beast. Will there be no end to my shame?

'I am going, Master,' I scramble to my feet and grab my rough shawl, not daring to meet Mistress Haggerty's eye. 'I am sorry to have made trouble.'

'Aye. Bugger off.' I catch a glimpse of his face and see a trace of pleasure around his mouth. He enjoyed kicking me. It made him feel like a proper man. 'Come near my inn again, and I will really make you screech.'

I limp along the street, shivering, and not just from cold. But at least my hurts are not worse and though the child squirmed inside me in protest, it quickly quietened. I have left behind my bundle, with its scraps of food and the farthings Mistress Haggarty gave me this morning, and am sorry for that, but even more sorry for the loss of regular work.

Doggett's eye is on me, calculating how much longer I will be able to pay for the squalid hutch under his stairs. The money in the jar under the straw will not see me through, and I will have to get used to hunger again. Not the hunger we had at the poorhouse, where we dreamed of full plates and puddings rich with sugar, but the hunger that brings fear. Fear that if I am not careful, or lucky, I might starve to death and my child with me. I find I do not want that any longer and am grateful not to have been kicked in the belly. I wish, of course, the child had never come into being but, now that it exists and constantly reminds me of its presence, I find I have sympathy for it.

On my return to the tenement, Doggett is perched on a sagging chair in the doorway of his room. He bares yellowed teeth in a leer and stands up. 'About your rent, sweetheart.' His hands reach towards my breasts. 'That is a mighty fine pair of threepenny bits you've grown there. Why make life hard for yourself? Let me have a proper feel and I might even let you off this week's money.'

Nausea floods my mouth, but I swallow it down and turn on my heel. He is not Chalke. What can he do? Turn me out on the street if I will not oblige him? There will be other loathsome cellars like his. Thank God there is still a little money left in my jar and a basket of straw is waiting to be plaited.

Chapter Fifty-Six

There is a tremendous thump at my door which I fear is the landlord after his rent and swearing he will throw me into the street if I do not step inside his room and oblige him. The man is almost as much of a brute as Chalke. Yesterday he was red-faced and unsteady on his feet from some bottles of illicit brandy he is swilling his way through. The tenants are all avoiding him. At least the raw smell of it distracts from the stink of human waste in the hallway.

But when I open my door, I see carrot-red hair and freckles. Mistress Haggarty's Sam, his lop-sided grin at seeing me fading as he peers over my shoulder at the kennel in which I live. His nose screws up at the poorly covered bucket in the corner that I am waiting for nightfall to empty. His eyes are so full of shock and pity that I think I might cry. Though these days I have precious few tears left to shed.

'How did you find me?' I say, though I know he cannot answer. Then I remember telling his mother about Doggett, my landlord. With such an unusual name his ramshackle house would not have been difficult to track down.

Sam's freckled fist holds out something wrapped in greasy paper. Food. Still hot. The smell prompts my belly to growl audibly.

'From your mother?' I try not to snatch. 'What a kind heart she has.' Now it is in my hand I rip open the packet to find a pair of roasted pig's trotters. Still warm from Mistress Haggerty's oven. Sticky and with the meat falling away from the fine bones. Evidently, she is still cooking the foods I introduced to her kitchen. I manage to stop myself tearing off a bite, but the thought of being able to do so, soon, makes my body quiver.

I look at Sam, who is searching through his breeches pocket and wonder how soon he will leave. How soon I can devour Mistress Haggerty's bounty. He pulls out a piece of boiled sugar, covered with fluff, followed by some farthings and halfpennies. He gestures from the coins to me before folding down his height to place them on the floor just inside my door. Then he shuffles his great feet. He has followed his mother's instructions and does not know what to do next. I wish I could ask if she is still in trouble with her husband, but could get no reply.

'You had best get home, Sam,' I say, helping him. 'But let your mother know how much this means to me. That she cared for me in my trouble.'

He knuckles his forehead in a familiar gesture of respect and turns back towards the stairs, stuffing his sweet into his mouth as he goes, lint and all. I imagine its taste and would have snatched it from him if it had been offered. I sense his relief at leaving, but am equally pleased at being able to crouch down against Nellie's wall and fall on my feast.

As well as being always hungry, I am never warm. Cold seeps into the bones, there is no escaping it. I dream of heat. Of thick stockings. Of flannel petticoats. My woollen shawl. Boots that don't let in water and chafe chilblained feet. To suffer hunger and cold together is cruel. What will I do when my boots fall to pieces? Go barefoot?

At least my child still lives within me. The days drag. The weeks feel like a candle guttering down to darkness. It is perhaps four weeks before I expect to be brought to bed. Or rather, I strive to be amused, *brought to straw*. The time will pass. I am awaiting release. A prisoner desperate to lose her chains.

I am half-dozing in Nellie's broken chair, still aching from my bruises and dreaming of spitted meat sizzling over a fire. Of a satisfying slab of Thomas's cheese. Of warm bread, fragrant from the oven and oozing with butter. Of Mrs Lamb's apple tartlets, their smell wafting around her kitchen like intoxicating smoke. So hot from the oven they threaten to scald your mouth, yet so tempting you don't care and sink your teeth into them regardless.

Then a noise in the passage outside jolts me awake, to find none of it real. My job is gone. Soon I could be starving in a doorway.

The door creaks open and Peg, who usually drags around like a wind-broken nag, almost dances into the cellar.

'I have news!'

'What has happened?' I think immediately of constables dragging Chalke away.

'The old bastard has been beaten!' She flashes broken teeth. 'Thrashed, like a cur that nicked the Sunday roast.'

'Beaten? By whom?'

'Nobody knows.' She rubs thin hands together, her face splitting in a grin. 'But his face is swollen as a pig's bladder.'

'Was he robbed?' I think back to the night I made the burned wine. Was that the work of men with a sister or daughter despoiled?

'A grudge, 'tis thought. Apparently, it was a great tall feller, with a face muffled in a scarf, who come on him just after dark. Broke a whip on his back, but spoke not one word.'

My heart misses a beat. *A great tall man, with a whip.*

'He was not caught?'

'Got clean away. There was no-one near.'

Master Chalke has suffered pain and I am more than glad.

'Peg…' I hesitate. 'Might it have been Thomas?'

'Your farmer?'

'I saw Jack at the Haggerty's, just before I was dismissed. He said Thomas went to the bookshop, looking for me.'

I cannot bring myself to tell the whole of it.

Peg looks thoughtful. 'I told you the man kept asking where you were. Why won't you let me tell him?'

'You must never say a word.' I shift in the chair. 'Look, Peg, there is food. Mistress Haggerty sent Sam, with it.' The second trotter had been tormenting me for hours and it is a relief to pass it to my friend. The fat has congealed, but Peg falls on the meat with a sigh of pleasure.

'A great lad called Ruben delivers the milk now,' she says, her mouth busy, 'so I wouldn't be surprised if Farmer Thomas spends his days searching for you.'

'He will not be looking now.'

'Why not?'

'Never mind why not. Put him from your mind.'

Thomas must have realised what happened to me and meted out his own punishment. It surely means he knows I did not willingly give myself to Chalke.

He knows nothing about the trade in children and, even if he did, what country farmer could set himself against men with sixty guineas to spend on unnatural lusts?

Since Chalke and his powerful friends have not come after me, enough time must have passed for me to be considered just another dismissed servant. And at least I tried to help girls like Suzy, even if little seems to have come of my efforts. I need now to concentrate on my own survival, before poverty reduces me to sheltering in some derelict doorway.

Chapter Fifty-Seven

Yet at dusk Peg is unexpectedly back, while I am forcing raw fingers to plait more straw. At least with Nellie lending me that old chair, I do not spend my days on the floor.

I can just make out the furrows in Peg's brow as she hunkers down beside my chair.

'The new maid has brought in a young sister,' she says. 'The little 'un is only nine. Plump and pink-cheeked.'

We look at one another and know her likely fate.

'I sleep on the kitchen floor now, since they share the garret room.' Peg presses her palms against Nellie's warm wall. 'Maybe the Mistress will hand me over to the parish constable. Now they don't need me no more.'

I put the straw on the floor and take one of her hands. The skin is rough and dry. The joints of her fingers swollen.

'I told you not to worry about that, Peg. I have a letter from Chalke's desk. From a surgeon they knew, at the Locke Hospital. The one who treated you all those years ago. It says you could not leave your bed or put a foot to the floor for weeks after your leg was broken. So how could have run into the hallway after your attacker? And killed him?'

Peg stares at me, slack-mouthed.

'I expect they silenced the man because he was making trouble for them,' I say. 'They are ruthless enough. And they planned for you to take the blame if the story ever came out.'

'Why?' She is round-eyed.

'To save their own worthless skins. And you were too young to defend yourself. When nobody cared enough to ask after the murdered man, they let you go on thinking you had done it. Just to be cruel.'

She rubs at her eyes.

'And I was scared of the rope. All these years. For nothing?'

'Peg, that letter proves your innocence. But I hope you will stay in the house a while longer. In case anything happens about my letter.' I glance round the cellar. 'At least you will have a decent roof over your head, and food.'

She scratches at the scab on her neck that never seems to heal, then pulls two tired-looking carrots from her apron pocket. Filched from the vegetable sack at the house.

'Here, have these. You're thin as a shotten herring. I still wish you would let me say something to your farmer.'

'No, Peg. Just stay at the house and keep your eyes and ears open. Something should surely happen soon and I need you there, to tell me.'

My hunger is constant and after she has gone, I think how Thomas would hand me a full pitcher of creamy milk. Take me to his farm and place a heaped plate of roast beef in front of me. But would he? Now he knows I have a bastard in my belly?

I think of him often, wishing I had my time over. After that visit to his farm, I should have trusted him. But the child was in my belly then. So it was already too late.

I finger the carrots and plan to save them for nightfall. Then pour water into my washing bowl to dampen the bonnet straw, to make it more pliable for plaiting while there is still some light. And try not to worry about the coming weeks and what they will bring.

Chapter Fifty-Eight

Early next day I make my way back to the Chalke house before they are likely to be abroad. I want to see the little girl for myself. It is a long walk, but I remind myself Peg does it regularly, despite a dragging leg. Without complaint.

When the new maidservant finally saunters out to empty slops into the gutter, I see a sharp face that suggests she thinks she knows everything. Though, of course, she is cruelly wrong about that. She hangs about the railings, perhaps hoping to smile at the gangly footman from the next door house. Then a slight figure skips up the steps to join her. The sister. Small, even for nine, with fair curls and a rosy, chubby face.

Why has nothing happened since my letter was delivered? Has Chalke's brother succeeded in hushing the whole business up? If so, there is nothing more I can do. Especially now that I am carrying my shame for all to see.

At least, since Master Chalke does not know about the papers I carried away, he can hardly link me to his disgrace and come after me. He will likely think a disappointed customer turned against him. And even if he does wonder, surely he will have too many concerns about his brother or the lawmakers to hunt down a pregnant beggar, hidden in the slums.

As I pause outside the Chalke house, I remember everything I lost from being sent there. A life of contentment and usefulness, with people who valued me. People who would now cross the street to shun me.

I no longer have even necessities and would be grateful for soap that smells of old bones and refuses to lather. For coals that are damp and billow black smoke in a grate. For back-breaking work, without thanks. I thought I knew about want, but know now that sacrificing that halfpenny to get my letter delivered could mean the difference between life and death for me. But what choice did I have? Suzy was young and unprotected. Like the child across the road. I am proud that at least I tried to do what was right.

I think that it is time for Peg to leave that house, but not before telling the new maid of the risks to her sister. She looks knowing, so I suspect she will not be as surprised as I was by the evils there are in the world and will arrange for the child to go elsewhere.

As I turn for home my mind fixes instead on the cold pease pudding which is all that awaits me in the cellar for my supper. My belly growls for it now, though I should save it until darkness falls.

I want my body back. The one I have now is misshapen. It aches. It behaves oddly and wants to piss all the time. Even my walk is more like a duck being prodded to market than that of a young girl.

I hate everything about myself. With no change of clothes, my skirt and bodice are stiff with dirt, the hair under my cap oily and matted. My head itches with fleas, but there is no soap and clean water must be bought from the water carts. The bed straw I paid for has gone frowsty and there is a foul stink from the night pail, even after it has been emptied.

I yearn to be clean. There was an old wash tub at the Buttermere house that I had taken to my room every week so I could crouch down in it and douse myself in jugs of hot water. Even at the Chalke house, on wash-days when I rose before dawn, I would give myself a rub down with a soapy cloth in the scullery. Now I cannot imagine my body being wholesome ever again.

The marks on the wall beneath my window track the days until the child is expected and I think of little else, since it rarely leaves me in peace, turning around inside me, like a carp outgrowing its pond.

My mind returns constantly to the night my world collapsed, like a finger probing a sore. I fall asleep thinking of it. Dream of it. Wake to it. Sometimes I am made so angry by the remembrance that I can scarcely breathe.

Next time I see Peg I will tell her to pack her few scraps together and join me in the cellar, though not before speaking to the new maid. Then we will face the hungry days to come together. I can do no more.

Chapter Fifty-Nine

My head aches, my throat is parched and scratchy, and I feel the itch of raised blotches all over my legs. I was so cold last night that I burrowed deep into the flea-infested straw, hugging my quilt and hessian shawl around me and burying my hands under my arms for warmth. Dreaming of afternoons in the Buttermere kitchen, with the warm weight of Puss on my lap as I darned stockings before the sparking fire.

The occasional sound of infants through the wall in the night make me feel less alone. Nellie is unexpectedly kind, but I must not take advantage of her in case she turns against me. She is such a strange mixture of hardness and softness. Bad and good.

There is a turnip in my hand, scavenged from the market, and I start to gnaw its hard, raw flesh. It reminds me of Thomas, talking about growing them for his beasts. I think of him often. Of his generosity and goodness. Hoping that the beating Chalke received proves my friend knows I did not go with my master willingly.

Hunger begins to make me properly afraid, sometimes making my head spin with weakness and my knees threaten to give way. There is an angry scream in my mind that I hang onto life by such things as a vegetable grown to feed cattle. But I have an irrational urge to see the Buttermere house again, even just from the street. And, if I don't go now, I will soon be too ungainly to travel far from my cellar.

I am weary and my feet drag as I set out, making a woman in the alley shake a fist and threaten.

'Take yourself off. I work this patch.' She is in a dirty pink wrapper, wearing a straw hat decorated with tattered ribbon. A tart, hoping for customers. Does she think a girl heavy with child wants her loathsome pitch? I stomp away, striving for dignity.

It is a relief to reach more respectable streets, though they bring that pang for what used to be. For what might still be, if Mistress Buttermere hadn't moved to York.

Overhead gulls fly and wheel, like scraps of paper in the sky. Mrs Lamb used to say they came inland when the weather was turning bad. Perhaps there will be more snow. The thought makes me shiver. I think I will never be warm again.

It was foolish to come. The house is empty. Mistress Buttermere and Mrs Lamb must still be in Yorkshire. And what could I have done anyway, had they returned?

I turn back towards the rookeries. When this child comes out of my belly I will not, of course, keep it. It would be a permanent reminder of what was done to me. Of what I have lost forever. And it will be a bastard, scorned by decent folk and expected to be as immoral as its fallen mother. I pray it will not be a girl. Peg says she has heard many of the lads from the Hospital enter the Navy, as ship's boys, and I think of Thomas and his boyhood longing to be a midshipman. The Navy might offer a life of adventure and possibility, even to a foundling.

I feel it stir inside me now. The oddest sensation. Something living that is part of me. Even this unwanted, unwelcome child deserves some kind of life. I would never expose it to perish on the streets. Nor would I leave it on the steps of the poorhouse. Most infants left there died, overnight or soon after. Their swift burials were in the ground in front of our building: the only things planted, dead infants. A paupers' boneyard instead of a garden of flowers.

The child itself will be innocent and I am determined not to hate the creature. That would be unchristian. Unfeeling. Unfair. But it will be a relief to leave it in the care of others. To try to forget its existence and the brutal night it was made.

My letter seems to have achieved nothing and instead I must concentrate on my own survival and counting down the days.

Chapter Sixty

The bitter January nights gnaw my toes and deny me sleep. I remember when I took the warming pan to make the Chalke's bed cosy, and afterwards would slip up to the garret and leave it under my own blanket. There was usually enough heat remaining for a snug welcome after locking-up.

Fleas remain a torment and I think back to how easy they were to catch in an ordered household, standing out like black seeds against crisp white bed sheets. Easy to trap with finger and thumb and crush between your nails. Here they breed in the straw and feast on me through the night. More shaming are lice that burrow into the seams of my clothes. I wish I had a candle, to scorch them out, but I have nothing.

The hours of darkness are hardest. The light goes at four o'clock. Without a candle, without a rush light, without even the glow from a few coals, this cellar is pitch black. There is no chance of plaiting straw. No way to read my precious book. I think back to how I hated cleaning spilled wax from silver candlesticks. Now I would pick off the residue with eager fingers if I could use it to make light. Or I might even be tempted to eat it. I have heard women with child sometimes crave to eat coal. If I had a lump, I would try it.

Servitude can be degrading, but at least provides food, warmth and light. Entertainment, even, for Mistress Buttermere owned a clavichord and often played pieces by Mozart and Bach. She knew I liked to sit on the top of the stair outside the music room and listen, even sometimes telling me who the composers were. Her fingers were swollen and heavy with rings, but could still coax magical music from a keyboard.

Here there is nothing to do in the dark but lie on the straw, listening for the rat who comes scrabbling in the night. In the early days I feared he would attack me, but he is not bold enough. My hunger makes me wonder about trying to catch him. What would his flesh taste like? I remember Thomas talking of the Romans considering dormice a delicacy. A country dormouse would be wholesome. Yet a London rat will live on unspeakable waste, and

I would need to eat the creature raw. I have not sunk that low. Yet.

'*Always believe things can get better, and they might*,' Mother liked to insist, after we moved from the top half of a house we shared with my grandparents and their canary to a single room with the great loom in the corner where it could catch light from the window.

They did not get better for her, of course. Unless she is in Heaven with the angels. I like to think she is, but hope she is not looking down on what I have become.

I think of Thomas whenever I take my book from the rush basket to read, grieved that its pages are already speckled by damp. I wonder what he does on his farm in this snow, with his milking cows snug in their byre, eating their turnips. I am convinced he was the man who horsewhipped Chalke and hope it proves he did not think I had gone with my master willingly.

I do not expect he would recognise me now. I glimpsed my reflection in a cheval glass yesterday, slanted in a milliner's window. I had not seen myself in a looking-glass for months and was shocked to realise the ragged girl with sunken cheeks was me.

I think of the Chalkes and still hope that the law might catch up with them. But there is no news and I have the copper coin taste of fear in my mouth. If they have been questioned, but not arrested, might they be looking for me? What if Jack has told them what an avid reader I was? But I dare not think that, for my only defence is hiding under Doggett's stairs.

Now, when there is that strange fluttering inside me, I sense a difference in my feelings towards the child. Not tenderness, but something close to compassion. It is, after all, one of God's creatures and, like me, was powerless against its destiny. I pray it will have the good fortune to be a boy, with better opportunities.

Peg still worries, now she is about to leave the Chalke house and share my straw pallet.

'I wish you would let Farmer Graham help you.'

'He thinks me a whore.'

'Does he?' She rummages in her skirts and holds out a fold of grubby and crumpled paper. Taking it from her, I feel something hard and round inside. 'If that is true, why did the lad who brings the milk ask me to get this to you?'

When I break the seal two bright sovereigns fall into my palm.

They are wrapped in a letter.

Broad Oak

Hannah,

I have learned of your plight and am ashamed for my sex and for not taking steps to protect you when I could.

But there is a place of safety here for you now, in Betty's cottage. For you and Peg, both.

My wagon travels its habitual route every morning, and though it no longer stops at your old workplace, Ruben has instructions to carry you back here with him whenever it suits you. Simply present yourself to him.

Alternatively, business affairs bring me into town on the first Monday of each month and I leave your friend Calypso outside The Red Lion in the middle of the day.

What is enclosed with this note represents an advance for giving lessons to the children in my village. Something I know you will enjoy doing. So do not look upon it as charity.

Please allow me the honour of being of assistance to you.

Your respectful servant

Thomas Graham

Peg and I stare at the coins. Enough to cover the rent until the child comes. And more, besides.

I frown at the stained and crumpled parchment.

'How long have you had this, Peg?'

'Not long.' She squirms and avoids my eye. 'I guessed them was coins in there. Not sovereigns, though.' She looks up, shamefaced. 'I suppose I was tempted. Because of that debt. But I didn't touch it.'

I squeeze her arm. 'You owe the Chalkes nothing, Peg. Remember? I have that surgeon's note. But I don't blame you for holding back the letter. It is in my hand now. Though, sadly, you must take the money back.'

'Why? What does your farmer say?'

'Foolish things. The man is losing his reason.'

'You are the one whose mind has gone. That will keep Doggett off your back till your time comes, and beyond.' She digs the jar out of the straw and holds it up to jingle the coppers it contains. 'How long will this last?'

I sigh and drop the sovereigns inside. She is right. This good man's generosity will keep us off the streets. I must keep it, but there is no way I am seeking out his wagon to take my sorry self to his farm. At least not until after the child is born.

I would burn with shame for Thomas to see me now. We are so short of money I was thinking I would have to sell my precious book. Reading has always been my escape, now more than ever, and the thought of sacrificing *Aesop's Fables* has been bitter.

Peg scurries off, after another scrubbing job for when she abandons the Chalke house. Perhaps after settling the rent, buying food and having my boots mended I could make more lavender bags. Buy an old table to work on and maybe a brazier in which to burn scavenged wood. And I shall need to make myself a respectable dress, for when I look for work after the birth. Two guineas should be enough, if I am careful.

But why is there still no news about the Chalkes? The new maid, Sara, having been warned by Peg, has sent her young sister off to a cousin in Highgate and plans, herself, to leave long before Lady Day. Peg says there is no other news of interest. Why has nothing happened? What is Sir Christopher thinking of?

Chapter Sixty-One

Peg alarms me again by pushing wearily through the door next morning, shaking snow from her clothing.

'They have gone,' she says.

I start up from where I was failing to get comfortable on the straw, fuddled. She has never come this early before.

'Who has gone?'

'The Chalkes. Those men come back, last night. Sounded like they would bring down the front door with their fists. They were wearing dark greatcoats again, but you could see the liveries underneath and one flashed a gold ring, when he took off his gloves.'

She flops down beside me.

'The master was shouting and cursing. The mistress was screeching, too, her face as red as a slapped arse. But the men took no notice. Pack one bag apiece, they said. And quick about it.'

She leans back against the warm bricks.

'There was a scuffle, but they was carried off, regardless. In a closed carriage.'

So, Sir Christopher has finally called the law down on those two. It seems forever since I penned my letter. Perhaps the pair of them are even now in Newgate. Chained to a wall. The news is more satisfying than a hot meal.

'Were there constables with them?'

'There was not. Just the men who come with the brother that other time.' Peg gestures to the bundle she has brought with her, dropped inside the door. 'One of them said Sara and I should clear off as soon as it was light, so I brought my stuff.' She looks around. 'I'll be sharing this place with you from now on.'

If no constables were involved this is not what I intended. It does not feel like justice. Have the Chalkes been taken to some place of safety and discretion? Might those men in greatcoats come after me now?

Peg frowns down at me.

'You all right? No more of them cramps?'

I shake my head. Discomforts are normal. But I decide to seek

Nellie's advice about new lodgings. Well away from here. And Thomas's generosity means I could also give her a small gift, if we are to move away. She has been so kind-hearted towards me that she deserves something.

'Peg, could you slip out and fetch an ounce or two of tobacco for Nellie?' I count coins from our jar, comforted by the glint of the sovereigns at the bottom. 'And three hot meat pies for our breakfast?'

Looking around after she has gone my heart sinks when I remember the night soil bucket waiting to be emptied, for I prefer taking it outside when there is nobody to see. But the stench is such that I grab it and lug it up the stairs. At least, after it is emptied, we will be able to properly enjoy our meat pies. Afterwards I will huddle down in the straw and try to rest. Tomorrow I think I might have my boots repaired.

Trudging back with the empty bucket, minutes later, I am nearly pushed over on the stairs by a scrawny youth in a hurry to get out of the house. He looks shifty, like so many of those who come and go in this dreadful place, but I am careful to ignore him. Most of my neighbours would knock you down as soon as look at you.

But when I reach the cellar, the door stands wide open. Because of being distracted by Peg's news, I had not used my key when I went out with the bucket.

I know from the scattered straw what has happened. The youth was after food, I expect, but found our secret hoard. The jar is still there, but empty. A screw of paper containing several ounces of dried peas has also gone. All that is left is the rush basket, some ragged stockings and, for some reason, my precious book.

I refuse to break down and wail, in case I never stop. This is cruelly unfair, but I cannot afford to let it destroy me. Tomorrow I will go back to that trader and exchange my gown for the cheapest he has. My wool shawl is long gone, but those darned stockings can be sacrificed as well. No matter if I have no change of clothing, since nothing can be washed anyway.

In the cramped booth behind the second-hand clothes stall, my nostrils fill with the stink from heaps of ragged garments piled on the trestle tables: for men on one side, women on the other. Some are limp and torn, others stiff with grease. All surely fit only for rag, yet destined for the backs of the poorest of the poor. Like me. My self-respect has withered and I know I cannot expect to retrieve it until after this wretched child is born.

Chapter Sixty-Two

I am plodding to the market next day, eyeing the rubbish and slush for pickings, when I recognise angel-bright hair ahead of me. It is Jack. Strolling in the winter sunshine. Presumably Chalke's brother's men were not interested in him.

Might he help me? Or at least tell me something about what has happened? I despise myself for the childish dreams that I had before I realised the handsome youth is as corrupt as the rest of them.

I hate him seeing me like this, but cannot be proud with my money gone and things looking so bleak. This young man is not as bad as the others. He was probably led astray at an early age by his beast of an uncle. He might even feel he owes me a kindness, after lying to Thomas about me encouraging Chalke.

I pull my patched gown into a better semblance of respectability and catch up with him.

'Jack…'

I notice a button hanging off his coat. His hair looks unwashed. The ribbon restraining it, frayed. This is a different Jack from the immaculate young man I remember.

'You again.' His nose wrinkles. 'What an unsightly lump you have become.'

'I need work, Jack. Could you help me?'

I am tempted to accuse him of losing me that precious job with Mistress Haggerty, though I did trick him about Black Spur and reminding him could make him angry. He might still have those golden looks, but I know him to be more devil than angel.

The brows rise over those sapphire eyes. Any suggestion of friendship between us gone.

'What do you think I could do? Uncle and I have our own troubles.' His mouth turns down. 'We were plagued by snooping constables and forced to close Mistress Jarrett's establishment. And even the printing business.' He scowls. 'Some busybody laid information about us. But they will sorely regret doing so, when we winkle them out.'

This at least is welcome news. That the awful brothel has been closed and the lewd books stopped. Yet Jack and his uncle walk free. And the Chalkes have perhaps been smuggled away by his titled brother.

Then my stomach lurches, for Jack knows I can read. It would not take much for him to suspect me.

'Uncle Twyford struggles to turn a guinea these days.' Jack kicks at a blown apple in the gutter, exploding its rottenness like a pettish boy. He scowls. 'Chalke, naturally, seems to have taken himself off to safety in Ireland. Men like him are never held to account.'

He stares at me. 'We are both short of prospects, are we not?' He scratches a chin that has not been shaved for days. 'After you are rid of your brat, assuming you regain your looks, how would it be if I found you a protector? Some generous gentleman to set you up in lodgings and pay for your favours.' He peers at me, uncertain. 'You are still comely and we could pass you off as a virgin. There are ways to deceive a man.' He moves a fraction away. 'Though you would need a damn good scrub first.'

I am demolished. If I did not have a child to live for, I would sink down into the melting snow and pray for death. I am defenceless, as I have been since Mother died. I am despised. I am being offered a future as a prostitute. And I stink.

'Anyway, Hannah, I cannot stand around consorting with beggars. I am meeting someone.' His hand reaches into his waistcoat pocket, idly turning the coins he finds there while deciding whether to be generous. 'Here.' Two pennies are pressed into my hand. 'But do not trouble me again while you are in that sordid state.'

Then he hesitates, and his brows meet as he studies me.

'You think yourself something of a scholar, do you not? Does that mean you can write, as well as read?'

'A few simple words only.' I make myself meet his gaze, but he still looks thoughtful.

'And you live around here?'

'Yes.'

'When is the bastard due?'

'In a few weeks.'

'Well, think about my proposition. I doubt I will be selling books much longer and another means of earning might be useful.'

Then he strides off. Glad to be rid of me.

I study the coins, which represent a penny loaf and a wedge of cheese. Perhaps even some raw onions. Enough to feed Peg and myself for several days. Beyond that, we will be going hungry.

Things must have happened since my letter was delivered and I am pleased that the place above the snuff shop has been closed. Yet Jack said nothing of arrests. Has that great lord silenced Sir Christopher? Will Chalke and his wife be living in comfort in Ireland, perhaps even pursuing their foul trade there?

I hurry to make my purchases and an old wife in the market with sympathy in her eyes, wraps my cheese in fresh cauliflower leaves. The rags I have wound around my hands, for warmth, conceal the lack of a wedding ring.

Weary, I return to our cellar. My legs and back ache and I will be glad to rest in my borrowed chair while I nibble some of the cheese. If only I had a fire to cook on. But at least I have the onions. I have a craving for them, sliced and sprinkled with vinegar. I might ask Nellie if she has any to spare.

Leaving the market, I noticed two figures standing close together in conversation beside a stall offering dried fruits for sale. A man with bright hair and a young lady with prominent teeth, wearing costly clothes. It was Jack, his arm tight around the girl's waist, while she gazed adoringly into his eyes. From the muted, companionable laughter I guessed it must be the cousin.

I remember his sneer. *What in God's name would I want with a girl who looks like a horse? Who has never opened a serious book in her life*? But I suppose if the bookshop might not survive, betrothal to a girl with some money might secure his future.

How different he is from Thomas, who has been like the brother I lack. Is it too late to try and contact him? To let him help me? I would be tempted if I were not such a lice-ridden bundle of rags. And if I had not so foolishly lost his guineas.

Chapter Sixty-Three

I want this thing over with, and to survive. Women of childbearing age carry death as well as life in their wombs. To perish while giving birth is commonplace. Too often one sees a large coffin, with a smaller one balanced on top, being conveyed to the graveyard. Perhaps that would be the easiest thing for me. After the pain and struggle, my mother's end had been peaceful. Almost.

Her face took on a strange pallor in her last hours, like cheap candle wax. Her eyes were staring, fixed on something other than her gathered family. The metallic smell of blood in the room was strong. The midwife shaking her head. The dead creature in the basin, under the linen cloth, with tiny translucent fists clutching at a life it had failed to grasp.

It is part of life for women to have babies and often die from bearing them. If not from the first, from the second or the tenth. There is nothing to be done about it. In the way that men go to war and sometimes fail to return, childbed for women can be a forced march into danger.

If I die it might be for the best, but I am afraid of what would happen, after. A tumbling descent into a flaming pit? Did I tempt Master Chalke without realising it? Churchmen would likely say so.

I have not been inside a place of worship since Christmas, when I crept into a pew one morning, but even though there were no other worshippers and the building echoed with emptiness, I was conscious of being a fallen woman in a sacred place. I suppose I should accept my tarnished soul and pray for forgiveness. Yet I cannot understand how God could have looked down on what happened that night, and turned away.

Better if I survive. I thought I had grown up at ten, but I was wrong. I know now that there are even worse things than dirt, hunger and injustice. And I do not want to die without having lived at least a little.

The child grows monstrous in my belly. It must be feeding on me, for one scavenged meal a day cannot be enough nourishment

221

for both of us. I am nothing but limbs thin as sticks and a stomach that gets in the way when I tie my boots. Sometimes I raise my shift and study my distended belly, patterned with blue veins. Occasionally now I wonder if the baby means to kick its way out of me. It will come soon. Only after it does, if I survive and give it into the charge of others, can I hope to retrieve my life.

Yet when I trace the outline of what might be an arm and it responds with what feels like a deliberate push, I feel a bond with the unwanted creature. It did not seek its beginning and I remember Mary at the poorhouse, who had never known her mother. Might my child grow up like her? Let it be a boy, I pray. Nellie thinks the way I carry my burden means it will be, and I tell myself she knows about these things.

My only relief these days is the warmth from Peg's bony body as we cling together in the night. Meanwhile the rent is due again, but we do not have it. Might I have to give birth on the street?

I place my remaining pennies in the landlord's outstretched palm and he stares at them with the suggestion of a sneer before pushing them into the pocket of his waistcoat.

'It is all I have just now. You will get the balance. Tomorrow.'

'How do you propose to manage that?'

'They need a pot washer at *The George*.'

'The job is promised to you?'

'No.' My lips are dry. 'But if they do not take me, I will sing in the market.'

'I doubt that singing for pennies will earn my rent.'

There is grit under my fingernails from this morning's scavenging for coal. If the jolting carts have a full load, a rattle of lumps sometimes falls onto the road. Nellie gave me bread and soup in return for what I collected and brought back in the skirt of my gown.

'I am not much short.'

'I have said before, Annie, that there is an easier way to pay your rent money.'

What kind of man will proposition a girl heavy with child? I refuse to sink to that. If *The George* does not want me, I will sing my heart out. Someone will surely take pity and give me a spare coin or two. My time is getting near and afterwards things will improve. They must.

THE SERVANT

Chapter Sixty-Four

My voice is not strong, but Mrs Lamb used to say it was sweet. So I stand where the women pass into the market and summon the courage to make a public spectacle of myself. *The George* did not want a woman about to drop a child, so I have no choice.

The first sound from my cracked lips is a croak. This is a noisy place, so I make myself think of fresh bread and how I might earn enough to buy a penny loaf as well as pay my rent. Then try again. Louder. The tune is a quaver, but I persevere despite the clamour surrounding me. Nobody even notices. Time passes. Finally, an elderly gentleman smiles and digs a generous handful of coppers from his pocket. Enough, perhaps, to appease our landlord. Then there is nothing, only indifference and the biting cold.

I am about to turn for home when a soberly-dressed woman walks by, a governess, perhaps, escorting a curly-haired child. The little girl has her teeth in an apple. She stares at me, tugs the woman's sleeve, and whispers. As they walk away, I hear: '*A slut, child,*' murmured by the woman. Perhaps the tender-hearted girl was asking for a coin for me. Instead, she lobs her apple in my direction. It lands at my feet and I snatch it up into my sleeve. Though not before noticing that she has only taken a single bite from it, probably because it is wrinkled from winter storage. My mouth waters. Nearly a whole apple is a feast.

I think of her as I trudge back to my cellar. What if her governess were careless? What if she strayed and became lost? Might she end in the hands of people like the Chalkes? Where are that wicked pair hiding? And why do Twyford and Jack still walk free?

After I get home and the apple is gnawed to nothing, I count out the money I have been given. Not quite enough, so I drag myself to Nellie's room.

'Could you lend me a penny?' It grieves me that I will be forced to sell my precious book, perhaps tomorrow.

Nellie stares at me, slumped in her doorway like a bundle of dirty washing, then reaches into her pocket for a coin.

'It is a gift.' She places a reddened hand on my belly. Gentle, but exploratory. 'I reckon you are pretty close to your time, Annie.

Don't go begging on the streets again. You and old Peg can share my soup until the babe comes. And welcome.'

I struggle up the stairs and thrust my money at Doggett, who takes it with a surly grunt and staggers back into his room, clearly drunk. I have another week's reprieve.

I shuffle along the passageway wondering whether I might try singing one more time. With Thomas's sovereigns gone, next week there will be nothing but *Aesop's Fables* between us and the street. Then the cramp bites into me.

Chapter Sixty-Five

As blood and water gush down my thighs onto the hall floor, I know I must get out of sight, so I hang onto the worm-eaten bannister and shuffle down the stairs. Trying to hurry, aware the child is coming days earlier than we thought.

Around me doors slam, children squabble and foul language signals arguments likely to end in violence. The familiar noises of the house. Then I unlock our door and slam it behind me, relieved at least to be safe from prying eyes.

I slide down the wall onto our straw bed and pull my ragged half-quilt under me. It will be ruined over the coming hours, but I refuse to give birth on dried grass, like an animal. At least there is that welcome glimmer of warmth in the bricks to lean against. One of Nellie's infants is unusually loud today, but its grizzling might mask any noises I make.

I consider distracting myself with my precious book, but do not want it soiled. Its pages are already speckled with damp. Better, instead, to think about finally getting my freedom back when this is over.

From the age of ten I have known I am unimportant, but I am a hard worker and have more determination and learning than most. I am barely sixteen, so there is surely time to make something of myself. To appear respectable again after the child is left at the Foundling Hospital. My son would be nothing to me but an unwelcome reminder and a badge of disgrace.

The pains, when they begin to properly bite, bring a flutter of panic, for Peg will not return from her latest job until dark and there is no money for a midwife. They squeeze, make me gasp, then stop, and make me whimper for my mother. Perhaps, when they get closer together, I will drag myself next door and seek Nellie's help.

I knew there would be pain, from my mother's labours and from the muffled cries one hears from houses where women have reached their time. But there is also draining exhaustion. I need sleep to summon the strength to push the child out and get my ordeal over. But I know there is likely to be a deal of straining before that happens.

I am moaning to myself when Nellie puts her head around the door, makes a clucking sound, and comes to kneel beside me.

'How long have you been like this?'

'I don't know. Two hours?'

'Let me see.' Nellie has borne half a dozen children and I am grateful to have someone help me, for I am not as brave as I thought. She shamelessly lifts my skirts. I am nothing but a great veined belly and white, spindly legs. Sweaty and soiled. I disgust myself.

'First ones is often slow,' Nellie says, sucking on her empty pipe. 'You are nothing but skin and bone, girl. When did you last eat?'

'Yesterday. Your soup. And I had an apple.'

There is no bread. Peg is not paid until the week's end and we have only a few coppers between us, which will be needed next week to stave off the landlord. After they are gone, if we are to eat again or keep this roof over our heads, I must drag myself into the street and beg.

Nellie looks me over. 'I will bring some tea. And a bite of bread to go with it.' She gives me a stern look. 'I will not want paying for it, neither.'

I let my eyes tell Nellie how welcome that would be, for I have no strength for pride. If she will feed me, I will let her.

The tea, when it comes, slopping in a chipped bowl, is nectar for I am desperately thirsty. The pains launch through my guts with more frequency now, like a tight-wound spring. But while I await the next surge, I dip bread in the tea and suck the pap gratefully into my mouth.

'That is good,' Nellie encourages. 'Get it down. You need your strength.'

The noise of the wailing child through the wall starts up again. It must be her own, since the babes she fosters will be in a gin-and-water stupor.

'Your little girl is calling for you,' I say, not wanting her to leave.

'Don't you worry. My Dorcas can see to her sister.' She gropes under my shift again, her smell feral, though my own is rank now. 'Let me rub your back. It helps.'

At least it is still light, though I cannot afford even a tallow dip and it could be night before the child comes.

'Want me to send word to Peg? Dorcas could fetch her.' She

clamps stained teeth on the pipe. 'You need someone with you.'

I must find a way of buying our friend another screw of tobacco, after this is done. Assuming I survive. 'Peg has a pot-washing job,' I say. 'We cannot lose her wages.'

'Then I will come, every so often, to check on you. Bang on the wall with your tin mug if you feel the babe ready to come out.'

I nod my thanks, wanting to beg her to stay.

It is unbearable to feel like an overripe fruit ready to burst. Yet surely expelling this great lump will split my body in two?

Perhaps it will die, as so many of my mother's did. Yet I cannot bear to think the burden I have carried under my heart these months, that has pushed at me with impatient limbs, might fail to draw breath. I pray, again, that it will be a son. For who would willingly bring an unwanted girl into the world?

As the hours pass, I begin to despair. I cannot do this thing. Darkness falls and Peg returns, to wipe my sweating brow and share the weary hours. Then Nellie brings us a rush light and a mouthful of gin. A bowl of water and cloths. More tea. More foul-tasting gin. Finally, the two of them urge me to push, though I weep from fatigue and misery at a body which has become a mess of blood and hurt.

The child slithers into Peg's hands in the thin light of dawn.

I had expected to despise it. Instead, when my trembling fingers touch the bloodied creature laid on my belly, there is fierce joy. Tears flood down and I am overwhelmed. This is life, created by me. Something all my own.

The infant that Peg places in my arms, wrapped in the scrap of clean linen saved for this day and looking outraged at coming into the world, is a girl. A precious daughter that will be part of me until I die.

How strange to be a mother. How right.

'I will bring the caudle I have brewed for you,' says Nellie, packing rags between my legs with rough tenderness. 'We must build you up. Then you need sleep.'

She and Peg make a nest in the straw for me with one of Nellie's motheaten blankets and a hot wrapped brick tucked under my feet that make me feel like a ragged queen. The need for sleep weighs my eyelids, but I cannot bear to lose sight of the precious scrap of life I have created.

I am in awe of her perfection. Washed with clean water provided by our ever-generous neighbour, the baby's skin is silken-soft. How guilty I feel about despising Nellie. Rough-spoken and rough-living she may be, and her care of children doubtful, but she has been my saviour.

I think my daughter wants to suckle and offer my breast. Try to squeeze a few drops of milk from painful nipples to tempt her minute, rosebud mouth. But I fail.

Nellie roughly draws out her own swollen breast.

'Give that child here. Plenty of time to feed her, after you are rested. You lost a deal of blood.'

She is right. The child's coming was an ordeal. I am beyond weary as I sip the caudle and watch Nellie encourage my daughter to tug hungrily at her nipple.

Peg has settled beside me, her back resting against the warmth of the wall.

'I will hold the little one while you sleep,' she smiles. 'She will be safe with me.'

Chapter Sixty-Six

I sleep late and wake to full daylight at the tiny window. Peg is still beside me, clutching a swaddled bundle.

'Why is she so quiet?' Its stillness panics me. 'Let me see her.' I am frantic until my daughter is in my arms and I realise her eyes are only closed in sleep. She is tiny, but fits perfectly into the crook of my arm.

Peg slips next door, to Nellie's, to return with more tea and another crust of coarse bread to dip into it. They are like mothers to me.

'Now you have had the child,' Peg says, accepting the morsel of bread that I pass her, 'we should talk about moving away. Maybe sending that letter wasn't such a good idea.' I recognise her old haunted look and wish I had not told her about meeting Jack.

I clutch my daughter with one arm and sip tea with my free hand. I am sore and weary still, but brimming with love for every child that breathes.

'Think of those girls, Peg. Used by evil old men. You were one yourself. Don't you feel for them?'

'Of course, I do. But Chalke is not locked away. Twyford and that Jack fellow walk free. And you said the apprentice asked whereabouts you live.' She shakes her head. 'After we have taken the babe to the Hospital, it's best if we disappear.'

My heart lurches at talk of giving up my child. To strangers.

'Those men might come looking for you, Hannah. Who else could have taken those papers from Chalke's house? And you said young Twyford knows you can read and write.'

'They cannot prove it was me. Not even Jack would think me capable of penning such a letter.'

'Maybe not. But they might think you told a tale to some gentleman of your acquaintance. Like Farmer Graham. He would have been capable of writing it. Wouldn't he?'

She is right. I could well be looked for. If only we still had those guineas from Thomas, they would have paid for discreet lodgings on the other side of London. Out of harm's way.

I try the child at my breast again, silent, but desperate for us not to be parted. Desperate for there to be some way to keep her.

Chapter Sixty-Seven

'I will call her Thomasina,' I announce.

Peg's brow wrinkles. I have said nothing to her of the constant memories I have of my friend. My regret that I did not trust him with my plight. That I want my daughter's name to have at least a connection with someone good and caring. It is all I can give her.

'They will likely change it,' she says.

'Perhaps. But until then, that is what I want her to be called.'

We have argued about the child in my arms. Peg feels almost as much for her as I do, but sees danger for my tiny girl, from the Chalkes and from their powerful friends. She worries that Jack knows we live in this neighbourhood. That he will direct those men in greatcoats with the closed carriage to where I live.

On my lap my daughter's head nestles in my hand, warm as an apricot on a sunny wall. Her bunched fist clings to my finger, the nails delicate as a lady's pearl earrings, and my heart squeezes with love. She is so fragile, her skin so fine, I fear my calloused fingers might draw blood.

Although her halo of fuzzing dark hair is almost comical, her beauty overwhelms me and I am consumed by tenderness and fear. She has nobody in the world but me and I am a powerless nothing. An object of scorn.

She needs a clean room, with no fleas to bite her, and a proper fire. Warmer clothes, not patched rags and clouts. Most of all, she needs nourishment. My nipples are raw, but though my daughter tries to suck, her face grows red with frustration until Nellie pulls out a breast dripping with the milk she wails for.

This living, breathing miracle is the child I expected to abhor. The child I tried to murder. The child I must give up. But the longing to see her grow, to surround her with love, pinches my heart. I keep remembering Mary at the poorhouse, with a thumb in her mouth, saying she had never had a mother to remember.

Could I not find a way to keep my baby? Some women do, though staying with me would have her branded a bastard. But even if I found work it could not be within a household, not with a child, even if I pretended to be a widow. Servants are expected to be single, so that they can concentrate on looking after those they work for. And hiding her away would mean leaving her with someone like Nellie.

I see no way out of my sacrifice, especially as Peg insists that keeping her will make it easier for the Chalkes to find and punish us.

Whenever Peg gathers Thomasina in her scrawny arms and croons a tuneless lullaby, I see the love on her face. What was done to her meant she could never hope for children of her own. She is even more unfortunate than I am.

'The babies at the poorhouse usually died,' I say. 'We would hear the mothers shrieking in the night. The babies whimpering in the early hours of the morning. Then silence, followed by the scrape of the shovels.'

Peg offers a gnarled claw for the baby to grasp. 'The place we are taking her to is different,' she says. 'The man who built it cared.'

'Why?'

'Maybe he saw it as a Christian duty.'

I consider this. I know there are good people in this hard world. People like Mrs Lamb, Mistress Buttermere and Nellie. Then there is Thomas, who cares for his farm labourers and the beasts in his fields, and who tried to help me, even though I had rejected him. But I must not think about him and how my life might have been.

Peg knows how torn I am. 'Nobody knows where the Chalkes are, Hannah.' She rocks the baby. 'But that brother might still be around, and if he has you taken by the beaks you will never see this child again.'

'Nor will I, if I leave her at the Hospital.'

'You might. If you can build a life for yourself. They say you can go back for a child, later.'

I have nothing to give my daughter but love. Not clothes, not bedding, not a decent roof over her head. Not even mother's milk. I stare at the damp mottling the wall, the frost crazing the inside of the window, and wonder how I could ever provide a fit home for her. Yet I am this child's only hope. Otherwise she has no choice but servitude, and perhaps a fate like mine.

I consider the unthinkable. Would I whore myself to keep my

child? It is a sure way of earning money, if you are young. Yet what gift would it be to her to have such a mother?

I wish now I could persuade a kindly old man to marry me. Marriage for a woman means children, year on year, and with them the pangs and risks of birth. Followed too often by the pangs of sorrow when so many of them die. It is the way things are.

But Mrs Lamb used to jest about finding herself an elderly husband, since a widower with a family might think a woman past childbearing an advantage. He would get a mother for his brood in return for giving her security. With a white-haired gentleman possibly indifferent in health, she might not have to suffer him long.

I had scorned the thought. How different was it from slavery? Service in a good household seemed more honest. But need has made me see what tempted her: an old husband, with a limit to the time you would be tied to him. The memory of Chalke's body brings bile to my throat. I do not wish ever to be touched by another man, not even a handsome one like Jack. But I think might submit to it, for Thomasina.

I cannot help remembering that Thomas is not an old man. Nor is he vain and immoral like Jack. I have that memory of walking with him in a meadow full of grazing cows, their jaws moving rhythmically and their eyes lazy with interest. Birdsong from the great oak in the centre of the field. Sunlight on spiders' webs in the lush grass. There had been mud in his farmyard, as he had said there would be, but that proved it was not a foolish fairy tale.

I think now I could have tolerated marriage to Thomas, especially if it meant keeping my daughter, for he might not have made too many demands on my body. Perhaps I should have listened to Peg and tried to deceive him. With my bleak prospects now, perhaps I was wrong to be so stubborn.

It still seems strange to love this child so much, remembering her beginning, but I realise I would do anything for her. To make her thrive, we tried dripping gruel into her tiny mouth, prepared by our kind neighbour, but she puked up the mess and howled instead for milk. To live, she needs a wet nurse, but there is no money, and there will be a limit to Nellie's charity. I rage against the unfairness of a world where I am forced to give up my darling child. To never see her first steps. Never hear her first words. Never read a story to her. All because I am poor, and disgraced.

Chapter Sixty-Eight

''Tis time, Hannah.' Peg struggles up from the straw.

'Must I take Thomasina to that place?'

My friend strokes my face with her calloused hand. She is as close to breaking as I am. It is a cruel thing to do and I am filled with furious tears. But I have nothing for my daughter but love. My gown is a rag and my boots squelch with every step. I have no work and cannot feed my child, or myself. I must do this, though the unfairness of it tears my heart.

Part of me prays they will have no room, for I must take my chance with their lottery. We have been told the Hospital only accept babies under three months old, and not all of those, since there are never enough places. And it enrages me that in order to apply I must display my shame before idle people of fashion.

Peg and I trudge the slow mile from our lodging, shivering in the wind since both our ragged shawls are lapped around the baby. Yet these last moments with Thomasina speed past. Nothing is said as we walk, the squeak of snow underfoot, but Peg and I know I could never do this cruel thing alone. I remember the desolate woman I saw that day, with Jack, and know I must look as defeated as she did.

By the time we arrive and Peg raises the iron knocker and hammers it on the door, my eyes are sore and puffy. How can I trust this building, with curving perimeter walls that make it look like a vast prison?

Yet the maid who eventually opens the door looks ordinary enough.

'Come,' she says, as I step into an echoing corridor. Her voice is not unkind, but she makes Peg wait outside, which renders me numb and I follow where I am led as if sleepwalking.

We enter a grand room, but with the grit of sand under our feet. Someone wants to save the fine floors from dirt tracked in by the poor women standing, like me, clutching their babies.

On the walls hang huge paintings showing scenes from antiquity or the bible. Can that be Moses, among the bulrushes? A few bored-looking couples seem more interested in the pictures than what is happening to us. Two young ladies, escorted by an officer in flaring scarlet, pass a pomander back and forth, to save their delicate noses. They nudge one another as a woman in a lace fichu motions to me to put my hand into a linen bag.

Obedient, my fingers grope. The balls inside feel smooth, like the billiard balls back at the Buttermere house, but colour has neither shape nor texture. There is nothing to guide me. If I take out a white one, Thomasina can have a place. If a black one, I will be sent away. If red, I must wait to see if any of the chosen babies are rejected for being sickly. My child's future hangs on a blind choice.

My fingers reject first one, then another, and the woman shakes the bag, to hurry me. I pull my hand out, then uncurl my fingers, almost afraid to look. *White*. I should be glad, but instead I sob. That I have fallen so far, when I did nothing wrong. That not only must I accept my fate, but am expected to be grateful for this charity.

Afterwards I remember intermittent things, some clearly, others hardly at all. A woman in a pristine apron scooping Thomasina from my arms and disappearing with her.

My hands shaking. My legs leaden.

'She is taking the baby to the doctor,' the first woman explained. 'To make sure it is not diseased.'

Indignation flared, then died. Would I want Thomasina left where there was sickness?

Then I was led into yet another room, this one with carpets on the floor. At a desk sat a lady in a midnight-blue silk dress, a book open before her and a velvet pincushion by her hand. Gold spectacles were perched on the end of her nose and a thin gold band was on her finger. Her knuckles were swollen, but those hands had clearly never laboured, except perhaps with a tapestry needle. The skin was speckled like a brown hen's egg, for she was an old lady. A gentlewoman, filling the years of her widowhood with charitable works.

She looked up from under the frill of her cap, her eyes the faded blue of dried lavender.

'How old is the baby?'

'Two weeks.'

'Is she baptised?'

I shook my head. I would have liked her christened, if I had known how it might be done. 'But I have called her Thomasina.'

The lady nodded and wrote in her ledger. Reading upside down, I watched her write *Thomasina* against a column of numbers with a pen that scratched on the paper. Then she copied the number onto a separate piece of parchment. Sprinkled sand over the inky marks. Delicately blew away the residue.

'Our children are all baptised into the Church of England by a proper minister,' she said. 'In our own Chapel.' Her eyes met mine. 'When they are given a new name.'

'She will no longer be called Thomasina?' Peg had warned me, but the reality of losing my child – probably forever – without even being able to name her, was yet another injury.

The lady's voice was patient, for she must have done this countless times. 'Our rules protect the child from knowing its origins.'

I stared at the split in my boots and felt my eyes blur. My baby must be saved from knowing what a dissolute woman her mother has been. But how would I know her again, if I were ignorant of her new name?

'If I were able to come for her one day…' My voice faltered. If Thomasina had still been in my arms, I think I would have run from the building with her.

The lady's voice sounded tired as she pointed from her ledger to the parchment beside it. 'We keep a description of each child. Of what it is wearing when brought to us. Of any physical characteristics. Your daughter, for example, has that mop of dark hair. Unusual in a baby so young. Then we record the date she is accepted. And her age. All this helps identify her, should there be the need.' She looked at me, expectant. 'Have you a token?'

I stood silent. Bereft.

The lady's gaze softened. 'A button, perhaps? Or a scrap of your dress would do.' Her fingers moved to the chatelaine at her waist, with its tiny pair of scissors, and I remembered the gingham square that Peg suggested I should bring. I fumbled it from my pocket.

'A pretty pattern,' the lady said, taking it, and I saw from her eyes she did not mock. 'You will always remember that and we will keep it with our records as a pledge. Between you and the

Hospital.' Then she took a long dressmaker's pin from the cushion and secured the fabric to the parchment, before folding everything into a package.

I was grieved to relinquish the square, having treasured it all these years, but wanted to invoke my mother's spirit to protect her granddaughter's identity with that scrap from her old dress.

'This billet will be sealed with wax before you leave and your daughter given a leaden tag, with a matching number, to wear throughout her time here. Then we could track her record back, should we need to. It is a very sure method.'

I could see it had been carefully thought through. Peg was right. These people meant well.

'We will take proper care of your baby,' the woman assured me, removing her spectacles and rubbing her eyes. 'She will be raised as a God-fearing member of society. When she is ready, she will have the skills to lead a useful life.'

'But what will happen to her now, Mistress?'

'All our infants go to wet nurses in the country until they are four or five, when they return here. The nurses are honest, clean-living women, and we have inspectors who check on them.' She glanced at my hands, twisting as if wringing a cloth. 'Have you heard of Master Hogarth? The famous artist, who died last year? Some of his works are on our staircase.'

'I have seen his prints.'

'Well, he was one of our inspectors in his spare time. As was his wife, Jane.'

I felt my eyes widen, for Master Hogarth was enormously respected.

'And when she is four or five? What then?'

'She will return here to be educated. She will be taught to read, though not to write. When old enough she will go into service.'

I tremble at the thought of her being at the mercy of an unknown family. Of a master like Chalke.

The faded eyes seemed to read my mind. 'None of our girls are allowed into the households of single gentlemen. And if they are indentured to a married couple, the wife must sign her agreement to take the girl under her protection.'

That was more than I had expected.

Then the door opened. My baby was there. Was in my arms

again.

'Now you must say your goodbyes,' the lady said.

My arms clutched the precious bundle, but after kissing her, murmuring that I loved her and shedding tears into her dark hair, I allowed them to take her. That place was her best chance, in case Chalke or his brother tracked me down and did me mischief. And there was always – I had to hope it – the possibility I could rebuild my life. That one day I might reclaim her.

It is almost impossible to drag myself away knowing Thomasina is left behind. For her sake I must somehow claw my way back to respectability. Find a way to be called her mother again.

I take one backward glance at those rows of windows, like judging eyes. Does she cry for me somewhere inside? Yet I have to place my hope in the Hospital, for there is nowhere else.

Peg is slumped close to the entrance and I see her lined face is as wet as mine. I do not know how we manage to trudge back to the cellar. Once, I expected to be free when the child left my body. No longer. I will never be free of my daughter while I live.

Back in our noisome room, Peg wipes her eyes roughly with her sleeve as if to signal further grieving is something we cannot afford.

'The tapster at *The Red Lion* wants a woman for rough work', she says. 'The pay is next to nothing, of course. But get in quick tomorrow, before anyone else gets it.'

I nod, not yet steady enough for speech. Is that not the inn where Thomas goes every month? But I will go there tomorrow, early. I must look forward, not back. I must get my strength back. Look fit for a decent day's work. Try to save up for a more respectable-looking gown.

I thought I would want to forget, for I have a hard and stony road to travel, like that poor man in *The Pilgrim's Progress*. But how can I forget, when my breasts ache to nourish my child and my mind struggles to picture where she is, and the stranger who tends her, instead of me?

Chapter Sixty-Nine

Nellie brings two cabbage leaves, scavenged from the market, for my aching breasts. Now that it is too late, with bitter irony, my breasts are engorged with milk.

After Nellie has gone, I nibble their green edges, pick out the stems and crunch them between my teeth. Then I slip the remnants inside my bodice. Hunger is humbling. Given the chance, I would lick out a stranger's dish and be glad of it. You see starving people in doorways, hollow-eyed and grey as wraiths, looking like the spectres they are destined to become. I will be one of them if I cannot find a way of putting food regularly into my body. My welcome job at *The Red Lion* provides scraps of food, if not yet the opportunity to show I can cook. But I need to look healthy and strong again. To look employable in a respectable household.

My days are a haze of grieving, hunger and fatigue. Part of me wants to die in the night, for my heart has been ripped from my body. But the child I tried to destroy – that I expected to hate, as a reminder of the harm done to me – has become my world. I cannot abandon her to make her way in this uncaring city alone. I must find a way to get her back. To somehow protect and nurture her. To make a new beginning.

Yet will I even be allowed to try? Peg saw Jack in the market yesterday with two of the men who had been at the Chalke house, again wearing greatcoats that failed to conceal liveries underneath. And they were asking questions of the stallholders. I remember the expression on Jack's face when he asked if I could write as well as read. We need to move away from here. As soon as we can.

Peg and I consult Nellie, who is drawing on her pipe and blowing smoke over her collection of sleeping infants. We have brought a bag of roast chestnuts to share, an extravagance Peg bought to try and cheer me. It is past their season and they are riddled with worm, but we are indifferent. The tiny creatures will be shrivelled by the coals and might provide useful nourishment.

We cram into the evil-smelling room, glad of the warmth from the fire.

'We need some cheap lodgings, Nellie,' I say. 'Do you know of any? Somewhere discreet?'

'Behind with your rent?' Nellie sucks on her pipe and regards us, perched on the end of her bed and surrounded by the gin-quietened infants.

'Someone is looking for me.'

'The law?'

I shake my head. 'Men who wish me harm.'

'A scrap like you?' She draws on the pipe again, thinking. 'Well, I expect I can ask around.' She hooks a chestnut from the bag. 'Don't fret, Annie. I won't go around blabbing.'

Two days later, she comes to stand in the doorway of our room.

'I might have some good news,' she says.

'Have you found us somewhere?' I have been skulking in our room, afraid to go out. Afraid someone might come and drag me away. To the river, maybe.

'I did find a place, but there may be no need.' She frowns at our cubicle, and its lack of comfort. 'A young cove was sniffing around yesterday when Doggett was out thieving more brandy. The man asked if anyone knew of a pretty girl hereabouts with curling black hair. Ripe to drop a child.'

'Did the feller say what he wanted?' Peg is avoiding my eye.

'Some tale about a long-lost relative. Not that I believed a word. Stared at me like I was made of dirt, he did. With eyes blue as poison bottles.' Nellie steps inside and positions herself against the warm wall. 'I didn't fancy the look of him. And cannot abide nosy parkers, anyway. So I told him there had been such a girl, in one of the basement rooms, but she had died. And her child with her.'

My heart races. It must have been Jack. He knows I live around here. 'Do you think he believed you?'

'Why wouldn't he? I have had enough practice needing to lie to men.' Nellie frowns disapprovingly at our window, open despite the bitter cold. 'So I demanded half a crown. To pay for laying out your corpse and cleaning your room.' She pulls her shawl closer around her shoulders. It is shabby, but of wool. 'I told him the blood on the bedding and on the floor had been terrible. That the job needed to be done quick, because you was starting to stink. That a man had to be paid extra to take you away on a handcart, as the other tenants was complaining.' She grins. 'It worked, for he cleared off, looking green. I don't expect he will be coming back.' She frowns at the open window again. 'He didn't leave no money, though. Mean bugger.'

Suddenly I find I can breathe again and Peg lets out her own sigh of relief. Jack came to find me and will instead have reported my death to anyone interested.

We should be safe now and will not need to move. At least here we have Nellie's friendship and grubby generosity.

But I wish I knew where the Chalkes are and if Sir Christopher did more than send a few constables round to be bookshop to curtail Twyford's activities.

'Does that mean you are staying?' Nellie asks.

'I think it does. But if anyone else asks,' I lick dry lips. 'Anyone at all. Please tell them the same. That I am dead and buried.'

Peg nods vigorously. 'You did right, Nellie. There are people who would do us mischief, given the chance. That tale of yours should send them away for good.'

It is a relief to think they will have stopped searching for me and I am hidden in our room, bending sore fingers to another pile of bonnet straw, when Nellie comes tapping on the door again. She has brought the treat of a bowl of stewed tea with her.

'You know what you said? That if anyone else asked after you, I should say you was dead?'

'Yes, Nellie. I must stay out of sight. For several months at least.'

I sip the tea, savouring it in my mouth. Not caring that it is bitter and stewed. Soon I might be strong enough to do a full day's work. To start saving up to go to that rag man and pick out a more respectable-looking gown. To work my way back towards being employed in some good wife's home.

'I ask because I was not so sure about the other one that come,' says Nellie. 'I rather fancied the look of him.'

My mouth is suddenly dry. 'What other one?'

'Another fine-looking feller. You sure can pick them. Though this one was a proper gent. Shook my hand and gave me his name, all proper like, together with a whole shilling. Master Graham he said. You know him?'

I stare at the tangle of damp straw in my lap. 'And you told him I had died?'

'I did. Though this one looked grieved. He even asked where they had taken your body.' Nellie looks at me and frowns. 'I should not have done that. Should I?'

'No, you did right.' I compose my face. 'Anyone who comes asking must think me underground.'

I finish the bowl of tea, down to its sour dregs, careful to avoid Nellie's perceptive eye. Thinking that if Thomas was not lost to me before, he certainly will be now.

Chapter Seventy

When I recognise the well-groomed bay outside *The Red Lion* my heart lurches. Forgotten is the whole afternoon's scrubbing promised by the tapsters. My instinct is to scurry away. If Calypso is in the street, Thomas will be nearby. Yet I find I yearn for a glimpse of him. I could surely manage that, since, from a distance, he is unlikely to recognise me as the girl he once knew. And, anyway, he thinks me long dead.

I knew this might happen from the moment they allowed me to scour their floors for a pittance and am forced to admit to myself that I hoped for more than a wage from coming here.

I duck into the doorway of a mantua makers. If I hide here, Thomas should appear soon. He may think me dead, but I need to know he is well: it gnaws at me that Chalke's family might somehow have discovered him responsible for that beating.

Winter still lingers. Even in this shelter, the wind wraps my skirts around my legs and cuts at my ankles. My boots have holes in them and with my hose beyond repair I might as well be barefoot. It is only when you are in danger of having no stockings you realise the difference they make. How can I look employable in any respectable household when my gums bleed and my breasts leak sour milk into my bodice? And I need sleep, not just for rest, but to escape yearning for Thomasina. Somewhere outside the city she feeds at another breast. Perhaps among green fields like those surrounding Thomas's farm.

Angry knuckles rap at the window glass and a scowling woman mouths at me to move on. She does not want her customers repelled by a bundle of rags on her doorstep. I creep back into the street, close to the wall, feeling weak as a spider's thread. Then I give myself a shake and remind myself that although a spider's thread is slight, it has strength. There is still no sign of Thomas. I know I should hurry round the back of the inn, but ache to stroke Calypso one final time.

The mare is harnessed to Thomas's trap rather than to the milk cart since, of course, he has given up the round. Presumably he is here about the regular business in town that he mentioned in his letter.

I cannot resist approaching the horse for a brief, comforting contact. A reminder of the life I might have had.

She is chomping towards the bottom of a hessian nosebag while a scruffy boy sits on a nearby wall, legs dangling. He is devouring a bun I suspect has been earned in return for watching the trap. I imagine its taste: doughy and most likely made from flour spoiled with sawdust and alum, but satisfying.

I approach, gaining only an indifferent look from the boy since he will hardly think me a horse thief. The money Peg and I earn does little more than keep us alive and my stomach is hollow as a gutted fish, so the smell of oats makes it rumble. Might I sneak a handful? The well-fed Calypso, standing on three legs to rest a rear hoof, would not miss it. Crumbled with water, it would make a meal. The boy is concentrating on his food and my fingers twitch with temptation.

I warm my chapped hands on the horse's flank, breathing in her familiar scent and remembering morning talks with her master. The big soft eyes of the mare blink at me, benevolent.

'How is your lovely foal?' I murmur into her swivelling ear. 'Does she wait in your field? Or was she sold at a local horse fair?' I am saddened that she, too, has no power over what happens to her baby.

Calypso shifts on the cobbles, long eyelashes blinking, her noisy munching reminding me of my need to get strong again. With a soothing reassurance, I slip my hand into the bag, but suddenly the boy is off the wall. Shouting.

'Hey! Stop that thieving!'

As he scrambles towards me, fists bunching with puny menace, I suddenly see a broad-shouldered figure approaching and pull my sackcloth shawl over my head. I am too feeble to do more than scuttle back to the mantua makers. If I can avoid the shopkeeper's notice, Thomas will probably climb into the trap and be gone in minutes. But a brindle-coloured dog bounds up to me and starts nosing at my skirts, tail thrashing. Before I can stop myself, I stoop to tousle his ears.

'*Hannah*?' Thomas's raised voice makes people stare as he hurries across the street. Standing before me in a brown velvet jacket, cord breeches and a white shirt, he is so clean that I cringe.

Close up, there is a faint air of horses, soap and good health and I edge into the doorway, burning with shame for my own sorry state.

'Dear God.' Rooted to the spot, he clearly thinks he has seen a ghost. Then he moves closer and removes his hat as if I were a lady, instead of a filthy beggar. 'Hannah? Is it really you?' There is the familiar sprig of rosemary in his buttonhole and I catch a hint of its sharp fragrance. 'I was told you were dead.' He twists the hat in his hands and I remember the last time he stood before me like this. There is a catch in his voice. 'I had been searching for so long. And then to be told you had died…'

We are silent in the bustle of the street, the stolen oats turning to dust in my hand. Thomas keeps twisting the hat, staring at the dirty scrap of hessian sacking that serves me for a shawl. The wreck of what I used to be. Then, 'Come across the road,' he says. 'Sit with me in the trap.'

I have not proper command of my limbs and fear I might collapse, but manage to reach the trap and slump against its wheel. In spite of the cold, my skin feels clammy. Peg and I shared some soup with Nellie last night and I think it was spoiled, for my stomach has been roiling ever since.

'You are not well. Let me help you onto the seat.'

Then my knees give way and I expect to crumple on the cobbles, but am instead gathered up and lifted, the fabric of Thomas's coat soft against my cheek. Mortified to be this close to his nose and eyes, I struggle.

'Don't fight me.' He places me carefully on the seat and feels my hands. 'You are frozen. Here,' he shrugs off his coat and puts it around my shoulders. 'This should warm you.'

I slump against the backrest, revived by the warmth in the garment. The way it smells of him. 'You have business here.' I say. 'I mustn't keep you.'

'You are my business now, Hannah. Thank God I have found you. I was in despair when I thought you had died. Friendless and in trouble.'

I shiver and he wraps the coat more closely around me, thinking it the cold that makes me tremble. But the temptation to let him take charge of me is overpowering.

'Are you strong enough for a short journey? We could be home in under an hour.' Those dark eyes study me. 'You are skin and bone. You need proper sustenance.'

He reaches under the seat, produces a stone bottle, and beckons to the boy by the wall who is watching us, big-eyed. He counts out copper coins. 'Take this into the inn and bring it back full of hot tea, with sugar. I will give you a good tip, but only if you are quick.'

Not many minutes later I am sipping the most delicious drink I have ever tasted.

'Forgive me,' Thomas says, hesitant. 'But I found out about your trouble.' His brow puckers. 'For Chalke to force himself on an innocent girl! Under his protection.'

This is a shameful subject and I have no words. But at least I know he did not think me a wanton.

'Tell me, Hannah?' His voice is gentle again. 'What happened to your baby?'

'She is gone,' I whisper.

His hand moves to rest on my shoulder. 'That is the cruellest thing. To lose a child.'

I realise he thinks my baby died.

'She is alive. But I had to leave her at the Foundling Hospital.'

His eyes are on my rags, the thinness of my shoulders, my dirt. I know how I look.

'You lost your place because of the child? And then could not afford to keep her?'

'They send them to the country, until they are weaned,' I say. 'Then bring them back, to learn a useful trade.' I wipe at my eyes. 'If they survive.'

'I have heard of the place. At least somebody tries to help the unfortunate.' His eyes flick to the street, but nobody is taking the least notice of us. Even the boy has disappeared, to spend his tip. 'When you disappeared, I feared you had vanished for ever. Then to be told you had died. London is such a vast, uncaring place. Sometimes I think I hate it.'

This is all too much for me. The coat, the tea, having someone care. I sway in the seat.

'You are safe now.' His brow puckers. 'But why on earth wouldn't Peg say where you were? I could have helped you. Did you not get my letter?'

'I made Peg promise not to tell anyone.' I hesitate. 'It was wonderfully kind of you to send so much money. But it was stolen… and I was afraid of what you would think.'

'You imagined I would blame you? When it was not your fault?'

I see from the downturn of his mouth the thought disturbs him.

'Most men would,' I say.

'Am I just another man, Hannah?' He sighs. 'In any event, I need to get you to Broad Oak, and well again.'

'How can I go to the farm?' I have finished the tea, but am grateful for the warmth of the bottle still clutched in my hands.

'I ask nothing but to be your friend, Hannah. And Peg's.' He smiles, though there is no gladness in his eyes. 'So, you must agree, if only for your poor friend's sake.'

It would not be right to go back to the farm with him, but could I bring myself to beg a few shillings? As a churchwarden, he will put a generous amount in the collection plate each Sunday. But I have already had two of his guineas and have lost them. Thomas is a kind and Christian man, but can no longer be a friend. Too much has changed. The girl that I was has been done away with.

Yet pride is for people with full bellies. If I do not let him help, how will I ever get my daughter back? I realise I must do it, not just for Peg, but for Thomasina.

Hector scrambles up into the trap and squeezes in beside me, leaning his bulk against my leg and resting a bony head on my knee. I fondle one of his ears, touched that he remembers me.

'I do not have milk today,' Thomas says, offering me a bundle in a napkin, 'but I have cheese and apples.'

I try not to snatch at the food Betty will have prepared for his journey and Thomas turns away, refusing to watch me hunch over it like a miser.

I devour the cheese, coveting the wrinkled pippins in the napkin as some women would gold bracelets. Even if I do not eat again today this food will give me strength to scrub those floors and perhaps get the promise of regular work. Unless, of course, I go back with Thomas to the farm.

'Are you still lodging in that dreadful place?'

I nod.

'Do you have things there? Or could we collect Peg and simply leave.'

I think of our possessions. Worthless, but including my precious book.

'There are a few belongings.'

'Then we will get them and then find Peg. She can help Betty at the farm. My housekeeper could use another pair of hands. There is nothing to keep us in the city.'

I finger the pennies in my pocket, all I have, and feel the humiliation of needing to beg. 'We owe the landlord.'

'Then I will settle what you owe while Hector stays with you in the trap. He will not let anyone trouble you.'

I hug the coat around me. The prospect of going somewhere safe, out of London, where I will not risk running into Jack, who believes me safely dead, is something I can no longer refuse.

Chapter Seventy-One

Only the rumble and lurch of the trap's wheels on the road keep me from losing consciousness as Calypso trots to our lodging. My directions were muddled, but Thomas has finally found the place.

'Our room is on the lower floor. Under the staircase.' I think of the stinking bucket in the corner. 'But I ought to…'

'You are staying here. With Hector.' He secures the reins and I see from his compressed lips he will not give way on this. 'Just tell me how much you owe.'

I sense eyes watching from the windows as I hand over the key on its greasy string and Thomas shoulders his way through the door. Shortly afterwards there are raised voices. Then a long pause. A slamming door. Thomas strides out, his eyes flaring with temper and the old rush basket clutched under his arm. He thrusts it under my seat.

'That rogue is lucky not to have a bloody nose.' He climbs back beside me. 'Now. Where can I find Peg?'

'She is washing pots at *The King's Head*. Opposite the old tannery. But if she leaves before finishing her work, she will lose her place.'

'Let her lose it. You are both coming to Broad Oak.'

My mouth opens in protest, but no sound comes. I am getting that awful feeling again. That I will swoon.

'Betty has had a room ready for you in her cottage for months. It is still there. She still had hope, though I had none.' Thomas twitches the reins and studies me. 'Though I think Peg must wait. You are deathly pale. I hope you can manage the journey.'

'I am sure I can.' If I keep talking, it might fend off the faintness. 'Did you lose your whip?' He is using one with a stitched leather top. No sign of the silver fox.

'I broke it.' He glances up from the road. 'On a rat's back.'

I look at his face. See the barely repressed anger.

'So it was you? Who attacked Chalke?'

'When I discovered what he had done, I forgot that I am a generally peaceable man. I considered killing him, but decided he was not worth hanging for and threw him in the gutter instead.

251

Where he belonged.'

'If you had been caught…'

It would have meant ruin. Prison, or worse. Thomas is not powerful enough to attack a member of the aristocracy, even a disgraced one, and escape justice.

'I was safe enough. The London streets are dark and few would interfere with a beating. Most men are cowards at heart.'

The harness jingles. The clip-clop of iron-shod hooves echoes off the stones of the road. Yet the street noises seem curiously distant.

'It grieves me to think of you in that pigsty,' he says. 'It is a miracle you survived.'

'I have no skill in farm labour,' I manage to say, 'but I can learn. I owe you two guineas.'

'You owe me nothing.'

'Betty has her own family to think of. And we cannot pay her.'

'Her husband oversees my cows, Hannah. And the cottage is mine. There will be nothing to pay. Besides which, she worried about you almost as much as I did. She will be overjoyed to see you.'

Wrapped in Thomas's coat, I am cold and then hot, by turns. There is a queasy lurch in my belly from more food than I am used to. A need to take shallow breaths.

He leans across and touches my forehead.

'You are feverish.'

The world is swimming again. 'I am going to be sick...'

He reins in the horse and I lean over the side of the trap to spew half-digested apples and cheese down his wheel into the gutter. I am beyond even feeling humiliated.

Thomas presses a soft handkerchief into my hand, then produces a silver flask. 'Take a sip of this. Not too much. It is brandy.'

I have never had brandy before. It tastes like liquid fire and makes me cough. I am desperate to lie flat somewhere, before I collapse.

'I need to get you home.' He pulls me gently towards him. 'Put your arm around my waist and lean against me. Do not worry, Hannah. I will not let you fall.'

I must have properly fainted, for I open my eyes as the trap jolts over a rut and draws up in Thomas's yard. Calypso lets out a great snort at being home and young Tommy runs from the stables to catch her reins from his master.

'Give her a rub down and some water. Then run to the lower field for your father. I might want him to go to the village for the doctor.' Thomas gathers me up like an armful of twigs and strides towards the open door of Betty's cottage. 'Let's get you inside.'

In a bustle the housekeeper appears in the entrance, drying her hands on a cloth.

'She is alive! God be praised.' She stares at me, her round face creased with anxiety. 'Whatever happened to the poor child?'

'It is a long story. Can I take her straight up?' Clutched against his broad chest, I sense his impatience.

'The room is still ready, Master. With a fire laid in the hearth.'

In moments we are through Betty's kitchen and up narrow, winding stairs into a low-ceilinged bedroom. There is a strong, clean smell, as if someone has recently polished the furniture with linseed oil. Thomas sets me in a chair by the fireplace and pulls out a flint while Betty turns down the patchwork quilt on the bed.

'Send for the doctor if you think it necessary,' he says. 'And fetch one of my mother's old night shifts from the house, while I light this fire.' He looks up from the task to smile at me. 'She was about your size.'

Flames crackle and a needle of warmth reaches me as the housekeeper hurries out. I glance at the bed. A proper bed, with pillows, and the luxury of a willow-patterned chamber pot peeping from underneath.

Thomas gets awkwardly to his feet. 'As soon as Betty returns, I will leave you in her care and go for Peg.'

I stare down my vomit-stained dress to my boots and think of the red-raw feet inside. The oozing blisters. The tattered remnants of stockings that stink. I cannot stop myself crying that every inch of me is shameful.

Thomas has gone to stand in the open doorway, and I am glad for I will not smell so bad from there. 'You have been terribly wronged, Hannah,' he says. 'I cannot undo that. But I intend to show you not all men are evil.'

'May I have a bowl of water? Soap?'

'Betty will see to everything.' He spreads his hands. 'We might get Dr Hodges to come and look at you. He is a good man and discreet.' He nods towards a truckle bed pushed against the far wall. 'That is for Peg. We thought you would like to be together.'

If I can hold up a little longer, I will be able to wash and then crawl into that bed. I yearn to collapse into its comfort. To close my eyes and lose myself in oblivion. For at last I am faint, not with hunger, but with hope.

Then Betty is back, pink-faced with haste, a white cambric garment over one arm and a jug of steaming water in her other hand.

Thomas nods approval. 'I will go and collect Peg now.' He pauses at the door, his voice a murmur I am not meant to hear. 'I suspect the weakness is lack of care after her confinement. And hunger, no doubt. Like a fool, I gave her some sour apples. Try her instead with a little bread and milk.'

The chair by the fire is comfortable and the temptation to sleep so powerful that I do not even care about his final low-voiced instruction as he turns to leave.

'And burn every stitch she's wearing.'

Whereupon he is gone and Betty is gently helping me out of my rags.

Chapter Seventy-Two

This has been no fantasy of my mind, for I wake in the feather bed wearing the soft cambric nightdress. Much too big for me, it bunches around my hips and smells of lavender and being blown on a line in the fresh air. A downy pillow is under my cheek, its cover edged with lace. Everything is a heaven of cleanliness.

I have never slept on a feather mattress before. You sink into its softness and it moulds itself around you like swansdown.

Then I think I must be dreaming again, for Thomasina is wailing in the next room. It is a lusty cry. Stronger than any I remember her making.

My feeble attempts to climb out of bed wake Peg, in the truckle bed next to me, and she is immediately at my side.

'Shhh… Go back to sleep, Hannah. It is not yet dawn.'

'Thomasina. She is crying.'

'No, no. It is only Betty's boy in the next room. Teething. Go back to sleep.'

I fall back against the plumped-up bolsters and struggle to clear my head. Betty's child? Then I turn my head into the pillow, eyes damp. We are in Betty's cottage. Thomasina is far away. Gone from me. Probably for ever.

I remember now, before I slept, having bread and milk with grated sugar and nutmeg sprinkled on its surface. Betty saying Thomas had gone to fetch Peg, while my spoon circled the bottom of the dish as if I were chasing the last speck of dust from a floor. After that had come long and blessed sleep.

Since then I have dozed on and off for days, waking only to have chicken broth or sips of watered-down canary wine. Peg will have been there that first night, but I was not aware of her until the next morning, when she stood at my bedside, a faded dimity gown secured around her with pins. Something that I suspect must once have been Betty's.

'Find me a needle and thread,' I said. 'I will soon make that fit. It will give me something to do.'

I am still weak, but feel like a wilted plant that has at last had water.

I remember hearing Thomas's voice on the landing outside from time to time, instructing Betty: 'She needs oatmeal gruel, with fresh milk. New laid eggs, coddled with best butter. Perhaps one of your custards.'

'Never fear, Master. She is young. We will get her well again.'

'And cut down some of my mother's old gowns, for when she is ready to get up.'

He never came in to see me, but I can guess who picked the primroses in that china jug on the windowsill by my bed. Who placed my *Aesop's Fables* there, together with *Robinson Crusoe* and a slender book of poetry.

Peg's gown is altered now and two morning dresses, finer than anything I have ever owned and that I have been sitting up in bed stitching to fit myself, lie waiting across a chair.

Nothing is too much trouble and it makes my eyes well-up that people have such kindness for a ruined girl. When I am strong enough, perhaps I should slip away early one morning and take my shameful presence back to London to seek honest work. I should be strong enough for that now.

'What else can I fetch you, Miss?' Betty never seems to resent the work I make for her. Nor the interest her master takes in a penniless rag of a girl.

'I would like a proper wash,' I say, fingering my lank hair. I have already had a basin and a cloth, with soap that smells of lemons, but want to sluice hot water over my head and body. To be certain no fleas or lice remain to infest this good woman's home.

'She wants a tub,' Peg grunts from the chair in the corner, where I had thought her asleep. 'Cannot abide not being clean as a parson's shirt on a Sunday.' She lifts a currant bun from the plate beside her and begins gnawing at it with reverence.

'That is no problem, for we have a proper tub,' says Betty. 'While you were missing, the master busied himself shifting the midden, to occupy his mind. He often used the tub, to clean the muck off. I will have Jed bring it up.'

A whole tub of water would be unimaginable luxury.

There is a big fire in the grate of the bedroom an hour later, as Betty bustles around me, filling the tub and helping me into the wonderfully soothing water. A folded towel is beneath me to cushion my still-protruding bones. She rinses my long hair from a jug until it squeaks between her fingers and I turn my mind from the unsettling thought of Thomas sitting where I am now, naked.

Afterwards I make my way downstairs in one of my new gowns, and wrapped in a faded paisley shawl, sit drying my hair before the kitchen inglenook. I am still shaky on my legs, despite eating four times a day and drinking from the jug of milk always at my bedside, a weighted net protecting it from flies. Then a draught tells me the door into the yard has opened and I turn to see Thomas.

'Am I disturbing you, ladies?'

'No, Master,' says Betty. 'But close that door before the child catches her death.' She is behind me with a brush, working tangles from my hair, and after doing as he is bid, Thomas comes to stare at it, curling almost to my waist.

There was talk of cutting it, when I first arrived, but I am glad Betty held her hand. He has never seen me without my cap. Then he looks into my face and his feelings are plain to see. Since having my daughter, I know what love looks like and it pains me, for to care that much for a fallen woman makes him almost as unfortunate as I am.

Most mornings now I get dressed and make my way to Betty's kitchen, where I address myself to the boys' shirts in her mending basket. It is a comfortable place to be, though it still grieves me to look at her plump-cheeked son, crawling around the floor under the watch of Peg, who has already made herself his nursemaid. But I can never take his wriggling warmth into my own arms without wanting to weep.

Chapter Seventy-Three

The birds wake me, early, and I ease myself from bed to tiptoe to the window on legs still stupidly weak. Peg is a lump under her bedclothes. A mist lies over the fields outside and dawn is breaking. Quietly I unfasten the latch on the leaded window and breathe in the clean, cool air.

At the edge of the nearest field, a figure in shirtsleeves leans on the split rail fence gazing into the distance. Thomas. The dog is at his side, tail enthusiastic for the morning.

I dress swiftly and slip out through the darkened kitchen to join him, Hector bounding up to nose at my legs.

'It promises to be a fine day,' Thomas says, looking me over. 'You have colour in your cheeks at last. Might you be strong enough for a walk, later? We could go down to the far paddock to see Aurora.'

'I would love that,' I say. 'Now my belly is reacquainted with food, my legs need to remember what they are for.' I look around for a stick to throw for Hector. 'It is shaming to starve. To be prepared to do anything to put a crust in your mouth.'

'It is only shaming to those responsible.'

'There are always people in want, Thomas. It is how things are.'

'There are men who dream of making a just world.' He shakes his head. 'I wish them joy, but would never wager on it happening soon. One must not hope for the impossible. All one can do is help those within one's reach.'

At last I find something to throw and Hector is not too proud to chase after a fragment of tree root.

Thomas gazes into the brightening distance. 'I feared you might be gone from me for ever,' he says. 'London is such a vast place.'

'But were you not disgusted, when you saw me in the street? I was rank.'

'You will always be a summer meadow to me, Hannah.'

Hector is back, pawing at my ankle, and I retrieve the root from his jaws to toss again.

'I have not thanked you properly for all you have done. For me, and for Peg. I am well enough to work now. Find something for

258

me to do.'

'There is time enough for that.'

'You have put a roof over our heads. You are feeding and clothing us. I prefer not to be an object of charity.'

'That is nonsense.' Thomas grunts at Hector to stop bothering me with the root. 'What I have given you is an advance of wages, no more. In a week or two, you can start getting involved with our cheese-making. Take on some more girls. Working here will likely save them going into service.' He gives Hector a rough pat for sitting obediently at his side.

'And you could start teaching the village children to read. What I have been doing for Betty's boys is not enough. There is space in one of my old barns for a little school.' His smile is insistent. 'You would be good at being both a teacher and a cheese maker. But you and your daughter need more than just a wage coming in, Hannah. You need a proper home. I can provide that. A farm is not a bad place to raise a child.'

'What are you saying?'

'That you should come and live with me. Both of you.'

I blink. 'You are a churchwarden. Your brother is a vicar. Having a bastard and her mother under your roof would shame not only you, but him.'

'Not if I give them both my name.' He glances at me. 'What did you call your daughter? You never said.'

I hesitate a moment. 'Thomasina.'

His arm comes around my shoulder to give it a brief squeeze, before releasing me.

'Though she will not be called that now. They give them new names. It is as if my baby ceased to exist.'

'But, Hannah,' he takes half a step closer. 'We could easily make her Thomasina again.'

My breath catches in my throat and I swallow hard. For an intelligent man, he is making no sense.

'Come,' Thomas says. 'Let us walk over to the yard. Wish Aphrodite a good morning.'

'I know you mean me a great kindness,' I say, as we reach the sty and I lean over the rail to scratch the sow's rough back. 'But you could not hide the truth. You would make yourself food for gossip.'

'I am suggesting we marry, Hannah.'

It was what I knew he meant, for he has asked me before. But I have no reply. Too much has happened since then.

'Hector had a grand morning yesterday.' Thomas smiles at the dog who is staring at us with a fixed expression, as if he understands everything that is being said. 'Ratting in the great barn. Look at him. He wants you to stay. He knows you belong.'

'A wife with a bastard would shame you, Thomas. Before your neighbours. Your relations, and friends.'

'They will think she is mine, Hannah. Country people are not so precious about such things. Many brides walk up the aisle close to their time, and nothing is thought of it, twelve months after.'

'But she isn't yours, Thomas.'

'As I have said, the world will assume that we were dilatory about formalising our union. It happens. You and your daughter are innocent in the face of God. And to me. So, who needs to know the truth? My house is lacking a daughter. In time she might even have brothers and sisters, God willing.'

I flinch at his words. At the picture it raises in my mind. Yet he is right. My child and I are innocent of any wrongdoing.

His strong hands rest on the edge of the sty, tanned from the outdoors. 'Do I need to say it, Hannah? Surely you know I love you.'

I cannot speak, for there is an ache in my chest for what might have been. I could not bear to be in his, or any man's bed, but could picture myself willingly sharing everything else with Thomas.

He lets out a deep sigh. 'Well, then, be my cheese-maker and schoolmistress. You could make a good life here. I will find you a snug cottage, if you will not make your home with me. After perhaps a year, the Hospital should think you able to provide a fit home for your child. I can make sure you have the character references they will require.'

'I am sorry, Thomas.'

'So am I.' He glances sideways at me, the gleam of humour in his eye suggesting he is not offended. Saddened, perhaps. But he is used to disappointment from me. 'Would I have done better in a more romantic setting? Proposed in a meadow bright with celandines? Rather than beside a pigsty?'

'I would prefer,' I say, facing him, 'to make my own way. I am a good cook, now. You should try my raised pork pies.'

'Don't mention such things in Aphrodite's hearing.' He reaches into the pen and gently tugs the sow's ear.

'You must know in your heart you should not tie yourself to someone like me.'

'If you could see into my heart, Hannah, you would not deny me.' He stoops to rescue a turnip that has rolled under the gate, tossing it back to the pig. 'I still think that to be sure of getting your daughter back as soon as possible, you need a husband.'

He is stubborn. But so am I, and even if the thought of marriage did not revolt me, I cannot let him ruin his life because of me.

'No, Thomas.'

'Let me speak.' He studies his hands and the sprinkling of dark hair on his wrists sends a tremor through me. 'I loved Liza, but it did not consume me the way my feelings for you do. I want a different marriage. One where the two of us share our work; our books, our thoughts. As if we were one person.'

I think now that I will cry, for what woman would even dream of such an offer, never mind refuse it? To hide my face, I bend over the sow as she noisily demolishes her turnip.

I remember Mrs Lamb joking about finding a rich old man to marry. *How hard would it be to keep someone's cold feet warm for a few years?* she'd said. *Then why not do it,* I'd asked. *Because, my girl, it takes a strong stomach to take on a gouty wreck. With an old man's noises and an old man's smells.*

And Mrs Lamb, as a virgin of over forty years, knew nothing of the assaults and degradation of the marriage bed.

But Thomas is not, of course, old. He has a fine figure and an intelligent face. He is a landowner and could have a lady for his wife if he chose, so what he proposes is not only abhorrent to me, but imprudent and nonsensical.

'Come. I will not rush you. With your history, it is not surprising you need time.' He offers his arm and we make our way towards the house, the dog at our heels. 'Let us see if Betty has some breakfast for us.'

Chapter Seventy-Four

I have always tried not to covet what others have. In the Buttermere house I enjoyed being surrounded by wonderful things and having the care of them. But this modest parlour, with its feeling of having been lived in by generations of decent honest yeomen, this I envy.

'It is unusual to so dislike the idea of marriage.' Thomas is studying my face as the salty tang of bacon drifts through the open door from the kitchen and the dog sprawls at our feet. 'Though in Catholic countries young women take the veil, as a vocation. Seeing themselves as brides of Christ.'

'I feel no vocation,' I say. 'How can I believe in a heavenly father, when he failed to care for me?'

'I can understand that, Hannah. After my family died, I stopped going to church.'

'You do not believe?'

'My belief dropped down a deep well. Though I expect to haul it back up again, one day.'

I nod. His feelings are not unlike my own.

'I know an evil thing was done to you, Hannah. But I hope you can learn to put it behind you.'

'I have never told you…what happened.'

'I know enough. Do not distress yourself by speaking of it.'

'But I cannot bear to think…of what men want from women.'

I am unable to meet his eye, and stare instead at a patch of mottled sunlight on the floor.

There is a pause and I wonder if he is digesting what a bad bargain he would be getting.

'That is no surprise,' he says, quietly. 'There are horses who have been so cruelly treated, they never learn to trust.' He pulls out a chair so I can sit, my hands in my lap, my eyes still avoiding his. 'But we could live as brother and sister. I have been alone so long that even a sister-wife would be a joy. We could have separate bedrooms, as the aristocracy do. The rest of the world will think us a regular married couple. The parents of a child.' He smiles. 'I would love a daughter. Especially one who might look like you.'

The idea of living with him is unsettling, even as a sister-wife, and the thought makes my stomach quiver. But how could I accept such a sacrifice, after all he has done for me? It would mean him never having a proper wife.

'As I have said, I am accustomed to living alone.' He shrugs, as if it does not matter, though it surely must. 'Continuing will be no punishment. But to have a companion, especially if that companion were you, would be the greatest blessing.'

If there is one person I could trust, it is this loving, generous man. But that makes it an impossible gift. What if he meets someone in years to come, a woman without a past, that he wants to make his wife? Someone who could give him sons?

'That is not sensible.'

'We could be married quietly, in our parish church,' he says, as if I have not spoken. 'It would only require the banns to be read.'

'It would not be fair to you.'

'Hannah, it would be more than I dared hope for.'

He stands in front of me, still in his boots, and the housemaid in me notices the mud tracked across Betty's clean floor. 'I am being selfish,' he says. 'For you could help me plan what to do with the farm. As well as bring a smile into my life again.'

I sense he is holding his breath and my own comes more rapidly in my chest. It is hard not to accept such generosity, yet I am spoiled goods and will always carry the shame – though I know in my heart I am still an innocent girl. Can I bring disgrace to a man who has done so much for me? What return would that be?

Through the window, I see wisps of cloud in the sky. Whipped egg white in a shining blue bowl.

'The Foundling Hospital would raise no concerns about releasing Thomasina to a respectable married couple,' he says. 'With a prosperous farm.'

I acknowledge to myself that he is right about the world believing he had fathered my daughter and was doing the decent thing by me. Such things are not uncommon. And gossip would fade when fresher scandals chased talk into dusty rumour.

It is too hard to go on without my baby. She is in my thoughts every waking hour. Where has she been sent? Might she be hungry? Cold? Unloved, certainly, for she cannot have her mother. And when I think this, I find my cheeks are wet. For Thomasina to have a future, I must accept this strange proposal and try to repay Thomas with hard work and loyalty.

Sometimes I even think it might be good to be held in his strong arms. Perhaps I could even bear the other thing, if it did not happen often. I have no knowledge of whether men exert their rights only on occasion, or every night.

'I like you better in your old work coat,' I say, reaching up to touch the velvet on his lapels with a finger, delaying an answer. The clothes are not new. He looks to have worn them often, perhaps to Sunday church, but they are not a working man's garments. 'When you dress like this, I see you are a proper gentleman. How could I be in your life, except as a servant?'

The look in his eyes does not change. 'If your family had not been persecuted and fled to England, you would have had servants of your own, wouldn't you?' He takes my fingers gently in his. 'Without you, Hannah, I have only my workers and animals to care about. When you seemed lost, the thought of you being in the squalor of the back streets haunted me. In want. At risk of harm.' His face creases. 'Not all men are beasts.'

'How could I not know it? After everything you have done?'

'Then I will ask you to marry me again. When I am wearing my oldest coat.' His smile broadens, I think to show he is not offended at being rebuffed.

'I like all your coats, Thomas.'

'But say you will consider my proposal.'

'I will. I promise.'

Hector gets up to stand beside us, his tail thrashing, as if approving our bargain. As if urging me to accept.

Chapter Seventy-Five

Late that afternoon we walk through the orchard together to the lower paddock, Thomas switching idly at the grass with his crop. It is easier to confide in him when we are not sitting across a table from one another. If we are to wed, he needs to know there could be danger in allying himself with me.

'I was taught that good overcame evil,' I say. 'I was sure when people knew what Chalke was doing, they would be outraged. That he would be stopped.'

Over in the great field, the cows – aware it is milking time – approach the gate like overweight dowagers drawn to the supper table. Peaseblossom, leads the way.

'Men have always wronged women.' Thomas slows his pace, my legs being shorter than his. 'I doubt it could be stopped. But proper punishment should be meted out. If you had confided in me, I would have set the magistrates on Chalke for what he did.'

'There was worse than what happened to me.'

'Tell me.'

I study the cows in their leisurely progress. 'I sensed there was something wrong in that house. From my first day.'

We pause at the hawthorn hedge bordering the lane.

'And I was not the first maid dishonoured. But there were worse things.' The hem of my skirt is dark with moisture from the lush grass. 'They had a locked room. One night I stole the key and looked inside.' I shiver at the memory. 'There were lewd books, with drawings. Receipts for vast sums of money. With girls' names on.'

Thomas looks uncomfortable. These are not proper subjects of conversation for a man and woman who are not related. 'London offers many temptations, I am afraid,' he says. 'It is well known.'

'I am not troubled about whores.' I surprise myself by my easy use of the word, but I am no longer an ignorant child. 'This was something I would never have believed.'

'Go on.' He gazes across the lane at the church tower, visible through the trees. I must ask him to show me the graves of his family. I would like to take them some primroses.

'Peg found an account book belonging to Mistress Chalke. The entries troubled me.' I close my eyes, but it fails to shut out the memory. 'The locked room revealed their meaning. That rich men came to the house for auctions. He was selling little girls. As young as six years of age.'

It is a relief to have it said. I steal a glance at my companion, not sure if he will have believed me, but see from the bleak look in his eyes that he does.

'Why did you not you come straight to me?'

'How could I?' I rip a nettle from the hedgerow, but drop it when I am stung. 'It was not long after he came to my room. I mistrusted all men.'

Thomas leans down, pulls a dock leaf and hands it to me.

'I wish, now, that I had killed him, he says,' lashing the hedgerow with the crop. There is a vein standing out in his forehead. 'I still might, if I get my hands on him.'

I touch his sleeve. 'At least he only came after me that single time. Afterwards, I got Peg to share my bed. It kept him away. Though the auctions continued.'

Somehow it is easier to tell him the rest. I glance sideways at him. He is still angry, but calmer and even gives a snort of laughter when I tell him of dressing up as a boy. I touch his sleeve again. 'They are dangerous people. The mistress threatened to cut my throat if I talked. A sensible man would avoid me.'

He shrugs. 'I could no more avoid you, Hannah, than stop breathing.'

I take a handkerchief from my pocket – a proper handkerchief, of fine lawn – and scrub at my stained fingers. 'After I got my letter delivered, I expected it would be the greatest scandal.'

'It should have been. Perhaps your magistrate was corrupt.'

'I would have sworn not.'

'But he seems to have managed to close the house where the girls were traded. That is no small thing, Hannah.'

The church clock strikes four and across the big field Jed opens the five-bar gate and waggles his stick at the herd to hurry them through. Beyond, the milkmaids wait on three-legged stools in the open-sided milking shed. In minutes they will be resting foreheads against the flanks of the cows, to empty those great swinging bags of their warm milk.

Thomas and I turn back towards the shed. Like the milkmaids, I wear pattens to save my shoes from the mud of the yard. Though the ones I wear now are of leather, soft as butter on my feet.

'You did a deal of good, Hannah. And you did it alone.' Thomas rests an arm on my shoulder. 'Few men would have troubled themselves. Even fewer been brave enough to act against people with such powerful connections.'

'Could you find out what happened to the Chalkes? If they have been put in some secret prison?'

'Are you sure you want to know? If the brother is as powerful as you think, it seems doubtful.'

'I would still rather know. And I worry about a little girl I saw. Who was in their horrible clutches.'

'Then when I am next in London, I will make it my business to ask questions. My lawyer is a trustworthy man. With clients in influential circles.'

'But be careful,' I lean into his arm. It is such a comfort to share this terrible knowledge. 'And promise you will not go after Chalke.'

'I promise.' He makes a face. 'As I said before, such a brute is not worth hanging for. And I have you to look after, now.' He whistles for Hector, who has been investigating the barn, and the dog comes obediently to heel. No rats for him today. 'I doubt we can make the world a good place, Hannah. But with people like you in it, there may be hope.'

A black kitten has clambered onto the thatch of the milking shed and is struggling to find a way back down. There is the faintest touch of white on its chest, like a floury fingerprint. As we pass, Thomas stretches up and transfers it safely to the ground, to wobble purposefully towards the cows and the hope of spilled milk.

'A determined creature,' he says, glancing at me with a smile as he takes my elbow to steer me towards the house. 'Brave beyond its size and also blessed with grace and beauty.

'I will be going to London tomorrow to order a seed drill and to visit my man of business about the papers the Hospital have requested. I will find out what I can then. Discreetly.'

I nod, satisfied. 'Tell me. What is a seed drill?'

'A machine for sowing seed – instead of having it scattered by hand. Too many families struggle to find corn at a fair price and I plan to grow more.' He offers me his arm. 'Come. We will sharee a dish of tea while I tell you my plans for the lower field.'

I am pleased he wants to discuss the working of the farm with me, but decide that if this lawyer of his knows nothing, I will go up to London myself. To discover the truth.

Chapter Seventy-Six

Our marriage was a quiet affair, with only Betty and her husband, and Peg in a new gown and a cap edged with lace, to hear the vows. Thomas has moved his clothes from the best bedroom into the chamber across the hall and I wonder what Betty thinks. Servants always know what happens in a household and she had clearly hoped for something different, for there were dried rose petals scattered among our wedding sheets.

Every night I lie alone in the four-poster bed where generations of my husband's family were born and wonder at my changed life. In the mornings Betty and I try out cheese recipes from an old book I have found and, every afternoon, I help the curate's widow teach some of the village children. Mistress Frith is a stooped lady of seventy and ready to hand over to someone younger. Thomas has spruced up that old barn and I am reading Aesop's story about the fox to nine bright-eyed youngsters, girls included, to encourage them to want to learn their letters.

Ruben continues to deliver the milk, always smiling despite his early start, happy to have regular work. Hector accompanies him, though Thomas talks of getting a terrier puppy, for we want Hector with us.

All I lack is my daughter. All I think of is when I can have her with me, now that I am a respectable married woman. It wakes me in the night. As the first fingers of dawn touch the curtains. As I help with the churning of the whey butter.

'Why do I not simply go to the Hospital, Thomas? Tell them I have a husband and a proper home, and demand her back?' I fidget in my chair. 'You could take me.'

We are sitting at the kitchen table, the clinking of crockery from the scullery making me feel I should be helping Betty.

'There are rules, Hannah. You would not want just anyone being able to turn up at their door. Asking to take her away.'

'So, what can I do?'

He takes a document from his pocket and spreads it flat on the table. 'You need to prepare what they call a Petition. We will do it together.'

'When did you get this?' I stare at the page of script.

Thomas takes one of my hands in his. 'I went up to the Hospital while you were teaching this afternoon. Spoke to one of the Guardians.'

'You went to London? Did you see her?'

'No, Hannah.'

'Why not?' Fear quivers my voice. 'Has something happened to her?'

He is quick to squeeze my hand. 'She was not there, remember? And they would no tell me anything, because I had no right to ask.' He hesitates. 'Though I am sure they would have said if anything was untoward.

'To release information, they need proof of the connection. Your daughter's date of birth. The day you took her to the Hospital. A description of the token you left with them.' My hand is squeezed again. 'It is good they are careful.'

He is right and I must be sensible. I seize the paper and study it. The wording is ridiculously formal to concern a tiny baby.

'All we need do,' Thomas says, 'is satisfy the Guardians that you have a respectable home to give her. Then they will provide directions to find her and a letter of authority to present to her wet nurse. Your baby might be a distance away. I was told some are sent as far as Bedfordshire.'

I bend over the instructions, scrutinising each word.

RULES to be observed by Persons claiming Children delivered into the Foundling Hospital.

A Petition must be delivered to the General Committee (which sits every Wednesday at 12 o'clock) setting forth, the Day the Child was delivered into the Hospital; the Clothes it had on; or any other Mark on its Body, or Distinction, or Token, sent with it.

If, after the Petition is read, and upon examining the Register, the Child be found alive, enquiry will be made into the Circumstances of the Party claiming, before the ensuing Wednesday, and if the Child be in the Hospital, it will be forthwith delivered, either upon an Indenture to Secure a Settlement, or without, as the General Committee may judge most proper (unless some particular Reason or Objection shall offer to the Contrary).

If the Child is not in the Hospital, it will be sent for and delivered, or if most agreeable to the Parties, a Letter will be given them to those who have the Care of the Children in any of the several Hospitals, Houses, or Nurseries, belonging to this Corporation, in order to the Delivery of the same, in the Country or Place where such Child may happen to be.

If the Child is dead, a Declaration from the Secretary of its Death, if required, will be given.

My heart turns to ice at that final sentence.

'Can we do this now?' I force myself to take a sensible breath.

'Of course. I will fetch ink and paper. Although, as you see, they only accept petitions on Wednesdays.'

'Nearly a week away.'

I twist my hands in my lap until he captures them again in his.

'We will write your petition now, Hannah, so that it is ready for me to take to London next Wednesday. If it is accepted, *when* it is accepted, I promise that we will collect her at the first possible moment.

'In the meantime, you must continue to build your strength, for you will soon have a daughter to look after. You should have beef steak for breakfast every morning. And a rest with one of our books after the afternoon lessons.' He releases my hands. 'Now I will fetch the writing materials. I see no reason why we should not have Thomasina here within a fortnight.'

As I await his return, I remember my faltering steps in that echoing corridor, and how the lady in the midnight-blue dress raised her eyes from the volume in front of her to ask me for a token to leave along with my daughter. The day I felt my heart wither inside me.

Somewhere in the Hospital's vast building a piece of gingham from her grandmother's dress keeps the link between us alive. Pray God it will see us reunited.

Chapter Seventy-Seven

'I have news of the Chalkes.'

Thomas settles across from me at the oak table, his eyes impossible to read as he takes my hands. He has ridden to London to order his seed-drill and consult his lawyer. To deliver papers about his affairs to the Guardians at the Hospital.

'Tell me they have been thrown in a dungeon.' I bare my teeth. Like Hector facing a rat. 'With the key at the bottom of the Thames.'

'Sadly not. As you suspected, Chalke is not the family name. His brother wears the coronet that would have been his had he been born half an hour earlier. No doubt why he turned to the bad.

'They are related to the great men of the court: one uncle is a bishop; another a king's minister.'

'And that's why they are not in Newgate?' I pull my hands free. 'How can that be a proper reason for people turning their backs? On children being disgustingly abused? It is wrong. Even if the perpetrators were related to the King himself.'

'Your magistrate will have been obliged to be circumspect.' Thomas shakes his head. 'But I am told he has had Jarrett and both the Twyfords taken up, for keeping a bawdy house and selling lewd books. They will be transported before the month is out. To shut their mouths. The Chalkes were a different matter.'

'They have gone free?'

'They have been spirited away. Perhaps to Ireland. Nobody appears to know.'

His hands close over mine again. 'Society cannot admit such a foul trade exists, Hannah. But at least it has been stopped. As I said before, that is no small achievement.

'Never forget, dear wife, that because of what you did, countless innocents have been preserved from horror.'

I find I have been holding my breath and let it out, slowly. Thomas is right. Wishing for the moon is for children and fools.

That evening I look over at Thomas as he lights a twist of paper from the fire. Then he applies it to his long-stemmed pipe, frowning as he concentrates on getting it lit to his satisfaction. His cheeks puff with effort, turning him for a moment into a handsome Toby jug. Apart from the candle on the table, there is only a flickering glow from the inglenook. Anyone would think us a long-married couple, sitting together in contentment.

I had not expected to have deep feelings again for anyone but my daughter. Yet this man stirs my emotions in ways I do not understand. Because of him we will soon collect Thomasina, and I crave to gift him something fitting in return. It is clear that he desires me. Perhaps I could even give him a son. Which is what every man wants.

He blows a thin stream of smoke towards the fire and smiles across at me. A log falls, threatening sparks to the rug, and he pushes it back with his foot. 'Time for bed. I have an early start tomorrow, to take in our Petition. You take the candle. I know my way around the house in the dark.'

'You are unbelievably good, Thomas. Taking a bastard under your roof. Giving her your name.'

He frowns.

'*Never* use that ugly word. Or I might consider becoming the kind of man who thrashes his wife.' He lays the pipe on the hearth. 'The child is your flesh, Hannah, and I do not give a single damn who fathered her. I consider her mine already.'

I rise and take the half step to his chair. Lean down and touch my mouth to his. Yet he holds himself still, only responding by stroking my cheek with a finger.

'Let us go up,' I say, taking the candlestick.

At the bedroom door, I place a hand on his sleeve to prevent him going to his own room. I am close enough to feel his warmth, smell his now familiar scent. My heart is pounding. My mouth so dry I can hardly swallow. Whether from fear or desire, I cannot tell. 'Do not go,' I say. 'Stay with me tonight.'

His eyes glint in the candlelight. 'I am a patient man, as all farmers must be. And we have a lifetime ahead of us, Hannah. Are you sure?'

I cannot think what to say, but use my grip on his sleeve to take him with me. The candle flame trembles as I lead the way into the room. Into his own chamber. Up to his own bed, that he has not slept in since our marriage.

To my surprise I realise that I need him to hold me. To kiss me. To put his hands on me. I do not want the other thing, but that will only last a few minutes and perhaps be less painful this time. I will close my eyes tight and wish it over quickly. Yet there is a curious ache inside me that makes me want our union to happen.

'Help me,' I say, fumbling at my laces. My gown does not require a lady's maid, but I have to say something, for he looks as if he might still leave and his closeness makes me strangely breathless.

'I know how difficult this must be for you,' he says, as his big hands fumble with the gown, 'but remember how precious you are to me. That I could never hurt you. That I love you.'

'Thomas…'

'Shhhh. Do not speak.' As he lets down my hair, no lady's maid could be more gentle. With a serious, unsmiling face he kisses the top of my head, my brow and my eyelids with slow deliberation, then steps away. 'We will simply climb into our bed and sleep in one another's arms. If anything happens between us, it will only be because you have reached for me first. When I know that you are ready. And unafraid.'

He will not hurt me, for I am precious to him. But I feel his need, like a kettle simmering on a fire. As the gown slips to the floor I tell myself: *I can do this*.

I find I want to. That my body needs his. As he whispers my name against my skin, fear slips away. Folded into his arms, I discover my husband to be not only tender and giving, but a teacher of amazing things. We fit so precisely, and I am astounded by waves of physical pleasure. It is a world away from my imaginings.

The dawn is a pale smudge through the bed curtains as I feel Thomas untangle himself and slip quietly from the bed. Thinking me still asleep, he folds my gown tidily onto a chair and walks to the window to look out at his fields and the morning. He is naked, all loose-limbed grace, his muscular chest lightly covered in dark hair that arrows downwards. A truly beautiful man.

Afterwards I cannot stop touching him, even if it is just to brush the sleeve of his shirt with my fingers or to bury my face in his chest so that I can breathe in his scent.

This must be what is meant about love between a man and a woman. What the poets write about. A joining of heart, of soul and of body – which will be mine for our whole life together.

Chapter Seventy-Eight

There is one last thing to do. Though when I tell Thomas I want to visit Mrs Roberts, Sir Christopher's housekeeper, he fixes me with that perceptive gaze that I have come to love.

'What, my darling wife, are you up to?'

'Nothing.' I promise myself this is the last lie I will ever tell him. 'But servants always know their masters' business. There must have been below-stairs gossip. About what happened.'

My husband runs a hand through his thick hair. 'I wish you would look forward, dearest. Not backwards.'

I put my arms around him knowing that if I am patient, he will give in to me.

'Well. If you are determined.' He sighs, kissing the top of my head. 'But I am going with you.'

I reach up to rub the dark stubble on his chin. He usually shaves at night, because he rises so early, but I find I like the way it rasps under my fingers.

'Mrs Roberts would never speak freely with you there. Take me to the house. In the trap. Then come back for me, an hour later.'

'And you are not planning to try to see the magistrate?'

I smile up at him. 'Even if he is there, why would Sir Christopher go anywhere near his housekeeper's room? It will just be two women talking over a dish of tea. And I want their French cook's recipe for ragout of rabbit. Mrs Lamb said it was the best she had ever tasted.' I meet his eye, unblinking. 'You know how partial you are to rabbit.'

Thomas knits his dark brows. 'You belong here now. Not in London, with its intrigues.'

'Humour me, husband. Drop me at the house. Then hunt down some of those seed catalogues you find so irresistible.'

The red-cheeked girl who answers the kitchen door is nonplussed at finding a lady at the servants' entrance. Behind her, I see Mrs Roberts scurrying to take charge. Under a velvet pelisse, my gown is plain grey, but of silk. My hair braided under a stiff-crowned straw Bergère, tied with a broad ribbon under my chin. My town shoes of kid.

'Can I help you, ma'am? You will be wanting the mistress…'

'Mrs Roberts…'

'Hannah?' Her eyes grow round. 'It is never you.'

.I remove my left glove and hold up my hand with its shiny gold ring. To let her know my dramatic change in fortune was not earned from forgetting myself.

'You are married!' She beams, having always been soft-hearted. She scrutinises me. 'And married well.'

'I am a gentleman farmer's wife now. He is the finest man and I am more than lucky.'

'Then I am pleased for you.' She takes my arm and ushers me inside. 'The tea went up to the master not ten minutes since. Will you share a dish with me?'

We walk to her room, like old friends, and over the refreshment I tell her what I want. To speak to Sir Christopher.

She stares. 'Hannah, you may have risen in the world, but he would never see you.'

'Tell him the person is here who wrote to him anonymously in February. About a monstrous crime. I think you will find he feels differently.'

She took some persuading, but eventually slipped away, leaving me to wonder if coming here might make my happy world unravel. But how else will I know what happened to little Suzy?

Eventually I hear murmuring voices. The bang of a nearby door. Footsteps. The rustle of Mrs Roberts' starched petticoats.

Soon afterwards, I am in Sir Christopher's study, standing before his desk. He is a small man, with a strong angular face. Weary and cynical looking.

He does not offer me a chair, but I notice a doll lying on the window seat and a familiar stripy cat curled in one of the wing chairs by the fireplace. I tell myself I am not in the dock. That I should not be trembling.

'Am I to believe you responsible for that extraordinary letter?' This will be how he sounds on the bench. 'That you composed and penned it yourself?'

'That is correct, sir.'

He lifts a book from the desk. A Bible. Holds it out.

'Read for me.'

I realise he is testing whether I have the education to have written to him and seek out a passage I have always loved for its beauty. Then I read it, slowly:

Charity suffereth long, and is kind; charity envieth not; charity vaunteth not itself, is not puffed up,

Doth not behave itself unseemly, seeketh not her own, is not easily provoked, thinketh no evil;

Rejoiceth not in iniquity, but rejoiceth in truth.

'Enough.' He gestures for me to return the Bible, but I keep it in my hand.

'I swear by this holy book, Sir Christopher, that my letter contained nothing but the truth.'

Stern eyes under bushy grey brows study me.

'I know it to have been the truth, Mistress Graham. From my enquiries. But who delivered it for you? My footman told me he saw a young gentleman.'

I do not know where to look, not daring to lie to him, yet fearful of what he might think of a servant girl dressed-up in breeches and her master's wig.

Then the cat jumps off her chair and comes to rub around my ankles. She remembers me.

'Well, perhaps it is best to pass over that detail.' He looks at the cat, his gaze thoughtful. 'I assumed what I was sent came from someone crossed in an illicit transaction. A gentleman resentful over a bad debt. Perhaps even – these things occasionally happen – someone with a guilty conscience. But never that it might have written by a young woman.'

'Why should my word not be good? If I had proof in my hand?'

'Why not, indeed, Mistress Graham. But you were wise enough to realise it would carry more weight if it appeared to originate from someone other than a servant girl.'

The magistrate rises from his chair, scoops up the cat and sets it by the hearth, where it arches its back and settles down on its elbows, rump to the warmth.

'I will not ask how you came by those documents.' He motions to me with his arm. But come and sit with me by the fire. Please.'

My legs are still quaking, so I am relieved to accept the invitation.

'Mrs Roberts tells me you have married,' he says when we are settled opposite one another.

'My husband has a dairy farm. He is a churchwarden.'

'You have done well for yourself, Mistress Graham.'

'I have been lucky. He is the very best of men.'

'Tell me. Does he know you are here?'

'He believes me to be visiting your housekeeper. Which I was.'

The magistrate's eyes crease. He laughs.

'I live in a house dominated by females, Mistress Graham. And am daily amazed at how they can make me do whatever they want.' He reaches down to touch the cat's back and she yawns, at ease with him, displaying whiskers fine as kipper bones. 'And your interest in coming here today... is what?

'There was a child in that evil place called Suzy. No more than six years old. I hate to think what might have happened to her. If it is known where she is, my husband and I could offer her a good Christian home.'

Thomas knows nothing of this hope of mine, but has a heart warm enough to agree to it.

'I recall the name.' He ruffles the cat's fur. 'She was one of those tracked down. But she carried measles into the house of her protector. Several people died, including the scoundrel who had bought her. Yet somehow the child survived. She is in the care of some charitable institution. If you wish, I will arrange for you to be sent a letter giving details, together with my permission to remove her.'

I study my gloved hands, trying not to think of what she must have gone through. Telling myself crying achieves nothing. Telling myself that Thomas and I will have two daughters now to love.

'Yet those evil Chalkes walk free.' I shake my head.

'They do not, Mistress Graham.'

He stares into the fire. 'Jarrett and both of the Twyfords are currently on the high seas, bound for the New World and a harsh period of well-deserved bondage. They were committed for running a common bawdy house and put up no defence when told that revealing the depravity of their trade would have earned them the rope. It gave me no small pleasure to see them convicted.'

A log crumbles, exploding in tiny sparks.

'As for Chalke, his brother clearly knew what the man was

doing, but did nothing as long as the business was discreet.'

He shakes his head. The grey eyes have turned dark. Impenetrable.

'But when the traffic threatened to come into the public domain, his Lordship could not have him questioned in open court. With such a stain on the family honour, the King would no longer have received him.'

Outrage makes me forget myself.

'Honour! From men worse than beasts...'

He holds up a hand.

'You believe a magistrate to be a man of power, Mistress Graham. And it is true that men and women's lives often lie in my hand. But I cannot always follow my private wishes.

'Those in power do not want the common people taking to the streets because their innocent daughters are being despoiled by the aristocracy. A mob is an ugly thing, eager to pillage the great houses of the town.' He lets out a sigh. 'I am the King's servant. It is my duty to preserve the peace.'

'So, Chalke goes unpunished?' My guts twist with anger.

The grey eyes fix on mine.

'You appreciate that this conversation is not taking place? That it must never be mentioned outside this room?'

I incline my head. What else can I do?

'That man could not be allowed to walk the same earth as his distinguished kinsman. But some sores are so foul they need to be cauterised in private.'

I see from Sir Christopher's face the distaste he feels.

'The family have an estate on the coast of Ireland. The Chalkes were supposedly being banished there when the boat carrying them from ship to shore capsized and sank. Unusually, the two sailors manning the little vessel were strong swimmers, while the Chalkes were not. A suspiciously convenient accident.' He studies me from under those bristling eyebrows. 'The aristocracy can be ruthless, even to their own. And I cannot find it in my heart to feel sorry for those drowned.'

He blinks and smiles. A bleak smile.

'Time has made me a realist. When I was new to the bench, I presided over a trial at the Old Bailey. A tutor who taught young girls had taken advantage of their innocence.

'A doctor stood up before us and testified to the damage that had been done to their young bodies. One of the children was produced and questioned. She was the only daughter of a shopkeeper, a man of neither influence nor education, but who had enlightened ideas and hopes about his girl. It was her mother who gave evidence, since the father could not trust himself in the same room as the man accused.

'Yet, inexplicably to me, the jury found the tutor innocent. They could not bear, I decided, after a sleepless night, to look into the darkness dwelling in some men's souls. And dismissing a child's evidence – especially that of a poor and young girl – allowed them to convince themselves it could not possibly have happened.

'And that vile man, Mistress Graham, was a nobody. Not a member of the aristocracy whose brother has the ear of our sovereign. A sovereign, moreover, known to have inconveniently high moral standards.'

He nudges a log that threatens to topple onto the rug further back on the fire with his boot, careful not to disturb the cat.

'Yet I have also seen juries refuse to convict men guilty of theft. To do it because they considered the value of a man's life greater than that of a sheep stolen to feed a hungry family.'

The grey eyes flicker and he straightens his shoulders. 'So, I tell myself there is always hope.'

Puss curls up, deciding nothing exciting is happening. We are simply two people she is comfortable with, talking in front of a fire.

'You have been fortunate, Mistress Graham, to escape the attentions of people who might have found it expedient to silence you.' The grey eyes flicker. 'Mrs Roberts says you're something of a *blue-stocking*. In future it would be safer to remember the teaching of the ancient Chinese general, *Sun Tzu*, who advocated only fighting battles you know you can win. Concentrate, instead, on your domestic concerns. Leave serious matters to your husband.'

'Yet perhaps I did manage to win, sir. With your help.'

He stifles a laugh as he reaches for the bell. 'Then perhaps you will take a glass of canary with me, Mistress Graham. To toast our modest victory and hope for better things in the time to come.'

After half an hour, the footman ushers me out through the front door, his eyes confused at recognising me. I smile and give him a coin before making my way down the steps and towards my waiting husband.

I know that Jarrett, Jack and his uncle are on their way to the Americas, to prevent tongues wagging and to expiate their crimes with hard labour. That the Chalkes were given the ultimate punishment, far from the public eye. The great ones of the land having decreed no good would be served by having their filthy linen publicly displayed.

And that little Suzy can soon be enfolded into our growing family.

Sir Christopher is right. There may be battles for me in the future, but for now I must concentrate on the welfare of my husband and those who work for him. And on the two little girls who will soon be safe under our roof.

Chapter Seventy-Nine

The waiting time was wearisome. Thomas delivered the Petition to the General Committee, although he was unable to see anyone except the clerk who took the paper from him. He then went back to London, to answer enquiries about our circumstances, taking with him our marriage certificate, a letter from the vicar, and a document from his lawyer setting out his land holdings and investments.

He tried, unsuccessfully, to keep that information from me, for it spelled out what a shoddy bargain he is getting in acquiring me for a wife.

He was told Thomasina lives in a hamlet near Barnet, not so very far distant from Broad Oak. There was rejoicing in our house when he returned carrying the letter addressed to her wet nurse, commanding her to deliver the child into our care.

Betty, Peg and I have spent every free moment refurbishing the old nursery for its new arrival. Stitching and knitting. Rescuing old toys and teething rings. Anything to help the time pass until we can collect her. And Betty was eager to offer to feed my little daughter alongside her own toddling son. They will grow up as playmates.

One day soon, I hope to have a reply to the invitation my generous husband has sent to Mrs Lamb, care of Major Harper's household in York. He knew my dearest wish would be for her to take her retirement with us at Broad Oak and thinks it a splendid idea. Betty, too, is overjoyed at the prospect of the farm again becoming full of life.

One hand is in my lap and the other has sneaked under Thomas's coat to grasp his strong thigh, for comfort, as he reins in the horse outside a tumbledown cottage. How fortunate my daughter is to have him for a father. How fortunate little Suzy will be, later in the week, when we travel to collect her.

It is more a smallholding than a farm. Nothing like the prosperous Broad Oak. There are ancient-looking beehives and some scrawny goats in an orchard at one side. Part of the thatch is mended with canvas and black smoke from the chimney suggests they are burning damp wood and cannot afford a sweep. But it pleases me to see a quantity of clean washing spread to dry on bushes: aprons and caps, children's clouts, woollen stockings and workmanlike smocks that must belong to the man of the house.

On the other side of a split-rail fence three children play under the gnarled trees, two of them boys, teasing a mongrel puppy with a stick. The third, a gangling girl of about eight, plays with a doll, rocking it in her arms. They look shabby, but in good health, so my spirits lift.

When she realises the trap is stopping and we intend to get out, the young girl clutches the doll against her pinafore and the cloth in which it is wrapped slips to reveal a halo of dark hair. A tiny fist grasping the girl's pigtail. My heart lurches in my chest. That is no doll. That is our daughter.

***

The End

End Note

Back in 2015 I visited London's *Foundling Hospital Museum* for the first time. It is an emotive place and I could not get the heart-breaking stories it told – about the tokens desperate mothers left in the hope that they might, one day, be able to retrieve their precious child – out of my head. My book, ***The Servant***, is the result.

Founded by Royal Charter in 1739, The London Foundling Hospital came into existence after seventeen years of effort by retired sea captain William Coram to provide 'Provision for Foundlings'. His eventual success was due, to a great extent, to his gaining the support of sixteen ladies of high rank, headed by the Duchess of Somerset. Their signatures on *The Ladies Petition* was presented to George II in 1735.

Some things are known – that sand was put down on the receiving room floor when women took part in the lottery for a place for their babies – others remain conjecture. I must therefore stress that ***The Servant*** is a work of fiction and will undoubtedly contain many errors and omissions, together with the occasional flight of fancy. I hope, however, that it will encourage everyone who can to visit the Museum and to spare a thought for the plight of the women obliged to seek its help long before the advent of women's emancipation and when social injustice was rife.

Although I consulted a multitude of books and sources whilst researching the novel, the following is a select biography of those I found most useful:

London's Forgotten Children, Thomas Coram and the Foundling Hospital by Gillian Pugh

Fate, Hope & Charity, Essays by Janette Bright and Dr Gillian Clark, exploring the poignant stories behind the Foundling Hospital tokens

Threads of Feeling, The London Foundling Hospital's textile tokens, 1740-1770, by John Stiles

Harris's List of Covent Garden Ladies – Sex in the City in Georgian Britain, by Hallie Rubenhold

The Secret History of Georgian London by Dan Cruikshank

The Pleasure of the Imagination by John Brewer, English Culture in the Eighteenth Century.

Longbourn, by Jo Baker

Anne Hughes, 'Her Boke', The Diary of a Farmer's Wife, 1796-1797, first published by the Farmer's Weekly

Old Bailey Online – The Proceedings of the Old Bailey 1674-1913

All mistakes, misunderstandings and anachronisms are my fault and mine alone.

My thanks must finally go to **The Historical Writers Association** for selecting *The Servant* for their **HWA/Sharpe Books Unpublished Novel Award 2020** and, equally, to my ever-patient husband and to my magnificent writers' group (**ninevoices.wordpress.com**) who have encouraged me every long step of the way.

I welcome feedback on my writing and can be contacted via my email: maggiedavieswriting@gmail.com

Printed in Great Britain
by Amazon